No Couches in Korea

Author's Note

No Couches in Korea is a memoir of Pusan from 1996-1997, with later reflections on how South Korea has changed through the published date of 2016. That means that about 98% is non-fiction and factual. However, there were a few author liberties, particularly with character origins, character names, character quotes, and a few incidents where I had to add a few things that didn't actually happen to characters. This was for better story continuity and character development.

However, everything about Korea itself at that time, is 100% as personally experienced, particularly the schools, the locations, the expat scenes, and everything else from that time period.

www.kevinmaher.com has links to *No Couches in Korea* YouTube, Facebook, and other author information. You can scan the following QR Code:

https://www.facebook.com/NoCouchesinKorea/

https://www.youtube.com/channel/UCM0XVTAjDRtHFkSNh IBiM9Q

NO COUCHES IN KOREA

Kevin M Maher

Wintermoon Books
Detroit, Michigan

ISBN: 0692674004
ISBN 13: 9780692674000

NO COUCHES IN KOREA

NO COUCHES IN KOREA

May, 1996. Four long bulky bags and an acoustic guitar all sat in a row on the short green grass between the road and the sidewalk, as I hovered nearby, peering towards Division Street searching for my cab. It was my last day living in Portland, Oregon—a city I had come to love—and it was my last night with the black-haired, green-eyed woman I'd been involved with for the last three years. For Sasha and me, it was no longer the beginning of the end: it was the end of the end. I was about to leave, I was about to go, I was on my way to teach English in Pusan (부산·釜山), South Korea. I was saying good-bye to all I'd known, including her.

Sad as hell, I stood on the curb among my bags on that misty May morning, waiting. Maybe the cab was late. Maybe it went to the wrong address—I didn't know. I left my things on the side of the road, put my hand into her mailbox, and ripped open the letter that I'd left with her key enclosed. Then I walked back into the apartment.

As I opened the front door, the morning's memories flooded back into my mind. I could hear the sound of the alarm clock as I embraced her— "Honey? Honey? It's the morning, honey..." But she was tired. She wanted to sleep more, so we simply embraced in bed. I could see it all, it had just happened hours ago, but that moment was gone forever. What had once happened every day might never happen again.

Several months earlier, I learned of the possibility that I could teach English in Korea. I called a recruiter, and he asked me, "Can you start immediately? Could you buy a flight for this weekend?"

"No," I said to the other side of the line, as I looked at Sasha looking at me from the kitchen table. She looked apprehensive that I was following through with my westward intention. "Give me more time, and I can."

The recruiter followed this, "Can you just call us back when you are ready?" He explained they always had teaching positions available, but they only placed teachers into urgent situations. I was okay with that.

Two months later, I called the same recruiter again. He was pleased, "Come by my office and sign the contract. Buy a plane ticket for Pusan. You will start on the first of the month."

I agreed with that stipulation. I also told him agree that I would arrive a week early to observe and learn from teachers before getting into a classroom. I made it clear that I had never taught before, but I was willing to try. The recruiter accepted my conditions, and I began to research about South Korean's second largest city.

So, there I was on the morning of my flight. I picked up the phone and dialed the taxi cab company. "Hello? Yeah, yeah, I'll hold." I played with the cord for a while. "Yes, no problem. I'm calling from 2339 SE Sherman Street. Yes, I was calling to confirm that my cab is coming. Sure! Okay. Five minutes? Okay, five minutes. Yeah...yeah...okay, great. No, no thank you. Okay, bye," and I hung up the phone. Sasha's cat, Shaddow, rubbed up against me. I petted her, feeling lifeless inside. I asked myself—and the cat—"So, is this really it?"

Joe and Sasha couldn't have been two more different friends. They were two people that I'd spent the better part of the last several years with, exploring up and resettling up and down the western United States. I was sure I would see both again, separately, but I didn't know when. Tattooed Joe, with black and white tattoos up and down his arms, in the West Coast tradition of the time. An intellectual wanderer with a penchant for low-paying jobs. A literature guy, a vegetarian, a musician, and a friend, who I often shared the open road of exploring relocations. Sasha, a similar soul, but more of an intellectual women's studies person, with a preference for loud music, literature of a different variety, and a political bent, quick to share her opinions. The two rubbed each other the wrong way often, but they both pulled out different aspects of myself, tremendously so.

Joe represented my perpetual wanderlust spirit, the unquenchable one—seeking connections, new spheres of existence, and different types of realities. Joe started in New York, I started in Michigan. After the last year living in Portland, he would continue northwest to work in the Alaskan canneries. I wanted to go so far west, to jump across the entire Pacific Ocean. We would later meet in South Korea, or that was the plan, as I would tell him if it was a 'go ahead' or not. Joe's influence was greatest on me because of his literature interests. He introduced me to writers who shared a wanderlust for travel just like I had. Jack Kerouac, Henry Miller, Ernest Hemingway, among others, simply fueling the flames deeper inside of me, with the hopes of mimicking their recording of experiences along with living it.

Whereas Sasha represented the opposite side of me, the one that had brought out the best in me, as a human being. The one that would make me aspire to be more with my life. She introduced to be literature that made me want to be a better human being. However, Sasha had hit the end of the road, and Portland was that place for her. She had no desire to go so far west, to be out of the west coast. Of everywhere that we'd been, Portland was her final stop. We'd all worked the national parks, tried different western cities, but this was her final stop.

As they pulled out different sides of me, I knew I would meet them both again, it was just a matter of time, but I didn't know in what context. Mostly, South Korea beckoned me. In Portland, Sasha and I had once found a toy store with a unique toy flower. You twisted the green stems, and the flower petals popped out into a display of colors. It held a symbolic value of some type for me. This should I, or shouldn't I, type of power. It went well with a wanderlust-souled person.

Now, on this day, I found myself with that same toy flower, with multicolored petals. I found myself holding one petal, and saying, "I will be back," moving to the next petal, "I won't be back." This continued, and I hoped that I wouldn't be back. I hoped that everything would turn out alright. I hoped that I'd connect and grow on some level that would give me greater insights into my own existence—culturally, spiritually, or however else.

Back in the apartment, the one that Sasha and I no longer shared, I sat down and addressed an envelope to Sasha with the key to be enclosed.

As I sat at the table, Shaddow brushed against my legs, purring loudly. She meowed. I looked at her. "This is it, kitty. This is it. When I step out this door, I may never see you again. Do you know that? I might never see you again?" Then, I sealed the envelope.

I knew my time was up. I stood, opened the door, and looked at Shaddow through my tear-filled eyes. "Take care of Sasha, okay? I'm going to miss her very much. Will you do that for me? And please tell your cat friends in Korea to take care of me, okay? Can you do that for me?"

I slipped through the door and walked down the driveway one last time; I could see myself embracing her by the door. I had walked her to her car earlier that same morning. She was leaving for her regular workday, and I was leaving to make the largest jump west that I could conceive of making.

Tears had welled up in my eyes. I clearly remembered the last exchange we had just shared with each other. "Sasha. I miss you already, and I haven't even left."

"Follow your bliss. Just don't end up back on your parent's couch in Michigan." There wasn't much else to say. A fear that everything you did in life would be worthless. The anxiety that you'd end in the same starting point. The gravestone marked with your birthplace and death place in the same location.

She got into her car, and I watched her. She backed up her car, and I watched her. I stared at her, and I waited for the last eye contact I might ever make with her. She gave it to me, and I tried to smile. I whispered to myself, "I need you to support me through this," and her eyes drifted away from mine towards the road. I watched her drive into the street and pull away. Tears welled up and rolled down my cheeks. And that was it.

So there I was; I still hadn't left. I could back out from it all. But, I shoved the envelope into her mailbox, and walked towards my four long bulky bags and acoustic guitar sitting in the green grass. I hovered over them, peering towards Division Street for my cab. It was my last day of 'that'.

Fifteen hours later, unable to sleep because of the anxiety, I got off the plane in Pusan, South Korea. I made my way through the airport, my progress impeded by people walking into me, at me, everywhere but around me. A young woman emerged from the crowd. "Adam?" A pause, "Adam Wanderson?"

I answered hesitantly, "Yes? How do you know who I am?"

In broken English, she said, "Easy, you are the only foreigner." She was a typical thin Korean woman with long black hair and almond-shaped eyes, just like everyone else in the airport. I wondered if foreigners were difficult to differentiate for her. "My name is Ms. Kim, I will bring you to hotel."

I carried my bags over my shoulders—she carried my acoustic guitar. In her car, she weaved into heavy traffic on busy expressways that I did not expect at one o'clock in the morning. An hour later, she navigated tiny little alleys, filled with people walking around. What multitudes of people did in alleys, at two o'clock in the morning, was a mystery to me. But they seemed to be eating, drinking, and walking around in these neon-lit busy pathways.

In one of these alleys, she stopped at what was my hotel. I emotionally, and desperately, wanted to ask her out, or ask her in—or to ask her anything that would keep her with me, and save me from being alone. She left without any deliberation, and I went and collapsed on the bed.

Unfortunately, it was 3am, and I was aware that someone would pick me up between 5:30-6am. I plugged in my alarm clock, and it exploded. No worries I thought, I would keep myself awake for the appointment. I could crash for days once they brought me to my new apartment. It was great that I arrived early, and had this luxury. I sat upright, with all the lights on, so I could get some shut eye, but not crash too hard.

My first morning in Pusan, my neck was sore from sitting upright all night. At five-thirty in the morning, I shuffled into the bathroom. I struggled to turn on the hot water, while amazed at the copious loose uncovered electrical wires above the shower head. This would be a consistent theme that I would see throughout Korean bathrooms, that is, wires of electricity, loosely hanging, near unprotected shower heads.

As soon as I was unclothed and wet, shampoo dripping down my head, I heard a *knock*.

"I'm in the shower," I yelled. I couldn't believe the guy was here to pick me up this early. I yelled again, "Just a second!"

Knock Knock Knock.

"Just a second! I'm in the shower! Coming! Just a second!" Why couldn't this guy give me a few seconds to get the shampoo out of my hair?

Knock Knock Knock.

He was so persistent that I hurriedly stepped out of the bathroom without a towel, dripping water everywhere. I approached the door and yelled through it, "Give me two or three minutes! I need to put on some clothes! I was in the shower! Just hold on!"

Knock Knock Knock.

"Just a second," I yelled, giving up. I proceeded to open the door slightly, peering through the crack. An older Korean woman with a tray balanced under her arm, pushed her way into my room. "Ahhh...thank you," I said to her, trying to cover my nudity. She placed the tray, which held two strange breads and a cup of coffee, directly into the middle of the room. Then she quickly disappeared again.

I proceeded to get back into the shower and rinse out the shampoo. I realized that I needed to be ready, for anyone, at any time. I went into hyper-fast speed, to be fully prepared, as quick as possible, to make that good impression. Then I waited, and waited, and waited, and waited. But no one else came by.

As time passed, I felt jittery and nervous about the upcoming day, that I began to pace. Soon I began to step in and out of my hotel room—over and over, anxiously peering down the hall. Before long, I began looking in and out of the hotel's front door while scanning the busy alley filled with people scurrying about in seemingly every direction. A stream of Korean faces peered right back at me. I tried to give direct eye contact to make that good first impression, but with everyone staring at me, how would I know who was the right person?

Before long, one Korean person from the crowd approached me, "Adam?"

"Yes, I am." I felt startled, nervous, apprehensive, and eager. Was I making a good impression?

"Welcome to Korea." We picked up my four bulky bags and an acoustic guitar, and threw them into his van. All the while, people flowed around us.

By seven a.m., we were in what I assumed to be my new workplace, an English language institute. It was in yet another busy alley. There appeared to be a billiards hall above my work floor, and some type of singing room below it. This little location, in a random alley, in a random building, seemingly on a random floor, would soon become my corner of this universe. An extremely hectically busy corner of the universe.

The driver helped me carry in my bags and then proceeded to spread them out across the middle of the teacher's lounge. The same small lounge that served as a major throughway for students going to class. Little did I know that my bags would remain there for half the day, unattended, while I could only later assume that kids and teachers alike, consistently had to step over them, or on them, depending on their attention skills.

My driver initiated a conversation with the older Korean woman who sat at an oversized desk. Everything was said in Korean, with an occasional "Adam" thrown into the conversation. The woman suspiciously glared at me continuously, and I smiled back, each time.

The driver turned to me—"This is your new employer." I smiled, nodding my head again. "Hello!" I waited for her to extend her arm toward me, but she didn't. I sat awkwardly, a slightly crooked smile hanging on my face. More Korean was spoken between them. They ignored me.

I glanced uncomfortably around the room, staring at my belongings sprawled out, and then at the clock. I tried to peek into the nearby classrooms. They looked small, very small.

When a foreigner entered the room, my driver angrily shouted, "You're late!"

The tall, bushy red haired man, shouted back a quick response, "What? We got plenty of time!"

The driver barked back, "I told you to be here twenty minutes ago!"

The foreigner ignored him. "C'mon, let's go," he spat out to me, a speckle of spit flying from his mouth.

Not knowing where we were going, I asked, "Should I grab my stuff?"

"Nah, we'll get it later." I grabbed my smallest bag with my documents and passport.

The two of us entered the elevator, and exited into the alley. Puzzled, I asked, "Who was that woman?"

"That was the boss, and my name is Louie, and that was our *hagwan*. (학원·學院). Our language institute."

So, what's next?"

"Didn't they tell you?" He adjusted his tie, "You're coming to teach with me at the middle school today."

He was my only connection to everything. "Teaching? Now? What? What about my stuff? I came a week early, and I need to rest."

"Don't worry," he assured me, "We'll be back this afternoon. Later, you have to teach there too."

"What? I don't know how to teach! What about the training they promised me? I came here days early to be trained to teach!"

"Typical, dude! They don't tell you anything. That's just like 'em. They put you to work the same day you arrive. I'm glad I'm getting out of here!"

"Where are you going?"

"I found another job. I'm going to Japan tonight to get a new work visa. I'll be back on Monday to teach at a different school downtown."

"So, how long have you been working at this one?"

"Two months," and then he paused. "But I've been in Korea for seven months." As he said this, we began walking over a large overpass. "Okay, you know where you're at? I won't be with you when you come back, dude, so you better pay attention. I gotta get home and pack. I'm sorry, dude, this is typical Korean bullshit. You know where you are, right?"

"What? I have no idea where I am at."

"Just remember how to get to this bus stop. Once here, take Bus 105 or Bus 111-1 or Bus 111-2. Okay, you got that? You got a pen?"

"Just a second. You can't take me back again?" I pulled out a pen and paper, "What buses did you say again?"

"It's typical Korean bullshit, dude. Buses 105, 111-1 or 111-2, but you can also come back on the 15—it's right around the corner from the school. But you can't come back on the 111-2."

"How will I know when I'm back? It all looks the same!"

"I'll tell you what: my girlfriend's teaching at the same school. I'll tell her to stay after her classes and wait for you. I'm sorry, dude, but I gotta get home and pack. Just typical Korean bullshit." He paused, took a deep breath, "Just typical Korean bullshit."

Once on the bus, there wasn't anywhere to sit. I had my bag in one hand, and my pen and paper in another. Suddenly, I felt a pull on my bag. "Hey," I yelled. A woman pulled my bag out of my hand, and sat it on her lap.

"Korean culture," Louie explained. "If you are standing, and you have a bag, it is second-nature for a sitting person to grab it from you, and place it on their lap."

"Thanks," I said in English.

Taking standing passenger's bags, and placing them on their laps, was one of those 1996 customs that faded away in time. It was such a commonplace gesture at that time, that I quickly adjusting to equally doing that for strangers, whenever I had my own seat.

Since this was my first experience with this custom, I suspiciously watched my bag on her lap, throughout the journey. However, it did free up my hands, to take notes on landmarks. However, every landmark I thought I saw, didn't turn out to be an actual landmark. Things like church crosses or bowling pins, weren't one-offs, they were just mass-produced over and over.

Once at to the school, Louie directed me to the classroom. "Okay, this is where you'll be teaching for two hours in the morning and two hours in the afternoon. These kids are fun: you have first grade. The other new teacher will have second grade. Okay, you know how to get here, right?"

"No, but that's okay."

Before long, students came into our classroom. Louie yelled, "It's Game Day!"

"Great," I muttered, sighing to myself, "This will really help me teach."

The kids screamed, "Game! Game! Game! Yeah!"

For the entire first hour, we played Hangman and Simon Says. "Simon says turn around," or "Raise your right hand," or "Touch your nose." I sat patiently through it, wondering how I would teach real lessons.

After the hour, Louie told me, "Okay, dude, I gotta go back. Off to Japan tonight. Good luck! So, just play some game for the next hour. Okay dude, you'll be okay. Sorry the hagwan is doing this to you, but I gotta go."

"What's a *hagwan* do for teachers anyways? Is there any training?"

"Typical Korean bullshit," is all he could say. "You'll learn. It's how things work in Korea. If you have a white face, they figure you can teach English. They don't speak English, so they will never know if you teach well or not. As long as you make them money, they don't care what you do, or what you say." Louie sighed seemingly resigned to something he didn't agree with. "Just be popular, be an English monkey." Then Louie left me alone, and I was officially in charge of my first class.

My class had about fifteen students. It was a typical classroom, a green chalkboard, white chalk, small desks like you'd see in any classroom anywhere.

"Hello, my name is Adam. I'm from the United States. Do you know where that is? USA?" I didn't get a response. I asked the nearest student, "What's your name?" She gave me a puzzled look. Her facial expression told me that I intimidated her. "What page are you on in this book?" No response again, and I was at a loss. "Do you guys like hangman?" I pronounced the word very slowly, loudly, and clearly, "Hangman?"

A kid screamed, "Yes! Hangman!"

Other followed suit, "Hangmaaaan!"

So we proceeded to play Hangman for the next hour.

As promised, Laurie waited for me after class. Louie's girlfriend was awkward, but kind. She was a slim girl in her twenties with long blond hair and blue eyes.

The first thing that she asked was, "So how was your first class?"

"I don't know. Louie could talk with the students, but they didn't understand a word I said."

"They only know a few words, whatever's in the book. Stick with the book, and you'll be okay."

10

The bus back was exceptionally packed. When we boarded the bus, I felt like my limbs were being separated and stretched from the crowd, as someone had pushed their way onto the bus, and caught my bag.

When we got off the bus, Laurie reminded me again that tomorrow, I would be traveling that route alone. Good luck to myself, I thought.

Later I handled these situations by writing down important locations written in Korean. I could show that to bus drivers, and they'd yell for me to get off the bus at the right stop. But, I didn't know that yet on my first morning, in a foreign country, on my first day outside North America.

***
3
***

Laurie brought me from that Middle School to the language institute, or hagwan. This time, I met the director. He was a Korean-Canadian man who spoke English as a native speaker, and he translated for the old woman—the owner. The same woman who had glared at me continuously, as I sat in front of her, just prior to sending me off to teach. The director was the English go-between for the owner and the foreign teachers.

"My name's Kamm," said the thin Korean man. He was smoking a cigarette vigorously, putting it to his mouth with big inhaling puffs and exhaling profusely while his arms jerked about. "So how was your first class?"

"Good—I think. I didn't plan to teach so suddenly after arriving, though."

"Well, Louie's leaving today," His eyes darted everywhere as his hand jerked his cigarette out of his mouth. "It's good you came a few days early!" He exhaled more profusely, adding to the smoky atmosphere of the school.

"Sure, sure, but I was hoping for training. That is why I came a few days early," I pleaded.

"You'll do fine," his smoke cloud said.

My bags were still lying in the middle of the teacher's lounge, as they had all day. I noticed one of my bags, the one mostly with books, had split open slightly. *You Can't Go Home Again* by Thomas Wolf had escaped.

"How about my belongings?" I inquired. "When do I find a better place for those?

"You can take them up now."

"How?" I asked. "Where do I live?"

"Okay, you have to take a bus up the hill. Maybe seven or eight stops, and your apartment is up on the hill. Don't take bus 169 up the hill, and coming down don't take 169-1. But you can take 169-1 up the hill, but don't take 169 down the hill."

"I don't know where the apartment is, though…"

"It's right up on the hill. What do you mean? Just take a bus up there, or take a taxi with your stuff." His arm jerked quickly, flashing red streaks in the air amid the smoke cloud, "Just say DAE-GYUNG-HA-PEE-TA-UN-AH-PA-TUH (태경해피타운아파트). Louie's up there, he'll let you in, Building #8, Room #400. Jesus Christ!"

"I'll help you," Laurie told me. Before long, we were on our way towards our Taekyung Happy Town Apartments. It took me a few months to recognize that the Korean pronunciation of Happy Town was so different, that I hadn't even recognized it as an English word.

Once we stepped out of the hagwan, we turned right into an alley filled with shops and restaurants, such as our future teacher haunt, The Blue Note Bar. That little alley had swarms of people meandering about at all hours of the day, and constant car traffic that honked their horns through it all. It wasn't much different than the alley I had stayed at for the hotel. I carried my stuff through the crowds, directly behind Laurie. But, the crowds were so thick, that she kept falling out of my sight. She was only steps ahead of me, and her blond hair stood out among the mass of black-haired pedestrians, but there were so many people in these narrow streets that she routinely disappeared from my view. Occasional cars pushed the flow of people to the sides. Most businesses were the size of a single garage, but they were crammed with goods to sell. In front of these shops, many vegetable sellers and street food vendors were camped out on floor mats, with their goods spread out, for the many passing by on foot.

Once we worked our way to the bus, we boarded the 169-1 bus in front of a pile heap of garbage. Aboard, our bus kept climbing up and up and up into the mountains. We had even smaller roads to navigate than the walkable alley down below. Not only that, but people were walking in the middle of these roads, much like the alleys, so the bus driver continuously laid on his horn, and stopping for, pedestrians. To make it worse, many of the hairpin turns were so sharp on the steep hills that he had to step hard on both his accelerator and his break, creating a constant jerking motion of the bus. Even worse, the bus was overcrowded, which meant that standing up on the moving bus, was a challenge. There were too many people, too many sharp turns, too many stops and starts, and too much steepness combined in one trip.

Once off the bus, we climbed up two steeper, short hills to our large twenty-five floor apartment building. However, our actual apartment was on the fourth floor, which meant we didn't have much of a view. Actually, we were four floors up, but we had a fifth floor address. This was because 'four' in Korean, was an unlucky number, as its pronunciation sounded like the Korean word for 'death.' Many apartments in Korea skipped the fourth floor, including our own. Not only was that true for our apartment, but it was also true for our hagwan, which was also four floors up, but given a fifth floor address.

Taekyung Happy Town apartment in Gupo(3)-Dong (구포3동), certainly seemed large from the outside, but not so large in the inside. Our living space in the inside, reflected that fact.

Being in the mountains, seemed like a great thing. But it was an inconvenient location in relation to the rest of the city. We were hidden up in a mountain that everything had to go down through the busy Deokcheon (덕천동·德川洞) area, before you could get anywhere else. Deokcheon was the location of where our hagwan was located at.

Once Laurie and I entered the apartment, I immediately received a "Hey dude!" Louie was in my future bedroom, "Hey, let me get these things out of your room, dude! Here, lend me a hand, will ya?" I stepped in, and started handing his things to him. Before long, the kitchen was filled with Louie's stuff.

After we had everything out, I looked around. The apartment had four bedrooms, but only one of the bedrooms had windows. We didn't have a living room, and this was because three of the four bedrooms were the previous living room. None of those bedroom walls reached the ceiling either. They were poorly constructed add-on rooms.

Our social space of the apartment was a dining room table with four chairs around it. This table was against the refrigerator, but it acted as our living room. Equally, we had little kitchen counter space, so this same table served as the kitchen counter to make dinners. In short, there wasn't much space in the apartment for four people.

"Dude, I gotta talk to Laurie before she goes to the girls' apartment. You want a Cass beer? There's some beer in the fridge." Louie already had a beer, "Make yourself at home, dude."

14

The two main beer brands in Korea at that time were Cass and Hite. They were fierce competitors, but generally Pusan was said to like Hite, while Cass seemed to be more of a Seoul (서울·首爾) preference, or so I had heard later. OB Beer would be a third but minor brand. We never saw any other brands of beer in Korea, at that time. Those three dominated the market fully.

It was barely past twelve noon, and Louie was already drinking. I was overwhelmed with Korea already—so was this what it does to you? Drinking beer in the morning?

Louie reminded me again, "Laurie will pick you up in one hour, so you can get back to teach your second shift at the middle school again." He paused, "Are you sure you don't want a beer?"

"No thanks. I have to teach again. I hardly slept either."

"Typical, dude. You gotta get used to it. But just tell 'em, man. You just gotta say 'no', and they back down. Let them know who is boss!"

"I can't do that. I just got here."

"Dude, now's the best time! Make it clear you won't put up with that shit. Otherwise they'll do that to you all the time."

Changing the subject, "So how many people live in this apartment?"

"Four people total, dude. Skate's the oldest, a middle-aged guy, and Stefano is his twenties, like us. Also there's Melvin. People say bad things about him, but you just have to understand he's different."

"How so?"

"You'll see. I don't want to say anything to affect your thoughts on him, dude. Give him a chance. He's different, though." He slugged down more beer.

"Okay, okay, I see. I just have to meet him, eh?"

"Yeah, he's okay dude, don't judge him too harshly though."

The front door opened and an older man entered—I assumed it was Skate. He was big and strong, with an unusually shaped head, high forehead, and narrow chin.

"Fuck, guys," was the first thing out of his mouth. "Glad to be done teaching for a while!" He paused, and looked me up and down, "You must be the new teacher? What's your name? Skate's mine!"

"Adam," I said. "Where are you from?"

"Albuquerque," Skate replied.

"Albuquerque? I can't say I've met anyone from Albuquerque before."

Louie proceeded to step over his own stuff again, automatically handing Skate a beverage. Skate changed the subject, "A bottle of Hite! Perfect! Adam, after teaching, you just need a beer."

"No thanks. I just got off the plane last night, I hardly slept at all, and it sounds like I have to teach all day," I complained.

Louie shook his head, "Typical Korean bullshit, huh Skate?"

Skate yelled, "Damn Koreans!" He opened his beer, "You'll see, man, you'll be trying to get out of the elevator, and they'll all stand there trying to get in as you're trying to get out. That's a Korean, man. I hate 'em!"

I reflected on Skate, how he could be a negative influence on my view of Korea. He would start me thinking on worldviews, how we influence each other by our words. This was his worldview however, not one that I should adopt himself. I asked him, "So why are you teaching here?"

"I don't know, I probably shouldn't. Koreans. The women are hot." Skate approached the window and yelled, "Fuck you, Korea!"

Louie turned to me and shook his head privately, as in, we just have to tolerate this guy.

"Koreans. You'll see, man," Skate said as he turned back from the window. "You talk to the owner at Kupo (구포·龜浦) Hagwan? She won't even look at ya!" Kupo was the name of our language institute, and incidentally, the name of our greater neighborhood in Pusan.

I responded, "Yeah? Was that the owner? She didn't look at me either."

"She can't speak English. She yells at the Korean teachers or secretaries to yell at you. You won't even know that you did something wrong. She doesn't even look at ya. I hate the bitch. All the Korean teachers down there are bitches. Korea. Just don't let them get to ya—isn't that right, Louie?"

"Stand your ground, dude," Louie responded.

There wasn't much to say to any of that on day one. I did reflect on how Skate seemed to be an anti-Korea person, whereas Louie just seemed more adamant about the negatives of this particular language institute. He didn't seem to have the issues with Korea itself, unlike Skate. I would have

16

to sort out all the different personalities, and form my own opinion on things later.

I changed the subject, "So what times do you guys teach?"

Skate responded, "Well, everyone teaches three classes early in the morning and three classes late in the evening. It's a split schedule, man. Everyone does it."

Louie cut him off, "Yeah, but dude, Adam will be teaching at the middle school, too. Triple split schedule. He'll have my schedule. It sucks: You'll be on buses, always trying to get somewhere to teach again. Enjoy this little lunch break, it's all you got until ten tonight. It sucks dude. That's why I'm getting out of this school. I was only here a month, and it was enough for me."

"Am I the only one who needs to do this?"

Just then, the front door opened again. It was a young man with Mediterranean features and curly black hair hanging into his eyes. He was wearing a collegiate baseball cap, had olive skin, and large dark eyes. He smiled at me, "Hey, it's the new teacher."

"Yeah, Hi. Are you Stefano or Melvin?"

"Oh God, no! Melvin? No, I'm Stefano."

Skate laughed, "Melvin! You haven't met Melvin yet, have you?"

"No, not yet," I told him. "Not yet."

"Fuck Melvin!" Skate yelled. "Fuck Melvin!"

"Why is that? What's Melvin like?" I inquired.

"Oh, you'll see," Skate told me. "You'll see! Fuckin' Melvin!"

Stefano asked me, "Where are you from?"

"I just flew in from Portland, Oregon. Just got here last night," I told him. "I don't have a good schedule, though. Louie, does anyone else have a schedule like me?"

Stefano quickly responded, "I do! She farms people out. There are seven teachers working at our hagwan, but there are four of us farmed out to middle schools during the day. She makes a lot of extra money that way."

"Really?" I inquired. "Hmmm...how does she make money on that?"

"Well, you figure she pays us about one million Korean won a month, but then she rents us out to the middle schools for the same amount. So the extra classes we teach at the hagwan are pure profit," Stefano explained.

Skate chimed in, "Damn!"

"Yeah, well, I gotta take a shower before I get back to my middle school again," Stefano said, as he grabbed a towel out of his room and proceeded to the bathroom. "This is one of the few good hours that we aren't all working, but we'll all be back on our buses soon."

"Do they even speak to us at the hagwan?" I asked both Louie and Skate. "No Korean person has told me what I'm supposed to do yet."

"Typical, dude!" Louie chimed in, "It's always like that. They won't tell you a word. Everyone will help you out, though. All the foreigners, that is. Some of the Korean teachers as well, but not all of them. My suggestion is to find a better school."

Skate added, "We'll show you everything you need to know at the hagwan tonight, no problem.

The telephone rang, and Louie answered, "Hello? Oh yes...just a second." He smiled and raised his voice, "Is there a Skate*y* here? Skate*y*?" I later learned that Koreans often added an "ee" or an "ah" sound at the end of words that were supposed to end with a consonant. "Skate*y*, your honey's on the phone!"

Skate picked up the phone, "Hello, sweetie. Are you dressing sexy for me today? You are? What are you wearing? Really? I'd love to see that!"

Louie turned to me, and spat out, "Skate has a lot of honeys!" Then he said a little louder, "Which honey is this one, Skate*y*?"

Skate was still on the phone, "So when will I see you next? Will you wear that miniskirt to class next time? It makes you look SO sexy!"

"Ooooooooo, Skate*y*, you sweet talker," Louie joked.

"Okay, honey," Skate continued. "Let's meet tomorrow for lunch. Promise me you'll wear the miniskirt I bought for you! Promise? Okay. Bye, sexy!"

Louie inquired, "Which one was that, Skate*y*?"

"That was one of the married housewives. Her husband treats her like shit, though. Koreans—they don't know how to treat a woman like a woman," he insisted. "She's a REAL cutie though, a real cutie."

"How many cuties you got, now?" Louie asked.

"Oh, I don't know," Skate responded thinking about it momentarily. "Hye-Jin is a real cutie. If she calls, be sure to get her number. I lost it somewhere." He reflected, "Oh, there's Jin-Kyung, the secretary—the legs on her!"

Louie responded, "What a lady's man!" I wasn't sure if it was a joke or just a response to what Skate was saying.

"Yeah, well, these Korean asshole men don't know how to treat a woman!" Skate got irate, "Mi-Young doesn't even sleep with her husband! Her husband won't even look at her if she's naked! Can you believe that? He'll tell her, 'Put on some clothes,' if he sees that! A sexy woman like that?" Skate slugged his beer down with that thought. "These men have no idea what they got!"

Stefano emerged from the shower, towel wrapped around his waist and black curly locks dripping down into his eyes. "Well, Adam," he added, "It isn't all doom and gloom though." He shook his head back, swinging his curly black locks out of his eyes. "I heard from people working on the other side of the city of Pusan. It's a completely different place over there. People don't stare, everyone is nicer. This area though, eeeh. We are socio-economically poor, living near a large dog market, and all."

Skate yelled again as he raised his beer to his mouth, "Koreans!" He paused momentarily, looked at the clock, "Hey Louie, you need another beer?"

Louie spat, "Yeah, Skate, just a second." He gulped the last of his beer, "Give me another."

"It's a different place here," Stefano added. "Well, regardless of whatever else, at least the streets are safe, and the people are honest, usually."

"Yep," I simply did not know what to say. I would have to experience Korea myself, and make my own judgements. All I could do was let their words linger around in my head.

"Yeah, things are definitely different," Stefano responded. "On the plus side, Koreans are giving, you wouldn't believe how many people have given me umbrellas, when they see me without one in the rain."

"On the other hand," Skate interrupted.

The door opened again interrupting all of them. A tall skinny guy with thick glasses came in. He looked awkward, so I figured he must have been Melvin. He had his Walkman on, and was listening to a heavy metal band at full volume.

"Hey guys," he shouted over the music. "What's going on?"

Stefano shouted back, "Hey Melvin, we're right here. You don't have to yell!"

"WHAT? What? I can't hear you! What? Just a sec!" He fumbled for the volume switch on his Walkman. He yelled again, "What'd ya say, Stefano?"

"I said you don't have to yell so loud!"

"Oh yeah," he said, as he pushed his glasses up with his forefinger while moving his eyebrows up and down, a funny grin on his face. "Schubblebee, sorry," he apologized. I'd never heard such a word before, but he said it real quickly, with all the syllables blended together. "So...uhh...you must be the new teacher?" He said as he pushed up his thick glasses with his forefinger, raising his eyebrows. "My name is Melvin," he yelled.

"Good to meet you," I said. "So where are you from?"

"What? Huh?" he was still yelling, even without the loud music.

"Where are you from?" I asked again.

"Schubblebee," he said again quickly. "Uh, yeah," he responded. "Spokane, and you?" Before I could answer, he yelled, "Hey, do you like Faith No More?" He shouted louder, "I'm listening to Faith No More!"

"Sheeesh, quiet Melvin!" Stefano responded back at him. "Don't yell! We're right here."

"Oh yeah, shoot." He walked over to the television set and turned it on.

"Melvin, what are you doing?" Stefano asked him, "You always do this—are you going to sit there and stare at that Japanese television station?" Stefano turned to me and said, "He'll do it for hours!" Melvin turned the volume down very low, almost inaudible, and sat right next to the TV, his face about six inches from the screen. "That's so bad for your eyes," Stefano shook his head.

"Shoot, Stefano, why are you always telling me what to do?"

I wanted to redirect their conversation, "So where are the other teachers?"

Skate responded, "Well, there are four here, and three are in the girls' apartment. Seven total."

"Yeah, dude," Louie interrupted. "Laurie and I are leaving, but you and this other guy are our replacements. The other guy will be here this weekend."

"Oh yeah? What's his name?"

"His name is Caden. He'll be living in the girls' apartment with Paris and Kristian."

I inquired, "What are they like?"

Melvin yelled, "Paris and Kristian hate me!" With a serious tone, he reiterated it, "I don't know what I ever did to them, but they hate me!"

"Adam, maybe on Saturday, I'll..." Skate began but was interrupted. "Oh, Jesus Christ!!" Melvin was shouting at the television, but then directed his attention towards the ceiling, "Sorry, Jesus. Sheesh! Sheesh!"

"I'll show you around Pusan on Saturday," Skate continued more loudly and forcibly ignoring Melvin.

Melvin shouted, "Basketball highlights!"

"Calm down, Melvin," Stefano told him.

Melvin turned to glare at Stefano and pushed his glasses up on his face. He raised his eyebrows, and his teeth showed as his upper lip raised slightly. "Buzz off, Stefano!"

Ignoring them, Skate continued, "It's a big city; I'll show you the highlights this weekend."

"Yeah, yeah! Go, Go!" Melvin yelled.

Just then, another knock on the door, and Louie's girlfriend Laurie invited herself in. She told me, "Time to go back to the middle school again. You ready to go?"

"Yeah," I told her as I picked up my workbooks from the morning class. "Well, see you guys later this afternoon."

"Okay, we'll see you tonight," I heard them seemingly say at once.

Stefano added, "I can take you down to the hagwan tonight. I go down later than everyone else."

"Cool. Sounds good," I told him. Laurie and I were on our way to start the rest of my first full day in Korea.

***

4

***

Laurie and I wandered down the steep incline toward the bus stop. It was the same one that we had just dragged the suitcases up, an hour ago. Time to go back to work again, already.

Two pale white people with blond ponytails among all black-haired Koreans. I had a Kurt Cobain haircut, but slightly more grown-out. I would keep it tied back in Korea, as it attracted significant attention the few times I did not. Just being a foreigner, attracted enough attention already.

People stopped what they were doing and stared. Kids surrounded us and shouted, "Hello."

"Do they always stare at us like that?"

"Well..." she paused. "You'll get used to it. But around here, they certainly do."

While we waited for our bus, we received plenty of pointing and looks. To get back to the Middle School, first had to go back to the Deokcheon rotary, which was where our Kupo Hagwan was located.

In 1996, Korea did not have a conventional spelling for English translations as it would later. Soft spellings were more common, so Deokcheon would have been Teokcheon or Tokchon. Equally, Busan was Pusan, and Gupo was Kupo. It would be a few years later when South Korea created a spelling policy and standardized the T's into D's, the P's into B's, and the K's into G's.

For the story's sake, I will standardize Deokcheon to its modern day spelling, but I always had a strong preference for Pusan with a 'P'. I have decided that I will keep Kupo Hagwan with a K, but modernize Gupo, the area in Pusan, with the G spelling.

Deokcheon was a huge mess of construction everywhere, and garbage heaps throughout. One in particular reached nearly to the second story of its nearby building. That garbage heap would mark the location that I needed to get to, to board the bus from the Deokcheon Rotary to our Happy Town Apartments. Find the oversized garbage heap, and I'd find my bus.

Pusan only had one subway line, but that wasn't near us. The city was under construction and someday two subway lines would go through Deokcheon. Equally, we had construction all the way up the hill towards our apartment as well. Our bus appeared to be re-routed through a narrow-laned dog market. A larger, wider, road was nearby, but unusable, due to the on-going construction.

As we walked across Deokcheon, we had to cross an overpass to board the next bus. There was a very old lady, always wearing red, with all of her belongings spread out on a mat. She had various items just hanging on the bridge overpass railings. I would continually see her as a permanent feature of that overpass, throughout all of my time living in Deokcheon.

As we walked, one man approached me, said, "USA #1," shook my hand, and said, "Welcome to Korea."

I let out, "Thanks," and he wandered off as quickly as he had come.

At our bus stop, I saw a small group of high school girls in their standard blue uniforms. One of the girls saw Laurie and myself, and she proceeded to nudge her friends to get their attention. Within seconds, several were pointing, which resulted in more strangers turning around to get a glimpse of the foreigners, too. This constant attention that we'd attract, had a strange mix of flattery, but also one of absolute exhaustion.

When our bus arrived, we got on, only to get more pointing and staring from the passengers. When I sat down, I took elaborate notes to help me with the direction. As I did, the older Korean man next to me, leaned over, staring at every pen scratch that I made.

When we got off the bus, we had to walk through the courtyard of the Middle School, to get to the front entrance. Korean middle schools consisted of two perpendicular buildings, three or four stories high, forming two sides of a perfect square. This arrangement allowed for a wide-open square of sand and play areas that made up their courtyards. This meant that walking through it, we were viewed by half the classrooms in the building. Additionally, the schools were fenced in, so there wasn't a back route option.

As we entered the courtyard, children yelled out the windows, "Hello! Hello!" There were several hundred, yelling at the same time. Intended solely to welcome us, the school reverberated with their shouts and echoes of "Hello! Hello! Hello! Hello! Hello!"

I waved my hand, as did Laurie. I asked her, "Do they ALWAYS do this?"

"Yes, always." She confided, "We're probably the first foreigners that most of the school kids have ever seen."

I could hardly hear her through the yelling. "WHAT?"

"YES!" She looked at me, to see if I could hear her, "YES!" This was followed by other words that I could not hear. I nodded my head anyways.

More and more children gathered at the windows, yelling and waving. "HELLO! HELLO!" Each one vying for more attention than the next.

I shouted to Laurie, "But you've been coming here every day for two months!"

She yelled back, "They are excited because they have a new teacher!" We continued walking, and I reflected on what fame must have felt like. This constant unrelenting attention.

Once inside, I put my shoes in a locker and proceeded to put on a pair of slippers. No shoes were allowed in any Korean school. While inside, everyone wore slippers or their socks. Shoes were stored by the entrance. This would be a custom that I would love. I never liked wearing shoes all day anyways, and this custom allowed me to leave them at the door.

When we entered the teacher's lounge, we passed by various teachers, and they stood and bowed to show respect. We continued through the large office space, where groups of desks were cluttered together, representing their respective subject areas. Laurie directed me to the English section. There were no partitions, everyone was in view of everyone else.

Laurie introduced me, "This is Mrs. Baek, Mrs. Lee, and Miss Kyung." They each shook my hand awkwardly.

Mrs. Baek said to me in broken English, "How you do? I'm head English department."

We continued with introductions and formalities, while steady streams of children peaked into the teacher's lounge and giggled. The other two teachers remained silent. There would be another day, where one of the two silent English teachers would break their silence, "You, me, go, you understand," to which I wouldn't understand. But I did quickly understand that the other two English teachers didn't know any English at all. Zilch, zero, nada, nothing. That being said, I think they were really good at teaching English grammar in the Korean language to their students. But, they had no ability whatsoever to use English.

Mrs. Baek continued, "The English Department would like very much to learn from you. We want to watch you teach."

"Mrs. Baek, I have never taught children before in my life. I came to Korea hoping that you could train me!"

"Oh...you never taught before?"

"They told me that if I came early, they would train me for a few days beforehand. Instead I'm working on my first day."

"Today is your first day in Korea?"

"Yes, today is my first day."

"Oh. Class begins now."

"If you could, could you show me how to teach a lesson?"

"Yes."

"Chapter seven. You will teach chapter seven. First, you will say a word, then the students will repeat the word. Then they will act it out." She pointed to a picture of a fireman, "Fireman. Fireman. What do firemen do?"

"I see," I told her. She continued teaching her method while I continued taking my notes. Meanwhile the kids kept coming into the office, screaming and pointing at me. I saw them, but I was busy taking notes, so I couldn't acknowledge them.

Minutes later, I went to teach my first actual lesson. As I pushed through the crowded hallway, the shouts of "Hello, Hello, Hello," were mixed with the repeated demands of "Hi-Five! Hi-Five! Hi-Five!"— something I was sure the kids had learned from Louie. I raised my hand and allowed the kids to slap it. They chanted, "Me! Me! Me!" Just when I thought I had heard enough, a second wave of it began, "Me! Hi-Five! Me!" They yelled all the way to the classroom."

Inside the classroom, there were only twelve students at twelve desks. The other students didn't leave, however. They peered in as many windows as they could. Each classroom had windows that could be seen through from the hallways, but placed at an adult's eye level, closer to the ceilings.

26

This height disadvantage didn't faze them however, as they took turns and lifted their friends to see, or took their own initiative and pulled themselves up to hang, watch, and shout. The halls echoed. I thought they might go home shortly if I waited them out, but they did not.

Numerous times, I yelled, "Go home!" But interruptions and yelling made whatever teaching I had planned not possible. "You kids have to go home!" But they didn't understand a word I said, and I didn't know how to say that in Korean. "I'm trying to teach! You kids have to go!" I closed the windows, but they simply opened them back up again.

I heard Mrs. Baek yell something in Korean down the hall, and the crowds began to disperse—at least temporarily. It was time to begin the lesson.

"Fireman," I said, and the children shouted it back to me. "What does a fireman do?" No one responded. "Fireman," I said again. They repeated it. "What does a fireman do?" No response. I tried to convey what I wanted with the "Shwaah" sound—my imitation of water coming out of a hose. The kids laughed, but no one acted it out. I continued to act like a firefighter. "You try, you try!"

Soon, more kids were back along the walls and doors, making it difficult to hear and speak again. More children waved through the windows and gave me their chanting, "Hello! Hello!"

After two hours of struggle, it was time to go home. Exhausted, I met Laurie once again. I was completely drained and ready to get out of there.

The kids continued to shout madly as we walked away from the school, "Hello! Hello! Hello!"

I shouted to Laurie as best I could "We need to teach them how to say 'Good-bye.' That is a word I would much rather hear right now."

***

5

***

Back at the apartment, I unpacked a few things. But I felt too exhausted and the time went by too quickly; soon I was on yet another bus, heading to the hagwan with Stefano. My third shift of my first day was about to begin.

"Okay, this bus always turns here. Remember, it takes an elbow shape," Stefano told me.

"Yes, yes," I responded exhaustedly.

"And see right here, it turns back on this main road. See that? It's an elbow shape. See?"

"Yes, yes."

"See, it's the same road, but its elbow shapes off the main road. That's where you'll always get off to get to the apartment."

"All right."

"Now, you'll go straight down this road from here—well, it *would* be straight, you see, but of course there's construction."

"Yes, yes," as I wrote down more instructions. "Everywhere there is construction."

"You'll also remember because you go through the dog market. Once you go through, you'll get off at the second stop around the next corner."

"Yes, yes, the dog market—Wait, what?" The dog market contained rows and rows of caged dogs along the sides of the road. Each cage was just large enough for the animals to stand, without being able to walk around. I saw close to fifty or sixty small cages, each filled with dogs. The market had a terrible stench. "I thought eating dog was illegal since the 1988 Olympics?"

"It was, and supposedly there weren't any that summer."

"But it *is* illegal, isn't it?" Butcher tables were set up next to the cages. The dog meat had been boiled and skinned, and you could see the entire musculature of their bodies—and the looks of horror frozen on their faces. Little skinless dogs were heaped in stiff piles. Next to them were dog limbs and other body parts sliced into different cuts. A head attached to the breastbone, the rest being cut into different pieces.

"Yeah, it's illegal, but the police ignore them—or they've been bribed. It's only illegal on paper."

"Ah, I see." As I nodded my head, I noticed back rows, beyond the main rows, of just dogs. In Korea, stores selling the same items were grouped together, competing for the same customers. This bus went through nearly a half kilometer of canine carnage, with even more depths within. One large mass of dogs, butcher tables, and dog cages.

"Gupo Dog Meat Market! Largest dog market in Pusan—maybe in all of Korea. Right between our apartment and our Kupo Hagwan."

"And we get to walk through it a minimum of six times a day! Ahh...Deokcheon-dong!"

"Care for some Boshintang (보신탕·補身湯)?" Around the market, there were many dog meat restaurants, filled with mostly older Korean males. It was believed to make the men more virile. I would have plenty of time to examine and reflect on every aspect of dog meat, while living in Deokchon-dong.

We got off the bus, and I noticed more people turning and staring at us as we proceeded through the crowded streets. We came across one woman who hadn't seen Stefano and myself until we were in front of her.

"Ahh...ahh..." Her eyes popped out at the sight of us. Her jaw dropped, "Ahh...ahh..." She tried to catch her breath. "Ahh...Ahh...Ahh..."

Stefano shrugged, and we made a turn and entered the school.

Kamm, the director, met me at the hagwan's main room, cigarette in hand. "Hey, how's it going there?" He puffed and let out a large exhale.

Obviously, it wasn't that great. "So can I observe classes tonight? I need to see how I'm supposed to teach."

"Yeah, yeah," he said, jerking his hand back and forth, creating a cloud of smoke. Somewhat dismissing my plea, "These guys will teach you everything you need to know! Have they shown you the books yet?"

"No, not yet." Kamm took another puff of his cigarette and blew more smoke into the cloud above his head, which was spread out over the teacher's lounge. I asked him, "All adult students at Kupo, right?"

"Yeah, yeah, that's right," he said. Then he motioned to Stefano, "Why don't you show him what to do? All the attendance sheets and crap, and the books you use."

"I have to teach right now," Stefano responded.

"Jesus Christ!" Kamm yelled. "What the hell? I have to do everything around here!" He took another deep puff from his cigarette. "Jesus Christ, take him to class, ya twit! Take him to your class, Jesus Christ!" He exhaled. "Jesus Christ, do I have to do everything around here!"

Stefano and I walked away, "Where did he learn his English?"

"He grew up in Canada, but he was born in Korea. Korean-Canadian."

"Ah...I see," and with that we entered into a small classroom occupied by five students who appeared to be of college age.

"Hello, everyone," Stefano said to them. "This is our new teacher, Adam. So, Adam, where are you from?"

"Hello. Yes, I'm Adam. I'm from the United States. I just arrived from Portland, Oregon." For whatever reason, Portland seemed easier to say than Michigan. Since it was the last place I lived, I continued to go with that, and I felt I knew it better as an adult than that of my home state of Michigan.

One of the students exclaimed, "Port-Land? Where?"

I pulled out a marker and drew a freehand map of the United States on the board. "Right here," I told him, indicating Portland with a large X. "And this is Seattle, and this is California. Anything else you'd like to know?"

"How old are you?"

"I'm twenty-six years old."

Another asked, "Do you have a girlfriend?"

The class giggled.

"Well, yes and no," I began to explain.

The student quickly followed that up, "Yes and no? What do you mean?"

"I had a girlfriend for several years until yesterday. Now I'm not so sure anymore. So, no, not anymore. So, that is a 'no', but because it was so recent, it feels like a 'yes.'"

Another asked, "Why did you come to Korea?" This would be a question I would get consistently asked on nearly a daily basis.

"Well, to teach English, and to see what it's like to live in another country."

Another asked, "What do you think of Korea?"

"I like it, what I've seen."

One of previous students asked, "How long you here?"

I didn't know if that meant until now, or into the future. I guessed and said, "Today is my first day."

A few gasped and one said, "Really?"

Another responded, "Short time, teacher!"

"Yes, yes." It proceeded like this, until they ran out of questions for me. "Well, why don't you guys tell me about yourselves?" I pointed to the student to my right, "You first."

"My name Moon. I twenty-two year. I am one brother, one sister."

"Have, not am. I have one brother." By saying this I felt I impeded on our conversation. They stopped talking. "Good, good," I tried to get the conversation going again, "Anything else?"

"No."

"Good, very good," I said, as I indicated for the next person to speak, "And you?"

"My name is John. I nineteen year old. I have two brother."

"John? How did you get the name John?"

Stefano interrupted, "They give themselves English nicknames."

I clarified, "Everyone does that?"

"Yes," a student responded, followed by group confirmation.

There was more silence, so I said "Good, good." Then I motioned to the next student. "And your name?"

"My name is Sharon Stone. I'm twenty years old. I have one sister."

"Sharon Stone?"

Stefano interrupted again, "They like to call themselves after movie stars or basketball players."

"Oh," I said. "Well, anything else?" There was silence.

I motioned for Sharon Stone to answer.

"No," Sharon Stone responded, and then all five students stared at me.

"Sharon Stone," Stefano cut in, "What did you do today?"

"Sleep and watch TV."

"That's all?" I responded.

"Yes," she answered.

"What did you do last weekend?" Stefano interjected.

"Sleep."

"Okay, how about Moon? What did you do last weekend?"

"Nothing," Moon responded.

"Nothing? How can you do nothing?" Stefano egged her on, "You had to have done something!"

"Watch TV."

"That's all? Watch TV? Only watch TV?"

"Yes."

"John, how about you?"

"Study," John responded quickly.

"What did you study?"

"Math."

"Do you have a test?"

"Yes."

Then there was silence for a while. All the students stared at us again, they waiting for us to ask more questions. Stefano asked, "Have you seen me juggle yet? I brought juggling sticks!"

"Ohhh," John said, "very good!"

"Can you juggle?" Sharon Stone inquired.

"Yes, of course," Stefano told her. We moved some chairs around and Stefano began juggling, his long curly black hair hanging in his eyes.

"Oh! Very good! Very good," Moon told him.

"You very good juggle!" Sharon Stone clapped.

After ten minutes, Stefano rested. They asked him some basic questions, and then it was back to silence once again.

Stefano turned to me. "Teaching is real easy. Just ask them questions. It's a conversation, and they just need to talk." He then announced to the class, "Okay, let's go home five minutes early today!"

"Yes!" Moon responded with a grin.

On our way back to the teacher's lounge, I asked Stefano, "Do you ever teach out of a book?"

"Oh, yes. It's better, but with a new teacher, they like to ask a lot of questions."

"Oh. Can you show me what books you use?"

We went to the bookshelf. Stefano pulled out a few books and showed me some of his favorites, and then we headed for the bus back home. They were just basic conversation books.

Years later, I would learn how to teach English very effectively. But throughout my time at Kupo Hagwan, I was told it was conversational English, and students wanted to talk. The reality is they didn't want to talk, and they had a large number of other reasons to be in an English class. They didn't appear to want homework either, although occasionally they'd ask for it. Few had time to prepare for lessons. Overall, they appeared to see it as a social activity. They had their own busy lives, and an hour a day was all they wanted to devote to English. Plus, they could make new friends for a month, and then we'd all go out afterwards. Kupo Hagwan was a language institute for adults. They would sign up for a daily class, meeting every weekday at the same time for that month. Then at the end of the month, they may or may not re-register again. Teachers might create followings among certain students, who would always take your class. Other students might rotate and try different teachers each month. Regardless, the end-of-the-month party with the teacher was always demanded, and a near tradition. They enjoyed hearing the American perspective on all of the various issues, even though, at times, I found hearing the Korean perspective to be quite repetitive after a while.

Because of a complete lack of training, and a very small library of actual teaching books to use, I mostly used a very ineffective way of just writing up questions on topics that I found interesting. So, we would explore something like, 'Games', and I would write out 25 questions or so to explore that topic. Since all the students wanted to talk to me, and not to teach other, I became the focal point. This meant that some students talked too much, and others not at all. Distributing and allocating speaking time became a continual challenge for me. Later, I would find that this continued to be a challenge for many.

Nonetheless, this is what I was limited to at this time. So, I spent my time generating discussion topic ideas that I would recycle to all of my many classes. On the plus side, this became an excellent way for me to get to know all aspects of Korean thought very quickly. With time, I could almost guess their collective answers on an entire range of topics.

Being a native speaker, I hadn't thought much about how to express or teach grammar, I wasn't adequately trained for it at that time, and I had few book resources to even do that. At times, I felt that Koreans knew English grammar better than I knew grammar. If I was asked a grammar question, I simply asked a student to explain it in Korean instead, and insisted it was better conveyed in this manner. I did this to avert the question, and because I felt they were more knowledgeable discussing English grammar anyways. Because of this, I focused more on the conversational aspect, and stressed this to students as being my specialty. I would let other teachers focus on their own strengths, and students would gravitate towards what they preferred anyways.

Since we had no program, few resources, an owner who couldn't speak English, and a director who didn't care; we were basically left to fend for ourselves. We taught however we wanted. If a teacher was sex-minded, he geared most his classes into sexual topics. Students that liked that, would take their class. If a teacher was politicized or religious, they would gear their lessons in that direction. Years later, I would see every kind of teacher in all kinds of different situations. Basically, they used the classroom as a venue to teach and argue for their own personal values or causes. Other teachers simply brought board games to every class. Their discussion would be generated around that game.

But, in 1996, with all of the teaching we had to do, the lack of training and resources, and without the internet, we simply did whatever got us through each day. We only had enough time to just rest between classes, let alone develop our teaching abilities or a curriculum.

I stuck with my own method of 'Topic Discussions.' I did everything from gay rights, gun rights, abortion, Middle East issues, Japan issues, smoking in public, and anything else I thought I wanted to know the

Korean perspective on. My general assessment was that most Korean students hadn't thought much on any of these topics. But, certain things would later prove to be immense winners, for example, Japan topics, which created passionate hatreds to come out of my students. I didn't personally find this appealing to hear, as I was equally as interested in Japan as I was with Korea, but it became a clear winner to generate student speaking.

The larger problem I had, was the overwhelming need to understand what they were saying in English. Particularly how to correct the enormity of errors in so many different aspects, while equally trying to encourage them to simply talk. I resolved this by avoiding correcting them. I created a mantra that said, 'Correcting students creates a fear of speaking.' In retrospect, I should have done more controlled conversation with grammar points. But without resources or teaching experience, I felt limited.

What other teachers did in their classroom, I had no idea. We never talked about it socially. We worked too much, we wanted to get to know each other, we wanted to get to know Korea, and wanted to forget about teaching during the few hours of the day that we weren't teaching. I would later become aware that certain teachers were game people, but it was very clear that no one actually knew how to teach English. We did the best we could, with the limited resources and support that we had.

By the end of the first day, I was exhausted. We left Kupo Hagwan at ten at night, and I had to wake up at five in the morning, to start my second day. I wanted to give Sasha a call, but I didn't know if that was appropriate or not. Maybe I would wait until the weekend, and I could try to find a letter, a stamp, and a post office to send something meaningful. I should send something just as one human being to another, even if we no longer had a relationship.

Not having teaching resources was just one of many issues. We also had limited information on basic things like how to make phone calls. It was also a time period prior to the internet. This meant we would become secluded, internally focused, and inbred-like close, as you will soon find out.

***
6
***

It was Saturday, my third day in Korea. Yesterday had been remarkably similar to the day before; I'd taught twice at the middle school—once early in the morning, and again in the afternoon. My evening had been spent at Kupo Hagwan. During the week, I had met Kristian and Paris, the two girls. They were worried about Caden, the new teacher—who would become their new roommate. Caden was to replace Laurie, and I was to replace Louie. They were hoping he wasn't a psycho, as they put it. Caden would arrive that night, so we made plans to meet the girls at the girls' apartment that evening.

It seemed strange to me that Caden and I were officially starting at the same time, the beginning of the month, but I already had so much bonding and connections with my immediate foreign community, simply by arriving a few days earlier. It was a theme that I would regularly see in Korea, this intensive family-like bonding that regularly occurred, filled with all the typical drama that any family might have.

For that first weekend, I had agreed to take a tour of Pusan, courtesy of Skate. We began with the bus route that took us to the nearest metro station, and I scribbled down more directions to places in this complicated maze of a city. Pusan had no street addresses, unlike in the West. To find a place, you started with an address that narrowly defined the area and then you delved further and further into specifics. So first you would find the larger general area and then ask around for the more specific area.

Skate and I made an outline of the places that I should see, with a focus on Seomyeon (서면·西面). Seomyeon acted as a focal point for the city, so if you had any hope to find anything international of any nature, if might exist there, but doubtful to exist anywhere else in the city. The bus took nearly forty-five minutes to reach the nearest subway station of Dongnae. Once at that station, we had subway access to four important areas in Pusan— Seomyeon, Pusan Station (부산역), Nampo-dong (남포동·南浦洞) and Pusan National University (부산대학교/釜山大學校).

The one great location we couldn't get to by subway was Haeundae Beach (해운대·海雲台). Interestingly, they were building a new metro line direct from Haeundae Beach through our area of Deokcheon. Skate explained to me that Haeundae was not only the most visited beach in Pusan, but the most visited in all of Korea. I would see it that night, after Skate's tour, as the others wanted to take me there along with the new teacher.

Once at Dongnae Station, Skate and I boarded Pusan's one subway line to Seomyeon. If we went to the highly visible Lotte Department Store in Seomyeon, we could easily find Young Kwang Bookstore, the best selection of English books in the city. This didn't mean they had a large English section, as it was almost entirely Korean books. But they would have a few desperately needed ESL textbooks, some Korean-English dictionaries, and some old classic literature. Being that our hagwan was so absent of teaching material, I hoped for some ESL textbooks, as well as a good dictionary. I also wanted to see what all they had.

While trying to get on the train bound to Seomyeon, I noticed passengers stood and waited immediately at the subway doors on both sides. "They always do this," Skate complained to me. "They wait right there for the subway doors to open, and the other people inside the subway do the same thing. When the doors open, one side pushed to get on, and the other side to get off." We walked into the mass and waited for the doors, while people behind me pushed me with their palms directly into my back. I looked behind me angrily, and saw a few old ladies. I just pushed my back backwards, to keep my balance. What would you say to old ladies pushing you? I would experience this as a very typical phenomenon throughout my upcoming year in Pusan.

Years later, they created extensive public campaigns to create awareness for people to wait to the side until everyone got off. But, in 1996, those rules didn't exist, and you always had a solid mass of people poised and ready to fight their way on or off at each station. The pushing was irritating to deal with, and different foreigners handled this differently. I learned to position my feet well, while others just pushed through harder.

As soon as the subway did come, we were caught in a mass of pushing and shoving. Skate yelled in my direction, "Koreans! No patience! It's always fuckin' like this!" The bag on my back got caught in the process, as the wall of fighting pushed me in different directions. Skate bullied his way through, which created the opening that we needed. I pulled hard, so my backpack would follow me through the mess. We maneuvered our bodies into open seats—which were fairly plentiful despite the appearance that people were actually fighting for space.

Three high school kids, in their school uniforms, came and stood around us. In Korea, children attended school six days a week, which included Saturdays. They noticed the two foreigners together and began to point, stare, and talk about us.

I ignored them, and opened my notebook to record directions and locations. One of the teens peeked at what I was writing, and then gestured to his friends. Skate yelled in Korean to the kids, "DO YOU WANNA DIE?" The three kids quickly moved and waited near the subway door. They immediately exited at the next stop. "When you've been here for as long as I have, you start to get so sick of this Korean bullshit!" He adamantly continued "I hate that shit! Can't they leave foreigners alone! Korea!"

With them gone, I looked around and saw two other boys, both standing. One pulled the other to himself, so that his frontal parts, was in the other's butt. Then he put his hands in his friend's front pockets.

I looked at Skate, "Gay?"

"Nah," He was still worked up about the other teens staring and saying things about us. "It'll get to ya! Koreans!" His face was still red with anger.

Regarding the two boys standing, I later learned that Korean males had no problem with doing what westerners might perceive as gay behavior. It was extremely common to see two men holdings hands, of any age. Particularly the hardest, most working-class men, often walked down the street holding hands, without any thought of it whatsoever. Young Korean men would often talk to other men, putting their hands on their thighs. These two young boys felt extremely comfortable, even putting each other's hands in the others' pockets, on a public subway train.

However, in contrast, when you spoke with Koreans in the classroom, they adamantly insisted that there were no homosexuals in Korea. They would say it was simply an American or Western phenomenon.

Throughout my time in Korea, I always found it interesting that westerners were more tolerant of homosexual relationships, but wouldn't want anyone to confuse them for being gay. Whereas Korea wasn't tolerant, but this type of behavior was well accepted. Years later, this constant holding hands of men would fade away, and I often wondered if it was because of western teachers commenting on this cultural difference.

Once we arrived at our Seomyeon station, we stood up to wait among the buildup of people at the door. Skate located a middle-aged Korean woman who was dolled up with excessive makeup. He smiled at her, through the crowd of people who had begun to push and shove. I looked at Skate, "Getting off these subways is quite an experience, isn't it?" He was focused on the girl with thick makeup—he hadn't heard a word I said. "Isn't it, Skate?"

"Huh? Yeah," he murmured. The subway doors opened, and the mass of people struggled through each other again. No one wanted to give way to the other. Just one big mass of desperate pushing and shoving. Once again, I felt my bag caught by people as they pushed through each other. Through it all, Skate remained focused on the girl, "Anyunghasaeyo"—"Hello"—he said to her in Korean.

"Hello." She smiled back at him, uncertain of her English pronunciation. All three of us stood in the crowd of people struggling to get around us, both of them awestruck in the middle of it. I struggled through the pushing crowd.

Skate still focused on the girl, "So beautiful, you know you're beautiful, don't you?"

She blushed, "Thank you!" Once we pushed through the crowd, there was a little space to walk comfortably again. Skate moved in her direction, and put his arm around her.

"Where are you going, beautiful?" He caressed her up and down the side of her back. She looked ghostly white from the thickness of her make-up. She was a similar age to Skate, both of them middle-aged.

"I go shopping," she told Skate, in broken English. I stood looking at him, observing his protruding forehead, the way his face narrowed down to his small little chin. The way he looked down on her, due to his height.

"Why don't you join us for coffee instead?" He stressed the word 'us.' Personally, I wanted to go to the bookstore myself. Maybe I was taking the wrong kind of notes, come to think of it. Was I watching a pro at work here?

"Do you know any good places, honey? A good place for a coffee?"

I interjected, "Why don't I give you guys some time alone? If you can show me the bookstore, I can entertain myself for hours. You can pick me up before you go home. Sound good?"

Skate smiled, squeezing the woman's arm, "You don't want to get coffee with us?"

"I can spend hours at bookstores at home. It's no problem."

"Okay, buddy, we can do that." He turned to the girl, "Did you hear that? We're going to show him to the bookstore, and then we can get coffee." She kept looking into his eyes. He asked her, "What was your name, beautiful?"

"Sunny," she said. He slipped his hand down her back.

"Sunny is a beautiful name," he told her, as we strolled out of the subway and into the street. The two of them stared into each other's eyes, as I took notes for future directions as we proceeded toward the bookstore.

Seomyeon looked like a mass of people among tall buildings to me at the time. Years later, I would classify Seomyeon as something like Gangnam in Seoul, or Shinjuku or Shibuya in Tokyo. Basically, it had shopping, restaurants, bars, markets, crowds, and everything else, in tall buildings that lined the streets. It was a focal point for everyone in the city. Seomyeon acted like an American downtown, but was absolutely nothing like one. It wasn't filled with parking lots, it was an area with people everywhere, more like a European capital's most central area. They had some sidewalks, but mostly it was a maze of people walking in the pedestrian-filled streets along with random cars pushing their way through it. It had a buzz of energy and atmosphere that drew people to it. The people appeared different than my neighborhood of Deokcheon. They seemed younger, to overall dress better, and had more spending money available to them. We navigated these streets until we reached Young Kwang Books.

"Okay, I'll see you in one hour, Adam," Skate told me once we arrived.

I knew he wasn't going to be back in an hour, but I gave him the benefit of the doubt. "Sure, take your time," I told him.

***
7
***

I browsed every English book available at Young Kwang. I read travel books, literature books, and teaching books. I studied the Korean-English dictionaries. Skate could take his time. Overall, the English section was small, but sufficient. The main thing was I now had access to reading material in my language.

As I browsed through the teaching books, I noticed a young girl of about fifteen who following me from one section to another. I smiled at her, and she gathered the courage to speak to me.

"Hello. Where you from?"

"USA."

"You English teacher?"

"Yes."

"I study English, I want teacher. You my teacher?"

"Actually, I just arrived three days ago. I can't teach private lessons right now; I don't know anything yet."

She ignored my words, "I study America next year. I want improve English."

"Oh, sure. Give me your phone number. I know other English teachers who might be interested."

"Thank you, teacher!"

She gave me her number, and I went back to browsing through books. This would be another thing I'd have to get used to in Korea: strangers regularly approaching me in the street and asking for English lessons.

A foreigner could accumulate a lot of money giving private lessons here. The catch was that we had very little time to actually teach a private lesson, and the second catch was that it was highly illegal. The Korean government regularly searched for, and deported English teachers for teaching outside of their hagwan contract. I never had time to teach privates, with our work schedule. The hagwan owned us, and being caught teaching anywhere but at the hagwan employer connected to our visa, meant we could be deported. The ironic thing was that our hagwan farming us out to a middle school day was also illegal, and we could be deported for that as well, unbeknownst to any of us at that time.

However the desperation for English teachers was immense. I would recall other times in the near future, when I would go in and out of the Pusan Airport, and have hagwan owners waiting for foreigners to come through immigration. They would try to recruit them to work at their hagwan at the arrivals gate.

"Hello, welcome to Korea! Would you be willing to teach at my hagwan?"

Meanwhile, one hour went by quickly and then two. Sometime during the third hour, Skate came back. "Fuck," he said in his greeting, "You wouldn't believe it. You just wouldn't believe it."

"What? What?"

"You wouldn't believe it! C'mon, let's get out of here! Too many English speakers in here. I'll tell you in the markets."

I bought an English-Korean dictionary and a few textbooks, and we headed into the markets.

He pointed, "You see that building right there?"

"Yeah—what about it?"

"That's where I fucked her!"

"You—really?"

"Yeah, you wouldn't believe it. An hour after meeting her, and I was screwing her. That only happened one other time before in my life. You ever had that? Screwing a girl within an hour of meeting her?"

"No, I haven't. How did that happen?"

"I think she's a crazy one, though. She kept calling me 'Ivan'!"

"'Ivan? Why Ivan?"

"Some American military guy she must have known or something. She kept saying, 'Take me to America, Ivan! Take me to America, Ivan!'"

"Are you serious?"

"Yeah, I'm serious. Even as I was screwing her, she kept telling me 'Ivan! Ivan! I knew you'd come back!' She was crazy."

"So how did it happen so quickly?"

"Well, we were looking for a coffee shop, and we saw that building. There was supposed to be a coffee shop on the fourth floor, but the shop was closed."

Seomyeon was filled with buildings with stairwells. We continued walking through the alleys of Pusan, weaving through the crowds as Skate described what happened.

"The shop was closed, and no one was around in the stairwell." We weren't looking for anything in the market or on the streets, but Skate occasionally mentioned what we were walking through. We passed by animal parts and other unusual objects as we walked and talked.

"So I pressed myself right up next to her on the stairs. She liked that— man, she really liked that. You should have heard her, too, she said 'Ooooo,' just like that: 'Ooooo.' It was the sweetest 'ooooo' I'd ever heard. Can you imagine that, an 'ooooo' like that? She let out little moans of 'ooooo.' It was such a beautiful sound. Right there in the stairwell. Can you believe that? Within an hour after meeting her!"

"So are you going to call her again?"

"I'm a little scared of her, actually; she kept calling me 'Ivan.' But I did promise to meet her Monday afternoon. I don't know if I'll go or not, but I told her I would. It's better to not give your number." He couldn't stop thinking about it, 'Ooooo,' can you imagine a sound like that? I don't know who Ivan was, but she was happy that Ivan came home today!"

Next, we went to Nampo or Nampo-dong by subway, which was the other nucleus for the city, along with Seomyeon. As we sat on the train, a beggar went through our subway car, and placed a piece of paper on every Korean's lap. When he saw us foreigners, he ignored us altogether, but the person next to me, they had their paper sitting on their lap, and I could see a note written in Korea. Only one person on the train gave him money, and everyone else ignored him and his notes. Then the beggar picked up those notes, and took them to the next subway car. It was my first time to see this method of begging on trains, but it wouldn't be my last time.

Another street observation was as we ascended up the exit at Nampo-dong. Whenever I saw Koreans carrying large items up the steep steps, complete strangers would grab the other end and help them carry their bags up the stairs. Once they reached the top of the stairs, the stranger would depart without saying a word. This was another of those habits that seemed fairly entrenched during my time in Pusan. A few years later when I moved to Seoul, it seemed to have disappeared. At the time it merely made me feel irritated, as they'd block all the stairs as they stretched across, slowly ascending upstairs.

Nampodong was close to the shipping ports, so it was one of those unusual places that you might see other white people in Korea. They were always Russian, usually sailors. They were rougher in appearance and attitude, and seemed to navigate in their own world, independent of any interaction with Koreans themselves. Nampo also had the larger cinemas of the city, and many smaller markets of goods being sold. In short, it was a very unique and interesting corner of the city.

We wandered the markets, as we walked in the general direction of Pusan Station, which was the main area for both the ships and the trains as they entered the city.

As we walked, Skate brought up the girl again, "Did you see all that makeup she had on?"

"All the women here wear a lot of makeup, don't you think?" I reflected on the little time I had been in Korea, how rarely I saw a Korean women without makeup.

"Yeah, her makeup was pancake thick. She looked like a china doll. When I was kissing her, it was sliding off her face, it was so thick." We continued to walk at a frantic pace through the market, until I stopped short at the sight of dried pigs' heads sitting on stakes.

I exclaimed, "What the hell are those?"

"Pig heads," Skate told me nonchalantly, changing the subject back to the girl, "Right there in the stairwell. She had a pretty little body, too."

"Pig heads? What do they do with pig heads?" I couldn't keep my eyes off them. Skate tried to move on, but I kept staring at them. Flies surrounded the heads in swarms, and no one noticed except for me—not even Skate. I wondered what kind of country put pigs' heads on stakes.

Months later, I would learn that they were good luck for the opening of a new business. I would see them commonly in such situations.

He inquired, "You're going out with the gang tonight?"

"Yeah. Why, aren't you?"

"No, I can't tonight; I have a date with Mee-Kyung. I wouldn't go out with the gang anyway."

"Is that the woman you were talking with on the phone the other day? The married one?"

"No, it's the one who works as a secretary."

We continued walking to Pusan Station, which was one subway station away. Out front of the station, there was a Wendy's Restaurant. Oddly, this was quite unique for Korea, and didn't last longer than a few years. After seeing the Pusan one during the 1996-1997 year, Wendy's left Korea permanently. During the upcoming year, it would remain one of my few western food sanctuaries in the city. I didn't care for McDonalds, so that left Wendy's, and there was only one in the city.

Across the street from Pusan Station, existed an unusual little street which they called Texas Town or Russia Town. Both names came from the many sailors that would pull into Pusan's port occasionally. Traditionally it was the American Navy ships, but more frequently, it consisted of Russian sailors. They would exit the port, and this little street would be filled with prostitutes, bars, and nightclubs that catered to them. From time to time, it was swarmed by large groups of Russian sailors on shore leave, however, I never happened to have been in the area when those situations occurred. Even though it was in the same city of Pusan, my part of the city was 90 minutes away, due to the mountain terrain, constant construction, and heavy traffic. So, in many ways, it felt worlds away.

Even more stranger to me was that some of the stores in this area had both Russian and Korean alphabets on their signs, and the Korean-looking people in the stores could fluently speak Russian. It made me think that this part of Pusan, might be one of the few sanctuaries in the entire city, where a white person walking down the street, might not get that unrelenting attention that was so common in areas like my own, Deokcheon.

As my Pusan tour continued, I asked Skate about our fellow teachers' social lives. Referring to our group, "Does everyone go out together often?"

"Yeah, they usually do. Not me. I can't stand a big group like that. I'd rather just go out with a friend or two, myself. Fuck going out with the whole gang. The girls are stupid, and Melvin is an idiot. Fuck 'em, I can't stand 'em at all! You'd probably get along with them, but not me."

"Aren't you curious about meeting the other new teacher, though?"

"I'm sure I'll meet him later. You know what I do at the hagwan? I just hang out in a room by myself when I'm between classes, listening to all the shit that goes on there. I can't stand it. I just hide in a room. The Korean English teachers are idiots, and the director is a bitch. Someone ought to tell her to fuck off. I can't stand her. She won't even look at me! Screw 'em all!"

With that, we completed a short exploration of Seomyeon, Nampo, and Texas Town.

When I reflected on Skate, he seemed like a good guy, who certainly reached out to help the new guy. However, he was also a contradiction, in that he had no interest whatsoever in any of the other teachers. Louie was a one-off situation. He had only taught at Kupo a few weeks, as a transition between jobs. His beer-sharing lunch with Skate was more incidental as he was just celebrating his transition from our hagwan.

Skate's main interest was focused on Korean women, particularly the ones in his own age range of the late thirties and forties. But, when I think back to the time I lived with him, I don't recall him ever bringing Korean women back to the apartment. I knew he went out often on dates, but I din't know what resulted in those dates. If I were to guess, maybe it would have been too shameful for a middle-aged Korean women to go into an apartment with a western guy who had an apartment full of westerner roommates. Maybe Skate simply used hotels. I would never know.

In regards to his attitude, it certainly came through strongly. He had a low tolerance for most people, regardless if they were Korean or a fellow westerner. There must have been something about me that was quite acceptable on the tolerance level. He didn't come across in any peculiarly negative or strange way to me, but he certainly rubbed most others the wrong way. I would have time to reflect on this more, in time.

***

8

***

That evening, back in the apartment, Skate began telling Stefano and Melvin *the* story.

"Yeah, right there in the stairwell! You believe that? Did I tell you the sound she made? You should have heard it. The first time I touched her, she said 'ooooo.' Isn't that the sweetest sound you ever heard?" This went on for a while, until even Skate seemed to tire of the repetition and headed off to the shower to get ready for his date with the secretary.

"He's a real ladies man," Stefano replied, but with a tone of voice that was difficult to interpret.

"Aw...shoot!" Melvin shouted. "Shoot! He always gets women calling him up. Skate's a real sweet talker!" Melvin didn't catch Stefano's tone of voice. I found it funny that Melvin never caught the subtleties.

Stefano told me, "We're going to Haeundae Beach tonight. You didn't go there today, did you?"

"Nah, not yet. We saw the markets and the bookstore," I told him, "but not the beach."

"It's a great place," Stefano said. "In the summer like this, you can sleep on the beach at night, listening to the waves. I've done that a few times after drinking."

"Wait, you can legally drink at the beach?"

"You can drink anywhere. They don't have those alcohol restrictions like in the United States."

As we talked, Melvin seemed a bit unsettled, or as if he was waiting for something.

I asked the others, "So have you guys met the new teacher yet?"

"He's down at the girls' apartment now. We'll go down there before we all go out," Stefano replied. "Melvin, what are you doing tonight?"

"Shoot, I don't know!" he responded. "What are you guys doing tonight?"

"I just told Adam we're going to the girls' apartment and then Haeundae Beach."

"Oh shoot, yeah right. Shoot!" Melvin paced the kitchen floor, crinkling his nose up, and pushing his glasses up closer to the bridge of his nose. His eyebrows twitched up and down. You could tell no one had invited him. He wasn't well liked at the girls' apartment. "Shoot, I don't know, I might go to the Monk Bar or something. Shoot, I don't know."

I didn't know what to say, so I told him, "Why don't you come to the girls' apartment with us?"

Stefano gave me an unapproving look behind Melvin's back. Melvin happily said, "Yeah, is that where you guys are going? I'll join you, then."

Within fifteen minutes, Skate was out of the shower and ready for his date. Then Melvin went into the shower to clean up. Stefano quickly asked me, "So, you ready to go?"

"Right now? What about Melvin?"

"He'll be down later. I work with him at my middle school every day. I need to get away from him too. Why'd you invite him with us?"

"I don't know—why not?"

Stefano laughed, "Oh, the girls are going to be mad at you!" Then he shouted through the bathroom door, "See you later, Melvin. We're going down to the girls' apartment now!" Before Melvin could react, we were on out the door.

As we walked, I asked Stefano, "What do you think the new teacher will be like?"

It seemed that the foreign teachers depended on each other for everything, and that every personality in the group was integral to the whole. Regardless of who they were, they were who you had to associate with. If one was a little weird or strange or angry or whatever, you dealt with them, as if they were a family member. You had no choice. So despite only having been in Pusan for a few days, I felt heavily invested in who the new person might be.

"We'll find out," he sighed with a bit of resignation. "So how was your day with Skate?"

"It was interesting, and now I know where the bookstore is."

We continued down the steep hill, the kind you felt in your calf muscles. "I don't always agree with Skate, but you have to form your own opinion of him."

The way Stefano worded it, it sounded like he, and perhaps the others, had experienced past conflicts with Skate.

It left me thinking about the complexities of the group, and how you never knew what kind of a personality might be added into the mix. "You know, I'm the one who will spend the most time with Caden. He and I are taking over Louie and Laurie's places at the middle school."

"Yeah, it's like me being stuck with Melvin. It sucks, man."

"That's what I'm worried about!"

"I wonder how Louie and Laurie are doing in Japan now. He has been here longer than any of us. Nine months total, and then Kristian for eight months."

"You've been here three months already, eh?" I inquired of Stefano.

"Yeah, it's hard to believe it has been that long!" Three months made Stefano seem like a veteran, someone who knew everything there was to know about Korea and Korean culture.

"Three months, that's a long time!" I really believed it was.

***

9

***

Soon, we were knocking on the door of the girls' apartment. Paris, a blond-haired girl from Texas, opened the door. "Come on in!"

The apartment opened directly into the kitchen, which doubled as the living room—the same setup as ours. They had the same inserted partitions that took away any sense of a living room, in exchange for more bedrooms. Their table was much like ours, in that it served as the centerpiece for everything in the apartment. There was no living room there either. The four bedrooms each opened off into the kitchen. Paris and the new teacher, Caden, sat at the kitchen table. Kristian's Korean boyfriend, who had given himself the English nickname Jeffrey, sat on Kristian's bed with her. They talked with the group through her bedroom's open door. There wasn't enough chairs for everyone to be in the same room. I sat next to Caden and introduced myself, "My name's Adam. We'll be working the exact same schedule at the hagwan, and at the same middle school every day."

He brushed his fingers through his brown hair, "Caden is my name." His bangs had grown over his eyes, demanding that he regularly push his hair back to see properly. Caden was a tall, lanky, and confident young person. You could hear the confidence with every statement he made. "What are you doing in Korea?"

I replied, "Well, I wanted to try living in another country." That seemed like an obvious answer, but I left it at that.

He pushed his hand through his hair again, "What are you going to do after that?"

"I don't know yet. I guess I'll have a year to think about it." Korean work visas were one-year contracts. When people signed one, they thought of it as a one-year, right of duty. I countered it with a question, "And how about you?"

"Oh. I write science fiction. I hope to write my third in a series of books during my year here. Then I'm going to go to med school." He tilted his head back, and peered through his overgrown hair. "I need time to finish this latest book, though. My goal is to publish all three before I go to med school."

"Interesting," I told him, nodding. With a slight pause, "Well, I hope to travel after this year, see more of Asia."

"Me too. Although I did teach English last year for two months in Japan."

"Oh? How was that?"

"It was great! That's why I came to Korea. That, and I needed time to publish these books before med school."

"So is Korea like Japan?"

Caden pushed his hand through his hair, "It is more like what Japan used to have been like."

Stefano interrupted, "Melvin is coming over, and Adam invited him!"

Paris shouted at me, "You invited Melvin! Never invite Melvin! I can't believe you did that, Adam!" She was partly serious and partly kidding. Her blue eyes narrowed in a disapproving yet forgiving look. To make sure I knew it was disapproving, she asked me, "What did you do that for?"

"Well, he seemed so sad and stuff! I couldn't just let him wander the streets tonight by himself."

"He's around enough as it is," she responded sharply. "All night long, he takes taxis around the city to all the different bars and hangouts. Believe me—we'll see enough of him."

Caden changed the subject, "So, Paris, what are you going to do after Korea?"

She smiled back, "Well, I have a marketing degree, and I hope to study Korean to make myself more marketable."

Caden followed that up, "How long have you been here?"

She pointed her index finger in the air, "One month."

"And how's your Korean?"

She smiled, "Not so good."

"Well, I hope to learn Korean this year while I'm getting published. I just got out of UCLA this year."

Learning Korean was one of those goals that every foreigner seemed to have when they came to Korea, and everyone believed that just by living in Korea for a year, they would naturally become fluent Korean speakers.

This was never the case, but every new foreigner seemed to arrive with this assumption.

I threw another question at Caden, "Have you taught kids before? The kids at the middle school are young and without English—pretty hard for me to teach."

"Oh, kids. They're easy! No problem. I've taught it all before. I also studied Zen in Japan, at a university. Actually, I've been a Zen Instructor for five years. I taught Zen at UCLA. Plus, I taught English in Japan last summer during those three months."

He had said two months before, but I ignored it. "You shouldn't have any problem at the middle school then," I responded, although I couldn't help thinking it was a bit strange he had no curiosity about it whatsoever. Overwhelming confidence, I guessed. "Well, I've been going there this last week, so on Monday, I can show you the routine." No response, no questions—he acted like it was something he'd done himself a million times already. A very confident, future-oriented fellow.

KNOCK, KNOCK.

Paris sighed with that look, and exclaimed, "That must be Melvin!"

KNOCK KNOCK.

Stefano smiled at me, "I warned you, Adam!"

"I didn't know—I didn't know," I smiled and laughed.

Paris opened the door, and I heard a big "He-Woa!" This was Melvin's favored pronunciation of 'hello.' "What are you guys doing?"

"Melvin," Paris sighed, sounding irritated.

Melvin smirked, pushed up his glasses, and said, "Are you gonna give me a welcome kiss?"

She snipped back, "Shut up, Melvin!" They continued joking for a few minutes. Melvin said a few sexual things, trying to be funny, which didn't go over very well. Caden continued to brag and push his hand through his hair. Meanwhile, Melvin paced back and forth, pushing his glasses upwards making funny faces as he did so. All the while, Stefano and I sat drinking beer.

Paris took her shower. She disappeared into her bedroom for a while, and came out wearing a very sheer miniskirt. You could easily see her underwear through it, and it was so light, it seemed as if any breeze would flip it upward. Stefano, Melvin, Caden, and I all had a difficult time not looking at her—or, rather, that part of her. Even Kristian's boyfriend, Jeffrey, seemed to be paying more attention to the group—which meant Paris—and less time talking with his girlfriend in her bedroom. Eventually Melvin said something that crossed the line, and Paris told him, "Screw you, Melvin!" She kicked him out of the apartment: "Get the hell out of here!" I had the impression that this conversation had happened many times before. Melvin left and started his nightlife early.

Eventually, the six of us took our evening bus to Haeundae Beach. The ride would take an hour—apparently, it took *two* hours during the day, but traffic wasn't as bad on a weekend evening. To get to the beach, first we had to get from our steep apartment way up in the hills, down to Deokcheon. Our apartment was nestled up against the mountains, and the only thing down was always Deokcheon. From Deokcheon rotary, we would navigate around the mountains in either one of two different directions. Pusan, as a whole, was a very mountainous city crammed up along the ocean's coast.

As there were six of us, we opted for two taxis down to Deokcheon. The four people from the girl's apartment took one taxi together, and Stefano and I took the other. We would meet at the bottom of the hill in Deokcheon, at which we would then take the longer bus ride that led directly to the beach. This would be my first taxi ride.

As Stefano and I took our taxi, the driver stopped for another passenger. I interrupted Stefano story that he was telling, "Why is he stopping for more people?"

"They want to double up on fares," Stefano quickly answered, while more deeply involved in sharing his story.

However, the man he stopped for, didn't get in. The taxi driver simply drove immediately away without saying a word back to the man. "So, how come he didn't take that passenger then?"

"He wasn't going in the direction that we are going."

I accepted that answer, and watched the taxi driver continue to stop for others. Eventually a very typical Korean man jumped into the front seat. He looked like everyone else around here, a short conservative haircut, with his dress shirt tucked in. His clothes, including his slacks and dress shoes, looked worn and cheap. His shirt was a yellow and brown checkered short-sleeved, buttoned-up, collared type of shirt. Most men at that time seemed to like either checkered shirts or checkered slack pants, or sometimes both. Particularly around Deokcheon, this was common attire at the time, despite that the colors violently clashed. Green, brown, and yellow checkered clothing appeared to be the most in demand.

I looked at Stefano contemplating our new fellow passenger, "Are you sure this is normal?"

"Yep, happens all the time around here."

Now we had three passengers, but this wasn't enough for the taxi driver. He continued to pull over for a fourth. The same drive-off occurred if the potential passenger didn't give the right answer, but eventually one must have said something right, and we had the car full of people.

Ten minutes later, we were at Deokcheon. Stefano and I paid what was on the meter, but the other two men stayed in the taxi, off to wherever they were going.

Once at the Deokcheon rotary, we regrouped with the others, and we walked past our hagwon to get to our next bus stop. As always, we attracted a lot of attention, being six foreigners together in a group. I heard people shouting and yelling and screaming behind us. Everything was loud and crowded in this area, but their noise seemed to demand our attention well above the other noise and yelling.

I turned to see a group of screaming high school girls, incidentally pointing and yelling at us. "What's going on?" I inquired of Stefano, "Why are they so excited?"

"Don't you see? It's us. They see us. That's why they're so excited."

"Oh. It's nice to be the foreigners!"

One of the girls approached us and handed out a few flowers. She gave them directly to Caden, Stefano, and me. I felt flattered by the attention.

Paris asked smiling, "What about ours?"

"Just a second." The girl went back to get two more flowers—one for Paris, and one for Kristian. Jeffrey, the Korean among us, didn't get one.

"What about him?" Paris indicated Jeffrey.

"Sorry." She went back to her friends and got one more for him.

After that, we bought some beer for the bus ride. It would be an hour to the beach. Nothing eventful happened, except the typical pointing and staring from the other bus passengers. I asked for translations to know what they said as they pointed.

"They are saying 'Americans' as they point to us. *Miguk-saram* (미국사람·美國人). Every time you hear that word, that is what it means.

This directed my next question, "What about the Canadians among us?"

Kristian signed. "They just assume that we are all Americans." She looked at one of the pointers, pointed back to their group, and said, "Hanguk-saram (한국어사람)? Hanguk-saram!" Then she pointed back at herself, "Canada-saram! (캐나다사람)"

I immediately asked Kristian, "What did you just say?"

"I just pointed at them and said 'Korean.' Then I pointed at myself and said 'Canadian.'"

"Ahh. Does that make them stop pointing and saying that?"

"Nah, I just makes them point and stare more, as they hear me speak Korean."

"Ahh."

Haeundae Beach represented 'the other side' of the mountain. As did the one subway line that went through Pusan at that time. It was where the attention became a little less, and things for foreigners seemed at least a little less 'full on' from the constant attention. At Haeundae Beach, the attention dropped considerably. Mostly because it was a major tourist attraction for the country, and the country's premier beach.

It was also a place that we might actually see tourists, particularly Japanese tourists at that time, and we would see some Japanese writing on various buildings. It appeared quite exotic and interesting to me, this idea that we might see Japanese people here. We never did, but I always imagined them to be holed up in some of the hotels.

In 1996, I don't recall ever seeing any Caucasian foreigners at the beach, but by 1997, the teachers descending onto the city would increase considerably, and then I regularly would. Years later, foreign-owned bars would pop up around this area, and come and go. But at this time, our focal point was the only bar we knew of, and that was the dance floor at the Hyatt Hotel. This was located on the beach side of the main street.

Hyatt Hotel was particularly expensive for us, on our teacher's salary. So, we did a little dancing, mostly for the interest of the girls among us. Then we would go a nearby store, and just buy our beer to bring to the beach. We would sit on the sand in the moonlight, and listen to the crash of the ocean waves at night. This became a Haeundae routine, on the weekend nights we chose this option.

At the beach, you would see small groups of people scattered about talking to their own group of friends. Occasionally, you'd see a few beach wanderers, who would look to join random groups. These people were usually older or middle-aged Korean men called ajusshis (아저씨) in Korean, which simply meant older man. Once these drunk ajusshi men saw foreigners, they always tried to join us, solely to practice their English on us.

It was a common experience for any foreigner in Korea, at this time. Usually it happened in bars and restaurants, but any open space was fair game, like buses and trains, and equally the beach was yet another popular place to experience this attention.

One older man overheard us speaking English, and it drew him quickly to lecture us, "You are in Korea, and you must speak Korean." He pointed accusingly at us.

As he said this, he then plopped down in the middle of our group, and began to interrogate us in English, "Where are you from?" It would be a general pattern that we'd experience. A mix of basic questions, but all designed as a way for the person to practice their English on us, and dominate our conversation options.

We collectively excused ourselves away from him, and moved on down to a more secluded, isolated, less well-lit section of the beach. Within ten minutes of enjoying each other's conversation, the cycle would repeat itself. A different ajusshi man joined us, "Where are you from?"

"Good to meet you," Kristian politely told the man, "But we have to meet *our friends* now." Basically our code word excuse to exit that situation. We quickly finished the large bottles of Cass Beer that we had, and went to the Hyatt Hotel's downstairs club. That would be enough for the beach for now.

Inside Hyatt's disco, there were many upscale Koreans dancing, drinking, and sitting around trying to look demure or handsome, depending on their gender. The dance floor was small, but lit up with strobe lights.

Caden and I sat at the bar for a while, watching the dance floor. Caden, I noticed, seemed particularly interested in Paris and her sheer miniskirt as she danced. He turned to me with a big grin, "Paris has been hitting on me all night. I am really going to enjoy living in the girls' apartment."

"Oh yeah? What has she been saying?"

"She keeps touching me and flirting with me."

"Well, that's something to look forward to while living there."

"It's gonna be a very good year," he told me as Kristian and Jeffrey motioned for us to join them on the dance floor.

Stefano was spinning Paris around to the music—it appeared that Caden was not the only one getting a flirtatious vibe from her.

After several more songs and our round of drinks consumed, we decided to get the less expensive bottled Cass beer from the convenience store and bring them down to the beach. Hyatt Hotel would be there, whenever we needed to escape another drunk wandering ajusshi.

On our way to the convenience store, we came across something that I would call a kimbap (김밥·紫菜包飯) shop. These types of shops had plenty of quick and cheap Korean food options, but the kimbab was one of the quicker and easier items to order and have within a few minutes. They were vegetables rolled in rice, and wrapped again in a layer of seaweed paper. We bought six of them, and they placed them in plastic bags.

Next was the convenience store, where we bought the largest bottles of Cass and Hite beers. We decided on ramyen (라면·拉麵), which came in a pre-packaged cup container. All convenience stores had free boiling hot water to add to these, before you left the store. We added the hot water to the ramyen, and had to carefully carry it along without spilling it. I watched Stefano and Paris diligently carry theirs to the beach. Kristian and Jeffrey carried the kimbap, which was individually wrapped in tin foil.

Caden and I carried the heavy Cass bottles in plastic bags, which wonderfully clinked in a salivating, anticipatory way, as we walked.

Haeundae Beach was a long, thin stretch of beach surrounded by skyscrapers, with mountains in the background. The moonlight shone through our beer bottles in the most amazing way. The setting couldn't have been more ideal, and the way the gentle breeze hit us, was a feeling that enhanced the magic of it all.

We found a place in the sand, surprisingly free of the beach wanderer group-joiner types. It was a little past midnight, so it was possible that the beach wanderer types had wandered off onto buses, or had simply passed out where they last remained.

Nonetheless, we located ourselves so it wasn't obvious from lamp post lighting that we were a group of foreigners, and we tried to sit out of vocal range of others. We wanted to get to know each other more.

Once situated, Kristian and Jeffrey sat a little distance from the rest of us for their own privacy, so the three of us guys centered on Paris.

I buried my own feet into the sand. Paris was playfully kicking at my covered feet. She was facing me in such a way that her panties were visible, and the feeling that she was flirting was inescapable. She was often looking down and focusing on her ramyen, but it made her appear obliviously unaware of what she was really doing. At times, she jumped up to shake any sand on her butt, then sat back down. At one point, she went through her purse, pulled out her Texas driver's license, and showed it to Caden and myself, "Korea has really aged me, look!"

I looked, took a sip of my own beer, and made a polite fuss about what a great photo it was—"You look like a cheerleader! Is that really you? Amazing!" The breeze continued to hit just right, and I sat and contemplated how I loved being on this side of the ocean. I loved the fact that way over there somewhere lied Japan, and then way over beyond there, Hawaii. Then on my side of the world, lied Oregon and California. I was just there, and now I am here. Stefano was evidently doing his own contemplation, and he wandered off closer to the ocean itself, and sat down alone by himself.

We sat in the moonlight drinking more beer, and Paris inquired, "What's he doing over there?"

Just a weekend ago, I wouldn't have known Stefano, so I wouldn't have known if it was out or character for him or not. But with me, he seemed to be a social person, who enjoyed being around other people. I reflected on the fact that this intensity of just being a foreigner and living abroad, created this intensity of friendship, as if you knew people significantly longer than you actually did.

We left him alone for quite some time, then I decided that I would leave Paris and Caden to join Stefano for a while, as if Stefano and I had been best friends throughout our lives. "Hey, man, how's it going?"

Stefano and I made some small talk, and then he confessed, "Did you know Paris and I have been flirting all night? I wonder if I should try to sleep with her..."

"I don't know, Stefano. Seems like a bad idea. Actually, Caden thinks that she's flirting with him, too. *Actually*, even *I* feel like she is doing that to me."

"She told me that she thought Caden was too arrogant."

I laughed. "I can't argue with that."

"So what do you think I should do?"

"You don't want to do that. She's your coworker. Things will go bad, and you'll both be miserable!"

"Well, we've talked about it: and it would be strictly for sex—no boyfriend-girlfriend stuff. No relationship whatsoever."

"I still think it's a bad idea. You'll ruin your friendship. You can't sleep with a friend!"

"Yeah, that's what I'm afraid of."

"So, repeat after me: 'I will not sleep with my friends.'"

He laughed. "Okay, thanks for the advice." Then we joined the greater group. We talked and drank and listened to the ocean waves at night. A bit later, Stefano and Paris wandered off to dip their toes into the ocean.

That left Caden and I talking together. "Hey," Caden confessed to me, "I think I might sleep with Paris tonight. She's really been laying it on me—especially while you and Stefano were talking over there."

"Really?" I responded. "Is that so?"

Overall, it was a memorable and fantastic way to get to know Paris, Stefano, and Caden. After a few more beer runs, we knew that Sunday was yet another workday, so we resigned ourselves to get in a taxi back to Deokcheon. We would call it a night for Haeundae Beach, but it was certainly a place that I wanted to get back to again.

In a much later reflection, I thought of Paris, and how isolating it must have been to be a single white female in Korea. Kristian had her Korean boyfriend(s), but Paris evidently had a stronger preference for western males, as I never heard of her express interest in dating Korean men. That probably left a deeper sense of seclusion and isolation, and loneliness. Particularly in the type of foreigner bubble that we lived in, and such a small confining work-centric bubble that it was. She was obviously looking for some kind of deeper connection herself, and a situation with two new guys along with Stefano, and the moment certainly presented itself to her as a gift.

For myself, I was still trying to get a sense of what Korea was, but I liked it a lot. In fact, I felt I could love it. We would see how things would play out, for all of us.

***

11

***

Within several weeks, I began to get into a pattern. There wasn't much time to reflect, it became a quick routine of seven days a week of non-stop teaching, with a slightly lighter teaching load on weekends than weekdays.

At the hagwan, there were patterns. The classes that started at six thirty in the morning, usually consisted of tired office workers. The later morning hours at the hagwan consisted of more housewives. I would be back at the hagwan to teach various classes between five and ten at night. These evening and night students were an eclectic mix. They often wanted to collectively go out at night, and they usually organized that every few weeks, as a class. They were always free to join us on Friday nights when we made ourselves available to any students socially.

Mostly I found the discussion topics changed significantly depending on who was in my class. For example, the oldest Korean male in any classroom, let's say his name was Mr. Kim, says, "There are no gays in Korea, Korean women don't smoke, and Korean couples would never live together before marriage."

Then everyone else in the classroom will adamantly agree, and say, "That is correct, there are no gay men in Korea, Korean women don't smoke, and Korean couples would never live together before marriage. Those (immoral) things only happen in your country, in the United States."

However, if Mr. Kim and any other older ajusshi Korean males were absent that day, the student stories changed considerably. Suddenly, little Marilyn Monroe would admit that she lives with her boyfriend, she smokes a half a pack of cigarettes a day, and suspects that she has a gay male friend. Then she would open up and we would discuss her boyfriend problems. You put Mr. Kim and the other older Korean males back in the classroom, and suddenly we are once again talking about how none of that stuff ever occurs in Korea, and they would all agree, including little miss Marilyn Monroe.

The Middle School was a completely different experience from the hagwan. I was dealing with kids, and I found disciplining to be a chore. Not only did the students not know English, but few of the English teachers did either.

In one class, I decided to punish a student for misbehaving. I told him, "Sit down, Tom! Where is your book? You don't have a book? Why won't you sit down! Now I want you to clean up the classroom!"

All the students continued to ignore me, and the few that paid attention to me, didn't understand what I was asking of Tom either.

I decided to demonstrate. I picked up a piece of paper and crumpled it, "You see that paper, you pick it up, and you put it here!" I angrily threw it in the trash container. Tom looked at me, but was rather confused. I demanded of him, "Okay, you do it!" He still didn't do it, and continued to have that confused look. I repeated my punishment again, picking up yet another paper, crumpling it up, and demonstrating. Before long, I had cleaned the room with my demonstrations, and Tom, nor anyone else, had any idea why. How do you discipline anyone, if they don't understand the punishment? Defeated I resigned myself to, "Okay, turn to page ten," I said. "Tom, you look at Archie's book."

When I did have time to reflect, I thought about connections. Was I connecting with anyone here? Was I engaging with the culture? As much as I wasn't sure about Caden at that time, he became the one person that I spent most all of my waking moments with, as he had the same teaching schedule that I did. He boasted to me about all his goals and dreams, which didn't seem achievable with our work schedules. It rubbed me the wrong way, for whatever reason. We did have one thing in common, in that we had both left a serious relationship when we came to South Korea.

He brushed the long hair out of his eyes, "Her name was Luna." He jerked his head back to keep the hair from falling into his eyes. "We lived together for two years before I came here."

"Yeah, really?" I thought about my similar situation, "I also lived with Sasha for two years, as well as dated her before that. Not easy to leave a relationship, is it?"

"Tell me about it. Luna was pissed when I told her I was going to Korea!"

"Sasha was, too. It was a hard time, especially the last few weeks."

"Luna and I just got in a fight, and she said she'd never speak with me again. Now she's dating my best friend! That made it easier to leave!"

"It wasn't like that with Sasha and me," I told him. "We wanted to hate each other, but we just couldn't. Listen to this: we decided to take our last trip together, down into northern California—the redwoods and such. Well, we were at this café eating breakfast—"

Caden began to venture into his story, "Well, with Luna..."

"Listen to this," I interrupted. "We were at this diner café, and things were going well, but there was a lot of tension because I was leaving. So I told her, 'you seem high strung on this trip,' and she got really upset: 'High strung? You're calling me high strung? I'm not high strung!' She told me, 'I don't have to take this,' and she wouldn't say another word to me. I pleaded with her to talk to me, but she wouldn't say anything."

"Women are..." I could tell Caden wanted the floor again.

"Listen, Caden, I'm not finished," I told him. "So, Sasha wasn't talking to me, and I stopped trying to discuss it with her. 'Let's just go home and forget about the rest of our trip,' I told her. That just made her angrier. She paid the bill and wouldn't even take my money as I tried to hand it to her. She walked back to our table, threw two coins at it, and stormed out to the car. What do you do in this situation on a road trip?"

"Yeah," Caden interjected, "it is easier if you hate the person. That's what happened to Luna and me. We hate each other right now."

"There's more to the story. So she jumped in the car and started it. I went around to the passenger's side, and she reached across the car and slammed the lock down from the inside. So now I was in a panic. Here we were, miles away from home and having an incident. Part of me thought it might make it easier for me to go to Korea, with an ending like that. Anyhow, I started knocking on the door of the car, 'Let me in!' She reversed the car while I was yelling, 'C'mon Sasha, open it up, Sasha! C'mon!' She spun the tires kicking up dirt. I ran like hell trying to chase her!"

"Damn!" Caden responded.

"Yeah, but you know what, she drove about a hundred yards, and then she just stopped," I told him. "She just stopped right there. I didn't know what she was doing; I thought maybe she was going to throw my bags out the window, but she didn't. She just stayed right there. I jogged to the car, and she let me in. She still hadn't said a word. We sat in silence for the next hour, driving back to Oregon. Then she turned to me and said, 'I'm sorry Adam, I'm sorry.'"

"That was it?"

"You see, we were so angry at each other, and neither of us wanted things to end. Then we laughed about it. But, y'know, I was afraid to laugh too much about it, because it felt like it could happen again any time."

"Do you miss her?"

"Of course I do. Maybe I shouldn't have left."

"I hope I'll be with Luna again. Have you written Sasha?"

"Yes, I've written her twice already. Have you written Luna?"

"Yes, three times. I think about her often, even if she is dating my best friend."

"That really sucks. If you went back, do you think she would still be dating him?"

"I don't know. I'm sure she was mad at me, just like Sasha was mad at you."

"Yeah. It sucks, doesn't it?"

That was the one thing that Caden and I had in common, and we talked about it often. The rest of the time, I just listened quietly to his big tales about all the things he was going to do.

As neither of us were currently involved with anyone anymore, we did discuss the Korean female teachers as potential dating partners. Describing them was problematic, though. "You know the Korean teacher with the long, black hair?"

"The thin one?"

"Yeah, that's the one!"

That described all of them.

I thought about Sasha at night, wondering if she was thinking about me as well. We had already drifted apart. It was 1996, and e-mail wasn't commonly available yet. Staying in contact by phone was nearly impossible with the time difference, and letters took forever to arrive. I had to reassess what exactly I was trying to hold on, when I had already clearly let her go.

I logically decided that a deeper connection with Korea is what I needed. I would begin to study Korean. I would try to make a Korean girlfriend. I would try to integrate and fully understand my new home, and everyone in it. I wanted to understand my students more. The one thing everyone continued to tell me was, "You should make a Korean girlfriend, then you will become fluent in Korean." This seemed logical to me. This seemed like what I needed to do. Make a Korean girlfriend, learn Korean, and I would have that connection that I so desperately sought. The answer became so clear, I wouldn't even consider rotating the colorful flower with the, 'Should I,' or 'Shouldn't I' petals. Just do it. There was no backing out of this. There was no 'resigned on the couch' with hopelessness, not that I would have wanted that anyways. I had a well-connected, logical plan.

I bought Korean books, I studied the Korean alphabet, and I spent my free time memorizing Korean characters. Yes, I had a plan.

***

12

***

It was my third weekend, and it was a Friday night. The Friday night routine involved a nearby cafe/bar, just around the corner from the hagwan, called the Blue Note. Many students saw studying English as a social event, and many wanted to see the foreign teachers in a social setting. This was highly encouraged by the hagwan, as it meant increased popularity/demand for our classes, which meant more potential income. Various teachers finished their evening at different times, depending on their rotating monthly schedule, but we all agreed to meet at the Blue Note Cafe as we finished teaching. Our respective students, and our fellow Korean teachers, were all welcome to join us. Many did exactly that.

Having taught the entire day, we had the other routine of trying to find some food to eat, between or after our classes. By this time, I had discovered foods like seolleong-tang (설렁탕) or galbi-tang (갈비탕·排骨湯). Both were a type of soup which included meat, clear noodles, and various additives like salt, ground black pepper, red pepper, minced garlic, and chopped spring onions. I would have wanted exactly that, if it wasn't already late on Friday with the other teachers and students already socializing.

Because of my late work schedule, I stuck with Odang (오뎅·關東煮) on Fridays. It was a type of street food that I was introduced to early on. Odang was a fish hot dog on a stick, and it rested in a wonderful broth. Whenever I needed some quick sustenance, for example, between classes, I would go and devour as many of those as I could. All the Kupo teachers went to the same whole-in-the-wall, which was just around the corner from the hagwan, and nearly across the way from the Blue Note Cafe. For many new teachers, myself included, street food was the best method to get food, until we learned to read restaurant menus in Korean. Simply approach the stand, devour as much odang as you desired, and pay them afterwards based on how many sticks you set down, all done without needing to say a word. Perfect for anyone on the go, or a mute-feeling foreigner.

On this particular evening, Caden and myself, approached our regular street food stand, which consisted of odang, and mandu (만두·饅頭). As we were the newest teachers, we had the worst schedules, finishing at ten at night, while the others would be well-drunk by an hour or two ahead of us depending on their last scheduled class.

Our night began with a Korean man who was driving past on his motorcycle. When he saw two white people like myself and Caden standing at this stand and eating Korean food, he turned his head to stare. A few walking pedestrian were almost hit by him, but it didn't faze him. He then parked the bike in that exact spot that he began his stare, threw his legs over one side towards us, and simply sat on the bike and watched us. We were like escaped zoo animals who had somehow amazingly learned to eat human food. He didn't budge, and he didn't feel an ounce of shame or any emotion whatsoever than that of awe that these non-Asian people exist in Korea outside of the television. When we paid for the odang and mandu, we walked away, the motorcycle driver simply swung his legs back on his bike, and drove away.

This man lingered in my mind long after the incident, as it struck me as something that many of the less shameless would have loved to have done when they encountered foreigners. A similar common story I often heard were from foreigners who lived in ground floor apartments. At night, they'd see the occasional tracer of a lit cigarette from the living room or bedroom windows. Upon exploration the next morning, they'd see a pile of thrown away cigarette butts on the ground.

After our regular attention-attracting activities from the outside world, we entered the inside world of the Blue Note Cafe. This was a typical Korean establishment that had large tables, huge chairs, but very community oriented, at least for the group that you were with. There were no western bars anywhere that I was aware of, nothing with barstools or billiard tables, although perhaps in Seoul's Itaewon (이태원·梨泰院), as I would discover later. Additionally, Korean bars required patrons to order anju (소주), which was a Korean word for mandatory side dishes to be served with alcohol. They were usually fruits or other items you wouldn't expect to be eaten with alcohol. Patrons were required to purchase anju regardless if they wanted them or not. It would be years later until Korea would deviate from this anju system.

Another thing Korean bar establishments often had, was western themes. These included images of cowboys or American movie stars, or items such as American license plates. The Blue Note Bar and Cafe was one of these typical places. The decoration was filled with American memorabilia. I was equally sure that I could find both an Oregon and a Michigan license plate somewhere on the walls, if I looked for them.

For the basic setup, the foreign teachers were given two large tables in a back room, which had booths and added chairs, able to fit at least 15-20 people, surrounded by four walls, and hidden from view. The Korean teachers always sat near the front entrance, which was the opposite side of the bar. Occasionally one of us foreign teacher would join them, or one of them might join us. The hagwan students, might have had both as teachers, but they had a preference for trying to join us in the remote and hidden back of the bar.

Some nights, we would have up to twenty-five teachers and students socializing after work, but it varied considerably. This Friday night, Louie had returned from Japan and he joined us for drinks.

As we entered the back room, Paris yelled loudly for us, in a unique, slight Texas way, which I always liked to hear. A tinge of Texas also existed in the bar as Texas license plates and American wagon wheel decor would have been all too common in most Korean bars.

As I sat down, a Korean student quickly told me, "My name Hyun-Ju. I want to say hello." She paused for a moment than spurted it out again and laughed, "Hello!"

"Yo, Adam," Stefano interrupted her to ask me, "Want a beer?"

"Sure," I shouted back.

"My teacher is Paris," the student who had just said hello, nervously told me.

Paris yelled, "Heck yeah," to the student and gave her a high-five.

Stefano shouted, "Yo, Louie, you want another beer?" He didn't hear him, so he shouted out again, "YO, LOUIE!"

Louie spat out, "What?" He was trying to put his arm around a nearby female Korean student. The student moved away from him.

"You need another beer? We're ordering more."

"Yeah, get me two!" Louie spluttered back. "One for me, and one for the honey! Isn't that right, honey?" His honey squirmed away as he tried to recapture her again.

"Where's Laurie?" Melvin inquired, as his index finger extended and pushed the bridge of his glasses up his nose. He squinted a few more times immediately afterwards.

"Laurie? Laurie who?" Louie winked.

"You know—*Laurie*," Melvin pointed at him accusingly.

Hyun-Ju asked me, "How long have you been in Korea?"

"Three weeks," I answered.

She was surprised. "Three weeks? You like Korea?"

"I like it," I told her. It hit me strangely thinking that I had just arrived in Korea, but the connections I felt with this group, were easily some of the deepest and strongest connections of my life, nearly equal with that of college roommates and family itself. I asked the group, "Where's Skate tonight?"

"He hates going out with us," Stefano responded.

"Skate? He hates me! He can't tolerate being in the same room as me," Paris shouted. "He thinks—get this—I'm too hyperactive!"

Kristian's arms were wrapped around Jeffrey, her Korean boyfriend. She shouted, "Tell them why! Tell them why!"

"Well, the first night I arrived in Korea," Paris exclaimed excitedly, "I was freaking out! I couldn't deal with how things were! Insane! He must have thought I was a freaking nut! He didn't know how to deal with me."

"This is the kind of girl who can't walk over an overpass without freaking out," Kristian shared with us.

"OHHH!" Paris screamed. "Kristian, don't even talk about overpasses!"

Caden asked the group, "So, when are we going to talk with the Korean teachers?"

Jeffrey turned to me and asked, "Do you want shrimp chips?" These were a mainstay of the drinking experience in Korea. They served these snacks at most bars.

A different student asked me, "What do you think of Korea?"

Paris still thinking about the previous conversation, "I hate those overpasses!"

Melvin attempted to position himself closer to a female Korean student. As he moved around the table, he knocked the shrimp chip out of my hand. "Scrubblebee!"

Caden blurted out again, "Who's gonna go with me and chat with the Korean teachers awhile?"

Nearly the same time, Louie inquired of a Korean student, "C'mon honey, where you going?" She grabbed her purse and squeezed herself to sit between two of her friends on an already overcrowded couch. "Awww...c'mon, honey," Louie added, "I'll behave."

"Beer is here!" Stefano shouted. "Hey Louie, here's two for you! Yo Adam! Hey, who else needs another beer?"

"Yuck, you smoke!" Melvin said as he moved to sit next to the pretty Korean woman he had been angling to meet. "I hate smoke! It's disgusting!"

The girl was speechless, and I marveled at Melvin's approach. He'd gone to all that trouble to tell her that?

Another student inquired of me, "How long you stayed in Korea?" This would be a question I would get a lot, I could see.

Caden specified his once open inquiry towards me, "C'mon Adam, let's go join the Korean teachers!"

"Okay, I'm game!" And off we went.

The Korean teachers were on the other side of the room in their usual Friday location. We approached their table, and they collectively stopped their conversation.

The first response was when one of them said, "We wondered when you would come and say hello. We saw everyone but you two." Throughout the evening, I had noticed that other teachers had made their rounds to say hello to them, at least for a little while. Caden and I sat at opposite ends of their table.

One of the teachers asked me, "What do you think of Korea?"

Another asked Caden, "What do you think of Korean students?"
The questions continued: "Why did you come here?" "How long will you stay in Korea?" "What food do you like?" "Have you gone to Seomyeon?" I answered as well as I could: "Three weeks...I hope to stay a year...I like it very much...Everyone is very friendly...I like mandu and galbi-tang...Yes, I've been to Seomyeon...Yes, I like Korea, it is very nice...yes...yes...yes...no, not yet...uh-huh...uh-huh...Yes."

Caden was muttering as well, "About three weeks, probably stay a year...yes, I like it...Koreans are very friendly...I like kimbap and ramyen...yes, I've been to Seomyeon, my first day here...yes, I like Korea, it is very nice, it is different from Japan...yes...yes...yes...no, not yet...uh-huh...uh-huh...yes...maybe."

The teachers occasionally broke into Korean, which was completely incomprehensible to both of us. We heard the odd "Adam" or "Caden" sprinkled throughout their conversation and looked at each other quizzically, as the questions kept coming. When they finally stopped, we sat there a bit overwhelmed, catching our breath. Within an hour or so, the novelty wore off and the questions dried up. Now there was only Korean spoken. We no longer heard our names. I thought about my decision to study Korean, and how necessary that would be, if I wanted to make these connections.

I turned to one of the teachers, Ms. Key. This was the first time I had an opportunity to speak with the Korean teachers, so I inquired, "What was your major in school?"

Ms. Key responded nervously, "English Literature." In retrospect she was nervous, because most Koreans who studied English in college, felt terribly inadequate with their English ability when among any native English speaker.

"Oh, really?" I said with excitement. Later, I realized they had all studied English—they were English teachers. But at the time, her interest in English literature was fascinating to me. "So, what are some of your favorite books?"

"I like Faulkner, Joyce, and Shakespeare," she told me. "And you?"

I was carrying J. D. Salinger's *The Catcher in the Rye* with me. "This is one of my favorites." I carried a book with me everywhere in those days, particularly because of all the buses I had to take to get to the various schools. "This is a really good book," I told her. "I can loan it to you after I finish. If you have any grammatical or vocabulary questions, you can ask me about it. There are a lot of idioms and slang in here." I opened the book, and pointed out a few.

"I'd love to read it!" she responded. "I love reading." Caden was talking to Ms. Nam, a teacher he had mentioned on our bus rides together. He was attracted to her, and talked about her beauty. This was my chance to match her name with her face. He had tried to describe her to me before, but our English vocabulary didn't capture what he meant. Maybe Koreans could describe their differences better in the Korean language than we could in the English language.

Melvin came up to the table and shouted, "Hu-woa! How are you?"

One of the girls shouted back, "Melvin!" She mimicked the tone of his voice.

He shouted loudly back, "Mind if I sit down?" None of the teachers said anything. One of the teachers, Ms. Hwung, made a gagging motion with her finger. Melvin sat down, and loudly inquired, "So what's going on here?" He looked to the girl beside her, "How are you, Ms. Key?" She gave him an awkward look back. "Ms. Key loves me!"

I heard Caden on the other end of the table, talking about his science-fiction novel. It sounded distinctly different from a few weeks ago: "I can't tell you what it's about, but it's going to be like a space odyssey."

Melvin shouted, "I tried writing once, y'know!" He looked through his thick glasses for our reaction, "It was all about women." He paused, then shouted, "About how mean they are to me!" He laughed loudly at his own joke. "Yeah, they're always mean to me. In my book, they're all bitches!" He laughed. "No, really, I like women though." Melvin gave a firm push of his glasses with his index finger and moved his eyebrows up and down. "Everyone's laid a Korean chick but me. Can you believe that?" Two of the Korean teachers excused themselves to leave as Melvin continued. "Louie is talking to a Korean chick! Skatey's nailed tons of Korean chicks! Why can't I lay a Korean chick?" He smirked and shouted this as he pushed his glasses up again.

He went on and on. The Korean female teachers were trying to look anywhere, but him. Some of the Korean teachers couldn't help but laugh— it was so ridiculous. This only encouraged him to continue with the same theme. He loudly shouted, "You'd think a good looking guy like me could lay a Korean chick!" He joked, "You'd lay me, right Ms. Key?"

Another of the Korean teachers couldn't take it anymore. "Just go away, Melvin! Just go away!"

"Awwww...c'mon. You know I was only joking!" Melvin's face contorted, his lips pushed back toward his ears. It wasn't a smile either— more like a grimace. It was hard to look him in the face. "If you guys can't take a joke," he continued, "I'll just have to see what the other guys are doing."

One of the teachers yelled at him, "Go, Melvin, go!" Within five minutes of Melvin leaving our table, Paris and Stefano joined us. It occurred to me that they were fleeing the back room, because Melvin had gone back there.

I was right. Paris shouted to us, "Melvin's talking about laying Korean chicks again!" We laughed. Stefano grabbed Paris' hand, and they headed out the door together. Oh-oh. Stefano grabbed Paris' hand, and they headed for the door. This wouldn't be good.

With the JD Salinger connection, I saw an opportunity to possibly share cultures, in a way that I craved desperately. I envisioned that perhaps Ms. Key could be that connection. Even though I didn't know her yet, perhaps I would have her help me study Korean. Perhaps I could help her perfect her English.

***

13

***

As the night went on, we continued to drink more beer. The Korean teachers suggested taking us to a singing room, which they called a *norae-bang* (노래방) in Korean; Karaoke was one of the more popular social activities in Pusan. Most Koreans loved the singing rooms, and I later found that Kristian had a spectacular singing voice. She let it be known, and even between classes, students would invite her to a noraebang for an hour.

Before we left the Blue Note, I needed to use the men's bathroom. One observation besides the half used soap resting next to the sink, was as an old well-used comb. The comb was connected by a string to the wall, apparently they had a problem with people taking them? I reflected how I had oddly been seeing that in most business establishments. After that, I joined the rest of the group, and we entered into the busy alley.

Between the Blue Note and the Noraebang, I witnessed the continuous nightlife that permeated every fabric of South Korea. This was the kind of society where it was common to see vomit in the streets, and passed out people from too much soju imbibed, the most popular Korean alcohol. Tonight was no exception. Despite this, unlike most societies that might have this element, I felt 100% safe. I never questioned anyone's motives or felt in any danger. The genuine nature of the Korean people, their honesty and their kindness, was always evident in the public spaces. Despite the staring and attention that I often received as a foreigner, I never experienced it as hostility, or anything than just pure genuine and agenda-free curiosity. This aspect of Korea always endeared me.

Before we went inside, Kristian, knowing the noraebang routine well, insisted that we stop at a convenience store first. We bought bottles of Cass and Hite, along with shrimp chips. I shortly realized that this was common practice for singing rooms. We were free to go out and buy our own drinks and snacks, even if the noraebang itself offered the same thing, albeit at higher prices.

The noraebang was a few doors down from the Blue Note, both within that same crowded alley as the hagwan and everything else. Many of these alleys were neighborhood focal points, pedestrian-friendly, and filled with things to do. This one was in the heart of the Deokcheon area.

Once inside the establishment, we were met with loud singing from dozens of private rooms, simultaneously filled with their own respective patrons. When we were assigned our own room, we walked by doors that were of a clear transparent plastic, and we would see what other groups were doing. They were sitting on couches, with a table in the middle, and with a television screen with the song lyrics scrolling by. In our own respective room, I saw a couple tambourines, which I later realized were standard features in all singing rooms in Korea. Additionally, a playlist book was available, with mostly Korean and English songs.

We had nine people in our party that included myself, Caden, Kristian, Jeffry, and five of the Korean English teachers. We opened up the beer, and I sat between Ms. Key and Ms. Nam, as Caden sat on the other side of Ms. Nam. This interaction with the Korean teachers was very meaningful to me. I hoped that I could connect not only with my immediate newfound western friends, but through the larger Korean society through them.

Shortly after we arrived, Melvin found us, walked into our room, opened up a beer for himself, and joined us. He had a knack for disappearing, and reappearing, and how he kept tabs on where people went, was always a mystery to me. But, I didn't mind, he certainly had his idiosyncrasies, but alcohol allowed me to accept him better, than I could when we were sober.

I couldn't sing, and didn't want to try. When forced, I found it better to choose a male singer like Bob Dylan or Neil Young—someone who didn't have much of a vocal range as the top 40 pop stars. Most of the English karaoke songs came from 1970s and 1980s. Kristian was the best singer among us, and she always chose the musicians with the highest vocal ranges. Her voice was stunning, and I had to ask, "Where did you learn to sing so well?"

"I majored in Christian Music in college," she told me. That made sense. The Korean teachers also had a natural knack for singing. It was almost cultural for them. As I was beginning to read the Korean street signs in the Korean language, I noticed the word Noraebang or노래방everywhere. Usually it was written vertical down the side of the building, but it felt like with any conglomeration of neon signs, you were bound to see the노래방 characters of the Korean alphabet among them. 노래방 was the first Korean word that I learned to recognized, simply because of their sheer volume of those businesses throughout Pusan.

As I sat next to Ms. Key, it felt great to have her say, "Okay, Adam, your turn to sing again!" That supportive nature of Koreans really struck me. It was not the first time or the last time, that I would experience that aspect of Koreans, always inviting you to something, always trying to make you feel welcome.

"Unfortunately," I told her, "I already sang every Bob Dylan song in the songbook, and even those I couldn't sing well!" Despite that, it still felt good to be included.

"One more," Jeffrey chimed in. "We love the way you sing!" Even Kristian's boyfriend was sure to flatter me, and make me feel great. This was a strong ingrained Korean custom, the art of flattery. I certainly did appreciate it however.

I shouted back, "Okay, okay, but only if...only if...Melvin sings with me!"

"Yeah! Yeah!" A chorus chanted. Melvin's voice was actually worse than mine.

"You choose the song, Melvin," I requested of him.

One of the Korean teachers shouted, "Surfin' USA."

"Yuh!" Melvin shouted, "Yeaaaaauhhh!" So, both of us stood up and shouted the words, absolutely slaughtering the song: "Everyone's gone surfing! Surfin' USA!" Ms. Key shook the tambourine. We stood and mimicked the motions of riding a surfboard. Everyone laughed. I secretly wondered how often people did surfboard mimicking for a good laugh, but it didn't matter. This was fun.

After the song, I asked, "Anyone else want some beer?" I collected more money, excused myself, and left, stopping at the bathroom along the way. Another one with the half used soap, and the comb attached to the wall. This was certainly a thing. As a note, I continued to see this throughout my time in Pusan, but I never saw it in Seoul years later, which made me wonder if it was a Pusan thing or a time-entrenched thing.

I came back with a half-dozen large bottles of beer to distribute around the room. It was normal practice in Korea, to bring bottles of alcohol from outside establishments, but it always felt strange walking by the front desk, knowing that something like this was so unacceptable back in the United States. We sang and sang, and at that moment I realized that there was nowhere else in the world I'd rather be than right there, right then, at that moment.

At the end of night, Melvin and I took a taxi back to our apartment. As we entered, I noticed that Stefano's bedroom door open was wide open, and he wasn't in bed.

Yes, that's right. Stefano's bedroom door was wide open, and he wasn't in bed.

You might be wondering why I would even care about this? But, in reflection, I began to view our little community as a family. As my family. I genuinely cared for everyone and everything in this group. I wanted to expand this family. I wanted to integrate this family. I wanted connection. I had a fear that two people dating within our family, was bordering on incest, and nothing good could come from it.

It was equally ironic that as I saw things this way, I didn't expand it to a larger "family" that I had begun to build. You'll later see what I mean by this.

14

The next day was a Saturday. Despite our teaching contract clearly stating that we only worked five days a week, our hagwan, typical of most Korean hagwans at that time, insisted that we work seven days a week. However, I didn't mind, as I saw it more as an opportunity to see and interact with the Korean teachers more.

As a reflection of the time, cowboy hagwans in 1996 were the norm, not the exception. They were basically a language institute without any rules to adhere to, or a reputation to honor. They did what they wanted for short-term financial gain, including not paying their workers.

At least our hagwan paid on time, which made me feel like I worked for one of the better ones. As terrible as it was not to pay the foreign teachers, the Korean teachers were paid even less frequently. The worst of hagwan owners *never* paid their employees. A teacher might work for months only to realize that he or she would have to forfeit any chance of payment. These circumstances led to an epidemic of "midnight runners," foreigners who left the country without notice, seemingly in the middle of the night. 'That teacher pulled a 'midnight run,' was a common thing to be said in South Korea at that time.

Nevertheless, despite working seven days a week, I was eager to see Ms. Key again. After all, she had intrigued me with her interest in English literature. I wanted to continue our conversation and our connection, so I quickly finished *The Catcher in the Rye* before the Saturday afternoon work shift began. I wanted to give her the book that day. I hoped this would establish a stronger connection between the two of us.

When our work shift finished, I saw her in the greater group of Korean teachers.

"Ms. Key, how were your classes today?" My strategy was to make a bit of small talk. "By the way, I have this book I wanted to give to you. If you want to ask me any questions about anything English-related, please do." I gave her my *The Catcher in the Rye*.

"Yes, thank you! I really want to read this." I was pleased.

Some dead air sat between us. "You'll really like it." I had to ask her out, but there were too many other Korean teachers around. I didn't know how to go about it. "By the way," I began, "Would you be interested in playing pool?"

She had a confused look. She looked at me, did a swimming motion, and quizzically asked, "Pool?"

"Yes, pool. We could shoot pool." I gestured as if I was hitting a pool ball with a pool stick.

She turned to her Korean teacher colleagues, "Pool?"

One of them caught the mime, and said "Pocketball?"

"Ahmm...yes, yes. Pocketball." Finally I was getting something together, I blurted out, "Yeah, we should all play pocketball!"

I had a few of *the* looks, like *why*? I continued to nod my head like I was insisting and determined. Three of the Korean teachers agreed including Ms. Key, and her best friend, Ms. Hwung.

"How about tomorrow, after we finish teaching Sunday?"

They agreed again to the date, and I was content. I had made a connection.

The next day, we finished teaching our classes, and we went to the pool hall, which was the floor above our hagwan, in the same building.

The four of us went together, and I chose Ms. Key as my partner. None of the teachers were able to play well, so Ms. Key jokingly said, "We think Adam is a 'Pocketball King.'"

Pocketball, I learned, was the Konglish word for billiards. "A pool shark is how we say Pocketball King," I told them.

"A pool shark," Ms. Key smiled, and I could see her sense of humor. "This was your job before Korea?"

I laughed. "It's all luck."

Throughout our play, I continued to be surprised by the supportive and encouraging nature of my Korean colleagues. How they cheered and clapped when I sunk a ball in. Their attentive nature, and how they brought out the best in each other.

However, after two short games, all three of them were too exhausted to play another. Again, the typical nature of Koreans, to accommodate you, even when they were tired. They probably just wanted to go home after the long seven day workweek.

Probably here nor there, but years later, I would reflect on the Korean Confucianism structure, the one that taught that older men are to be respected and honored and allowed to dictate what everyone else does, nearly at all times. Foreigners were completely disregarded within this structure of respect, but I always wondered if I was that ajusshi in the classroom. Despite being peers in age, was I just like the ajusshi, the one that they humored, and tolerated until he left the area. I would never know. Being that foreigners were perceived as outside any Korean cultural norms, I think it would be a fine line if we authentically experienced the genuine or the humored. Perhaps it didn't matter, as at the end of the day, it all made you feel good.

Nonetheless, after our billiard outing, I was then referred to as the "Pool Shark," by the Korean teachers. I didn't mind, it made me feel like I was part of their world.

From that day forward, I continued to talk to the Korean teachers as often as possible. I hoped I was making a connection with Ms. Key, but in my heart, I just wanted that Korean connection. I wanted to have a Korean girlfriend, a Korean relationship. I wanted to have that conduit with the culture, the language, and I wanted that inside insight into things. I wanted to be a part of their group too. But, I was about to make a mistake.

A week or two later, as I spoke to Ms. Key and her best friend, Ms. Hwung, I asked them, "So what did you two do last weekend?"

Ms. Key blurted out, "Ms. Hwung had a date!" As I inquired more, it turned out to be an arranged date. Ms. Hwung was nearly thirty years old. In Korean culture, particularly true in the 1990's, a woman must marry before thirty, or it was assumed that she would never marry.

This was an interesting phenomenon about teaching English in the Korean hagwan system. Most Korean teachers were both female, and in their late twenties, just about to turn thirty. The social nature of the adult English hagwan system meant it was an opportunity for Korean females of marrying age, to potentially find a suitable marriage partner. They could listen to each other's opinions, in a conversational English environment, on many issues, and size up a person before any date could even occur.

"And how was the date?" I inquired of Hwung.

"He was nice," she told me.

Genuinely curious what Koreans did for dates, I followed it up, "And what did you do?"

"We had dinner, and walked around Haeundae Beach."

"Really? Sounds romantic," I told her.

"It was," Ms. Key interrupted. "But entire time, she wishing it you!" Usually when I quoted the teachers, I often corrected their grammar for them, but this I wanted to leave alone, as it was. I wanted to leave it deliberately vague to reflect upon, and to think about how each time two people from two different native languages communicated, there was always that vagueness of interpretation.

I was stunned. Was she serious? Was she joking? I inquired, "Is that so?" I felt embarrassed, but I couldn't help wondering what that meant.

"She tell me. She wish him you!" Ms. Hwung seemed to shrink away, as Ms. Key said that. How would I interpret that?

I was confused. Maybe she was interested me. If it was true, I found this introduced a seed of possibilities with it. Of course, Ms. Key was the one I was attracted to, but Ms. Hwung was equally attractive. I didn't know if I should take any of it seriously, or if they were joking around. The power of suggested opportunities had a powerful effect. Cultural differences. I definitely didn't want to dismiss or discount it though.

***

15

***

At this time, I began to take studying Korean more seriously. As each teacher had their own individual teaching schedule, I would sneak out to restaurants by myself, with the idea that I could eat or get a snack, with an hour of studying Korean attached. This happened because we might be scheduled to teach from 5-7pm and again at 8-9pm. This gave us an hour break, here and there, to ourselves.

I could combine this hour with a dinner, which on this particular day, is exactly what I did. I ordered my galbi-tang soup that I always liked. Unlike Korean people who always ordered in groups, foreigners often enjoyed eating by themselves at times. This created situations that Koreans weren't used to dealing with. For example, as I was studying, I would order my food, and then proceed to move all of the utensils and other items away from me, so I would have space for my Korean language material and notebook paper. This usually resulted in the older staff, usually an older ajumma (아줌마), an older woman, to come back to my table, move my book and paper out of the way, and place the utensils back in what they perceived to be their proper place. This used to annoy me significantly, but in later reflection, maybe they simply didn't have individual people coming into the restaurants who studied or read by themselves, something that more group-oriented Koreans would never do.

The other phenomenon that often occurred was that Korean ajusshi men would see you eating alone, and invite themselves to your table. This resulted in this typical conversation that I would experience often, including on this day.

"Where are you from?"

"*Miguk-saram.*" I'm American.

"How long have you been in Korea?"

I would answer the respective time, five weeks, in this case.

"Have you tried Korean food?"

"Yes, and I am eating it right now."

"Can you use chopsticks?"

"Yes, I am using them right now."

"What do you think of kimchi?"

"I like it, see my kimchi is already half gone."

It was always had a scripted feel, intended with great curiosity and interest. But, to be receiving the questions so regularly, made me feel annoyed. They were genuine questions, but had the assumption that you lived in some strange alien bubble without any experiences in Korea, despite that you were eating Korean food in front of them. It's as if the experience of seeing you eat Korean food was such a shock, they had to question you about it, to see if it were real.

On this particular evening, because I wanted to study Korean, and avoid those conversations, I excused myself from this ajusshi, and I went back to the hagwan. I would study my session in the main teachers' lounge.

As it came closer to my next class, one of the more fluent English speakers, Ms. Jang, came and told me, "I know someone who has a crush on you, Adam."

The lounge had other teachers who could overhear, so I felt a little embarrassed. But, I looked at her, and inquired, "Are you joking with me? Who?" I hoped it was Ms. Key or Ms. Hwung. Please be a teacher, and not a student, I thought to myself. "You're kidding me, right?"

"Seriously, one of the teachers has a major crush on you. She gets nervous every time you come into the teacher's room."

"I have to teach soon, and you're making me self-conscious!"

"It's true," another Korean English teacher added. "It's so sweet. She is excited when you arrive, and she is so nervous when you are here."

"One of the teachers? But you're all here right now."

"No, it's none of us in the room." That ruled out Ms. Key and Ms. Hwung. "It's one of the Japanese teachers!"

"Really? There are Japanese teachers here? Where are they?" They weren't really Japanese teachers, I would later find out. They were Korean teachers who taught Japanese classes at the hagwan. They stayed in a different section of the hagwan, in a Japanese teachers' lounge upstairs.

Kristian joined the conversation, "She's pretty, Adam. She is always talking about you. You're a lucky man."

"I want to know who it is. Can I meet her?"

One of the Korean teachers excused herself and ran upstairs. A few minutes later, an attractive woman with slightly curled hair came down the stairs. She made her appearance nervously, but she had a nice bounce to her hair, as she walked. I half felt I was in a shampoo commercial with slow-motion cameras and a song be played.

She was easily the goddess in the room. Just on appearance alone, she felt to be a completely different league than me. I felt I had a shot with the other teachers but this one? We all know how beauty plays in male-female dating however. The beauty industry doesn't make billions for nothing in what it promotes. Being told directly that a complete goddess of a woman has a 100% interest in you, was a complete game changer. It turned everything upside down. Why pursue a Ms. Key or Hs. Hwung when you had no idea if the interest was even mutual?

She nervously smiled at me, "I'm Eun-Hee."

I equally shared her anxiety, but managed, "Good to meet you—how are you?" It was hard to even say that.

"Good," she hesitantly replied in English.

"Her English isn't very good," one of the Korean teachers confided to me.

"Beautiful," I pondered aloud. Eun-Hee stood awkwardly and then motioned that she had to get back upstairs to prepare for her class.

"You're a lucky man," Kristian told me.

I inquired, "She doesn't know English?"

"No, but maybe you can exchange Korean for English lessons," Kristian stated. I contemplated this great idea as I got ready to teach my own class.

Of course I had been interested in Ms. Key, but I was unable to even secure a date with her, and ended up with a group pocketball event instead. Then I heard Ms. Hwung might be interested in me, which confused things more. I still wanted that Korean connection, that woman to get to know, that gap to be filled. Meeting Eun-Hee that day, hit me like a cupid's arrow.

***

16

***

Years later, I would find out just what a strange part of Pusan it was, that I lived in. At the time, I thought it was typical Korea. There was a large dog meat market in Deokcheon, and I often tried to defend its existence to my Korean students who were embarrassed by it. "It's just like India, they don't eat cows. They must look at Americans as barbaric for slaughtering and eating our cows. I'm guilty of it myself all the time. Who am to judge Koreans for eating dogs? It's just like Americans eating cows."

Still, most of my students would insist that they don't eat dogs. I was never sure if I should believe them or not. Years later, I would learn it was mostly an older Korean male ajusshi thing to eat dog.

Again, perhaps because of this dog market, it attracted a certain kind of Korean. I had often saw drunk men during the middle of the day, but one particular man was stumbling around in the middle of the street and it wasn't even twelve o'clock noon. It was particularly amusing, as while I was watching him from my bus window view, plenty of people in the bus were busy turning around to look at me, point, and say miguk-saram to each other, indicating that a white person was among them. Actually it literally meant an American person, but it was used for any white person despite nationality. Meanwhile, the bus driver was honking his horn at him, and trying to get around this wandering intoxicated man. I felt like the attention was on the wrong person. Shouldn't they be staring and pointing at the commotion out the window, and not at me?

Then, of all things, I watched the man pull down his pants, and they dropped to his ankles on the road. He proceeded to urinate in the middle of the street, and his piss stream landed directly at the spot that his fallen pants were at. I watched his pants soak up with urine, and all the while, the bus passengers were busy pointing and staring at me. It didn't seem right, but certainly made me aware that a white guy in Korea was the stranger local sight of the two events.

Despite these oddities, we were in a foreign bubble among ourselves. While I knew all of my colleagues, and even many of the Korean colleagues, it occurred to me that Caden still hadn't met Skate.

One of the reasons was because Skate isolated himself at work, just as much as he did from the girl's apartment. He couldn't stand his coworkers, his managers, or anything else about Korea. The moment he wasn't supposed to be teaching in a Korean classroom, he simply vanished and hid out of everyone's view.

They met as Caden and I waited at a bus stop at six forty-five in the morning. We heard loud, heavy footsteps, and Caden turned around to see a man running down the street. "Look," he pointed out to me, "It's another foreigner." The expat community in Korea was so small at this time, that any foreigner, particularly one in our backwater area of Deokcheon, was indeed a shock.

I turned around. "Hey, it's Skate!" When he was within hearing range, I yelled, "Weren't you supposed to teach at six thirty?"

"Yeah, I'm late. Fuck!"

Caden extended his hand, "Excuse me, I don't think we've met."

Skate yelled at him, "Fuck off!" And that's how Caden met Skate.

After my own morning classes, I took a bus back to the apartment. Typical of the steep hills, my bus driver met an oncoming bus in one of the narrow roads. They couldn't get around each other, and both refused to back up to let the other one through. Respectively, they got out of their buses, and proceeded to wrestle each other in the middle of the street. They avoided punching each other, as they simply pushed and pulled at each other's jackets, resulting in jackets pulled above their heads in the struggle. Ultimately, one of them backed down, got back in the bus, reversed it, and let the other one through.

Later I learned that Koreans don't inflict physical damage to each other, as they are then responsible for the hospital bills of the other.

With the interesting excursion up, and finally back at the apartment, I saw Skate sitting at the kitchen table. He wasn't usually back this early in the morning, so I asked him, "What are you doing here?"

"That bitch fired me."

"Why? How? Just because you were late?"

"It's not just that," he reflected. "That bitch." His eyes were filled with outrage. "That bitch doesn't even fucking speak English. She wouldn't even look at me. She had me stand in front of her desk as she yelled at one of the Korean teacher bitches!" He continued to fume, "She was reading a book while the Korean translated! I was so pissed!" Skate looked right at me and said, "I told her, 'If you got something to say, you say it to me, you bitch!' and I slammed her fucking book shut! That bitch was so pissed, she fired me right there. The bitch!"

"Man, that's harsh," I told him. "So, what are you going to do now?"

"What can I do? Just look for another job. I can stay here until the end of the month, and still get paid."

"So, in some ways, you're better off."

"Yes! I've been calling schools from the newspaper, and I have interviews. I can go to Thailand for a few weeks, get my visa, and come back. Relaxing on the beach—imagine that!"

"Yeah, a lot of people go to Thailand." I'd heard of a few expats who had a bad hagwan, cut their financial losses, and retreated to Thailand to spend what remaining money they had left. They'd come back to Korea and sign a different one-year contract at a different hagwan, ideally in a better situation than the one they left.

"Yeah, Thailand! I'm going to sit on the beach, and find me some young Thai girl. It'll be great! You know, you can even buy a wife down there. Get some fifteen-year-old bitch to marry. You gotta get them young, before their minds get all fucked up."

Without judgement, "So you'll stay in the apartment while being paid, AND go to Thailand! How do I get fired?"

The entire week, Skate hung around the house, telephoned different girlfriends, and got pissed drunk every night. Some nights he'd come home half annihilated and sit in the middle of the kitchen floor, cursing out Korea and its people.

I either ignored the rants or tried to change the subject. Personally, I was glad he would be leaving soon. Our situation at the school wasn't ideal, but his negativity made it worse. Once I inquired of him, "So any last things you want to do before you go?"

"Yeah! You know, there's one Korean teacher I really want to tell to fuck off! You know Ms. Hwung? I just want to call her a fuckin' goddamn bitch..." Skate trailed off into a long stream of nearly indecipherable curse words.

"Really? Why?"

"Because she is one! And I just want to go up to her and say, 'Ms. Hwung, you're a fucking—fucking...You wait until you've worked with her for a while, and you'll know what I mean."

***

17

***

Weekdays were uneventful. The week was devoted to two things—work and sleeping to work more. This made the Friday's stand out as something eventful. This Friday, Paris went to work wearing a sleeveless shirt. She wore it with the intention of going directly from teaching to the Blue Note Bar with all the rest of us. It never occurred to any westerner that a sleeveless shirt might be a problem.

The hagwan owner, already upset about Skate's behavior, reacted strongly to Paris' blouse. She called in a few of the Korean English teachers, and yelled at them. Then they calmly translated to Paris that her shirt was inappropriate, and they asked her to go home and change it. She did as they asked.

This caused me to reflect on how different the perception of clothing and what revealing means between the two cultures. Seeing a woman's upper arms meant nothing to a westerner. But in Korea, you'd regularly see Korean men feeling so ashamed and embarrassed to see an upper female arm that they'd give their jacket or any covering they had, to cover up that perceived immodest behavior.

Meanwhile, short mini-skirts were completely one hundred percent acceptable and didn't create any arousal, shame or anything else. Legs were commonly revealed, and no matter how short a mini-skirt could get, you would never hear of a woman ever being told to go home and put a longer one on.

Another cultural difference was the concept that women looking and staring at themselves in public mirrors meant nothing in Korea. All of the females I worked with, had mirrors on their desks both at the hagwan and the middle school. They spent significant time, in public, fixing themselves to their perceived perfection, in full view of everyone else. Even our main teacher's lounge had a wall-size mirror, and most of the Korean teachers spent most of their time between classes looking at all sides of their bodies their attire, and their face. They pulled out more make-up, viewed their butts from various angles, and simply did all of their vanity in full view of everyone else, without any shame or embarrassing about it whatsoever.

This was in strong contrast to myself or any westerner. The only time I ever looked at myself in any public mirror, was when I thought I was alone in the bathroom. If someone suddenly entered that same bathroom, I would quickly turn on the water, and pretend that I was about to do anything else, but actually examine myself in the mirror.

Once I'd learned that Eun-Hee had a crush on me, I quickly developed a reciprocal crush on her. As our usual Friday night was to go to the Blue Note Bar, I hoped that Eun-Hee might join us. While the Korean teachers were looking at themselves in the main mirrors, I asked them if Eun-Hee was planning to accompany them tonight. No one knew if she had or not. I was too reluctant and shy to ask her myself, particularly since it meant I would have to enter her teachers' lounge upstairs. I resigned it to chance and hopefulness that she might.

After my last class, as I walked from the hagwan to the Blue Note, I spotted Eun-Hee. She was with Kamm, the school director, and they were eating inside a nearby fast-food restaurant called Lotteria, a Korean version of McDonalds. This was the centerstone of a four-way crossing within our busy people-filled alley. The energy of people that converged outside of the Lotteria was the highest and densest within these alleys. I stood still among the moving crowds, as the people passed around me, wondering how I could ask her.

While Kamm and Eun-Hee emptied their trays into the garbage, I debated about going up and asking her if she would join us. I decided to busy myself with nearby merchandise displays in the street and to pretend that our meeting would be completely accidental.

They seemed to fiddle around in there forever, and it enhanced my anxiety. I looked in and saw Kamm going back to their chairs to gather their jackets, books, and cigarettes. This was becoming too awkward, so I decided that I must approach them directly. I felt I might never gather the courage to speak with her, if I didn't make an effort now. I gathered my breath and confidence, and met them directly at the entrance. My voice crackled and I said, "Hello, Eun-Hee."

She reacted oddly to me, appearing unsure of what to say. She didn't smile. Meanwhile, Kamm jerked his hand quickly, so that several cigarettes stuck out an inch or two from the pack. I inquired of Eun-Hee, "What are you doing tonight?"

She looked embarrassed and proceeded to hide behind Kamm. He pulled out a lighter. His gas was turned up too high, and it burned the front of his cigarette with a torch-like flame. Eun-Hee remained behind him, seemingly scared or embarrassed, and then she blurted out something in Korean. Kamm turned to me and said, "Fuck, dude, she doesn't even speak English," as he inhaled a quarter of his cigarette in one puff.

I motioned with my hands, pointing to myself, "I," I said, "am going to," motioning in the direction of where I was going, "The Blue Note," and pointed to the bar. Then, pointing to her, I said, "You go?" I made a walking gesture with my fingers toward the bar.

She continued to hide behind Kamm, with her arms extended over his shoulders. She shook her head and then said 'No,' out loud, several times. I was confused by the entire episode, but I nodded my head up and down in an understanding anyway. I knew Kamm was a married man, probably going home to his pregnant wife shortly, so it didn't dawn on me to invite him out with us as well.

"Okay," I said, "But if you change your mind, I'd love to see you there." Then I turned away and strolled down the street, unable to make sense of it. I turned around briefly and saw Kamm and Eun-Hee walking the other direction down the street, with a big cloud of Kamm's smoke rising up and over his shoulder.

Once inside the American license-plate filled bar, I noticed the usual Korean English teacher crowds, and I sat among them. I was somewhat equally shy about Ms. Key, and especially Ms. Hwung, because of what Ms. Key had said to me. I knew that I missed being in a relationship, and I knew that I wanted to pursue a relationship. I didn't know who that might be. Knowing Eun-Hee expressed interest in me, she appeared the obvious choice now.

I sat down next to Ms. Key, with Ms. Hwung on her other side. There were six teachers in total, and a teacher named Ms. Jang on my left side. As I sat down, I exclaimed, "You wouldn't believe what just happened."

"What happened?" Ms. Jang, the most fluent of the teachers, quickly responded. She was the same one who initially told me of Eun-hee's interest.

Ms. Jang was also the fiancée of King. He would become someone I would shortly meet, but also one of the few Kupo Hagwan teachers to had ever completed an entire year contract. I hadn't yet met King; but I had heard he went back to the United States for a few months, and that he would return to sign another teaching contract to be with his fiancée.

"Well, I just saw Eun-Hee with Kamm in Lotteria, and I asked her if she wanted to join us. She hid behind Kamm and shook her head no. Does that make sense? I mean, why would she hide behind him like that?"

"Maybe she was just nervous?"

"Do you think so? I'd love to talk to her."

"King and I are good friends with her. I'll talk to her about it, and we can arrange a double date for you guys, if you're interested."

"I'd love that! By the way, when is King coming back?"

"He's here now. He's in the back room with the other foreign teachers."

As we were talking, I saw Skate come in. Ms. Key raised her voice in surprise, "Why is he here?"

"Probably saying good-bye to the other teachers and students," I said. Skate went back to the back room toward the other foreign teachers.

In broken English, "None like him. He always angry."

I thought about it. "You're right: he is very angry. Angry guy."

We continued talking, and before long, Skate left the back room and walked toward our table. As he approached, several of the teachers diverted their eyes downward as he stopped next to Ms. Hwung. He bent over and whispered something in her ear, and she jumped up and shouted, "You asshole!" Skate, with a grin on his face, calmly walked away and out of the bar. He had obviously said what he had wanted to say. "Did you hear that?" She was irate, "Did you hear that Asshole!"

"What did he say?" I asked innocently, recalling his words earlier in the week.

Ms. Key confided to the group, "I heard it, it was really bad!"

Ms. Hwung, her face red and her jaw clenched, "What an asshole!"

"I can't believe it," I said, sharing her feeling. "Don't worry about it—you know what he's like." I tried to make it seem less than what it was, but I knew it was pointless. It had been a rotten thing to say.

"What an asshole!" I heard her say several more times. Skate had successfully ruined her night, and in the process, everyone else's as well. The conversation continued in that direction until I excused myself and joined the other foreign teachers in the back room for a while.

Once there, I met King for the first time. He was strong and tall, with blond hair, blue eyes, and a red goatee. He wore circular, wire-rimmed glasses. He was the center of the discussion as I came in.

Paris turned to me and said, "Where's your girlfriend, Adam?"

I blushed and King said to me, "They were telling me about Eun-Hee and you. You're a lucky man!"

Paris shouted, "Adam," to get my attention. "Is she out there now?"

"No, but I met her outside before I came in," and proceeded to tell them the story.

Paris inquired of me, "So, where have you been, then?"

"I was out talking with the Korean teachers, but things turned sour because of Skate," I told her.

"He's such a jerk. He told us what he was going to say beforehand. I'm so glad he's leaving!"

"I told you he was a jerk," Stefano reiterated to me.

"Well, I kind of knew already," I told him. "But as the new kid, I'm required to soak up all of the information from everyone. But I do agree: he's a jerk."

Paris reminded us, "He won't even talk to me!"

Kristian added, "Things used to be cool before he came. I remember when King, Dan, and Dave were here. They were before Skate. It was different before he came, right, King? I'm so glad he was fired." I had never met Dan and Dave, but the teachers were constantly changing at the hagwan. They always had a difficult time retaining teachers, mostly because of the hagwan's breeches of contracts.

I inquired of them, "What was it like before Skate?"

"Well, back in those days, everyone used to hang out in your apartment, even the students and Korean teachers. But since he came, they stopped going there. We used to rent movies every Friday night. There is a reason that we are all now at the Blue Note Bar."

King reiterated, "We use to have huge parties in the apartment, but yeah, Skate ruined that."

"Really?"

"And the hagwan was different, too. No one knew what he was going to do next, and he's racist," Kristian added. "Did you hear him going on about fuckin' Korea this and fuckin' Korea that?"

"Yeah, all the time," I told her. "All the time!"

"I don't even know what he's doing here, the way he hates everyone and everything so much."

"So I heard you're pretty good at shooting pool, Chief," King grinned.

I laughed, "Well, not really, but I played against some of the Korean teachers the other day."

We talked in the back room for hours, and I learned more about King and Kristian. King had been in the Peace Corps, in Africa, for two years before coming to Korea to teach English. Just watching his presence among the other teachers, I could tell that he was both deeply respected and knowledgeable on many subjects.

"You should have been here when Kristian first came," King told the group.

"Oh man," Kristian laughed. "I was really different then!"

"She was so quiet in the beginning."

"I was always into the Church when I first arrived; I was such a little goody two-shoes!" She laughed. "I went to a Christian university! I had never even smoked or drank before I came here!" She looked down at the cigarette in one hand and the cold beer in the other.

"You're not anything like that now."

"I know, and it's only been nine months. My parents wouldn't recognize me now!" She laughed. "But my brother used to smoke pot and stuff. When I go back, I want to hang out with him."

King grinned, "So what did you think of us, when you first met us?"

"Heathens!" Kristian screamed and laughed. "Bunch of heathens! Y'know, I was a virgin before I came here as well." She squeezed Jeffrey's hand.

Kristian was from Regina, Canada, and had long, blond hair sprayed high in front. She hadn't received much physical attention in Canada or in her church, but Koreans gave her a lot of attention. She soaked it up.

Paris shouted with her slight Texas twain, "You should see her flirt with the guys!"

Kristian laughed and fluttered her eyelids at one of the Korean men at our table. She smiled seductively. Her boyfriend took it all in stride, but his English wasn't very good. He couldn't understand us when we spoke naturally. The students were more familiar with the slow speed of the classroom. When we spoke to one another, it was rapid, idiom filled, and nearly impossible for a student to understand, if we didn't want them to understand.

We utilized this often.

Around one in the morning, an older ajusshi type joined us and began asking us the typical questions. "What do you think of Korea?"

Ignoring him, we continued to pour drinks for each other. One of the rules of Korea was that we must pour for others, not for ourselves.

The Korean ajusshi caught this and lectured us, "You are in Korea, and you must follow Korean rules. He poured from our pitcher of beer into our respective glasses. "Now you must pour for me."

We did as he requested. While sometimes we entertained these types of men, but usually we felt like they were just using us to practice English. We started using more idioms and a quicker type of English, hoping that he would get bored. He did not.

Ultimately, one of us picked up the pitcher of beer, and began to pour for themselves. The older ajusshi shouted "No," and knocked the pitcher out of their hand, sending the beer flying across several people, soaking up their clothes. I was one of those people and the beer had embarrassingly soaked up my crotch parts.

We decided that it was a good catalyst to end our evening, particularly since the next day was a Saturday, another work day. We ended our night.

18

Pusan National University. PNU, as we'd call it, was the heart of the foreign teacher expat community in 1996. It was the most convenient, because it was further north than Seomyeon and Nampo-dong, making it more accessible to a larger area of Pusan. Not only that, but it was the largest university on Pusan's only subway line, at that time. Construction was everywhere, as the city had at least five subway lines planned. So getting to that subway line, meant a reprise from the noise and chaos of construction throughout the rest of the city. That being said, it was a very crowded, insanely crowded, subway ride each time as well.

For us, we could take the bus from Deokcheon for about one hour to Dongnae Station. Then we would transfer over to PNU within a few stops opposite of the Seomyeon direction. The heart of our expat English teaching community met at Monk Bar. It was a jazz music bar named after Thelonious Monk, with a large wall-size portrait of him, on their wall.

Equally, coming out of the PNU metro station always gave a great feeling. Partially because we were going out socially, but mostly because the station exit overlooked both the student-filled streets in front of you and the mountainside scenery in the background. Something about peering over the horizon gave a feeling like something good was going to happen.

Then we meandered that PNU area to the Monk Bar, navigating streets that were filled with college kids, young people, and a few intellectual types. The kinds of people that were significantly different from our Deokcheon types of people, who were a more working class, rough-n-ready type of person.

For westerners in Korea, we were finding our way to our own community of like-minded individuals. This subset of western folks, a half a world away from their origins, but all converging to call somewhere quite unfamiliar as home. All determined, with all their own hopes and dreams, of connecting, of integrating, of being accepted, of learning, of discovering, of being one among the Korean people themselves. An exchange of cultures, an exchange of experiences, and a chance to grow, to learn more about yourself, and to see your own culture through different eyes. A group of people I felt a kinship and connection with, one that at times I longed to be with. A group that fully understood me. They simultaneously understood in great complexities, all of my current situations and issues on most levels. The kind of stuff that was too unrelatable to describe to anyone else, anywhere else in the world.

Among that larger group—King and Ms. Jang, Kristian and Jeffrey, Stefano and Paris, Caden, Melvin, and myself, had all agreed to meet at PNU on that Saturday night. The main reason was because of Louie and Laurie. They had returned from their visa trip to Japan, and Louie had started his new job. As for Laurie, she was planning an escape route from Korea altogether, in the form of a graduate program in London. We wanted to make a good night out to celebrate the two events. Because of the stress of the long and monotonous work week, the celebrative nature of the events, and that Pusan had a 2am curfew when the bars closed, we planned to go to a few U.S. military bars later, just to keep it going.

We arrived at the entrance of the Monk Bar, drifted down the stairwell, and oozed into the venue with the full view of Thelonious. The gentle wafting of jazz music reverberating through all of the speakers, filling us with comfort and excitement. We then spilled into a large table in the middle of the bar, one that would accommodate the largeness of our group. The drinks rolling in, and we got to talking once again.

A bit into the drinks and conversation, Louie spat out to me, "Hey dude, how's the middle school?"

"Good, good," I told him. "It was hard at first, but I'm getting used to it now."

"Well, remember dude, you just got to teach students one good thing a day," he told me. "Especially nouns, they love nouns! Y'know, they go home and their parents ask them, 'What did you learn today? If they can say 'table' and 'wall' and all those everyday things, parents really think they're learning."

"Yeah, that's a good idea, I'll remember that."

"Yeah dude, you hippie!" He remarked on my longer blond hair, despite that I always tied it back. Louie was drunk before we arrived, which wasn't uncommon for anyone who lived in South Korea, including Korean people themselves. The alcohol flowed in this nation.

Paris asked Louie, "So how was Japan?"

He spat out, "It was great, Paris!" He turned his hat backward. "I got so drunk I raided the ship's kitchen!" He laughed heartily, "Both Laurie and I!"

Laurie sat beside him, and looked embarrassed. "Only Louie," she said.

"Aww...c'mon, Laurie honey, you too, you too," Louie insisted. "It's so expensive there, like five thousand won! Five bucks! Can you believe that? For a sandwich? C'mon!"

Paris laughed, "So you raided the kitchen?"

"Aww...c'mon, you wouldn't raid the kitchen, Paris? C'mon? Five thousand won for a sandwich! Heck yeah, I raided the kitchen!" He laughed heartily again. "You should have seen me in there, too—I had slices of bread all laid out, and I just started splattering *kimchi* all over them. Mmmmmmm. Kimchi sandwiches!"

"*Kimchi* sandwiches? That's so gross, Louie!"

"No, it was good. You just splatter that *kimchi* between the pieces of bread...delicious." Louie rubbed his stomach. "I must have had twenty of them."

We listened to Louie's stories and drank beer until we were beyond drunk. Melvin kept leaving the bar and coming back. "So where do you keep going all the time, Melvin?" Louie asked him after this had happened a few times.

Melvin responded, "What...Huh?"

"What are you, deaf? Why do you always do that...'What...Huh?' You heard me!" Louie shouted back to him, "Okay, now. Once again, what did I say, Melvin? What did I say?"

"You said, 'Where do you keep going?'"

"Yes, that's right. Now, where did you go?"

"I went over to the Road House," he said as he pushed his glasses with his index finger, contorting his facial features.

"You went there by yourself?"

"Yeah. I think I'll go down to Rock and Roll next."

Louie suggested to him, "Why don't you just relax with us, Melvin?"

"You guys are drinking beer. I don't like beer," Melvin responded. His voice was loud, kind of slow and rough. "I prefer a man's drink! Whiskey on the Rocks!"

"Oh, a man's drink, huh? Well, why don't you order one and sit with us?"

"Okay, but you know I never get drunk."

Stefano jumped in, "Melvin, what are you talking about? You *always* get drunk."

"It's true, Stefano. I don't get drunk," Melvin claimed again.

"Well, just drink your drink, Melvin, and show them what a big boy you are," Louie smirked.

Within a couple hours, Melvin was trying to stand and knocked over chairs. "I never get drunk, you know."

"We know, Melvin, we know." Louie encouraged him, "Need another drink there, buddy?"

Nearby, saintly King was talking about his Peace Corps experiences. I leaned over to his direction. "I've been thinking about the Peace Corps myself someday. What kind of things did you do?"

"Well," King began. He said it very slow and clear manner, as if he was going to deliver a prepared speech. He was a well-traveled person, compared to the rest of us. "Well, I taught AIDS education in Ghana," he said in a clear, monotone voice. When he spoke, he reminded me of the writer William S. Burroughs. "In fact," he began, "One of the things I taught them," he paused, "Was how to wear a condom." He laughed while his eyes went glittery. "I showed them how to unroll a condom," he began to demonstrate with his hands, "and I had a banana with me." He said this very slowly and clearly, "I held up the banana and rolled the condom over it. I told them it would help prevent pregnancy and disease. Do you know what happened? The next day, I saw bananas wrapped in condoms hanging from everyone's front door." We all laughed.

Caden, shortly thereafter, pushed his hair back, and told me about his situation at the middle school. Specifically to me, he said, "Mrs. Baek offered me a job there! You too, she said."

"I don't want to work there, Caden. I hate teaching kids."

"One point six million won a month, a great apartment to live in, and less teaching hours per week. It's so much better."

"Yeah, but we have a great community of teachers at our school. I wouldn't want to be stuck out there in that location of the middle school, isolated from everyone."

Louie yelled loudly at Caden, "Go for it, dude!"

I asked Caden, "Anyhow, how are you going to get out of your contract?"

"I'm going to make things miserable around Kupo. Make it hell for them like Skate did. Make them fire me. And if that doesn't work, I'll tell them they lied to me. I'll say that I was contracted to teach kids, and the hagwan doesn't teach kids, but the middle school does." Caden really liked the kids at the middle school. His bragging didn't go over with the rest of the teachers, but I think the old ladies at the middle school liked his tall stories. He reminded me of a kid himself in some ways, and I think he related to them well.

Paris yelled to be overheard through the loudness of the Monk bar venue, "Is Skate out of your apartment, yet?"

"No, but he goes to Thailand in a few days."

"Kristian and I have been talking, and we think Caden should move up when Skate leaves. The new teacher can move in with us." I think the girls were tired of living with him.

"The new teacher?" I asked. "Is it a man or woman?"

"No one knows, yet."

"Typical, dude. They never tell you anything," Louie sputtered out. He stood and shouted, "Hey guys, let's go to the Legion and Dallas Bar!"

"What's that?" I asked.

"It's a sleazy military bar," Louie told me. "It's a big late-night hangout. English teachers, American military, Korean prostitutes—everyone goes there!" In 1996, Korean bars closed at 2am. American military-serving bars were one of the few exceptions.

So we paid our bills and stood outside, waiting for a taxi. Melvin stepped into the alley, and Paris and I laughed at his evening attire. She laughingly pointed at his socks, "Look at that!"

"I know—he always wears that around the house, too," Stefano chimed in. Melvin was wearing yellow basketball shorts with black Daffy Duck socks pulled up to his knees. This was accompanied by sandals and his Seattle Supersonics T-shirt. He always wore the same clothes.

"I wonder what underwear he's wearing," Stefano mused. "Maybe Tweety Bird?"

Paris laughed, "Go find out!" She pointing at me.

"Gross," I told her, but I was drunk, so I snuck up behind him and mimed pulling down his shorts. Paris laughed hysterically as I built up the anticipation. When I couldn't resist anymore, I pulled the shorts down— "Voila!" He wasn't wearing any underwear. Paris and I laughed hysterically. Melvin just stood there, his shorts down to his knees.

"Shoot! Shoooot!" he yelled. "Adam! Come here! Let me do that to you!"

I ran from him until we called a truce.

Than half of us took taxis to the military bar. Melvin took a taxi home.

***

19

***

Stefano and I were two of the people who took the taxi headed for the after-hours bars. The Dallas Club and Legion Bar were the two clubs for people who wanted to keep drinking after curfew. There were mostly US military guys, and Korean prostitutes, sitting at most tables. They flirted with each other, or simply waited for each other. Among all of that, members of the recent English Teacher community filled the periphery, generally looking quite out of place there. They were looking for that connection with each other, the opportunity to continue experiencing this living abroad existence, and looking to see what was in all these niches and crannies throughout their new home of South Korea.

There was also a large dance floor filled with couples grinding to the music. Because the bars were closing throughout the city at 2am, there was a sprinkle of constantly arriving English teachers all converging from around the city, at the same time. We saw Skate at the bar, which Paris and a few others weren't too happy about. People in our group began to get tired and go home, but Stefano, Skate, and I stayed well after everyone else. The sun was coming up, and I began to regret not leaving with the others. Stefano was at the bar, talking with an African American military friend of his, and Skate had also found a few friends to talk with. As I was still relatively new to Pusan, I had no desire to leave in a taxi by myself. I was dependent on Stefano—or Skate—to get back to the apartment.

First, I tried Stefano, "You ready to go home soon? I'm really tired."

"Not yet," he said, and continued with his discussion. He turned back to his friend, "So how much longer are you in the Army?"

I sighed and went over to Skate. "Are you going home soon? I'm tired, and I'm not sure how to get there..."

Skate angrily responded, "Why don't you ask your nigger-loving Jew friend?"

Ignoring Skate's bigotry, I stumbled back to Stefano again. "You ready to go home, man?" I didn't see Skate follow behind me, as I approached Stefano.

Stefano turned to me again, "Not yet."

Skate leaned over real close to Stefano, and whispered in his ear, "You fuckin' nigga-lovin' Jew!" Then he proceeded to quickly punch him in the side of the stomach. Stefano fell off of his barstool and into the person beside him.

Stefano got up. "What's your problem, Skate?" They began to push each other, but were immediately restrained by nearby military soldiers, including the African-American guy, who hadn't heard the whispered comment. With a little bit of posturing, Skate, the much larger guy, walked out of the bar, as his restrainers let him go.

Stefano yelled at the guys holding him back, "Let go of me, let go of me!" He was fuming, but he wasn't in range to strike at Skate, so they let him go as well. He stormed his way towards the bathroom, and knocked over a table with his flailing hands. It landed on a prostitute's open-toed high heel shoe.

She yelled at him in perfect English, "You idiot!" He didn't hear her, or anyone else, he simply charged through the bar, angrily knocking more objects out of his way. His flailing arm caught the back of a chair, and sent it flying as it hit a military man in the back. This brought a table of his friends to their feet. One of them stood up, and pounded Stefano hard— one fist to the face. Stefano dropped to the ground between a capsized table and a nearby chair.

Another of Stefano's bar friends, Mike—a black belt in taekwondo, and another English teacher stepped in. Mike yelled, "Lay off him! It was an accident!"

Mike lifted Stefano from the ground, and we walked him out of the club. Skate was waiting outside, and as soon as he saw Stefano, he asked very pleasantly and kindly, "What happened to you, Stefano?"

"I don't know," he told him, "They just started pounding me. I don't even know what I did." Stefano was too drunk to recall.

"You must have done something to piss that guy off," Skate stated in a friendly tone. "If I had seen that, I would have stepped in for you."

"I don't even know what I did," Stefano reiterated.

"I think it's time to go home," I said. Tomorrow, I would tell Stefano everything that had really happened.

"Dude, those military guys are assholes, man," Skate told him, putting his arm around him. The sight made me feel sick. "So you don't know what you did to bring that on, huh?"

"No, I have no idea. All I remember is a guy punching me, and then I fell to the ground."

"That sucks, dude," Skate told him. Mike hailed a cab.

The cab came, and all three of us got in, Stefano in the middle. As the cab driver drove us home, Skate expanded on his desire for revenge against the soldiers who had assaulted Stefano—he didn't know that I knew what had really happened.

"PU-SAN-JYUN-MOON-DAE (부산전문대학·釜山專門大)", Skate told the cab driver. From across the city, it was our closest landmark for a driver to navigate towards our direction. Once near there, we would gesture to him directly to our apartment. Without the Korean ability to communicate, it was the most efficient way to get home.

While in the cab, Stefano yelled in pain, "My arm hurts! I can't even move it! OH MY GOD!"

Skate began to play doctor, "I think you may have a broken your arm." Skate pushed down hard on various areas of his arm.

"OWWW!" Stefano moaned. "Don't touch me there!"

"It must be broken," Skate told him as he pushed again on the arm bone at the same time.

"Well, don't touch it then!" Eventually, we were home again, and I was relieved to end this long evening.

The next morning, I woke up around noon. Everyone was still asleep. I was reading a newspaper at the kitchen table when I heard a yell: "OWWW! What's wrong with my arm? AHHH!" Stefano came out of his room. He inquired of me, "What the hell *happened* last night?"

"I will tell you later," I whispered to him, with a gesture toward Skate's room. "I saw everything, and I'll tell you later." Skate was still in there with his door closed.

Skate entered the kitchen shortly thereafter, and played dumb again regarding the incident. Stefano called Mike on the phone. He recollected some of the evening's events, but he couldn't recall why the soldier had punched him. I sat quietly, waiting for Skate to leave.

Once he did, I told Stefano the entire story in detail. "I did recall arguing with Skate," Stefano told me, "but I didn't know what it was all about."

"Yep," I told him.

"I can't wait until he's gone."

"Just a few more days," I told him. After that night, I couldn't look at Skate anymore. Whenever he was in the apartment, I would walk down to the girls' place or stay down near the hagwan—anything and anywhere until he left. Stefano was doing the same thing; we kept meeting each other at the girls' apartment instead of our own. We both needed a break from Skate, but I also suspected that Stefano didn't mind being babied, by Paris.

And that is a subtle hint that Stefano and Paris did get involved with each other. In reflection, maybe that is what needed to happen. With our isolation from living in South Korea at a time before social media, without cellphones, with few English resources, with language limitations, with cultural limitations, and all the rest. It is only logical that relationships would develop as well.

On the other hand, I would say that I was personally closest to both Stefano and Paris both individually and collectively. They were the people that I enjoyed spending time with the most. The reason I was hesitant about them getting together, is the fear that the closeness could be severed if they got together, and then subsequently broke up.

***

20

***

Within a few days, Skate left for Thailand. He found a new employer and visa sponsor, but the system dictated that he left leave the country to process the new work visa.

With Skate gone, Stefano and I began to hang out in the apartment again. Stefano loved to cook; he danced about in the kitchen, one arm in a sling as he pulled out pots and pans and opened the refrigerator with the other. "What the hell?" he asked, irritated. "Why do we have so many cartons of milk and orange juice in the refrigerator?"

"I think one of the orange juices is mine."

"But there's a ton of them in here! Look at this—there must be eight or nine cartons of orange juice here! Also the milk, there's six of them. Why do we need so much milk and orange juice?"

"I don't know, Stefano. I don't even drink milk."

"I have one orange juice in here, and one milk. What the hell?"

"Must be Melvin's."

"What the hell? Did his parents take care of him his whole life? He never puts anything away," Stefano walked around the room, working himself up more as he talked. "Look at this shit; why is this clothes hanger on the kitchen table? Damn it Melvin!" He used his one arm to fling the hanger into Melvin's open room. "And all this shit—he never puts anything away. He's a pig!" Stefano went back to the open refrigerator again. "All of these cartons just have a little juice left in them, none of them are full, and they're all nearly empty. What an idiot. I'm cleaning out this fridge. We need to clean this place."

I had a lot of other things on my mind at the time, mostly Eun-Hee. Sasha was completely out of my mind, and it was nearly impossible to contact her anyway. I did send her the occasional postcard, but more as an already old friend, as opposed to a previous girlfriend.

Joe was still in Alaska, and I continued to send him the occasional postcard from Korea. He was waiting to see if going to Korea was a good idea or not. I was encouraging him, as an experience. I told him that I had a few prospects with some of the Korean teachers, including Ms. Key, Ms. Hwung, and Eun-Hee. I wanted one of those to happen, it was going to be circumstantial as to which one.

I focused most of my thoughts on Eun-Hee and the notebook in front of me. She was the one that I was most smitten with, of all of them. I was thinking of writing to her, something simple that she would understand. It would give me a chance to practice writing Korean, as opposed to my current study method of just reading street and menu signs everywhere. While I was thinking of what to say, I asked Stefano, "So, do you ever think you'll go back to Israel?" He had studied one semester there and often talked about it.

"Yes, I would love to," he said, as he began pulling everything out of the fridge. "I'm going to throw out all this stuff. We are going to find out exactly whose is whose, and get rid of the rest. Look at all these cartons. It's the same in the cupboards, and Melvin never throws shit out, even when it's empty. He just puts it back. Irritating!"

With his one arm, he tossed things in the trash, and sorted out whose items were whose—the Stefano pile, "Adam, is this yours?"—And into the Adam pile, or the probable Melvin pile.

"You know I've always wanted to go to Israel," I said to Stefano. "But I'd love to see more of Asia—Thailand, Vietnam, China...Nepal."

"Once I clean this out, everyone gets their own shelf!" Stefano exclaimed.

"Pretty cheap flights to Thailand," I said as I stared at my notebook's blank page.

"Good beaches in Thailand. But Sinai in Israel is the best."

"Oh, yeah?"

"The best. We use to get high in Sinai and sit in the sun all day." I had heard Stefano talk about this a thousand times, but I still liked to hear it.

"And backgammon! I miss backgammon. Do you play backgammon?"

"A little bit, but I'm not so good." We'd had this discussion before, too. I liked it every time though.

"We'll have to play backgammon someday. I've been missing it."

The front door opened, and in came Melvin. "Hu-Woaa! Whatcha doin', Stefano?"

"What the hell, Melvin?" Stefano was fired up again. "How much orange juice do you drink? There are six empty orange juice cartons here! Are you sure you're thirty-one years old? Have you always lived at home?"

"Shoot...awww...shoot...shut up, Stefano," Melvin said as he pushed up his glasses. "Why are you always picking on me?"

"Because you do stupid things. You're an idiot!"

I sat listening as I began a list all the possible things I could write to Eun-Hee. I had my Korean-English dictionary by my side; I wanted to write it in both languages to clear up any confusion. In the background, Stefano and Melvin let out their respective grievances.

The phone rang, and I got up and answered it. "Hello?"

"Hey, dude! It's Louie! What are you doing tonight?"

"You're looking for a drinking partner again tonight?" I asked Louie.

"C'mon, dude! You up for it? Come by after you get out of work."

"You live over an hour away by bus."

"Melvin's been coming over. Even Paris came over once. Why don't you and Stefano come over?"

"Not on a weekday. This weekend I will, though."

"Put Melvin on the phone."

Louie was desperate for company because Laurie was done with Korea. She was planning to leave anyway, and her plans for London had finally worked out. "Just a second, Louie." I turned towards the kitchen, "Melvin! Louie's on the phone."

"What? Huh?" Melvin said.

"Louie's on the phone."

He got up, and I handed it to him. "Hu-Woaa?" he shouted into the phone. "Huh? Aw shoot! Huh? What time? Just a sec...What? What? Oh, yeah...hahaha...yeah, what time? Yeah, okay..."

Stefano turned to me. "I'm going to get some cleaning supplies so we can clean this place up today. This apartment is a mess! We're all going to pitch in money and buy all the things we need. But first I'm going to get some cleaning supplies."

"Good idea," I said as I returned to my note-writing to Eun-Hee.

Stefano slammed the door shut as he left, and it was just Melvin and myself. Once Melvin hung up the phone, he shouted at me, "Whatcha doin?"

"Writing a letter, Melvin."

He shouted back, "Is it that Korean chick?"

"Maybe."

"Oh." Minutes later, "You like Getty Lee? From Rush?"

"He's okay."

He shouted back, "He's okay?" He paused, "He's the frickin' best. Who do you like? Who do *you* like?"

"I don't know, Melvin. I don't like that kind of music."

"Aw, shit...Shoot, I mean," he retracted his swear word. Hey, I got something serious to ask you about."

"What's that, Melvin?"

"Do you like comics?"

"No," I said. I could see the disappointment in his eyes.

"Oh...I was just asking, y'know. I collect comics."

"I know. You have them pasted all over your door and hanging from your walls."

Melvin laughed. "But I *really* like Japanese comics."

"Why's that?"

"More pornography. You should see it."

"I don't think I want to see that, Melvin."

He laughed hysterically. "Do you like anime?"

"What's that?"

"Japanese comics," he said seriously, as if anime were fundamental to life, art, and all things living. Years later, I would appreciate the art and style of comics, but at that time in my life, I had no deep understanding of them.

"Melvin, I don't know anything about comics."

"Huh?" He nodded his head. He hummed for a while. "Hey, why does Stefano give me a hard time?"

"Because you don't throw away your food, and it spoils. Plus, you have empty cartons filling up the fridge."

"The Korean teachers don't like me, either."

"Look, Melvin, I don't know. I'm going to the bathroom." When I got up, Melvin was still talking. As I walked behind him, he whirled his chair around vigorously to see me. I went back behind him the other way, and he again whirled his chair again. After a few more repetitions, I finally went to the bathroom. He continued to talk through the door.

When I came back out, he asked, "Have you heard the new Rush album?"

"No, I haven't."

"It's pretty good."

I could see that he wasn't going to stop talking—about Rush, or comics, or anything else—so I told him, "I'm going to my room to read." I went into my room and put on some soft music. I wanted to relax.

KNOCK KNOCK

I yelled through the door, "What?"

Melvin shouted back, "Can I come in and talk?"

"I'm busy." I silently got up off my bed and locked the door, "I have to do some things."

He shouted back at me, "Why doesn't anyone talk with me?"

"I don't know, Melvin."

He shouted again, "Can I come in?" I heard him turn my doorknob.

"I'm busy; talk through the door." I felt like a jerk, but I just wasn't interested in this particular conversation right now. I sat in my room and planned my letter.

That evening, I brought a simple note to the hagwan, written in both English and poorly translated Korean. I felt anxious about presenting it to Eun-Hee, but I was determined to follow through with it nonetheless.

I approached the table where she was sitting. This made her nervous; as she was probably wondering how to communicate with me if I said anything.

Instead, I just handed her my gift. She smiled pleasantly. As she browsed over it, she saw that I had misspelled her name. She gestured, indicating the correct spelling. I smiled, embarrassed.

We gestured back and forth a few more times, until the nonverbal communication became too awkward. I then wandered awkwardly over to the other side of the teacher's lounge to pretend like I had my own class preparation to do.

***

21

***

There are a few quintessential Korean experiences that really shape a person's long-term memories of the place. I was about to have a few of them.

Teaching in the hagwan was unique in several ways. First, unlike in a typical language teaching position, you were a "cultural ambassador." This meant that students wanted to know about your culture, and about what you thought of theirs. Second, teaching in Korea was a popularity contest. This meant that what you taught wasn't important; being liked by the students was. You would never be fired for not being able to teach, but you could easily be fired for not being popular. Students paid money for classes because they enjoyed attending them, not because the teaching content was good.

Because of these dynamics, classrooms could become quite casual, often stressing interesting conversation above language acquisition skills. Because of this, I often threw out the lessons I had prepared in favor of interesting topics suggested by students. As usual, that day, I began by asking, "Okay, before we begin, anything you guys want to talk about today?"

Six students sat at the same table as I did. A young, serious man quickly blurted out, "Erection!"

I looked around at them, "An erection?"

"Yes," he assured me, "Erection."

I looked at all of the students again, scanning their faces for smirks, enthusiasm, smiles…"An erection? You all want to talk about an erection?" I looked in the girls' direction, and they nodded their heads in agreement.

I was puzzled, obviously not sure how to make this into an appropriate topic.

"You not know erection?"

'Well, sure, I know about erections. But what exactly about an erection do you want to know?"

"You know, American erections."

"American erections?"

"Yes, Bill Clinton. American erections."

"Bill Clinton? And Monica Lewinsky?"

"Who?"

"Monica Lewinsky?"

One of them asked me, "Who is Ma-Nee-Ka?"

"Monica, yes. Repeat after me, Mo-ni-ca." I raised my hand to my mouth and awkwardly gestured as I said, "The blow job?"

"Blow. Job?"

A few repeated after him, "Blow job."

I inquired, "Is this the erection you want to talk about?"

"Yes, president erection. Who will win this year?"

I paused for a second. "Who will...win?"

"Republican or Democrat?"

"Oh...the presidential *election*!"

"Yes, the president erection."

"You mean between Bill Clinton and Bob Dole?"

"Yes."

1996.

1996, Nirvana, Kurt Cobain. A Tower Records had opened a store in Pusan. On the news rack, on one of the magazine covers, there was a famous photo of Kurt Cobain, an American legend of the 1990s. I bought this magazine, solely to bring it to my classrooms, to stimulate conversation with my students.

"Sharon Stone, do you know this photo?"

"No."

"Okay, okay, MJ, do you know?"

"Who is that?

"You don't know either? How about you, Tom Cruise? No? Really?"

And on and on it went.

I discovered that none of my students had ever heard of, or had seen an image of, Kurt Cobain. Wasn't he the icon of our generation? Didn't they love American icons? Didn't their chosen English names alone signify some interest in knowing this type of thing?

Korea. Where the music you don't expect, lives on, and the music you'd hope to talk about, had never arrived. When I did inquire of the American music they knew, it was usually Michael Jackson, Whitney Houston, and the most mainstream of pop music. The music that I felt that people in the 1990s were really listening to, such as Nirvana, Pearl Jam, Red Hot Chili Peppers, was something that hadn't arrived yet.

After those class, I retreated to the teacher's room—I needed a break.

Paris was there, and she was freaking out. "Adam, we need to get to the American Embassy!"

"Why?"

"The North Koreans are attacking! There are sirens going off right now!"

"What?"

"Come on, let's go! They can skylift us out of here!"

"What?"

Eventually, we settled Paris down, and we all got to rational thinking again. There was nothing more to do, than simply go back and teach our regular scheduled classes, as if nothing was going on.

Over the next few days, I had discovered that a North Korean submarine was shipwrecked—or was it subwrecked—on South Korean territory. Sirens were going off, as they did with any scare from the North.

Over the next few weeks, we found that the North Korean submarine crew had basically tried to shoot their way home, walking north. The captain had killed many of his own men, as he didn't want anyone releasing information on their mission as they had run aground. South Korean civilians were being killed as the remaining North Koreans tried to make their way north. Ultimately, the story goes, one of the North Koreans actually made it home.

This was interesting to me, as once I became aware of South Korea, I realized that there were constant international incident scares in the international media. But living in South Korea, none of those had any meaning, and didn't effect anything in the day to day life of the Korean people. From the international media, however, it felt like the beginning of the next Korean War, or something that could spark off World War III.

116

Over time, this kind of thing became so incredibly commonplace that most South Koreans were indifferent toward these events. No one thought much about it, and only the newest hagwan teachers would go into a panic. Even worse, when an incident did make international news, panicked family members back home would reach out to their North American sons and daughters, demanding them to get home out of harm's way. The longer we stayed in Korea, the more desensitized we became to the sirens, the political badgering, and all the rest. After a while, we refused to entertain any of it.

When I later asked students about the incident, there was just complete indifference. A complete non-event.

***

22

***

I was getting used to my neighborhood and my routines. Next to our apartment, there was a local convenience store, interestingly named, Happy Mart (해피마트). Our apartment was named Taekyung Happy Town. The Korean pronunciation of *happy* was so different from English, it took me several months to realize it was the same word. It sounded like HAY-PEE.

Inside the Happy Mart, lived an old ajumma and ajusshi. These were two words that every foreigner quickly learned, as they were so often used throughout Korea to refer to older people. When anyone wanted customer service, they simply yelled out ajumma for the old lady, or ajusshi for the old man, and they would come running. It wasn't long before foreigners became accustomed to yelling it out as well.

The ajumma and ajusshi of the Happy Mart, not only worked in the store, but they also lived in it. They had their sleeping mats just behind the cash register. This wasn't uncommon, as many store owners in Korea, particularly at this time, lived in the same store that they worked. If we went there late at night for our Cass or Hite beer runs, we would wake them up. But, they were always happy to see us.

Typical of most Korean store owners, they said a mix of Korean and English words, dependent on what they would know in English.

"Hello," I'd say in Korean, as I placed my beer on the counter.

"I love you," one of them might say back to me.

Then the other might count the change back, "One, two, and three. I love you."

I usually gave a smile, but I noticed Stefano, would usually give a, "I love you too," right back at them. It was endearing.

In general though, ajummas and ajusshis were a mixed bag. While they were often the first one to give you their own their umbrella in the rain, they might also be the first one to push you hard in the back, while you were already trying hard to get on, or stand on, a bus.

To be fair, bus drivers drove hard on both their brakes and accelerator, particularly with the steep hills around our house, so you did have to secure yourself firmly on any bus. As they pressed both petals at the same time, the buses would continuously rock upward and backward, sending many passengers flying hard to the bus floor. So, I could understand the urgency they had at times, to get on a bus, in addition to fighting the sheer large crowds for a seat.

One of the more unusual scenes I experienced was when I was waiting for a bus, and saw a group of old ajummas with wrapped parcels resting on their heads. As the bus opened their doors to let us on, they impressingly pushed people in front of them with their free hand.

I scrambled on quickly, mostly to get out of their way, but once on the bus, I felt something whiz by my head. As I turned around, I saw another large item whiz by my head. Than a *kaplunk* as one of those items hit hard squarely into one of the seats that I was aiming to sit in. As I was about to say something, they pushed hard past me, and their entire group quickly occupied every last seat. That was the nature of the rough and tough ajumma. I often had to remind myself that many of these old generation people were not that far removed from the 1950's Korean War themselves. In short, they had a heart of gold, but also had a tremendously thick layer of aggressive self-serving skin.

The people of Deokcheon were equally an interesting lot. This part of Pusan seemed to have significantly larger percentages of older people than anywhere on the subway line. We called the other part of Pusan, 'The other side of the mountains.' This included the beaches like Haeundae, as well as all of the nightlife and restaurants centers like PNU, Seomyeon, Nampodong, and so forth. Over there, it seemed that people stared significantly less, and had at least some familiarity with foreigners.

Over on *our* side of the mountain, we were surrounded by a significantly lower socio-economic stratum of the Korean population. More people sold more vegetables on the sidewalks, and their clothing looked more well-worn and so forth. Many older ladies walked bull-legged, with the look that they had spent their entire lives bent over working rice fields. They had sun-drenched rougher skins, as opposed to the other side of the mountain, where the Korean women preferred walking around with umbrellas, and jumping scared at the sight of a pigeon. Our people, on our side, were quick to slice and dice up dog meat, live octopus, you name it, and they had no issue with handling any living thing whatsoever.

I also noticed a clothing preference among these older women. They preferred bright clothing, a lot of loose-fitting floral patterns. Bright shirts and light loose pants that vibrated with an eclectic mix of colors. Large visors were worn by most of the women, while they permed their hair up high, and made sure to style it on top, displayed and sticking out above their visor. Meanwhile the men of Deokcheon preferred dress shoes and belts, but their slacks and dress shirts had this low quality, and mismatch of colors. Men preferred items such as checkered black and gold pants, with checkered black and green dress shirts. Their socks could be almost any color, which just clashed all the more. Yet, they all wore these with pride, and a sense of self-confidence. No one, ever, once looked down-and-out. They all appeared extremely self-assured, and sometimes even aggressively so.

Another fashion type, generally popular with older Korean men, but not completely unheard for older Korean women, were fishnet jackets that they'd wear over their dress shirt. These were generally airy, and I think their predominant purpose was for the men to carry things in the many zipper-enclosing pockets. These fishnet jackets could be any color, but red seemed to a more popular choice. They always clashed with whatever checkered pants or shirts they wore.

This being said, the older generation and their fashion attire varied significantly from the younger generations below thirty years old. The women were incredibly fashionable with tight jeans, mini-skirts, wearing a lot of black, and a ton of make-up. So much make-up, that you would hardly recognize the woman without it, despite seeing her every day at somewhere like the hagwan. The younger men weren't as stylish in the 1990's as they'd metro-sexually become in later decades, but they were still worlds apart from the older generation of the time.

Another oddity was the way that Korean men carried their young babies. I never once saw baby carriage in the western sense. Most women simply threw a blanket-like material around their back, with the baby wrapped inside. The baby's head dangled nearly perpendicular, loosely flailing all over the place, as the mother navigated crowded streets, shoved people, and rode jolting bus rides. I later reflected that maybe because babies became accustomed to sleeping under such bizarre circumstances, it gave them the uncanny ability to nap almost anywhere in any awkward position, as they became adults.

Despite the appearance of the older generations, they always had a heart of gold, and I always felt extremely safe, and comfortable sharing their streets with them. If I was looking for a street address, it was not uncommon that they'd spend the next fifteen or twenty minutes with me, helping to navigate me to that place. If it started to rain, and they saw I didn't have an umbrella with me, they were generous enough to give me their own umbrella, and go without one themselves. Equally, I was never once overcharged for anything, anywhere. In fact, there were a few specific incidents early on that I recalled intentionally trying to leave tips at restaurants, only to have servers chase me down days later as I walked past their place again, determined to get that change back to me.

Overall, I found my new home in South Korea to be challenging, exciting, intoxicating, never dull, and just plain rewarding. The one thing to top it all off, would be if I could just secure that Korean girlfriend, which was the one thing I felt I needed to make the transition most complete. That much needed link to connect me more to the culture, and less to the foreign bubble that I loved, but wouldn't have minded to break away from.

***

23

***

Another week would go by, and when I went to the Blue Note, I was surprised—and nervous—to see Eun-Hee there with Ms. Jang and the other Korean teachers. It was the first time I had seen her there. I tentatively approached their table and asked if I could join them. Ms. Jang quickly told me that I could certainly sit down and join them. As I did, they moved the chairs around the table so I could sit next to Eun-Hee.

It was a bit awkward at first, as Eun-Hee was busy talking to another teacher in Korean. I began to talk to Ms. Jang in English. I drank my first beer very fast, wondering why I was even sitting at the table at all, if I couldn't even get a chance to talk to Eun-Hee. I contemplated leaving. Eventually, I said to Ms. Jang, "Ask Eun-Hee what her major was in school." I couldn't think of anything else to say.

Ms. Jang interrupted their conversation, and asked Eun-Hee in Korean, which she then translated to me, "She said she majored in Japanese."

"Oh, Japanese. That's why you teach Japanese." It continued like that for a while, until I discovered that she had lived in Tokyo for a year during university. "If you ever want to go to Japan," she told Ms. Jang to tell me, "I can show you around."

I rather foolishly laughed and said, "Tomorrow. I want to go tomorrow!" I was joking, but they didn't understand that I was trying to be funny. Eun-Hee didn't seem to know why I was laughing, and I didn't think Ms. Jang understood, either. My words sat there, frozen in the air. "Actually, I would love to go to Japan someday with you," I said in all seriousness. Ms. Jang translated to Eun-Hee afterward. It felt so formal. As I ordered my next beer, I wondered if this was even worth pursuing. No matter how uncomfortable the conversation was, I sat there bearing it awkwardly. Finally, Eun-Hee announced through Ms. Jang that she was tired and was going home to bed.

Before she left, I asked her if she would like to go out for a date sometime, and she agreed. Eun-Hee told me, through Ms. Jang again, "I love movies, and I would love to see you play pocketball." Apparently my fame as a pool shark had spread through the hagwan since the day I'd played with Ms. Key. I wasn't sure why, but now I was grateful of that.

I now spent more time thinking of Eun-Hee and how I could get to know her better.

Sometimes King invited me to play pool, as I was jokingly a pocketball legend, by my other expat friends. Around this time, I wanted to shift the conversation to be about Eun-Hee. "So, King, you think she's interested in me?"

"Chief, that's all she talks about," he said in his soft, monotone voice. "Whenever she sees you, she gets nervous."

"Four ball in the side," I said. "Feeling's mutual," I added.

"You know one thing I like about you, Adam?" King said to me.

"What's that?"

"You have a soft monotone voice like mine." Only King would recognize or communicate such a thing.

"It's not good for singing, is it?"

In his monotone voice, he said, "So what! I have a voice like that, and I sing like shit!"

"Me too," I said in mine. "Six ball in the corner." We went back to playing. I inquired of him, "So, are you gonna go talk with Ms. Jang? Maybe we can have a double date with Eun-Hee?"

"Yeah, I'll do that," King said to me. "Ms. Jang and Eun-Hee are good friends. It'll be fun."

"When?" I asked anxiously.

"Oh, I don't know." We went back to playing billiards—or pocketball, or pool, or whatever you call it—killing yet another afternoon. I had hope.

***

24

***

Shortly thereafter, I met a new *miguk-saram* as the Koreans called all Americans. He was the new teacher who would be taking Skate's place. A Korean woman who couldn't speak any English brought him to the apartment and dropped him off. Confused, wondering where in the hell he was and what the hell was going on in this country, he tiredly announced to me, "My name's Huck."

I looked at him and saw a very thin man wearing wrinkled slacks and a button-down shirt that was too tight around the neck. He scared me slightly, as he looked like he could be Melvin's brother. They both had curly brown hair and the same build.

"My name's Adam," I told him, but I was afraid to say more. I was afraid this guy was going to be too similar to Melvin, and I didn't want him to attach himself to me. Then I'd have two Melvins to contend with. So I pretended I was busy with errands that afternoon. Meanwhile, Huck's belongings were all over the kitchen floor, in bags and suitcases. "You might actually be moving down to the girls' apartment," I told him. "They're living with this guy named Caden who they can't stand anymore. He may be moving up here." I really didn't want to listen to either Caden's babble nonstop, but apparently Paris and Kristian were even more fed up with it.

I had Bob Dylan playing loudly, and Huck told me, "Dylan rules. He's one of my favorites."

"Yeah, I really like him too," I admitted.

He asked me, "Can I take a look at your CDs?" I casually tossed them to him, hoping not to have a bonding experience with Melvin's double.

In his tightly buttoned shirt, Huck looked as if he could hardly breathe. He had on an oversized suit jacket. It was as if his much larger father had given his eldest son the suit coat off of his own back.

Regardless of my negative opinions, Huck was looking through my CD's with enthusiasm: "*Tom Waits*! I *love* Tom Waits! Look, the Jayhawks!

Yeah, Minneapolis! Soul Asylum! Hey, it's The Replacements. Oooooh, it's Husker Du! *Bob Mould*? I love that guy! I love Sugar! Minneapolis!"

"Yeah, I used to spend a lot of time in Minneapolis. I really got into the music scene there," I told him.

"Yeah, First Avenue is a great club," he said. "I use to go up there to see all kinds of bands."

"Where are you from?" I asked.

"Missouri, but we'd drive up through Iowa to see bands in Minneapolis. It's the best music venue in the Midwest, if you ask me."

"Yeah, that's right," I said back to him, "that's right." Our conversation went on about Minneapolis bands—something I really loved but never got to talk about. No one else here knew how great that city and its music and culture were, but Huck did. I wasn't a Minnesota native either, but I would have been proud to have been. By the way, "You don't have to wear that tie and suit and stuff, Huck," I told him. "Relax."

"Oh, no problem," Huck said. "I don't mind. This is all I brought with me—suits and ties, ties and suits." He spoke in a slow, singsong voice and then shouted, "Minneapolis!" He looked around some more. "Hey, you got some books here?"

"Yeah, I do," I said to him. "I have a shelf of them in my room, my favorites and the ones I'm about to read. If you need some things to read, I put them in the big cabinet once I finish them." I gestured to the one near our back window.

"Do you mind if I take a look?"

"No, go ahead," I told him.

"William Burroughs! Good, very good," he said. He said it like some old beatnik in his singsong voice. "Jack Kerouac—*On the Road*!"

"My favorite book, Huck."

"It's a good favorite book to have, yes siree, *ON the ROAD*."

"Louis-Ferdinand Celine is in there, too. Another teacher, King, turned me on to his writing."

"Haven't heard of him—I'll have to check him out. You got some real good books, here, yes siree. Which one you reading now?"

"*The Dharma Bums*."

"More Jack Kerouac! Mighty good, mighty good," he said to me. Huck wasn't anything like Melvin, I realized. Huck was pretty cool.

That evening, I brought Huck down to the school, and we talked all the way. Just like Melvin tried to bring up comics in conversations, I always threw something out about traveling. We all try to connect with like-minded souls. I casually asked him, "So, did you do any traveling in the States?"

"Yeah, we took a big trip last summer. A few of my friends took a tour of the national parks out west."

"Oh yeah?" I asked. I worked at several national parks myself. But I was reluctant to tell him now. The coincidences were too frequent, and it felt like I was lying. We had too much in common. But once we shared our stories in detail, there was no mistaking that they were all true experiences.

As we were walking, I told Huck, "Okay now, I have to be at work for three hours tonight, so do you know where you're at? You might have to get back home on your own, or wait for one of us. Do you really know where you are at?" I asked him several times as we walked through the dog market. He seemed sick to his stomach, but he said he knew, and I left it at that.

At the hagwan, it was business as usual. Paris met Huck and told him, "Don't unpack. You're moving down with us, and Caden is moving up to the guys' apartment."

"Fine with me," Huck said in his "everything's cool" tone of voice. Caden was all spread out at one of the teacher's tables with his laptop computer. He was playing a video game at high volume. He yelled and screamed and pushed his mane of hair back with his right hand as he played.

Paris pulled me aside, "I can't wait to get Caden out of our apartment. He plays those games all night, screaming and yelling like that."

Caden shouted from the teacher's lounge, "Gotcha! I GOTCHA!"

Melvin came in, "Hey, is that *King of Fighters*?"

"Yeah, man," Caden told him. Melvin sat and stared at Caden's computer screen, and I got a preview of what my apartment was going to be like within a day or so. Huck, the cool guy, was going to the girls' apartment. Caden the annoying one, would soon have his stuff spread out on our only table, playing video games day and night.

After we taught our first evening classes, we came out of our respective classrooms only to find that Huck had attempted the walk home alone. After we finished our work shift, Stefano and I took the bus home to see that Huck's stuff was still in the living room, but he wasn't there.

I called the girl's apartment, "Paris? Have you seen Huck? He's not here, although his stuff is?"

"We haven't seen him here," she told me. "He doesn't even know where this apartment is yet."

"Let's all go looking for him, before it gets too late."

We met Paris and Kristian, as we began down the steep hill from our apartment towards the Deokcheon rotary. It would be a twenty-five minute walk down, but who knew if he even walked up this hill, or went in a completely different direction altogether from the hagwan. Additionally, there was so much construction, and re-routed roads and alleys, there was no possible way to cover them. He could be anywhere.

We walked past bull-legged old ladies wandering down from the hills, and intoxicated soju-drinking men, sitting outside of various drinking establishments.

"You look down the side streets on the left, and I'll look down the side streets on the right," Stefano told me. The girls went further down from us, searching closer to the school. I remembered my first few weeks in Korea, when everything looked the same—Huck could be anywhere. An hour went by, and the sun was already down. "I don't think we're going to find him," Stefano stated.

Just as a complete hopeless feel engulfed us all, I saw what looked like Huck crossing one of the main roads, far down the hill. I sprinted down the road as fast as I could. "HUCK!" I shouted, "HUCK!"

Huck stopped. "Oh my god!" he said, still cool and collected. "I thought I was permanently lost! I didn't have anyone's phone numbers. All of my money and stuff was in the apartment. I've been walking for hours!"

"You're lucky you wandered across this street. I don't know how we could have found you either.

Paris, Stefano, and Kristian joined us, and we walked back home up the hill, getting dinner along the way. "This is GOOD," Huck stated, probably hungry as hell and exhausted beyond belief. "This is REALLY good." Ironically this might have been exceptional, as for the rest of the time that I knew him, he generally had most of his meals shipped from the U.S., in their processed food boxes.

"*Anything*'s good after a twenty-hour plane flight and an additional seven hours of wandering around lost."

"You said it," Huck calmly replied.

***

25

***

Time went on, and the apartment situation changed. It was now me, Stefano, Melvin, and our video game addict, Caden. His game-playing equipment was spread out all over tables at the middle school, the hagwan, and now my apartment—I was now stuck with him almost twenty-four hours a day. I was spending even more time with Paris, Kristian, and Huck in the girls' apartment. Stefano was dating Paris now, so it had become our de facto hangout place.

Other times, I went out with students to the noraebang—my singing was still awful—or I let them take me to Korean attractions or tourist sites. If you took up student invitations to places, you found yourself really getting to know the country and city well. Sometimes, I just took long bus rides by myself and read books in the back or roamed the city, exploring on my own. I was getting more into a venture out and explore everything and anything phase.

Caden was still trying to get out of his contract at the hagwan to work full time at the middle school. I think most of us secretly wished and hoped for that as well. We knew it was unlikely, though. Our contracts were attached to our visas, and they were employer-sponsored. Changing employers was impossible, unless an employer allowed you to cancel your contract. On the other hand, rules were broken all the time—it was actually illegal, for example, for the hagwan to farm us out to the middle school—or any school—for additional profit.

Eventually, the issue came to a head, and we all got to hear it develop in the teacher's lounge.

Kamm was talking to Caden, smoking his cigarette vigorously. "So, you're going to the middle school, you think?"

"If you'll let me out of my contract," Caden said with confidence, pushing his hair back.

"You really think we're going to fucking do that? What the fuck?" Kamm said it in his squeaky tough-guy voice, eyes darting every which way.

His hands jerked back and forth, the little red light of the cigarette creating tracers in the dimly lit teacher's lounge.

Several days later, at the middle school, it was just Caden and I and Mrs. Baek among a thousand young kids yelling "Hello!" and "Hi-five!" Mrs. Baek met us in the lounge, told the children to give us a moment's peace, and stated, "Caden, we can't hire you here. Your hagwan won't let us. Your director yelled at me for two hours, and I couldn't say or do anything. Your boss was so angry at me. She's not going to release you from your contract."

That was pretty much the end of the whole thing right there. Both Caden and I were pulled from the middle school—Caden's heaven, and my hell. We would work full time at the hagwan after the end of the month. I much preferred teaching the adults and being around my coworkers and the Korean teachers, plus, the hagwan was much closer to home than the middle school.

Caden, however, was crushed. He had already told Kupo that he was going to quit, secretly thinking they couldn't do anything about it. His plan was to work at the middle school illegally. It didn't work that way, and he ended up finishing his schedule until the end of the month. He was ready to move on, he said, back to Japan.

The very last day at the middle school, after his last class, he closed all the doors, and locked them from the inside. He cleared the desks from the middle of the room, and he sat in an awkward lotus position with his two index fingers pointing upward. It was one of his Zen rituals; after all, he had been a Zen practitioner or something in UCLA—or so he'd often claimed. After I finished teaching my class, I went to talk to Mrs. Baek. I wanted to thank her for everything I had learned from her. She asked me, "What do we do about your friend? I am so worried. He has been in there for thirty minutes. He let out his last class extra early."

Poor Mrs. Baek. Eventually, Caden did stop asking Buddha for guidance and came out. We went home and packed his bags on what was to be his last day in Korea. From then on, I was no longer teaching at the Middle School either.

It would be the last time that I would see Caden. After he left, I didn't think much about it. It felt good to me. But as the years went by, I reflected more about him, and how had I been a bit more mature myself, I might have learned a lot from him. He had a lot of ambitions, dreams, and goals. He certainly had more than I did at that time. If I had met him at a different time in my life, I might have respected that significantly. I might have even joined his dream sharing, with that of my own, if I had even had my own at that time. At the very least, I might have dismissed the perceived bragging more, and cherished more of the many great things that we often talked about instead.

For that matter, Skate as well. For whatever negatives he had, I truly did like the guy at the beginning. Through his negatives, he taught me tremendously the impact that his type of thinking had others. If it wasn't for the very nature of this living abroad experience, the way it pushes people together, who you might not have gravitated towards on your own, it all just gave me better perspective on life, and the many varied aspects of it. I had to be eternally grateful of that guy, just for that alone.

***
26
***

It was 1996, and something really special was about to occur. Louie was living in Seomyoen, and he called me about *The 1st Pusan International Film Festival* (제1회 부산국제영화제·第一會釜山國際電影節). It would later be well-known as one of the most important film festivals of Asia.

With the sudden withdrawal of our hagwan from the Middle School, I suddenly and unexpectedly had some free time immediately in the middle of my teaching day. This wouldn't last long, and coincidentally perfect.

"Come on, dude, you can stay at my place," Louie insisted. "Just come on down to Nampo-dong." Our Deokcheon place took nearly sixty to ninety minutes of traffic to get there.

"Nah, I still have classes at the hagwan, but I'll definitely spend every chance I get there," I told him.

"You won't regret that," he assured me.

I navigated my way to Nampo-dong, an area of Pusan that wasn't too far from Pusan Station itself, and a large nightlife, restaurant, and market area of Pusan. Much like Seomyeon, it had many neon-lit streets and alleys, with just about everything someone might want to meander around and enjoy. Much like Seomyeon, it acted much like any downtown would. It was a destination, a neon-lit crowded destination. On top of that, it was a fantastic location to go to the cinema, as its cinemas were plentiful enough to host such an event as the First Pusan International Film Festival, or BIFF, as they'd later call it. The B in BIFF, because later Pusan would become Busan.

Wandering around the event with Louie was fantastic. I still had my long hair, perpetually tied in the back, but this worked out to my favor here, more than anywhere else in Pusan.

"Yes, sir, welcome to the film. Follow me, sir." They would usher me immediately to the front rows, where the film directors and other important people were designated with all of the amenities.

I attempted to buy a ticket for some events I went to, but seldom did I actually need it. "Welcome, sir!" Unused tickets accrued in my pants pockets.

I watched Taiwanese films, Japanese films, Korean films, and just about anything that was scheduled with English subtitles.

Louie, equally, had the same treatment. We went to different films, talking about them later. "You should definitely see this Korean film, Louie. It is kind of like that American film, the one with two prisoners on the run, and the authorities chase them. You can't miss that."

The event had so much meaning to me. It made me miss this aspect of being back home in the United States, but equally enticed by the fact that it also existed here. Plus, I was having such a different experience with it, being perceived in such a way from the Korean people. The assumption that I must have been something much more than I actually was. These beautiful little events would became the bigger cause of how I would later feel that Korea was just as much a home, if not more, than anywhere else ever was, for me.

***

27

***

After the BIFF, and back up in Deokcheon once again, King and Ms. Jang had finally arranged my first date with Eun-Hee. However, the day before our double date, we had the rare holiday from school. I had been out with some of my students; they had wanted to show me Kyongju (경주·慶州), the most historical city of Korea, rich in history and culture. I had enjoyed my day tremendously, but I had also received a bad sunburn which had burned my face bright red. It wasn't the look I wanted for my big date with Eun-Hee, but I was just thankful to be going out with her. Rather than delay it, and risk missing the opportunity, I just went for it, sunburn and all.

King and the girls were going to pick me up at the apartment, so I went home immediately after my Saturday classes and cleaned it thoroughly. When Stefano came home, he saw me and said, "I can't believe you're cleaning, Adam. I thought I was the only one who cleaned around here."

We both surveyed the apartment. Everything was spotless. I couldn't tell him my real motive, so I just muttered, "Yeah, well, it was getting kinda dirty."

"No, this is really amazing. It looks great."

"Well, I figured it was probably my turn."

It was well after the time they were supposed to pick me up, and I just hoped that they would arrive before Melvin got there. I didn't want him to be part of Eun-Hee's overall impression of the date.

Finally, King called me on the phone, "Hey Adam. Well, Ms. Jang and I are down at in Deokcheon right now. Eun-Hee is at the beauty parlor getting her hair and nails done."

"Really?" I was shocked. I didn't expect her to be at a beauty parlor. I immediately felt flattered.

"You're just a lucky guy," King said. "Well, we'll see you in about fifteen minutes."

"Sounds good." I hung up and anxiously paced the floor, looking for things to clean.

Stefano could tell something was up. Eventually, I had to admit it: "I have a date with Eun-Hee this afternoon."

"Ahhh...I see how you are," he joked. "So, that's why you cleaned the apartment." We talked about meaningless things for a while, but I couldn't really concentrate on anything. I continued to check the window to see if they were coming to the apartment door.

Eventually, King did come to the door, but I didn't see the girls. When I opened it, he said, "Eun-Hee is nervous about coming up to the apartment." He paused, "Because Melvin lives here."

"Understood," I laughed. So I followed King down to the parking lot. I couldn't help but smile. When we got to the car, Ms. Jang motioned for me to sit in the front, next to Eun-Hee, and she got in the back with King.

In the car, Ms. Jang asked me, "Are you drunk?"

"No." This was a strange question. "Why?"

"We could see you walking through the parking lot, and your face was all red."

I laughed. "No, no, no, I have a sunburn. I went to Kyongju with my students." I recalled that Koreans don't get sunburned, but their faces often flush red when they've been drinking.

"Oh, how did you like Kyongju?" Ms. Jang translated for Eun-Hee, and I responded—and so on, back and forth. Then we all sat in silence for a while.

"Ms. Jang, can you tell Eun-Hee that she looks beautiful this evening?" I felt obligated to comment on that. Several more translations, culminating in a brief "thank you" which was followed by more silence. King and I started talking in English, and Ms. Jang and Eun-Hee began speaking in Korean.

The first place we went to was a Korean restaurant, where we sat cross-legged on the floor and ordered several Korean foods that I had never tried before. I enjoyed it immensely and added it to my food list for future visits. I sat next to Eun-Hee again, but I had to turn to talk to her, and she wasn't turning to talk to me. There was more awkwardness, and two different languages being spoken. I enjoyed talking to King about the Peace

Corps and the books we'd read, but I really wanted to talk to Eun-Hee. I asked her, which was translated, "So what did you do yesterday?"

After a few translations, I had an answer: "She says she stayed home and watched television yesterday."

"Ah...ask her what she watched." I knew nothing about Korean TV, but I wanted to keep our "conversation," strained as it was, going.

After the meal, Ms. Jang told me, "We were all discussing it, and we would like to go out for coffee now. Would you like that?"

I knew the conversation wasn't going well, and more awkward silences didn't interest me too much, but I agreed: "Sure, sounds good." I didn't have a better suggestion, and I really did want to try to communicate with Eun-Hee more. So we left the restaurant and got in the car again. Eun-Hee drove one block and parked again. Then we went into the coffee shop. We could already have been on our second cup, with the time we wasted moving her car one block and parking, but I didn't object.

At the coffee shop, we experienced yet more awkwardness, each of us talking to the wrong person yet again. After more green tea and Korean coffee, we all agreed to go play pocketball. Maybe that was one thing they assumed I'd enjoy. Although I didn't know the real reason, we were on the move once again. We got in the car again, drove another two blocks, and we parked in front of a billiards hall. This was much more time-consuming than walking, but it appeared to be Eun-Hee's preference.

When we entered, King went to get us a table, and Ms. Jang went to the bathroom. Eun-Hee and I were forced to communicate directly with one another. I sheepishly told her, "You know, I think you look great tonight."

She looked at me, perplexed. "What?"

"I think you are really pretty tonight." No response. "You," and I pointed to her, "Pretty." I gestured and hoped she would understand.

"Pretty?" she said.

"Pretty." I nodded my head. "Beautiful."

She smiled when she understood the word "beautiful." "Oh, thank you. I know."

I looked at her perplexed—*I know*? What kind of response was that? Then it dawned on me that she was joking. So I smiled back to her, and we stood there for what seemed like hours until finally King and Ms. Jang came back.

We played pocketball, and Eun-Hee and I were partners. Every time she made a shot, I acted excited and would slap her hand with mine. When I made a shot, she did the same with me. It was the only bonding experience available to us. Throughout the game, King and I talked, and Ms. Jang and Eun-Hee talked, but Eun-Hee and I couldn't connect with words. But on one occasion, Ms. Jang turned to me and said, "Eun-Hee told me you have the most beautiful blue eyes." It made me smile.

"Thank you," is all I could say. "Nine ball in the corner."

***

28

***

Later that week, I met with King, Kristian, Paris, and Stefano at the Blue Note Bar after work. "Heard you had a date," Paris casually mentioned to me.

"Yeah."

"How was it?" Stefano asked.

"It was good, but hard to communicate."

Paris didn't know Eun-Hee, so we spent about ten minutes trying to differentiate her from the other Korean teachers.

"She's the one with the long black hair. She has dark eyes, and she's thin. She dresses like a fashion model."

"You've just described every Korean teacher at the hagwan."

But eventually, we worked it out. "I know the one," Paris finally said. "She's the one who Kamm always flirts with!"

"What?" I asked her.

"Yeah, Kamm always flirts with her. Or at least he used to."

"Yeah, but now she just she pushes him away," Kristian chimed in.

"Kamm?" I was stunned. "Kamm, the director?"

"Yeah, her and Kamm used to always hang around each other," Paris told us.

"They used to..." Kristian said. "They used to, but she doesn't come in with him in the mornings anymore."

"Kamm, our director?" I said stunned once more.

"They used to get pretty physical at the hagwan," Paris said.

"You know, Eun-Hee acted pretty strange once in front of him," I thought back to the time in front of the fast-food restaurant.

"Well, they used to go home together and come back together," Paris said.

"They used to," Kristian said again. "But if you notice now, it's not like that."

"Kamm is married," King added, "And his wife is pregnant."

"Yeah, see, he wouldn't be with Eun-Hee," I told Paris.

"But that doesn't matter here," Stefano told us all. "In Korea, women are only for marriage; they just breed children and take care of the house. Married men can still have girlfriends."

Korea always prided itself on its low divorce rate during the 1990's, particularly in contrast to the United States' high divorce rate. We often reflected that it was probably because women had such a low status, and being a woman and a divorcee was so negatively stigmatized in Korean society. It meant that men could do anything they wanted, with little recourse for a woman to fight it.

"But Kamm?" I stated once again.

"Sometimes women send their men to prostitutes when they're pregnant," Stefano insisted. "Men are not considered unfaithful to their wives here. It's a different culture."

"That's true," King responded. "But Kristian is right. Whatever was happening, they've stopped since Eun-Hee has known you, Adam."

"That is so sleazy of Kamm, though."

"In the West, it's sleazy. It's common here," Stefano reminded us.

"No, Kamm is a sleazy man anywhere," Paris replied.

"True, true," we all agreed. Eventually, Stefano and Paris went home together. Then it was just Kristian, King, and I.

"You know, all the Korean women are attractive—and so sweet," I told them, working on more beer.

"Yes, that's true. I'm glad I have Ms. Jang," King told us.

"If things didn't work out with Eun-Hee, I wouldn't mind dating some of the other Korean teachers," I told them.

"Oh yeah, what do you mean?"

"Well, when I first got here, I really thought Ms. Key was attractive."

"Ms. Key?" King questioned. "Some people really like her, and some really don't."

"Yeah I know," I said. "I've brought it up to different people, and they either think she's the ugliest or the most attractive, but nothing in between."

"I've met a few other teachers who've said the same thing," King said. "It's interesting, because I can see how she might seem exotic."

This was one of the interesting things about intercultural dating. When I saw Koreans with westerners, I always wondered if they knew exactly what kind of westerner they had, as the one they had, seemed like someone who shouldn't have been able to date that type of Korean back home. But likewise, when most Koreans saw foreigners' choices in Korean women, they often questioned us. I think that they thought we were choosing strange or weird Koreans to date. Equally, when I saw Koreans choices in westerners, I also generally perceived them as choosing some of the weirder westerners to date.

We talked about it a little more, and I asked them about something else that had been on my mind: "Y'know, I think Ms. Hwung is interested in me. But I don't know."

"Ms. Hwung? She's kind of a bitch," Kristian told me. "To me, anyway."

"Really? Well get this..." I described the time at the hagwan when the three of us had talked. "Ms. Key said that Ms. Hwung had a date, but she really wished it was me. So what do you think about that?" I drunkenly asked. "Ask Ms. Jang about that; I'd really like to know. But I think Ms. Hwung likes me. What do you think?" They both just looked at me skeptically. "Ask Ms. Jang. Really," I told them while working on who knows what number beer.

A few days later, I was sitting in the hagwan getting ready for my classes. Ms. Key came up to me and nearly shouted, "HERE!" Then she slammed down *The Catcher in the Rye*, the book I had loaned to her shortly after I'd arrived. At that moment, I didn't understand why.

***

29

***

The following weekend, Paris and I worked the weekend shift along with Ms. Hwung and several other teachers. It was a Saturday afternoon, and between classes there was a brief break. Ms. Hwung came up to me in the teacher's lounge. "I want to talk with you," she said stonily.

"Okay," I said, "What about?" I had forgotten the conversation with King and Kristian, so I couldn't imagine why she might want to speak with me.

"You know what about," she said angrily. "It is something you said."

"What did I say?"

"You know what you said. Think back several days ago."

"Several days ago?" I said innocently. I couldn't think back to anything between us a couple days ago.

"You don't know? You don't fucking know. You fucking asshole!"

"What? What did I say?"

She yelled at me, "We will talk about it today, after work!"

I was a little nervous; I really had no idea what, but it was obvious that she was pretty angry about something. Take in mind, I am transcribing all of her words into well-spoken grammatically correct sentences, but the actual conversation was filled with broken English, and sentences that could easily be misperceived by either one of us.

After teaching our weekend classes, Paris waited for me to go home with her, but she could see that I was hesitant. "Aren't you ready to go?"

"Well, I need to talk to Ms. Hwung about something."

"Ooooooh...Adam and Ms. Hwung...She's a pretty one."

"Well, I don't know what it's about, exactly, but I think it's important."

"Quite the stud, Adam." I waited for Ms. Hwung to get out of her class.

When Ms. Hwung arrived, I asked her, "Where should we go?" She told me she knew a place, so we walked off in one direction, and Paris walked off in another. I could tell she was extremely curious about what Ms. Hwung wanted with me.

We went to a cafe, just Ms. Hwung and I, and she asked me once again, "Do you remember what you said?"

"No, I don't know," I said to her.

"You don't fucking know?" She yelled at me, her eyes wild. "You told everyone that I liked you, you fucking asshole!"

"What?" I said.

"You fucking asshole! You fucking asshole, why did you say that? Answer, you fucking asshole!"

"I don't know," I pleaded. "I didn't know, I thought maybe you did."

"You ask me, I will say NO! You fucking asshole. Why did you tell everyone! Why? ANSWER!"

"Well...well...well," I sputtered with my head down. I was being scolded like a child. "Well, remember that time with you, me, and Ms. Key?"

"She was joking! You fucking asshole! I can't believe you said this!"

"What can I do about it now?" I pleaded with her, feeling afraid that I'd ruined her reputation somehow.

"I want you to not talk to any Korean teachers again. NO KOREAN TEACHERS! I want you no talk to anyone! EVER!" She yelled "EVER! YOU NEVER TALK ANYONE AGAIN. NO KOREAN AT KUPO HAGWAN! EVER!"

"But you don't understand," I pleaded. I was embarrassed and shocked. "There is some kind of misunderstanding here," I told her again.

"Well, I would like to know, WHY YOU SAY SUCH THINGS!"

"It's a misunderstanding."

"What happened? What happened?" She muttered again, "You asshole."

"I think you have things confused," I told her. "I never told anyone you liked me."

She demanded, "THEN WHO DID?"

"I don't know," I said. "But this was based on the conversation that happened the other day."

"YES! YES! WHAT WAS IT?" She continued to demand while muttering, "You fucking asshole," under her breath.

"We were at the Blue Note Bar, and we were discussing misunderstandings, you see. We were discussing how hard it is to know what's going on for us foreigners."

"WHAT?"

"Just listen, please, just listen," I said to her. "We were discussing misinterpretations," I knew I was lying to her, but in a sense I was telling the truth. "We were discussing misinterpretations, and I said to them, "Yeah, like this one time I was talking to Ms. Hwung and Ms. Key, and Ms. Key said to me, 'Well, she really liked her date, but she really wished it was YOU, Adam!' So you see, I was telling them about how sometimes with the differences in cultures and languages you really don't know what people mean when they say things."

She thought it over for a while, and she seemed to relax a bit—although she still looked as if she hadn't completely ruled out killing me. We continued to sit in the restaurant drinking beer. She told me about herself and her family and her life. I firmly resolved to myself to never talk to—or about—this woman ever again. Afterward, I walked her to her bus stop, and then I walked to mine. Then I went up to the girls' apartment, knowing everyone except Melvin would be there.

As I walked through their door—and I just walked in as if I lived there myself; our group was that close—I was immediately greeted with curiosity.

"So what did you and Ms. Hwung do?" Paris winked at Stefano. "Adam left with Ms. Hwung after our classes today."

"Ms. Hwung?" Stefano said.

"Yeah, Ms. Hwung," Paris grinned. Then she asked in her sweet Texas drawl, "So, Adam, are you going to tell us?"

Stefano inquired, "What's this all about?"

"Look, I just came here to see what you guys are doing after classes today," I told them very seriously. "I really won't talk about it. It wasn't good, and I don't want to talk about it."

"C'mon, Adam, what was it about? You can't come in here and say that. Now we're *more* curious."

"No, I'm serious," I told them. "It was a misunderstanding that had to be cleared up. It wasn't good, and I don't want to talk about it."

Huck butted in, "He doesn't want to talk about it. Just drop it, Paris."

"He can't say it was bad and not talk about it. C'mon, Adam." Paris egged me on.

"If he doesn't want to talk about it, we can't force him," Stefano said. He must have sensed it was serious, too.

"So whatcha reading, Huck?" I inquired of him.

"MO-bee Dick!" he said in his singsong voice.

"Adam, you're just going to let it die like that? Tell us, tell us!" Paris demanded, still joking with me.

"So where are you in the book now?" I asked Huck.

"Captain Ahab's lookin' for the mighty MO-by!"

Paris wouldn't give up on me, but I insisted that it was a misunderstanding, and one I didn't want to ever talk about again—which was the truth. Huck and Stefano backed me up, bless their hearts.

"So he's looking for the mighty Moby, eh?"

"That's right, sir! Always looking for the mighty Moby, but he just can't snag the ol' fish."

I redirected the conversation, "So we all have a big holiday coming up soon. Where are we going to go?" Chu-sok (추석·秋夕) was upon us in several weeks. It would be a four-day holiday. I had been working every day, including the weekends, since I had arrived in Korea, so this break meant a lot to me. It meant a lot to all of us. Chu-sok was similar to American Thanksgiving, a time of family, meals, and spending time together. Most workplaces shut down, and most employees went back to their hometowns.

Paris said excitedly contributed, "Let's go to Hong Kong!"

"The Philippines are closer, and there are beaches!" Stefano argued.

"The mighty China!" Huck added in.

"Thailand!" I told them all.

***
30
***

I had increasingly mixed emotions about the chance of a relationship with Eun-Hee. The incident with Ms. Hwung had ruined my friendship with her group of friends at the hagwan and at the Blue Note Bar. Ms. Hwung and Ms. Jang seemed to have had a similar conflict, and Ms. Jang seemed to be avoiding that group of teachers as well. As a reminder, Ms. Jang was the fiancée of King, and the one I had shared with about regarding the Ms. Hwung misunderstanding.

I was still interested in Eun-Hee, despite my pessimism about it working out. She and I had planned another date with the help of King and Ms. Jang—we were going on a bowling excursion. I was encouraged to try again after watching Huck with his new possible girlfriend. Her name was Helen, and she was a Korean teacher from the hagwan. She also taught Japanese, just like Eun-Hee, and she couldn't speak English very well, either.

Shortly after my Ms. Hwung incident, Huck had organized a spaghetti dinner at his and the girls' apartment for the whole hagwan. He'd asked the teachers if they would go or not so he could plan. They consistently told him, "Yeah, we'll be there, we'll be there." He was expecting them.

I was skeptical at this point. "They're not going to come; there's a big division between our two groups. They really don't know what we're talking about, and we have no idea what they're talking about."

Stefano interjected, "Korean culture dictates that they say yes to invitations, but that doesn't mean they'll come." In short, we all had our reservations.

The day of the big spaghetti dinner, I arrived an hour late. I was not entirely surprised to find that almost everyone in attendance was of our regular foreign teacher group: I saw Stefano, Paris, Melvin, Kristian, Jeffrey, King, Ms. Jang, and Huck. One other person outside of our group did come, however; she was a very special guest of Huck's. During the dinner, Huck spoke in broken English so she could understand. You could see a spark between the two of them. The rest of us were excited that a new person had joined us, although we were somewhat disappointed that none of the other Korean English teachers had come. This confirmed both Stefano's philosophy, and perhaps my own. More cultural differences.

Huck and Helen spoke in simple English, and then they went to Huck's room for a more private discussion. The door was open, and they talked and talked. "Huck...glad...you...here," Huck said it very slowly, using his hands as props to help explain himself.

"Helen...glad...too."

"Is Helen enjoying herself?" He used more gestures to express himself so she could understand. "Enjoy," he said, "Same happy. Same same." He made two equal signs with two fingers extended. "Is Helen happy?"

"Yes."

"Huck happy too."

They continued like that throughout the afternoon and into the evening. Eventually she had to go home, but she didn't want to. We all knew Huck had found his Korean sweetheart.

The following weekend was my next and last date with Eun-Hee. In the afternoon, we went bowling. The old veterans of Kupo—Eun-Hee, Ms. Jang, Kristian, and King—explained that they had all used to go bowling every afternoon after our morning classes. They wanted to start doing this again—would others be interested in joining them? We ended up with four couples. We had Huck and Helen, Kristian and Jeffrey, King and Ms. Jang, and Eun-Hee and me. Half of us were Korean, and half were American or Canadian.

There was a bowling alley nearby, so I walked over with King and Huck, but Eun-Hee insisted on driving her car there. We waited at the bowling alley for her for about ten minutes.

Once inside, things settled into to a good afternoon, despite the fact that I still couldn't communicate with Eun-Hee at all. But we gave each other frequent glances as if to say, "If I could only speak your language!"

The Korean way of bowling was to give everyone high-fives when they scored a strike or spare. When they didn't, you tapped your closed fists together as if to say, "better luck next time."

The afternoon consisted of Huck's exaggerated expression, "Striiiiikkkee!" Every time I scored, I slapped high-fives, but I always held Eun-Hee's hands in mine for a bit longer. She was excited when I bowled well, and I was equally enthused when she did. I noticed encouragement from all the Korean teachers, which bolstered all of our spirits. Eun-Hee and I were still uncomfortable with each other, and after the games, we had another awkward moment. I asked her, "So, did you have fun?"

Perplexed, she began searching for someone to interpret what I'd said to her. At that moment, I felt it was all hopeless; it was useless trying to communicate. I excused myself to go to the bathroom. When I came back, Ms. Jang asked me, "Eun-Hee wants to know what you said to her."

"Did she have a good time?" This was followed by several minutes of Korean.

"Yes, she had a good time," Ms. Jang turned to tell me.

"Good." I nodded my head, trying to look pleased.

A few days later, back at the hagwan, I watched Huck communicating with Helen. "Huck...teach English...to Helen." His gestures explained it all. Meanwhile, Eun-Hee and I would stand on opposite sides of the room, ignoring each other, but we both knew we liked each other. If I could only communicate with her!

On another occasion, my students wanted to see a picture of my old girlfriend, Sasha. I had begun to miss her more than ever because of our wonderful conversations and our ability to connect with each other. So I brought the best picture I could of Sasha. It was a picture that I had taken about a week before going to Korea. I remembered it like it was yesterday. We went to a minor-league baseball stadium in Portland, and that day we'd found a way to sneak into the empty ballpark. We sat and talked on second base, among complete quietness in the middle of the city. It was a beautiful sunny day. I was beginning to feel like I had really lost something with her—the ability to communicate, for one.

So, since I had this photo, I showed it to them. My students had regularly asked me about girlfriends and ex-girlfriends. They saw a western woman; it occurred to me that she probably looked as exotic to them as they did to me. Regardless, one remarked, "Beautiful!" He joked, "Why are you here?"

"Does she have a new boyfriend? If not, I want her phone number!"

After my class, my students were still talking about the photo, and Ms. Hwung overheard them. "Oh, who is this? Your girlfriend?"

I told her, "My old girlfriend. We're not dating each other anymore."

"Look! It's Adam's girlfriend!" Ms. Hwung passed it around among the Korean teachers, including Eun-Hee, "It's Adam's GIRLFRIEND!"

"Well, she's not my girlfriend anymore. We broke up when I came here," I tried to explain.

"Your GIRLFRIEND is beautiful, Adam," Ms. Hwung continued. "Isn't she BEAUTIFUL, Eun-Hee?"

In the background I heard, "Huck like Helen. Helen like Huck?"

I took my picture away from them. I knew I couldn't explain this to Eun-Hee. We hadn't been able to establish the channels of communication to explain *anything*.

And sure enough, several days later, I saw Eun-Hee leaving Kupo. I ran to catch up to her. "Today. Eun-Hee. Adam. Pocketball? Movies?" I used my best Huck impressions to communicate with her.

"No," she said. "No," she confirmed it. "No," and I resolved myself to not try anymore. It wasn't worth the time or the effort, and I was sick of it all anyhow.

***
31
***

We were still planning our big holiday trip, but things weren't working out with that, either. We all wanted to go somewhere, but no one knew where exactly. Also, Stefano's and Paris's relationship was beginning to sour. Paris confessed to me once, "I don't even *like* Stefano. I got into it for the sex, and now I can't stand him. He's always bitching about something."

Then it was Stefano's turn: "We don't even have sex anymore—it just stopped. I don't even know why I go over there now; we just argue all the time."

Whenever I visited the girls' apartment, I heard them bickering. "Shut up, Stefano! Just shut the hell up!" Paris screamed at him.

"Just listen, Paris! Listen!"

"Shut up! I said shut up! Don't you ever shut up?"

Our big four-day vacation was beginning to seem more unlikely. Stefano confessed to me privately, "I just want to go somewhere by myself. I don't want to do the group thing."

When I was with the others, they said, "So where are we ALL going? What are we ALL going to do?" Paris would know Stefano wasn't involved in it, but it was still, "Where are we ALL going?" It was if it didn't matter that Stefano wasn't involved. It seemed like a division was forming, and things would never be the same.

Sometimes Huck and I talked about it, but he'd already made plans to go to Shanghai with Helen that weekend. I really felt isolated, and caught in the middle between Paris and Stefano, but it turned out that Helen's parents wouldn't allow her go. Huck and I started talking about our own travel plans. "So where should we go, Huck?"

"China!" he said in a big happy voice.

"It'll be hard to get visas." But we made a tentative plan to do that. Then we shifted the conversation to one of our other shared interests—hiking. So I suggested to him, "Let's go hike a mountain!"

"Seorak-San (설악산·雪嶽山)! That is THE Mountain in Korea to hike."

He shouted back, "Seorak-San!"

So Huck and I made big plans for a big hiking experience. The girls weren't interested in that idea, and Stefano planned his four days for a southern Korean island—by himself.

Huck and I constantly talked about it, and it became our plan—it was going to happen. Melvin was also left out, but he asked Huck, "Where you goin'?"

"We're going to hike a mountain!"

"Can I come?"

"Sure, why not?" Huck told him.

Later, Huck reported their conversation to me, and I quickly responded, "Huck, why did you invite Melvin? I can't hang with him for four days straight. I see him every day as is!"

"I didn't know he wasn't welcome."

"We'll be miserable, Huck. Four days? I can't do it."

"Sorry, Adam, sir. I didn't know. What can I do now?"

"Well, just pretend like it never happened. Just don't talk to him about it, and I won't talk about it, either. Maybe he'll forget about the whole thing."

I already spent most of my free time at the girls' apartment, and when I was home, I usually went to my room and locked the door so I could be by myself. It wasn't unusual for me not to talk to Melvin for weeks at a time.

Huck came up to me in the hagwan sometimes to report that Melvin had been asking him about the trip.

"Just don't say anything about it," I told Huck again. "He hasn't brought it up to me yet."

Eventually, however, Melvin cornered me as I came through the front door. "So are you and Huck going hiking on the holiday?"

"Well, Melvin, we really don't know," I told him. "Maybe not, a lot of traffic that weekend. I'm not so sure. Well, I'm pretty tired. I gotta go to sleep." I went into my room and proceeded to lock the door.

It went on like that for those several weeks beforehand. "I want to go hike a mountain," I told Huck. "But, I don't want to talk about comic books and Rush. Has he ever gotten into a conversation with you about those kinds of things?"

"Yeah," Huck said. "He came down here and said he had something serious to say. Then he asked me if I liked comics."

"He does that to everyone, Huck," I told him. "So we'll just pretend like nothing's happened. He'll forget, I'm sure he will. If not, I have a plan."

Then the night before the big hike, Huck and I went to the store and bought what we needed. Then we went over our hiking plans. We also went over what we'd dubbed "The Melvin Factor" once more, outlining our strategy for preventing him from tagging along.

Paris was in the apartment and overheard our conversation. "The Melvin Factor!" She repeated it several times, laughing every time.

"Yeah, but this is serious, Paris," I told her, "You can't tell Melvin. I don't want to spend our vacation with him!" Mountains and hiking were spiritual things for us, and the Melvin Factor would ruin it all, I explained carefully.

When I got home from Huck's, I saw Melvin sitting alone, in the dark, at the kitchen table. I snuck into my room quietly and grabbed my toothbrush. On my way to the bathroom, I heard Melvin's voice in the dark. "What time are you going tomorrow?"

"Oh, I don't know, maybe nine or ten o'clock." I was meeting Huck at six. I continued, "I have to talk to him tomorrow morning. I'm supposed to call him at eight, actually. Well, I gotta go to bed."

The next morning, shortly before six o'clock, I woke up, slowly opened my door, and looked toward Melvin's room. His door was wide open. I had never seen him sleep with his door open before, so I went back to my room and decided not to use the bathroom at all. I carefully and quietly threw on my prepacked backpack, grabbed my towel, and turned my doorknob slowly to close my bedroom door. Next, I quietly tiptoed through the apartment, carefully opened the front door, tiptoed down the stairs, and exited into the parking lot.

It was a quiet, peaceful morning and the world felt good. On my way down the hill to Huck's, I went behind a bush and took a piss, since I hadn't been able to do so at home. I laughed, feeling great as I walked down the hill with my backpack on, and my towel draped on my shoulder. It was good to feel alive. I was getting away for four days!

At Huck's apartment, I opened the door and was surprised to see Huck all ready to go. I asked him, "You don't mind if I use the shower, do you?" Before long, we were on our way, walking by staring Koreans and talking excitedly about the trip.

We had to wait an hour for a bus. I looked anxiously around, hoping that Melvin wouldn't show up. Then we were on the bus and down the road. It was an exquisite feeling, taking off like that. Anything was possible; we had no routines or obligations for four days.

Some Koreans on the bus came up to us, "Where are you going?"

"Hiking!"

"How long have you been in Korea?" "What do you think of Korea?"—all of the questions we were always being asked. It didn't matter. We were out of the city of Pusan and not working for four days!

A few hours later, we were far into the countryside, at the foot of a large mountain. We walked and talked. "So, how are things going with Helen?"

"Pretty good."

"She's really pretty, Huck. But be careful. I never told anyone exactly what happened with Ms. Hwung, but it really affected my view of the Korean teachers. Do you really want to know what happened?"

"No, no, I don't want to know."

"Well, I trust you Huck," so I told him anyway. He never told anyone else, either—he was that kind of guy. "That's why I'm a little bitter toward them these days. They gossip and stuff. I don't know, but I don't want to be involved in any of that." I was probably stretching the truth about them myself now, but such is the politics of other.

"I see where you're coming from," he said, stressing all the main words like he was singing a song—his singsong voice again. I knew he didn't feel the same way as I did, but he understood what I meant.

On our way up the mountain, we stopped at a Korean Buddhist temple and just enjoyed the beauty of it all. Huck took out his camera and shot some pictures of the whole scene. It was a good time. We even made it to the top fairly early. I pushed Huck HARD; he was drop-dead exhausted. I liked to hike fast going up, so I could relax the rest of the time. He wasn't used to it, but he didn't complain. He did tease me a bit later in front of the others later, though—"Adam hikes fast! All that time in YELLOWstone and SeQUOIa!" and he would stress words and syllables like 'yellow' and 'quoi' in his own way.

Along the way, we were often stopped by Koreans who wanted to have their pictures taken with us. We had to stand patiently, waiting for hikers to find their film and camera and get the shot set up, but it made them happy. By the end of the trip, I thought we could easily have been featured in dozens of different photo albums. I could just hear the photographers explaining to their friends: "Yeah, I was hiking this mountain, when I saw TWO foreigners—yes, TWO of them; can you imagine? Well the proof is right here! Count them, why don't you? Just count them! ONE! TWO! See, I don't lie, I don't lie!"

The hiking culture of Korea turned out to be quite unique. For one, Koreans wore a lot of hiking gear. They had all of the hiking amenities, and bright hiking attire to match. Walking sticks were preferred by just about everyone, and the trails had few switchbacks like you'd see in the United States, which meant that the walking sticks were more badly needed. There were also plenty of temples overlooking the views, which were usually filled with people resting. In these rest areas, Koreans would camp out for a while, imbibing soju alcohol and eating snacks together.

When we got to the top, we slept with a view of an expansive mountain range. It was just as crowded there, as it was coming up the trails. Throughout the hike, we often had to wait in long lines to get through the narrow mountain pathways. However, it was all enjoyable, and sharing the hiking experience with hundreds if not thousands of Koreans, was more like an event, as opposed to any type of hiking I had done back home.

When it was time to go back down the mountain, we took our time. Both of us brought some books. I had *The Moon and Sixpence* by M. Somerset Maugham, and he had his *Moby Dick*. We basked alongside rushing river streams, reading and resting in the sun.

"So, what's ol' Moby doin' now?"

"Ol' Moby still can't seem to catch that whale! How's Maugham telling his story over there?"

"Well, Gauguin is now in Tahiti, enjoying life."

"Ah yes, that's right."

Eventually the big weekend came to an end, and we were back in the city of Pusan. Melvin was waiting for me.

"Where the heck were you?"

I nonchalantly told him, "Huck and I went hiking."

"You knew I wanted to go! If you didn't want me to go, you should have told me. I would have made other plans!"

"Well, Huck and I had been making hiking plans and buying food and such, and you were never around." Melvin was always around, and we all knew that.

"You could have told me you didn't want me to come!"

"I'm sorry, Melvin, it was pretty rotten of me."

"Shoot yeah, it was rotten. I could have made other plans!"

"I know, Melvin, I apologize. Well I'm tired. I gotta go to bed. Good night."

"Ahhhmm...shit...oops, I mean, shoot. Aww...shoot...aawww, good night."

I did have to question my own ability to not straight out tell him I didn't want him to come. At the same time, it seemed implied.

Korea had a funny effect in this way. Each of us outsiders from Korean society, and slowly repelling each other even. The more the society gave you that outward stress, the more you wanted to internally retreat. But if we weren't collective outsiders from the greater society, what pull would we naturally have to each other anyways? What did someone like Melvin and myself have in common? We worked in the same school, lived in the same apartment, but did it mean we had to spend holiday weekends together too?

Was I in the wrong for avoiding him, or was he in the wrong for ignoring my many obvious non-verbal cues? My final conclusion was that I was in the wrong. But I wouldn't have done things any other way.

***

32

***

Things continued to change for me in Korea. I still went down to the girls' apartment from time to time, and we still spent time all together, but it became less and less. Paris and Stefano continued to argue more, and Huck spent more time with Helen. So I began to see what else was going on in Pusan and who else I could meet. Equally, I began to spend more time alone in my room or on the back of buses. I continued to read constantly. During those days, I always had a book in my hand.

More than anything, I began to feel tired of Korea; the thrill was gone. I had become more conscious of the attention that Koreans gave me in the streets, and it was getting harder to bear. I was moving in a downward spiral. My desire for connections seemed to be severing. I didn't appreciate the connections with the foreign community, how tight that was, as I was too anxious and eager to find some connection with Korea, the country I now called home.

Once, for example, I was trying to get a subway ticket, and a Korean man stood staring at me. It was common to catch people staring, but this man just wouldn't look away. I walked by him with my ticket in hand, and he turned his full body so that he could continue to stare at me. I walked around him in a complete circle, and he turned with me, unfazed. It took him an entire rotation to realize what I was doing, and he laughed afterward, but I was getting sick of this stuff. I wanted to not be the center of attention for a while. Maybe I could have tolerated it at another time, but not anymore at this time. It didn't help that the greater expat community, outside our own hagwan, seemed to be toxic with similar stories. All of the negative stories built up, and I ignored all of the many positive and amazing experiences that I was having in Korea with Koreans.

"I'm sick of it," I told a couple expats at PNU's Monk Bar, "I can't stand the attention! You try going into a store?"

"Yeah, and they fall all over the place trying to hand you every item within their reach, until they chase you out of there. Been there, dude! No browsing to be done there!"

"Yeah, exactly. I'm getting sick of that stuff! I want peace!"

Sometimes I brought it up in class, but my students would usually respond, "That's Korean culture; you're a foreigner." I would plead back, "But it's not your culture; you guys don't stare at *each other*!" Still, it never seemed strange to them that I would get stared at. They'd respond, "Why wouldn't you?"

So I was getting more withdrawn and sick of everything. There was one Saturday night, alone in my room reading, I decided I could still catch the last bus downtown. I grabbed my book, stuffed some money in my pockets, securely locked the door, and headed out on the town—being sure to buy a bottle of beer for the bus ride. I would again go down to the Pusan National University (PNU) area of the city, which was quickly becoming a magnet as an expat bar district. It included bars names like Monk, Tombstone, Hard-N-Heavy, and Rock & Roll. It was the largest collection of foreign bars of anywhere in Busan, and most of them brand new to accommodate the sudden increase of foreign English teachers suddenly arriving.

The PNU bars appealed to a small expat community from all over the city, who came from far and wide to get a bit more informed and reach out to a greater community. I was still cocooned with my hagwan colleagues, but PNU was the best location to meet up with people like Louie, Kristian, and King, who had moved on to other parts of the city, away from Deokcheon.

On that particular night, I was on the subway line to PNU, and I saw an attractive Korean woman reading a book. I hardly ever saw people reading books in the Korean subways. Locals seemed to passively watch whatever was going on in the subway while biding their idle time—staring at foreigners and pointing at them, was one of the common pastimes, I reflected sourly. Foreigners were so rare in 1996 that if I saw a non-Korean face, I stared too.

So it was exceptionally remarkable to me, to see a woman—a young woman, near my own age—reading a book on the subway. I was impressed, and I looked over at her several times. Then, as if fate had struck, the passenger next to her got up. I was standing at the time, so I took the empty seat. I opened my book to begin reading and I glanced over at hers.

Not only was it in English, it was *The Catcher in the Rye*! I couldn't believe it. I had to ask her, "Do you know English?"

"Yes," she said. "Where you from?" Our conversation sparked from there.

"Look, I need to get off the subway to meet some friends. Would you care to join me?"

"I am going home, but okay, I will go with you."

I felt elated at the possibility of finally meeting someone. I led her off the subway, and we talked as we navigated the narrow alleys to the Monk Bar.

"I saw you on the subway before?"

"You have?" I asked.

"Yes, you were with four friends. It looked like you were going somewhere and it was a weekend." Here I was, in a city of three million people, and this girl had seen me before.

I was a celebrity; the whole foreign community in Pusan were celebrities. If people saw us, they didn't forget it. I could imagine them explaining to their family and friends, "Yeah, I saw that guy with the long, yellow hair—the one who looks like a girl—again today. He was with that other foreigner who had curly black hair, and those other two yellow-haired girls again." I could see it all over the city of three million, little celebrities. In Manhattan, residents might take note if they saw Woody Allen walking around Times Square. But this was just regular me, walking around in this huge Korean city. At least I wouldn't be written about in any gossip magazines.

I led the fascinating Salinger-reading girl to the bar where I was going to meet the others. King called out "Adam! Where've you been?"

"Actually, I met this girl"—I motioned to her. "What was your name again?" I whispered to her. "Hyun-Ju! I met Hyun-Ju tonight!" King and I spoke for a little while, and then a few other friends came up.

"She looks good," King told me quietly.

"Yeah, and I met her on the subway. She was reading Salinger!"

"You're always a lucky guy."

The music was loud, and my friends kept interrupting us, so I turned to Hyun-Ju. "Let's go somewhere quiet, just us, and we can talk."

"Okay," she said. We held hands as we walked out. She led me to another place where we talked all night, well past her midnight curfew, but she didn't care. "I love talk you Adam, I late now. I go home now."

"Well, let's leave," I told her. But she didn't go home; we just walked through the Korean streets, and she showed me parts of the city that I'd never seen before.

I was in heaven again. Eventually the night ended, and I kissed her at four in the morning. We discussed excuses for her to give to her family. She was twenty-six years old, but Korean women lived at home until they were married. Americans forgot all about curfews when we moved out of the house at eighteen; it was one of those big cultural differences you would never think about. Before I left her, I asked, "Meet me tomorrow night? Would you?"

"Yes," she said excitedly. "I want."

The next day I told my friends all about her: "Yeah, she was reading Salinger!" and "She's so intelligent," and "I think I could fall in love with a girl like this!" and "Imagine I met her on a subway," and, "She remembers seeing me in Pusan months ago."

That evening, I went to meet Hyun-Ju again. We had arranged to meet in a park overlooking Pusan, and I was excited. I was nervous and wondered what she would look like. Usually, when a woman dresses up for you, she looks incredible. Last night, she had just been on her way home from work. What would she look like tonight?

I waited and waited, and eventually I saw her coming up to me. She looked different, though. She didn't look as pretty, and her clothes were much less attractive. "Hello Hyun-Ju, how are you?"

"I good." I held her hand, and we talked and talked. Let me rephrase that: she talked and talked. Everything seemed different. Like we weren't able to communicate anymore, and she was telling me all kinds of things that didn't interest me. "I had boyfriend," she confided. "I broke up. He want sex."

"Really? It bothered you that much?"

"I Seventh-Day Adventist. I went church today."

"Really?" I said again. That changed my perception of her—no interesting Eastern wisdom combined with Western knowledge. I asked her, "Do you read English books very often?"

"No!" she said. "I no like reading. Friend's book."

"What do you like to do?"

"Church, TV, shopping, sleep!"

"Oh." This wasn't the girl I thought she was the night before. I asked her a political question: "What do you think of the possibility of North Korea attacking South Korea?"

"I don't know."

"Hmmm...Really?" I said. "But it's in the newspapers every day. You don't care about it?"

"No."

She was holding my hand and swinging it awkwardly as we walked through the park. It didn't feel like we were exchanging any ideas at all, despite a lot of talking happening. I was disappointed. Then I started to notice oddities, like the way she jerked her head upward whenever I asked questions. "Are you hungry?" I asked.

She jerked her head quickly, "What?"

"Are you hungry?" I said again.

She jerked her head in my direction. "Yes. Hungry. What you like?"

"Surprise me, I'm a foreigner. Take me anywhere."

We went to an expensive restaurant, "You quiet, Adam. Why?"

"I'm just tired; I don't know."

"You want see movie?"

"Sure, sure. Anything you want to see in particular?"

She jerked her head up from her food, "What?"

In Huck-talk, I said, "What movie you want see?"

"One Hundred One Dalmatians?"

"Really?" Wasn't that a kid's movie?

Korea seemed to play only the largest blockbusters, so maybe it was largely irrelevant. "You no like see it?"

"What else is there?" I asked her.

She jerked her head up from her food. "What?"

So, we went to see *101 Dalmatians*. People throughout the theater were eating a strong-smelling dried squid. Just as Americans eat popcorn at movies, Koreans ate dried squid. Because the movie theater was crowded, the stench of dried squid permeated everything. The intense chomping it took to masticate dried squid added to my irritation.

Next to Hyun-Ju and I were two high school kids, in uniform, who alternated between snacking on dried squid, popcorn, and bubble gum: CHOMP CHOMP CHOMP. Then one of them opened a bag of potato chips: RIP—CRISP CRISP CHOMP CHOMP.

I gave them a nasty look, but they seemed oblivious. I wanted to scream at them in Korean, "Shut the fuck up," but I was privately forced to curse the language barrier once more.

Several times, I thought I heard people behind them kicking one of their chairs, but it didn't deter them whatsoever. CHOMP CHOMP CHOMP.

Out of the corner of my eye, I thought I saw Hyun-Ju give them the evil eye, but I didn't directly see her do it. She looked over at me, and I rolled my eyes upward as if to say, "Those idiot kids."

She turned to me, "What?"

After the movie, I asked her about it. "Did you hear those kids chomping their gum and crunching their potato chips? It was like that through the entire movie! I couldn't believe it! So loud!"

"What kids?" she said. "Who loud?"'

We got back on the subway. Before she got off at her subway stop, she said, "I don't think we had a very good time. I'm sorry. Maybe next time, okay?"

"It was a fine time, I liked it." Then she was on the other side of the subway door, and I was moving on. Once I got off the subway, I wandered around Pusan for a while before getting on a bus to the apartment. I felt lonely, disappointed, and sad. I kept thinking if I'd been with Sasha, the evening would have been different. Sasha would have held my hand in the movie theater, and afterward we would have talked about how annoying loud chips and bubble gum could be. I felt lonelier than ever.

I continued to stroll around the Nampo-dong area, stopping dejectedly at a leftover sign from earlier this year: *The 1st Pusan*

International Film Festival. I recalled how Louie had corralled a few of us, extricating us from our hagwan bubble to enjoy the festival—the first of its kind in Asia. Film staff personnel assumed I must have been a foreign director visiting, with my long blond hair looking artistic in a ponytail, and we were able to get some great viewing seats. I wondered if Hyun-Ju was even aware of the festival. Sasha would have scoffed at the idea of *101 Dalmatians,* or any blockbuster movie. We would have spent every moment available at the film festival. It made me question what I was exactly looking for here in Korea?

***

33

***

It felt good to get back to the apartment and shed away the stresses and disappointments of the day. "You know," I told Stefano, "I really missed Sasha after that date."

"I know what you mean," he said.

"I just kept thinking I could have been with her; we would have had a much better time."

"When I was in Israel, there was one woman I knew I could love, Miriam. That's the woman I want to marry."

"I don't know if I feel that way about Sasha," I told him, "but I just can't date these Korean women. Their culture is so different. I should just be Holden Caulfield from *The Catcher in the Rye*. But instead of catching kids turning into phony adults, I'll be *The Catcher in the Rice Field*—saving people from drowning in cultural misunderstandings."

Stefano laughed. "I know what you mean. Give me a western girl any day. Why do you think I was dating Paris?"

"You've been telling me that, but now I think I finally understand. The culture's so different here, I just can't relate. Yes, *the Catcher in the Rice Field*."

"I guess some people manage, though—you know Melvin has two girlfriends now?"

"Really? Two of them? *Melvin*?"

"Yeah, he met one at an animation festival. Her name's Pumpkin. He's crazy about her. He said she's not pretty, but they have all the same interests. Especially animation and comic books."

"Melvin found someone, and I can't? Maybe I need to go home. And who's the other girl?"

"Get this, he's brought her here a couple times. She spends the night!" Stefano and I started laughing.

"With Melvin? Get out of here! Where's Melvin now?"

"He's with her now. He'll probably come back with her again tonight!"

"Get out of here! No way!"

"See what you've been missing? You've been gone so much, you've been missing it all!"

I remembered that I finally had some good news to tell Stefano. "You know, I have a really good friend, his name's Joe, he might be coming to Korea soon." The same Joe that I had worked with in the national parks. He'd driven Sasha and me up to Oregon, the first time we met.

"Really? When?"

"Well, he's finishing up seasonal work in the Alaskan canneries. Hopefully he'll be placed in Pusan, so I can be his Catcher in the Rice Field."

"Alaska?" Stefano stated, "I worked the canneries for a summer myself."

Yep, I was with good people. The kind of people like Joe and Stefano who liked adventure, different experiences, and were willing to try out new things. I would have liked to have Joe placed here with Stefano, simply to overhear the conversation that they might have about Alaska. I wanted to live their experiences through them talking about it.

But, there wasn't any guarantee that Joe would be placed at Kupo Hagwan, let alone Pusan. Korean recruiters sought out native English speakers with college degrees and placed them—extremely randomly— anywhere that had requested a new teacher. There wasn't a matching system for a potential teacher to find the school ideal for him or her, or vice-versa. Each recruiter profited by being the first to fill any vacancy. The quicker they filled it, the quicker they would receive their commission. Money was the bottom line through and through.

Eventually, Melvin came home—with a beautiful girl on his arm. I couldn't believe it. "Hu-wooaa guys!" Melvin said as he came in. "This is— uhhh—Moon-Kim."

"Hello, Moon-Kim."

"She doesn't speak English," Stefano told me.

Melvin announced loudly, "Well, we're going to bed now."

They went into his bedroom, and Stefano whispered, "Listen to this." Our walls were so thin, it was not hard to hear everything he said.

"Do you wanna lie down? Huh? You wanna lie down? Huh? Huh? What? Do you wanna lie down?"

Stefano and I doubled over, laughing quietly. I whispered, "What the hell's going on in there?"

"I don't know...listen."

"What? Huh? Do you wanna lie down? What?"

We laughed and laughed. "Man, Stefano? Let's turn on some music!"

And Melvin's voice came through the wall again, "Why not? Huh? What? Do you wanna lie down? Huh? Why not? You wanna lie down?"

Stefano turned on the music, and both of us were relieved to not hear them anymore.

Melvin came back out, wearing only his oversized basketball shorts, his black Daffy Duck socks pulled up to his knees, and his blue rubber slippers that he always wore around the house. He walked by us, smiling proudly while he pushed up his glasses. "Huh?" he shouted? "What?"

"Nothing," I said. While he was in the bathroom, I turned to Stefano, "That was quick; did anything even happen?"

"Did you notice he's wearing different clothes now?"

"I'm so glad we didn't hear that!"

"Me too."

34

Melvin had several more dates with the animation-loving Pumpkin, as well as with his bedroom girl, Moon-Kim. Then both of them suddenly stopped associating with him. Every time I saw Melvin, he would ask, "Did I get any phone calls?"

"No, none today"

"What...huh?" He would push up his glasses.

"No phone calls, I said"

"Moon-Kim didn't call? Pumpkin didn't call?"

"No."

When the phone rang one particular afternoon, it was almost comical. Melvin jumped out of the shower at the first ring: "I GOT IT! I GOT IT!" He ran, wet and barely covered by his towel. "HU-WOA? HU-WOA? WHO IS IT? What? Oh, shoot...huh...yeah, just a second...ADAM!"

I went to the phone. "Hello, Hyun-Ju. How are you?" She called me all the time now.

"Good, I work now," Hyun-Ju told me. "I have break. What you doing?"

"Nothing." I paced around the room, staring out each of the windows and twirling the telephone cord.

"Why you not call?"

"I don't know." I paced back and forth, bored.

"What you doing?"

"Nothing. Well, I gotta go," and I hung up the phone.

Two minutes later, the phone rang again. "I GOT IT, I GOT IT!" Melvin screamed. "HU-WOA? HU-WOAAA? Huh? What? Aaww shoot. WHO? Oh, shoot. Just a second. ADAM!"

I went go back to the phone again, not asking who it was, "Hello, Hyun-Ju. How are you?" I paced the floor as she spoke.

"How you know it me?"

"It's always you."

"I back at desk again. Working. It busy."

"Oh yeah?"

"How come you not call?"

"I don't know."

"You never call; I call you always!" She laughed.

"Yeah. Well look, I gotta go." I hung up again.

Several minutes later, the phone rang again. "I GOT IT! I GOT IT!" Melvin sprinted through the apartment. "HU-WOAA? HU-WOAA?"

This time, I grabbed my book and ran for the door. As I went down the stairs and into the parking lot, I heard Melvin yell from the window, "Adam! Telephone!"

I ignored him and walked on down to the girls' apartment.

As I walked into their apartment, Huck was on their landline, stretching out his chord, as he spoke, "HELEN? Huck! No phone call today. Huck cry. No phone call? Huck sad today. Huck cry. Helen, today what do?"

Paris told me, "Everyday it's like this. Huck calls her all the time. He doesn't do anything else."

"Oh yeah?"

"Helen good day? Huck BAD day!"

"She's Korean—she's not supposed to have foreign men call her. But he calls her every day. Huck's really fallen for her," Paris told me.

"It's pretty sad," I said.

"It's pathetic!" I couldn't agree with pathetic, because I had a lot of respect for Huck. But it was hard to watch.

"Huck wait by phone...all night...Huck sad."

I told Paris about my date the other day and how it had made me think about Sasha. I also told her about my friend Joe, who might come to Pusan to teach English. We talked until Huck was finally off the phone.

"What's going on, Huck?" I asked.

"She never calls me anymore."

"I think you call her too much," Paris observed.

"Oh, I know," Huck replied. "I always do this to girls. It's just what I do."

"That's fatalism," I told him. "You just gotta do some other things, forget about her for a while. Hang out with us—hang out with me."

"It's hopeless, guys—I can't," Huck admitted. "I always do this. It sucks. I do this to all the girls I meet. It always happens, and it always sucks."

***
35
***

Another weekend arrived. Our group had new routines in place: Huck stayed home by the phone, and Stefano went off by himself—and everyone tried to avoid Melvin. We felt fractured as a group. Kristian had completed her contact, and subsequently left us. She was living over in Seomyeon, much like both King and Louie had respectively made their move over to the better side of the city. It gave us a more isolated feeling in Deokcheon. We worked too much, and had little access to the greater expat community, except on weekends. Their neighborhood was the more desirable, so we we had to go that way to meet up with people, as few wanted to come to the dog market-focused Gupo and Deokcheon.

Our hagwan owner didn't hire anyone new the last month. So, it was only Paris and Huck in the girl's apartment, and Stefano, Melvin, and myself in our apartment. Each individual was so fractured and isolated, that hanging one-on-one with any one of them, made you feel more depressed.

The only salvation of group unity was getting Kristian, Louie, and King to meet up with us in one of the few expat bars of Seomyeon. PNU had the community, but Cowboy Bar in Seomyeon was the exception in that much large bar district. It was the only anju-free establishment that we knew of in Seomyeon. Anju was that required purchase of an expensive side dish that you were forced to purchase with your alcohol. The only ones who'd meet from Deokcheon, were myself and Paris. She was the only mentally able to cope with another human being left of our Kupo Hagwan group. Just her and I.

At Cowboy Bar, Louie made an announcement: "Well, I'm going to Southeast Asia for a month! He looked everyone in the eye, mimicked Skate, and made a huge smirk, "I'm gonna get me a good Thai girl!" He now had a much more desirable teaching position which gave summer vacations.

"I want to go," I thought to myself. "I need to travel. I'm sick of this place!" It didn't help that our hagwan didn't have any vacations, not even the weekends off. I would have to go teach every day until who knows when.

"Really?" King responded to Louie. "Ms. Jang and I are going to Europe for two months. I can't wait to show her Amsterdam and Paris and Stockholm! We're going to have a good time!" King also had one of those jobs that allowed some freedom and teacher vacation time.

"I want to go," I thought to myself again.

"Thailand's going to rock my world! They have everything down there! I'm going to see Vietnam, Cambodia, Thailand, Malaysia, Singapore, and Hong Kong, I'm gonna have me a good ol' time!" Louie continued.

Thailand held a huge mystique for expats in Korea. It represented all that Korea was not. Ying to Yang, North to South, Not-so-Friendly Northeast Asia to Super-Friendly Southeast Asia, and Cold to Warm.

A drunk Korean ajusshi man joined our table. "Where you from?"

We had to go through the ritual again, for the umpteenth time. Are we going to have to talk about our respective countries in some superficial way now? He seemed to move on.

"What do you think of Korea?"

Someone tried to answer, but his English was so weak, he didn't understand the answer.

"How old are you?"

Ah, does it matter?

"Have you tried Korean food?"

What do you think, we live in Korea?

I got deeper into my thoughts. Leave me alone. I'm sick of guys like you staring at me and asking me that. I need to get out of here. I am so sick of this place.

In retrospect, these feelings I had were simply temporary. No doubt, never having a day off from work, took their toll. It affected me psychologically. Losing that group unity, the one we all counted on, to collectively get us through each day, was gone. We had no support from our Korean hagwan owner, or manager, or fellow Korean teachers. We were in a bubble, and any attempt to connect outside that foreign bubble, was largely ignored. Even the curious questions people asked us, seemed as an attempt at free English lesson for a Korean person to practice Basic English skills. They had no depth to what they asked, and no deep interest about us.

On the other hand, one could make the argument that if we simply studied Korean, we could tap into that depth. But working seven days a week, it didn't allow time to study or practice.

A few weeks later, both King and Louie were on their vacations, and I felt sadder than ever. Huck was miserable and depressed. Stefano was just absent entirely. I was miserable and depressed.

Paris could sense I was down. She invited me out to drink a beer near the hagwan, "Why are you so sad all the time?"

"I think I'm missing a relationship like the one I had with Sasha," I said after drinking many beers.

"Don't think about it; think about other things."

"I just don't feel like doing anything anymore. I think I need to go home. I think I need to go somewhere else."

"You gonna leave us?"

"I don't know. Maybe."

"What about your friend Joe? Isn't he coming to Korea?

"He is, but they could place him anywhere in the country."

"What if they placed him in Pusan though?"

"Well, we're good friends, and he's an adult, and I'd want him to experience Korea anyways. But, for me, I just can't take it anymore: the culture, the hagwan—*the staring*. I motioned to a nearby table, "Look at those guys pointing at us over there."

"Go screw yourselves!" Paris yelled at them. That just encouraged more people to stare at us.

"It never stops. I can't take it. I think I just miss what I had, and I miss Sasha. I miss the way things were before I came here."

"You're really serious?"

"Yeah, I just can't deal with it anymore. The other day I was at a bus stop—Paris, are you listening?"

"Yes, of course." She was making googly eyes and funny faces to other people who continued to stare at us. This made them stare more, so it was better to reign her in.

"I was at this bus stop, and this older Korean man—it's always the older Korean man—he was staring at me, and he motioned to shake his hand. So I shook it, and he started saying stuff in Korean. He wouldn't let go. And of course, I didn't know what he was saying."

"So what happened?"

"Well, he kept talking, and the crowd started laughing. He put me in a powerless situation, there was no way to handle that situation properly. Who knows what he was saying in Korean."

"It can be like that."

"But I don't want to deal with it anymore. I don't want to be gawked at. I miss my old life. I just want to go back to the way things were before."

Sasha became a symbol for my old life. This place where I could just read books, interact with people normally, and connect with everyone around me. A place where people didn't stare at me, didn't ask me weird questions, didn't follow me around stores, and they didn't point at me all the time. I wanted a normal existence. I wanted to relax in a public space.

I had been thinking of Sasha so often that I decided to call her again. I couldn't afford to do that very often due to the costs of international calls. In 1996, we didn't have the Internet for cheap calls. Just ten minutes on an international call cost a small fortune. People overseas generally communicated through the postal system. But when it seemed essential, you'd make that quick call, extremely conscious of each minute that went by.

On the phone, "Sasha?"

"Adam? Adam? I can't believe you called! ADAM!"

"I've been thinking about you."

"I've been thinking about you, too."

"Really?" I said. "Well, I was thinking I might come back home to Portland. What do you think about that?"

"What? It's so sudden!" She hesitated, as this was something we hadn't planned on before. "I don't know. What's going on over there?"

"I don't know; I'm just so sick of everything. I just can't stand it anymore."

"Did something happen to you? Are you okay?"

"Yes I'm fine," I laughed. "Well, what do you think about that? Would you like to see home in Portland?"

"This is so sudden. I'd have to think about it. I mean, how do I know you won't change your mind again? What's going on over there?"

"Nothing. Nothing, Sasha. I just realized I miss you. I just realized I should be with you."

"This phone call has got to be costing you a fortune."

"Well, I'll let you think about it," I told her. "You need time. Think about it."

About a week later, I was still thinking about it so often that I wrote her a letter every other day. I called her again.

"Sasha?"

"ADAM! How are you? I'm so GLAD you CALLED!"

"I've been thinking about you so much lately."

"Me too. I felt so dizzy after you told me you might be coming home. Are you still coming home?"

"Of course I am. I'd been thinking about it a lot before I even called you the first time."

"I'M so EXCITED!" She screamed. "So when are you coming home?"

"I don't know; I have to give my month notice first."

"I thought it might be right away." She seemed disappointed.

"Well, I just wanted to see if it was still a possibility before I did anything."

"Please come home, Adam. I want to see you SOON!"

"Sasha, I will come home. I will. But I gotta go now. Soon we'll be able to catch up on everything. I'll be home soon."

"I hope so, Adam."

"I think about you all the time, Sasha."

Sasha. The representative of stability, sensibility, settling-down, but with an added touch of political opinions, hard-core aggressive music, and social causes. Wasn't I settling down in Korea anyways? What did I find so repulsive about staying in one place that I rejected staying in Portland? I certainly wasn't seeing the world sitting in Deokcheon. Going back to Portland implied movement, going forward, moving on. I craved that.

'Should I' or "Shouldn't I' with the flower petals, and of course, I should.

Then I went be back to my daily reality again. Everyone was miserable at Kupo Hagwan, and Melvin was drunk all the time because of the two girlfriends he'd lost. Everything had gone to hell, and no one was happy. I took extra-long bus rides so I could read books, but I always got worked up because people were pointing at me.

Then there were the weekends where we'd all be stuck with a drunk Melvin. On one particular evening, he was so drunk that he knocked over chairs and couldn't stand upright. "Fuck! Aaww fuck...I'm so drunk. Dear Lord, forgive me for swearing."

We got in a taxi, and Melvin yelled, "Paris, touch my dick! Touch it! Touch my dick, come on!"

"Gross!" Paris shouted. "That's gross, Melvin!"

"Awww man! I'm sorry, Jesus! Forgive me, Jesus! Aaaawww...sheesh!"

I told Melvin, "You sure swear a lot for a so-called Christian!" We laughed about it for weeks.

He was getting drunk all over Pusan—in the apartment, on the streets, everywhere. I was too, actually; maybe that's why I kept running into him. "Hey Melvin, whatcha doin' here?"

"Gettin' frickin' drunk!"

"Oh yeah, me too."

Stefano was the smart one. He went off completely by himself to get ripping drunk. But then again, he was trying to avoid further petty arguments with Paris.

Then there was Paris. She was sad that Kristian wasn't working and living with her anymore. She and I were always tight running with the same people, and now they all just escaped us. We were all just 'out there', out alone, out there with our own thoughts, out there in our own heads.

A new girl, Mandy, had agreed to work at our hagwan for one month as a temporary replacement. Then she was going to work in a town in a faraway corner of Korea. Paris and Mandy bonded quickly and hung around all the time that month. I personally couldn't stand Mandy; she talked too much, and she never listened to others. She was one of those types who only wanted to hear her own voice.

Typical of most of our conversations, Mandy asked me, "What are you doing tonight, Adam?"

"I'm thinking of going down to the Monk Bar."

"Why don't you go down to the Monk Bar? That's where we're going!"

"Yeah, maybe I will," I said.

Maybe I was just sick of everything, so I had begun to avoid them, too. It seemed like everyone was avoiding each other, and everything sucked. I still liked Stefano and Paris, but things were changing yet again. They asked me, "What have you been doing? We never see you around anymore!"

"Not much." That was true—I spent my time reading books in the back of buses. What else would I be doing?

Things with Sasha were going well, but there was one problem with that, too. "Well, Sasha, I think I'm going to quit next month. Then I just want to travel to Southeast Asia for two months. I promise I'll be home for Christmas. I promise!"

"Are you coming home or not? I miss you, Adam. I want to see you sooner than that. Adam, come home."

It broke my heart, but I said, "No, I can't yet. Can you wait? After I quit, I just want to see a little of Asia, and then I'm there for good."

"Don't make me wait—anything can happen. Please come home. Shaddow misses you too!"

"I miss both of you!" I told her.

"Really? Shaddow too?"

"Yes, Shaddow too!"

"Shaddow, do you hear that? Adam misses you too. Can I bring Shaddow to the phone? Can I? Can I? Can I?"

"MEOW MEOW," Sasha said into the phone. It made me laugh.

I was still determined to make my Asia trip, but the next day I gave my one-month notice to Kamm.

"What do you mean you're going to quit?" Kamm yelled at me. "You can't quit! You signed a contract!" Smoke seemed to come out of his ears, as well as his mouth. "We'll have to get another teacher if you quit!"

"I have to get back to Oregon. It's important."

"Well, what the fuck?" he shouted, smoke all over the place. "You can't even stay two more fucking months?"

"No, I have to go. It's important."

He shouted at me, "Well, what the fuck!" He got over his disappointment quickly, however. He and Eun-Hee were happily together again, despite Kamm's pregnant wife. They were all over each other, and they always had their free hours at the same time. We all knew who had arranged that.

But none of it really mattered to me anyhow. I was going to be out of this place soon.

***

36

***

Mandy left at the end of that month, and two new teachers moved into the girls' apartment. They were from somewhere in Florida, good friends, and from the same town.

Everything was set in motion for me to go. I had been planning my trip to Southeast Asia and talking about it with Sasha. She objected to the idea, but I felt it was one last thing I needed to do before settling down with her. So I was kind of disappointed to meet the new teachers, because they seemed interesting.

Once they arrived, Stefano and I went down to see them together. It was nice to be going down to the girls' apartment with Stefano again. Paris was actually civilized to him. As soon as we came in, she shouted, "The guys are here!" Huck and Melvin didn't matter—Stefano and I were "the guys."

We all sat around the table. "Yeah, we're from Florida," said the taller, giraffe-like one. "I'm Monica. This is Linda. Yes, we're good friends from home!"

It was nice having group unity again. "Well, we've been working as lifeguards for two years," Monica continued, without taking a breath. Linda had short cropped hair, and she hadn't said a word. "We just came off the airplane! Six-hour layover in Tokyo." Linda sat there quietly.

I asked, "So Linda what do you think of Korea?"

"Well," Monica spoke for her, "We haven't seen much yet. Just got here you know, bud." I was already "bud."

"So, LINDA, both of you worked as lifeguards?"

"Yes. I told you that, Adam," Monica smiled. "Both of us worked as lifeguards!"

"So, LINDA, what part of Florida are you from?" I asked, specifically to Linda.

"We're from outside Tampa," Monica interrupted again, speaking for both of them. "We're both from the same place!" She smiled again as she said it.

Linda got up to use the bathroom, and Monica told us, "She follows me everywhere. I didn't want to come to Korea with her. She's a psycho. Been following me for years! Four years now! I came here to get away from her, and here she is! Can't go anywhere without this psycho following me!" Linda came back from the bathroom and quietly sat down again. "And as I was saying, Linda and I are going to give Korea a try, see how it goes. If it sucks, we can always go back to FLOR-i-da!"

"So you guys have known each other for four years, LINDA?"

"Yes," MONICA chimed in again. "I told you that. Four years!"

"Oh, that's right," I admitted I had known that already.

Later, at the hagwan. Monica told us, "Well, I have six classes of little monsters. They hate me; they all hate me, I love kids, though, I can teach kids all day long. Linda and I love to teach kids. They like women teachers more."

"Is that right, Linda?"

"As I was saying," Monica continued. "They really hate me, but I tell them to shut up and be quiet, and they listen."

Paris, who had been acting pretty different herself, arrived. "Girls! Where've you been? You left without me?"

"Well, you were sleeping, and we decided to let you sleep," Monica continued to talk on and on.

I was getting tired of the chatter, so I tried to sneak out of the hagwan immediately after classes. Paris caught me and asked, "Where are you going, Adam? You're leaving, and you never hang out with us anymore."

"Yeah, well, I'm just kind of tired."

Monica shouted, "We used to be the four musketeers!"

"Yeah, the four musketeers!" Paris echoed, "We miss you!"

"It's not the same without you," Monica stated.

The "four musketeers?" I'd just met Monica and Linda a week ago.

I still went down to the girls' apartment, mostly to get away from Melvin.

"Stefano's a sex fiend!" Monica exclaimed to me one night.

"Stefano?" I asked.

Monica shouted, "Yes, Stefano. He's always hitting on me." She was a very tall woman with a loud vocal voice, and I couldn't imagine little Stefano hitting on her.

"Stefano?" I said again, stunned.

"Everyone hits on Monica!" Linda told me.

"Yeah, Stefano is always hitting on me!"

I went back up to my own apartment, which I generally avoided, "Monica says you're a sex fiend, Stefano."

"What?"

"She says you're always hitting on her."

"She said the same about you the other day."

"What?"

But as much as I hated it, I still went down to visit them out of boredom. Eventually, I learned that Huck was a psychopath, too. "He's a freak!" Monica insisted. "You should see him around here!"

"What's he do, Monica?" I said in a bored voice, not wanting to hear bad things about my friend.

"He's a freak! He hides in his room all day!"

Linda parroted her, "It's true, Adam, Huck is a freak!"

"I can't believe you're leaving," Paris told me.

"We're going to miss you!" Monica told me.

"We love you, Adam!" Linda insisted.

So, here I was, ready to move on, and we have a super loud one, and a super quiet one. It certainly added a much different and needed dynamic to our bubble.

37

Two weeks left before I left on my Southeast Asia trip, I got a call from the hagwan.

"Adam, are you going to be at the apartment for a while?"

"Yes. Why?"

"Well, your friend Joe is here. He's going to take your place at Kupo Hagwan. Can you train him? Show him around?"

"Sure, sure, no problem." I was shocked. This was Kamm's work, no doubt. Of all the hagwans that Joe could have gone to, they put him here to replace me.

"By the way, we hear you're leaving. Very sorry to hear that. You were a very good employee. Well, if you change your mind, we'll need more teachers in the spring; perhaps we could arrange better pay. Come on back, and we can arrange for you to work at one of the colleges, even."

The fact that college jobs were given to very unqualified foreigners in Korea, was very interesting. They literally had no minimum requirements whatsoever, and universities went to recruiters just like a hagwan would do. They simply put in a request for any random person who requested to come to Korea in late August, and they make them a college professor two weeks later in September. Who they made into their university professors, was completely circumstantial. Most people like myself came, worked seven days a week, with classes from 7am-10pm, but then someone else might be randomly placed in a job with only 10-12 contact hours a week, with five months of paid vacation, and treated like a full college professor. The way Korea operated was completely insane.

Equally ironic was that since I quit my position, and had a half year of teaching experience, I was now qualified to teach in a university faculty position. I understood the recruiter logic of making an enticement for me, as it was full acceptable in Korea. I didn't understand universities not having any faculty standards whatsoever though.

"Thanks, good to know," I told the recruiter.

As it always goes, before I left, I continued to see how interesting and cool Korea actually was. For example, a few of us discovered 'Booking Clubs,' an unusual way for Koreans to date and get to know each other. The system worked that groups of men would go in, buy an expensive table, and order hard liquor with a bucket of ice. Outside the club, people known as 'pickies' would pick out random groups of girls walking by with their friends. The enticement for the girls was that they'd drink for free, and meet some guys. Inside the Booking Club, employees moved the girls to different tables of guys, trying to find a good match. It was an ingenious way for single people to mingle, without having to approach or be approached by anyone. The pickies did all the work.

Another place I was getting to know was Texas Town/Russia Town near Pusan Station/Nampodong. It was a rough place, filled with sailors and girls that catered to sailors. But with Pusan's limited choices of interesting venues, it became a favored area among the English teaching community. While PNU's university area had about 5-6 bars that catered to foreigners. The rest of the city was heavily anju-focused at big large tables, more compatible for groups of friends who only wanted to socialize together, as opposed to the foreigner's desires for interaction with other bar patrons.

Texas Town/Russia Town filled that niche. It had bars with pool tables, and dancing poles, and a strange unfamiliar element that put some spice into going out. There was one odd night where Stefano, Melvin and myself, were together, maybe from the olden days, and a photo was taken. It was one of a few photos that I had in those days, back in a time before digital cameras, back when people had to develop rolls of films. The flash went off, Melvin had his eyes wide open, eyebrows up, mouth wide open, with an expression of 'Huh?' Stefano was in the middle, black curly locks hanging in his eyes, and his Stefano smile of beer contentment. I equally had my content look with a beer, signifying this previous time. With the three of us, an old Indonesian man, probably a sailor, completely out of place with us, but seemingly completely in place with the environment. He looked as if he was part of our group, just by association of some sort. All around us, an unfamiliar element of random girls walking around, who knows how they got there, some dancing, some not, all out of our price range to even talk to, or socialize with. But, we weren't the only English Teachers hanging around, it became another de facto teacher hangout place, even though none of the bars catered to us whatsoever. PNU and Texas Town. Pusan 1996. The entire city was filled with alcohol, but those were the two areas that a person might find this developing English teacher expat scene. Just when I thought I'd had enough of Korea, entire other elements opened up, making me question what I was questioning.

As it was getting into the colder months, I began to use the Ondol Heating system of Korea. A few things about Korea, people didn't prefer to sit on furniture like couches or chairs that removed one's body from the floor. They instead threw down small tables or sleeping mats, so people had direct contact with the linoleum-covered floors. Shoes were not allowed to be worn in the house either, so it was said that the floors should be so clean, that you could technically eat a meal directly from the linoleum itself. Under the floors, existed the ondol heating system. It heated the linoleum, giving a wonderful warmth to the body during the winter months. You wanted as much contact as you could get with the floors. A couch or a chair, would only separate you from that. Couches were cold, too cold.

It's funny that when you think you are done with a place, you suddenly realize that you were just beginning with the place.

***
38
***

It was ironic that Joe arrived, and that he represented my wanderlust, as my wanderlust was propelling me forward.

He came in wearing all black, like always, and his hair was cut short on top. He had a rough growth of beard, longer than the hair on the top of his head. He looked like he had just come out of prison. Joe had tattoos up and down his arms, all black and white. Koreans feared tattoos, as only gangsters wore them here. But here he was on my doorstop, and I couldn't have been happier.

"So how's Portland? How was Alaska?" We caught up well into the night. I would immensely enjoy these Cannery updates, and even more so when Stefano was around, to confirm, enhance, and augment the stories.

But for that first night, "You know I'm leaving in two weeks, right?"

"Yeah, that's what they said. You coming back?"

"I don't know. I'm going to Southeast Asia, than back to Portland for Christmas with Sasha."

"Did you have to stay at some weird hotel downtown when you got here?"

"Yeah, I did! What an introduction, eh?"

He said matter-of-factly, "Yeah, it was something," Joe never got too excited. "You hear that new Neil Young CD?"

"No—he has a new CD?"

"Yeah, take a look." He put the CD on and passed me the case. "I was listening to it on the plane over here."

"Oh yeah, Neil Young. Love to hear this."

"Listen to this, when I was in Alaska, I met this guy, his name was Chuck. He was telling me about the 'sniff of confidence'!"

"Oh yeah, what's that?"

"This guy was always talking about things like that. He said when someone knows something, before they say it, they breath in really hard, giving the sniff of confidence," then Joe demonstrated it, and I laughed.

"So, how about those Korean girls you wrote me about? What ever happened with that?"

"They're all crazy, Joe. This culture's so different. You'll find out. Everyone finds out."

"Oh yeah?"

"Yeah. And the Korean teachers!" Now my *Catcher in the Rice Field* was showing through. "You never know what they're talking about. They're all pretty and stuff, but they're from a different world. You have to be careful what you say around them. They love to gossip. The teachers who teach Japanese are cool, though. I went out with one of them."

In reflection, I was rationalizing decisions, trying to put context to my excuse for more perpetual wanderlust. I was rationalizing why my Korean relationship didn't work. When one of your wanderlust-fueling friends comes to see you, and you've already made some decisions, you are kind of stuck with storylines sometimes.

Joe asked, "Oh yeah?" Was he really taking any of this seriously? I would imagine he was already dismissing this, and would make up his own mind, much like I dismissed Skate's Korea rants when I first arrived.

"She couldn't speak any English, though. It was tough." I continued with my storyline. "Anyway, now that you're here, I'll introduce you to everyone. Huck and Stefano are the coolest ones here. I really liked Paris too, but something weird has been going on since Linda and Monica arrived. Now, Melvin's okay. He's kind of weird, but you have to give him a chance. You'll see."

"What do you mean, 'Weird'?"

"He's pretty sad and lonely here, I think, but he's harmless. I'm just telling you. Huck's sad now, too, actually—pretty messed up because of a breakup with a Korean girlfriend. But you'll like him; he likes to read, likes good music, likes national parks...He's a cool guy."

That evening I brought Joe to Kupo Hagwan and showed him around everything I had come to know. The teachers and students were scared of him, they told me later, because they thought he looked like a convict. "Hide those tattoos," I told him. I was still beeming on the inside, just to have the guy around, I could have cared less.

I continued to visit Huck and the girls, and Monica continued to dominate every conversation. "Huck's a freak," she told me again. "Mopes around all day, freak! Hides in his bedroom. You know what he did the other day? We were talking one night after we got home from the bars, and the next day he left a note saying, 'Could you please be quiet?' He couldn't even come out and tell us himself, the freak!"

"Well, you should have more respect for him, Monica. You come home drunk and noisy. He's trying to be cool, and you're making it tough with your noise!"

"I don't mind that, but why doesn't he just be a MAN and come out here and tell us HIMSELF!"

"What do YOU think, Linda?"

"Adam," Linda reiterated, "It's all true. It's true. He couldn't even tell us himself!"

"Well, I've known Huck for a while, and he's just trying to be cool about it. C'mon, he has to live here with you guys."

"He's a freak!" Monica insisted.

"He is, Adam, you don't have to live with him!" Linda assured me.

"Joe's a freak, too! I'm sorry; I know he's an old friend, but he's a freak!" Monica insisted.

"He is," Linda parroted. "Monica's right. He's a freak!"

"We love you, Adam, but I'm sorry, Joe is a freak!"

"Really? Now why is that?"

"He's a downer on the school. I was just talking out loud in the school, and he said to me, 'Why are you always talking?' Can you believe that? He doesn't even know me? Freak!"

"But you *are* always talking," I said.

Monica laughed. "Adam, we like you, but Joe is a freak. He thinks he's so cool, too. What the fuck is his problem? He's a downer. He doesn't drink either!"

"It's true," Linda agreed, "It's all true!"

"I'm sorry, but I just don't see how you and he can be friends."

"We're pretty similar, actually. We have lots of the same interests. Plus, he's intelligent."

"He's too intelligent," Monica said, "And he's an asshole about it. I like intelligent and witty people, but Joe is all high and mighty about it."

"It's all true," Linda added. "He's a freak!"

"You don't know him yet. You just don't know him like I do," I insisted.

Most of the time, I showed Joe around Deokcheon, just him and I. Portland was a huge conversation topic, as it was on my mind more, and it was a shared location we both knew well. I dreamed to again explore the aisles of Powell's Bookstore, self-proclaimed 'largest independent new and used bookstore in the world.' But, of course Korea dominated most of our conversations.

"Hey, I'll show you more of Pusan this weekend," I told him one day at the hagwan.

"Yeah, I gotta find the broccoli." Joe was one of those guys also into raw foods, vegetarianism, and the like. Something very Portland about that. Pusan just wasn't the kind of place you'd find non-Korean items very easily. But I was up for the challenge, solely for the purpose of seeing more of the city before I left.

Paris overheard us. "What about us? How come you're not inviting us?"

"Too many people, Paris," I told her. "Joe can't explore Pusan with a horde of people."

"We all used to do things together, Adam! Ever since Joe came here, you don't even hang out with us!"

"I was at your apartment the other day, Paris."

"Well, you could have invited us this weekend. Maybe we'd like to go— wouldn't we, girls?"

"We used to be the Four Musketeers!" Linda shouted at me.

Monica added, "I don't know what's happened to you since Joe came!"

"I'm just saying you should invite us once in a while," Paris added.

I did try to hang out with them sometimes, but I just didn't like it. Once, when we were all on the bus going to get drunk, I saw the obnoxiousness of it more clearly than ever. Monica was babbling nonstop about something, and Paris was yelling—she was already drunk. Linda was quiet as always, but she agreed excitedly with Monica whenever a pause came up. "That's right, Adam! Monica's right! Stefano's a freak!" It was always the same.

Korean etiquette was to keep conversations quiet on buses, so people continued to look back at the loud foreigners, wondering when we'd shut up. I was embarrassed. One older Korean man stood up and shouted, "Ssshhh!"

"Did you hear that man?" Paris asked again, "Did you hear that idiot?"

"I can't believe he'd do that!" Monica quickly responded.

"Freak, Monica's right," Linda quickly added, "Monica's right. Freak!"

Paris announced, "I'm going to go sit by him!" She placed herself next to the old man, who tried to push her out of her new seat. "Hi there," she told him as he shoved her. Fluttering her eyes and looking back at us, she cooed, "So, you like what you see?"

Everyone laughed, except me. I just wanted to go sit in the back of the bus and read like I always did. I was ready to go. I wanted to hide from everyone.

The whole evening went on the same way. We walked down the street to different expatriate bars, and we got the stares that we always did. Paris yelled at a passerby, "What's your problem?"

"Freak!" Monica shouted after him.

"Monica's right! Monica's right!" Linda replied.

I didn't want to hang around with them much after that, so I just stayed in my own apartment with Joe, Stefano, and Melvin.

On Joe's second weekend in the apartment, we did a second extensive search for broccoli. Finally, on Sunday night, we found the green stuff, and Joe stocked up significantly.

Stefano had separated our refrigerator shelves, so we had our Stefano shelf, Adam shelf, and Melvin's shelf—Melvin's once again filled with empty juice and milk cartons. My shelf was usually half empty, so Joe utilized that for the first week.

With bags filled with broccoli, and Joe not being so familiar with the shelf rules, he cleared away some of the empty cartons, and placed his new finds on Melvin's shelves.

Stefano, Joe, and I settled down around our small kitchen table. Conversation went into a mix of Korea and Alaska.

Melvin, possibly unaware anyone was even in the house, came out with his loud music in his headphones. He stopped for a second, looked at us, pushed up his glasses, and said, "Huh?" Then he walked into the bathroom.

We went back into our conversation.

Then Melvin slowly went to the refrigerator, opened the door, and looked at his shelf. A little bit of a pause.

"BROCCOLI? WHEN did I BUY BROCCOLI?"

"Ah, that's mine, Melvin," Joe interrupted.

"Why would I buy broccoli?"

"Ahhmm...Melvin."

"I don't remember buying broccoli. I don't even LIKE broccoli!"

"Um, Melvin, that's my broccoli," Joe tried again.

Stefano loudly yelled, "Melvin!!"

"What? Huh?" He looked at Stefano, pulled his headphones away from his ears, and then muttered to himself, "SHOOT, Why would I buy broccoli?"

"That's my broccoli, Melvin. I bought it today," Joe reiterated.

"I was going to say...SUGAR...I don't even like broccoli!"

I told Joe, "I forgot to mention that we each have our own shelf."

Melvin, quick to tell him, "You got to put it on your own shelf! Shoot! I don't eat broccoli!" Reflecting back to himself, "I hate broccoli!"

"Uh, Melvin...there's only three shelves in there," Joe told him.

Melvin insisted his point, "Well, shoot! Don't put them on my shelf. I can't eat broccoli!"

"Ah, Melvin...that broccoli is for me, not for you."

"Then you eat it then, I don't want it."

I told Joe, "Here, you can put the broccoli on my shelf."

"Good," Melvin ever insistent, "I don't even like broccoli...sheesh."

I was going to miss Melvin's peculiarities, at least in spurts anyways. One morning, Joe, Stefano, and I were sitting at the kitchen table when we heard Melvin's alarm go off. Stefano told us, "Now listen to this, Joe! He does this every time!"

"AAAAAAAAAAHHHHH!" Melvin shouted at the top of his lungs.

"Okay, next is the Rush song, 'Fly by Night,'" Stefano added.

Ditterditterditter—"FLY BY NIGHT, AWAY FROM HERE!" The song came blasting through Melvin's bedroom door.

Joe joked, "Broccoli? When did I buy Broccoli? I don't even like Broccoli!"

Melvin exited his room in his shorts, Daffy Duck socks, and rubber slippers. He pushed up his glasses.

"Huh? Whut's goin' on?" Melvin shuffled off into the bathroom.

"Hey Joe, has Melvin asked you about comic books yet?" I asked.

Joe gave a quick *hah*! "He asked me that on the first day!"

"Quite the character, quite the character. Someone ought to write about him."

39

I was once again enjoying Korea and the expatriate community, and things seemed better again, but I was already committed to my travel plans. I had shipped several boxes direct to Sasha's apartment in Portland. It would take a minimum of two months before they would arrive. In the meanwhile, I would travel in Southeast Asia. Everything was set in motion, and all I had to do, was go with it.

I now had my hesitations. My emotional lows and negative feelings towards Korea had subsided. I saw it more as a temporary phase, rather than a seemingly permanent condition. I had connected, I had connected to a community. Even Monica and Linda, I could see, they also had that sense of the community. The concept of The Four Musketeers. They had intrinsically grasped the exact concept that I had been seeking myself.

I could appreciate the nature of living of Korea, the way people helped each other out, on any level. I might have had my complaints on the employer level, but my colleagues were step-ups, who rose to the occasion, and we all helped each other out immensely. If I ever had a situation out in the public, I could equally count on the fact that I was always safe, and anyone who could help me, would help me. It was the nature of the Korean people, and I hadn't quite seen for how great it all was previously, when I was in my lows. Their only true crime was asking me repetitive questions of curiosity, and staring excessively. Of all the crimes around the world that people do to each other, staring and curiosity were of the most minor of offenses.

Soon my last evening was upon me. Everyone I had known, came out, and we all got ripped at the Blue Note Cafe—students and teachers and everyone available, for the last time.

Louie slammed his beer down, "Hey Melvin," he splattered out. "How come you haven't been coming over to get drunk with me?"

"What? Huh?" Melvin pushed up his glasses with a big smile. "What'd ya say?" I had to smile, I would miss Melvin, just the way he looked made me laugh.

"Remember Adam, you always have an extra bedroom at either one of our two apartments," was a common statement I'd heard from various members of our close-knit group.

King and Ms. Jang sat at the table. "So what should I take King? What do I need for this trip?" I wanted his infinite travel wisdom.

King shared his words of wisdom for one his last times, "Well, Chief..."

It was my last night, and I felt sick as hell. I wasn't sure about traveling now, and I felt sad that I was leaving these people I had come to know. Now the realities of my decisions were hitting me. These were the wheels I had put in motion, and I had no choice but to move on with what was next in life.

After we left the Blue Note, I hung out at the girls' apartment all night. Paris, Linda, and Monica slumped against the walls, crashed out tired on the living room floor.

"I'm going to bed, Adam," Paris told me. "Just be sure to wake me up, and say good-bye before you leave." King and I continued to drink beer. Everyone who taught at the hagwan had to wake up at six in the morning the next day.

"Hey, why don't you bring my small pack with a lock to put around your waist?" King told me. "You'll need some security for the important stuff."

"I couldn't take that from you, King," I told him. "That's been to Europe with you twice and spent two years in Africa."

"No, I trust you. Just ship it back to me when you're back in Portland."

"Are you sure? I mean, I need it, but are you sure?"

"Yeah, of course. Take it," he said. "Don't worry about it!"

"Okay" I replied. Soon, Huck's alarm clock went off; he had set it to say goodbye, as he and Joe were going to walk me to the train station before their classes.

"Good *morning*!" Huck exclaimed.

"Morning," I said. "Well, I guess I better go get my stuff and say good-bye to everyone up at my apartment, too."

I cruised up the hill and slipped into my old place at Taekyung Happy Town Apartments. Stefano was in the bathroom, so I went to my room and got all my stuff together. Stefano met me in the kitchen and asked me, "Hey Adam, when did you get home last night anyhow?"

"Ten seconds ago!" I replied.

I said good-bye to Stefano. Joe joined Huck and myself for the walk to the train station.

We walked down the hill one last time, and I said my final good-bye to the girls and King. I gave Paris a big hug, "Paris, take care of yourself!"

"You're going to make me cry!" She reiterated. "You're really going to make me cry!" She tried to fight back the tears. It caught me as well, and I wiped the tears from my own eyes.

I felt a great affection for Paris. I always enjoyed her time, her nature, and her bubbly personality. She stuck with me through my own highs and lows, and I hoped I had done the same for her. In some ways, we were experiencing the same need for connections. We were locked in our little community, and my desire to connect with a Korea through a relationship failed at every turn. Her attempt to connect on a closer level with Stefano had failed. We both went through that subsequent isolated stage, and I was escaping it. Regardless, I felt great bond ship and connection with Paris, and I never really appreciated it, until I was saying my final good bye to her.

Joe and Huck joined me, each grabbing a bag. We headed down the steep hill for the last time, through the dog market, and navigated our way to the Gupo train station.

Joe and I made jokes along the way. "Y'know, I don't even need to say good-bye to you, Joe!" I told him. "I know I'll see you again. Huck, y'know how many times I've said good-bye to Joe now? All over the West Coast, and now on some other East Coast! Yeah, I'll be seeing HIM again!"

We wandered down the road, trying to make light of the situation. At the train station, I wished them well and vanished through the ticket booth and onto the train platform.

It would take six hours by train, and I stared out the window the entire time, reflecting how beautiful I found the rice fields, the mountains, and the way the landscape looked. It occurred to me that I knew a lot about my colleagues, my hagwan, my students, and the expat Pusan scenes, but I didn't know much else about Korea. Had I really even seen it at all?

Up in Seoul, I went to Itaewon for the first time. This was a large American military base neighborhood in the center of Seoul. There were many western bars, with things like pool tables and dart boards. It felt like the kind of neighborhood where one would never have a true Korean experience. It seemed to be some great sanctuary, but perhaps in some ways, might actually hide a foreigner from the true Korea experience altogether. It was a place where no one ever looked at you, or paid any attention to you. It was a place where Joe would have easily found his broccoli, and they even had some western amenities like Doritos or other types of beer besides Cass and Hite. There was a place called Nashville, which had authentic country American music and served hamburgers on a grill. It was completely inconceivable that such a place could exist in South Korea.

On top of that, at night, I found a Blues Bar, with an actual blues musician who happened to be Korean. I didn't feel like such things could have existed in Pusan. It seemed like a different world up here, one with so much depth. It made me feel deep regret that I only experienced Korea from one small corner of the country, and never had a chance to see how much the country might vary from place to place. Seoul gave me a glimpse into this entire other Korea altogether. I longed for it.

But, with that, I was off to Kimpo Airport with a flight to Bangkok.

***
40
***

I was probably in the wrong by taking a long two-month trip throughout Southeast Asia. The trip was tedious, long, fantastic, and made me long for more, if I only had money to have continued. In fact, it made me question if I had a mistake.

I had convinced myself that the entire Asia excursion was a fluke of absolute luck, my one and only opportunity to ever get outside of North America, and now I had to get 'back to my real life,' as if my real life implied a rejection of my desire to travel and see the world. I had agreed to just settle down, and I had committed to that.

I did my best to send postcards from Bangkok, Chiang Mai, Koh Samui, Penang, Singapore, and Kathmandu. Phone calls were the worst, I wasn't a phone person, and I hated the way the phones cut out in mid-conversation. So, therefore, I seldom made them.

Once I knew my exact arrival date, I called Sasha over a very poor—and expensive—telephone line to give her the news.

"Hi."

"Who is this?"

"It's me, Adam."

"Adam?"

"Can you hear me?"

"Adam, where are you?"

"I'm in Kathmandu. I booked my final ticket, and I'm coming home!"

"We need to talk."

"Can you pick me at the airport this coming Sunday?"

"Why didn't you come home directly from Korea?"

"I can't wait to see you!"

"We have a lot to talk about when you get home."

"Yes, we do! I'll arrive at three thirty in the afternoon, from Hong Kong." I was excited to see her, but the tone of her voice made me uneasy.

"Okay, I'll see you then."

We were disconnected. Several days later, I was in Hong Kong.

After a few uneventful final days in the beautiful city of Hong Kong, I found myself on my final international flight. Hello to Oregon, and good-bye to Asia. I wondered if I would ever get to see Asia again in my lifetime. As I flew over South Korea, I looked down to see if I could make out the details of Pusan from a plane window. I wanted to see if I could recognize Deokcheon, Seomyeon, or even Taegyung Happy Town. I thought about my friends and what a strong part we played in each other's lives. I wondered if Joe, Stefano, and Melvin were sitting around the kitchen table, and what they might be talking about. I wondered if Paris or Louie or King or Huck might be looking up at my plane right now.

I thought of Sasha, and the promises I made to her. Yes, we'd live together again, and it would be wonderful to spend time together again. But what if we'd changed? How could I stop dreaming of traveling and resign myself to the two weeks of vacation that came with a typical American job. Could I settle down to that kind of life? Did I want to? Maybe I should be with someone who shared my love of travel and also wanted to live abroad. But, at my core, I missed what I'd shared with Sasha. I missed going to cinemas, browsing bookstores, and tasting food from international restaurants. I missed taking part-time courses in the evenings and talking about what we'd learned.

When my plane landed, I felt nervous to see Sasha. For one, I hadn't showered in twenty-four hours. My hair looked greasy, and I must have looked travel weary and thinner than usual—and I was very thin as it was. I got off the plane and looked around for her with worried anticipation. For several years before Korea, we had hardly been separated, and I remembered how anxious we would be to see each other after even a day or two apart. But today, it just seemed unreal. I couldn't make sense of it. I had missed her tremendously while I was freezing in that cold hostel room in Nepal. I couldn't bear the thought of not being with her again during my lows in Korea. But now I was finally home, and I kept having the same reoccurring thought—should I be here?

I looked into the crowd and saw that straight black hair, even longer than usual. I gave her a smile and hugged her as she approached. "It's so good to see you." I felt like I was going to fall from exhaustion right there;

194

everything was too surreal. I had anticipated this meeting with bright eyes and excitement, maybe even some yelling or screaming—maybe she would run right for me and jump into my arms. Instead, there was a subdued smile and, "It's so good to see you." It's as if we were asking, 'So, who are you now, and why are you back in my life?' We walked along quietly, not knowing what to say. I told her—and myself—that I hadn't slept or showered in a long time; I was just out of it. It was the only thing that would explain the awkwardness.

"Well, lots of things have changed with me since you've been gone," she told me. I didn't understand what she meant, but I just nodded my head. We got into her car, and I couldn't believe what a tiny little city Portland really was. It was a workday afternoon, and there was hardly any traffic from the airport to her apartment. I sat on the passenger's side, trying to think of things to say to this woman I'd been so eager to see. "Well," she said, "This is Powell's Bookstore. Do you still remember it?" I told her I did, and she asked, "So, what do you want to do today? I have the day off." I didn't know what I wanted to do. Had it always been like this when we were together, or was this new? Why did everything seem so unfamiliar?

Powell's was as beautiful as ever, one large city block of books. As usual, there were a few people getting signatures for various political causes out front. I knew that if I were to go on my usual walks around the city, I'd pass the same homeless street kids over by Portland State University. But familiar as it was, everything seemed so distant. I couldn't understand why things seemed so—*off*.

Once at her apartment, I set my bags in the middle of the floor. I took a shower and I wanted to curl up in bed and sleep—hopefully with her at my side. She had one of those convertible couches, the types you pulled the cushions out, and suddenly you had a bed.

But she told me, "I'm just going to type on my computer while you're resting. Maybe I can rent movies for tonight, too." Is this what I wanted to come back home for?

I slept well that afternoon, and that evening we watched videos. I tried to cuddle with her, but all she could say was, "I'm trying to watch the movie. Why do you always want to do this during movies?" I backed away, confused. "Things have changed," she told me. "You can't just come back here like this and expect...Well, I'm not the same person. It takes time."

I nodded my head. "I understand," I said, but I didn't.

"By the way, I have an *X-Files* friend that I watch the show with. He's in this apartment complex."

"Oh, okay," I told her. "So you'll go over there on Fridays? Or does he come over here?"

"Either way. You don't mind, do you?"

"No, not if that's what you do. Well, let's get some sleep." She slept with her back to me, on the far side of the bed.

Korea seemed far away. A world away.

41

The next day, Sasha got up early to get to commute to work, a reminder of the American way of life. When I woke up, I explored the apartment for the first time since having sealed the envelope. I played with Shaddow, I hadn't expected to see this little critter again. My plan that day was to use her computer, write a resume, and schedule job interviews. When I turned on her computer, I saw a file that had recently been saved to her hard drive: *E-mail from Janet*. I had never touched Sasha's files in the past, but I was so uncertain about what was going on with us now. I clicked open the file.

> *Well, I'm glad Adam is finally settling down, and I'm very glad that you can be with him again. You deserve to be in a stable relationship, and I know you love him a lot. I'm very happy for you.*
>
> *As far as the mystery man, I say you should go for it! It's harmless, and I'm sure Adam had his fun in Asia. Why don't you enjoy life and just see what the mystery man has to offer? It couldn't do you any harm.*
>
> *Things in Los Angeles are going well. I'm still writing, and Bryan has been taking German classes through the university.*
>
> *Well Sasha, again I'm very excited for you and Adam's new life together, and I love you. Bye for now, Janet.*

Mystery man? *X-Files* friend? Could it be possible? What else could I do but start rummaging through her files? I was invading her rights as a human being, I reminded myself. If she ever found out, I wouldn't be able to face her—or myself. Still, I kept looking, stopping on a file labeled *Encounters*. I clicked on it, reading with burning curiosity and a little guilt. It was pure writing, from the soul. From a literary point of view, I had to admit, it was pretty good. It was a big file, so I scrolled to the most recent entry:

> *Today, I met a mystery man in the laundry room of the apartment! While I was putting in my whites, he was putting in his darks. I was embarrassed to put my underwear in the washer, but I did it—and we were talking about the X-Files the whole time! The X-Files! He was a handsome guy with glasses, and he really liked to talk. It could have ended just like that, but quite by accident I ended up with his keys in my laundry bag. About twenty minutes after I got back to my apartment, there was a knock on my door; he was wondering if I'd picked up his keys.*

This was dated about a month ago, probably right about the time I had arrived in Kathmandu. I read another entry dated about two weeks ago. While I had been squinting up at Mount Everest, probably picking my teeth in thought, she had her second encounter with the mystery man.

> *The mystery man stopped by my apartment again today! He brought over several X-Files magazines. I was trying not to look too excited that here he was here at my place. He seemed kind of nervous, and while I would have liked to lock lips with him then and there, I controlled myself and tried to arrange a meeting when we could talk and have coffee. He agreed to this, and I just wished we'd arranged a specific date. My parents are here for Thanksgiving now, so it looks like I'll have to wait a while.*

Next I read an entry written the day before I'd arrived. While I was in Hong Kong, figuring out how to order Chop Suey in Chinese; she was making other plans:

Last night was my last night of freedom before Adam enters my life again. After talking with my fantastically wonderful gay couple co-workers, Vance and Frank, I've decided to act on the mystery man. Vance thinks I should go for it, but Frank thinks I should just be thankful Adam's coming home. I'm also weighing in the factor of Janet's advice. And you know what? I'm going to act on it! I deserve it! What harm could it do?

So last night (again, my last night as a single woman) I was reading my new book in bed, when I decided, "What the hell—I'm going to go over there and see if he's home." I put on my shoes and walked over there and knocked—no one! My last night, too, but I didn't give up. I wrote him a note about the X-Files (a witty one, I think) and told him he should come over tonight so we could talk about it. So when I went over again, I left it on his door. Every hour I went over there, checking to see if the note was there. It was. So much for my last night as a single woman! Finally, about two in the morning, I fell asleep with my book in my hand.

The most recent file was dated yesterday. This was what she must have written while I was snoozing away last night. I was probably dreaming with that jetlag feel, the one where I tumble off the bed and hit hard against the planet earth. Meanwhile, she was at her computer typing this:

Well, Adam came back today. He looks much different than I remember. He seems more worn out from traveling. His hair is longer, he hasn't shaved in a while, and he seems thinner than I remember. I love Adam very much, but I really want to see what this Mystery Man is all about.

Anyhow, I came home with Adam from the airport, and on my door was an envelope from Richard. Yes, his name's Richard—he signed his name in the letter. Richard

said he would love to see me tomorrow night for coffee so
we can meet and talk! I can't wait! I'm going to have to let
Richard know about the situation with Adam. Of course,
discretion is a must.

Shocked? Yes, I was very shocked. But it was understandable considering how long I been gone, and the situation I put her in. I didn't know how this would play out, but having information seemed better than not having information. I would keep silent about it, but now I had a secret window to see how things were going.

Then I opened my resume files, so that they would show to be the most recently opened items on her computer. Once I turned the computer off, I simply sat and thought about things. I wanted to leave Portland right then, but there were two problems. One, I didn't have a car. Two, everything that I owned was being shipped to Sasha's house from Pusan. At the minimum, I had to wait until they would arrive. There was always the chance that this was harmless, and I didn't have anything to worry about. She would see him tonight, and I now had access to her files to see how it went.

I put on my winter coat and walked around the streets of Portland. My hands were burrowed deep in my pockets, and I walked fast, trying to take it all in. I walked for hours to think out the implications of my situation. What would I do now? I couldn't stay in Portland if things went bad. Where would I go? Damn, damn, damn! Why had I made myself so vulnerable? It was like a chess move that I had never anticipated.

I bought a bouquet of flowers to surprise Sasha for when she came home from work. I wondered how she would get ready for her coffee date, what she'd choose to wear, and how she'd get around to telling me about it. I hoped he'd be a creep, a real bastard—someone who would make her appreciate the guy she already had. Maybe he would immediately make some chauvinistic remark and piss her off. Maybe things would end with her in my arms, acknowledging that all men were assholes—except me.

When she opened the front door, I greeted her warmly, as if I knew nothing. I shouted, "Sasha!" I gave her a big smile, and a warm hug, and extended the flowers. "I'm so glad to see you! I bought you flowers. I rested today, and I feel better than yesterday. How was your day? How was traffic?"

"Oh, they're beautiful. This is so nice." She put her coat over her chair. You could tell she was in a good mood, which was hit-and-miss with her. I never knew what she was going to be like from one day—or hour—to the next. "What a welcome," she said joyously. "Oh Adam, I feel so tired, but you know what, I made plans to see a friend tonight." She took off her work clothes and walked to the bathroom to run a bath. "I made these plans before I knew you were coming back; I hope you don't mind."

I followed her around the house, talking rapidly. "Oh, you have plans?" I inquired, "What time? Is it a friend from work? Will you be out late? What are you going to do?"

"Well, actually, it's a man. He's only a friend." She checked the bathtub. "I made the plan weeks ago. It's only for a few hours, and we're just going to have a cup of coffee. It's nothing special."

"Oh, that's really nice," I told her. "Friends are very important. It's very healthy to have friends. I hope you have a good time." Then, as she took her warm bath, I began sharing stories. The Hong Kong flight was still on my mind, "Yeah, Sasha, there was this old couple from America on the flight. You wouldn't believe them!"

"Really?" She wasn't really listening to this; she seemed more concerned with being as clean as possible, I noted suspiciously. But I wanted to engage her.

"Yeah, you would have been shocked! They came to Hong Kong only to shop for two weeks. They said they paid five thousand dollars for flights and hotels, but that didn't include all the things they bought."

She continued her bath, "Really?"

"Yeah, real ugly Americans. Plus they kept complaining about Asia to me."

"What'd they say?"

"They said, 'I bet you're glad to be eating some real food instead of all this rice.' I love rice. They kept saying how backward things were in Hong Kong."

"So what'd you tell them?"

"Nothing. I just listened. They're old, and I can't change their opinions. I just listened and tried to read my book as much as possible."

She angrily questioned me, "Why don't you ever stand up and tell off ignorant people like that?"

"I can't change them, Sasha. People will just go on believing and reconfirming what they think reality is. How does being angry about it help?"

"I just don't understand you." She shook her head in a disappointed manner.

"But listen to this, there were also all of these Chinese babies on the plane, about twenty or thirty. Apparently, a lot of Americans adopt Chinese babies now. But there is legal law that they have to fly there and pick them up. Isn't that interesting? All over the plane there were Chinese babies being adopted by classic American families, real perfect couple types. A pretty weird sight, don't you think?"

"Yes, Adam. Yes, it is." Soon she was out of the bathroom and going through her closet. She asked me, "What should I wear tonight?"

I treated it as a rhetorical question and continued talking. I knew she was deeply interested in women's issues, so I said, "You wouldn't believe the women in Asia, how much less valued they are than men."

"Yeah? What was that like?"

"You wouldn't believe it," I said, and just started sharing everything I could remember—Korean husbands and their girlfriends, Korean women considered unmarriageable after thirty...I kept going, and she was getting pretty worked up.

"I can't believe that," she kept saying. "That makes me so angry."

"Yeah, and there's more."

"I gotta go, Adam. Can you tell me later? Will you be here when I come home?"

"Of course I will—I can't wait to see you tonight! Are you having dinner? I could make you some dinner if you're not! Are you?" Actually I wasn't a dinner making person, but I wanted to find out her plans.

"Thank you, but it's not necessary. I don't know if I'm eating or not."

I opened the door for her, as she put on her coat, "Well, my dear, have a good evening. I'll see you tonight!" I told her.

"Thank you, I will," she said, and she was out to see her mystery man. I closed the door behind her and sat down sadly on the couch.

I turned to the cat. "It's just you and me tonight, Shaddow."

But I tried not to get too upset about it. I spent the evening rifling through her books and deciding which ones to read while I was there. I tried to watch television, but the interest wasn't there. Then I paced around the house for a while, glaring out the window. Finally, I decided to take a bath myself. I was in the tub when she came home.

She called out, "Adam?"

"In the bathroom, Sasha, c'mon in," I yelled. I felt relaxed, finally. "How was your evening?"

"Oh, you know," she said. "He was a nice guy. We had coffee and talked for a while."

"Oh really? But you had a good time? What did you talk about it?"

"Not much. There's one thing he said that really bothered me, though..."

"Yes?" I said, "And what was that?" I was hoping it was something really offensive.

"Well, he told me it must be hard to meet men as a feminist. I never thought about it, but I think he's right."

"Oh yes, of course," I told her. Was she going to be impressed by that statement? What were the implications of that? I was trying to analyze it.

"But I kept thinking about it after he said it," she confessed. "I wonder..."

That night we laid down to sleep, and she wanted to know more about women in Korea. I told her as much as I could remember, and she became more and more outraged as I continued. I tried to get close to her, but she was too upset. "I could never live there," she kept saying. "I would never live there."

Several days later, I went back to her *Encounters* file.

I had the big date with the mystery man. As soon as I walked into his apartment, he seemed very nervous. Everything was immaculately clean. There was one thing he said that really bothered me, and I can't stop thinking about it: "It must be hard to meet men as a feminist."

Also, I was surprised at how cool Adam was with everything. I was worried how I would tell him, but I just walked in and told him I had plans. He was very understanding.

I wondered how different I might have taken things had I not read the files. If I knew nothing, would I have assumed the absolute worst? Something about knowing the exact situation you were in, had a comforting effect.

I would continue to just figure this out, day by day, and see what would happen. Now that I was now fully immersed in this experience, it was difficult not to get too wrapped in all of the emotions of it as well. But I didn't have any other choice.

***
42
***

A few days later, I was offered a temporary office job in downtown Portland. It helped me pass the time during the day, and I was home about an hour before Sasha each evening. Things settled down for a few days after her date, but then she said she had something important to share with me.

Over plates of spaghetti at the kitchen table, she asked, "Have you noticed anything different since you've been back?"

"I don't know. What do you mean?"

"Do you feel like I'm a little colder?"

"Well, I was expecting a bigger reception, but it was a stressful day for both of us."

"Well, I don't know how to say this, Adam, but things have changed."

"How so?" I had to play it cool, as if I didn't know what was going on.

"I don't think I want to be with you and live together again."

"It's a big step," I said. "I know we were planning it, but it's hard to just jump right again, isn't it? It takes time to get to know each other again, right?"

"Yes, that's exactly what I was thinking."

"Well, why don't we just see what happens?"

"But it's just not that. I just don't feel the same way about you now." That hit me to the core. I couldn't twirl my spaghetti on the end of the fork with that blow. I put my fork down, stunned. "I want to date other men. I want to be a single woman and go out on. I want to fall in love."

I sat there, thinking about how sad she had been when I left Portland, and her reactions when I expressed interest in returning to her. It made me reflect to that first day in Korea, the one where the book, *You Can't Go Home Again* by Thomas Wolf, escaped from my bags. It had a new meaning, on many levels now.

"I don't want a boyfriend in my life right now."

"Well, I don't know what to say to that, Sasha. I don't know how serious you are about this, and I'm going to have to think about it for a while. But no matter what happens, I'm still glad I'm with you right now."

That was actually a lie, it was nice to see her again, but under different pretexts and circumstances would have been much better. Leaving Portland made sense. In context, that entire experience in Korea was fantastic, as difficult as it seemed along the way. This experience though?

This would take time to internalize. What if this was the end? What would I do? I hadn't considered this option. I was having my own deliberations in Asia. But, I hadn't considered that likewise she might have had her own hesitations. When I reflected in my core being, I could see the wanderlust building immensely had she welcomed me back wholeheartedly. Still, I simply wasn't prepared to make this decision so soon. Perhaps, she was pushing something along that was going to be the ultimate outcome in the long run, despite my intentions, or lies to myself that I was going back to settle down.

This infected the bedroom, or should I say, the Convertible Sofa Bed. Sasha's apartment didn't have a bedroom, the couch in the living room was one of those convertible types that transformed into a bed at night. I wouldn't say either one of them was warm. Not the bed nor the couch, in either form. The couch began to represent the anxiety I'd feel, as I had to play out this situation. I couldn't relax on it. The bed converted that emotion horizontally. The flat kind without a horizon, one that limited your sights.

But, I was caught up in my circumstances. I couldn't see any of this clearly. My mind was muddled. When I needed to clear it out, I found myself drawn towards Beaverton, Oregon—a Portland suburb with Korean businesses. I would take busses out there, just to read the Korean storefronts. They took on a different, more personal meaning after I had experienced Korea. Being in Beaverton, made me feel like a more complete person, bridging two worlds, one that I had just begun to learn to straddle.

But now, I was simply living in the Portland world. Struggling to re-define the relationship I had with Sasha, she said, "Maybe we can live together in the same apartment and have separate rooms. We could be roommates and have the ability to date other people."

"Sasha, I'm open to anything you want. But I don't think we're capable of maintaining a relationship under those circumstances. I like the idea because I value our friendship, but I wouldn't feel comfortable if you brought dates home, and you probably wouldn't if I did."

But it was weird: I *did* like the idea. I liked it because it was so wrong that we could see how messed up things could become. What would be the result of that? It was an intriguing thought. But, that was a prime example of how linear my thinking had become, caught up in my immediate circumstances. I needed to get my mind back, the one that once said, "I'm moving westward, and more westward, and so far west that I'm going East, without any discussion on the matter whatsoever." The mind that never deliberated with that toy flower, the 'Should I' or 'Shouldn't I' nature of deliberations. You made your decision, put your heart into it 100%, and you went with it, without looking back.

With that, I patiently waited for my boxes to arrive from Korea. I wanted to let things play out more before I made any drastic change. I hadn't thought through all of my options either, so I felt I had to buy more time. I was still felt horizontal on that sofa bed, with the limited horizons. Still caught up in external circumstances, I wanted to ride out this bumpy road, just to make sure it didn't indeed lead to a dead end.

One evening, as we were enjoying a conversation, the doorbell rang.

Sasha went to her door, and I overheard her say, "Well, hello. What are you doing here?"

"Hi, Sasha," a man said. "I think someone stole my bicycle from the storage shed, and I wondered if you'd heard anything about it."

I stayed in the living room as they talked. Despite their expressions of shock, it was evident that they were glad to see each other.

"You don't mind if I use your phone, do you? I have to call my workplace and tell them I'm going to be late."

"Late? Don't worry about it, Richard. I'll give you a ride in my car."

"No, you really don't have to. I can just call and tell them I'm going to be late. It's no problem."

"I'm getting my coat. I'm going to drive you. Don't worry about it."

"Well, I still need to use your phone." That's when I got to see Richard, the mystery man. "Oh," he said as he entered the living room, "I didn't know someone was here. You were so quiet in here."

I shrugged my shoulders. "Good to meet you. My name's Adam."

He got on the phone, and I observed him closely. He had thick glasses, short hair, and—I was sure—an obnoxious personality. He was kind of a geek, and Sasha had always had this fascination with geeky people. Portland in general was a city that attracted that type. After seeing him, I was relieved. I had imagined Richard as an attractive man. He wasn't.

"Well, I'll be back in a little while. I'm just going to give Richard a ride to work," Sasha told me. Then they went out the door together, and I didn't see her again for another two hours.

When she came back, she said to me, "He arrived too early because I gave him a ride. So we went to McDonald's for coffee until his work shift began."

I interrogated her, "What does he do?"

"He's a server at the Blue Moon. But he wants to be a professional juggler."

"That's kind of an odd to aspiration to have, don't you think? A professional juggler. That sounds like a joke right there."

"What's so odd about it?"

"It's just strange, that's all. What kind of person aspires to be that? He seemed kind of obnoxious, if you ask me."

"Well fine. He's just a friend, and I don't think there's anything wrong with having friends," she told me. "And anyway, if we're talking about aspirations, what kind of twenty-six-year-old man has all of his belongings in three bags on my floor? Why don't you get some things? Why don't you live like a normal human being?"

"I like to travel, okay? I don't like material things."

Things went downhill from there.

That night seemed like a good night to sit on the couch and write a letter to Joe:

January 11, 1997

Hey Joe,

Where you going with that gun in your hand? Hey Joe, you know I caught my old lady running with another man. Just thought I'd write a few lyrics from Jimi Hendrix! Sort of getting settled in Portland again. If spending a lot of time reflecting on a couch is called settling, then I am very settled in already. Nah, fact is, I don't know what I'm doing here. But I was thinking of all you guys. Hope you're all doing well in Pusan, and the Kupo Hagwan schedule isn't too brutal this month! Give my regards to Huck, Stefano, Paris, Melvin, Monica, Linda, and all the rest!

안녕히계십시오

Adam

***

43

***

I had some previous colleagues who played darts in a downtown Portland bar. I knew they would be there on a Friday night, so I dropped by their Dart Bar.

"Adam! Long time no see!"

I looked at my round-bodied, bearded, old friend, "Yeah, I know right!" I was eager to share my stories.

"Where've you been recently anyways?"

"You wouldn't believe it! I went to Korea where I was teaching English, then I went to Thailand, Nepal, Singapore, Hong Kong, and all around. I just got back." I was expecting his jaw to drop. Who would announce that, right?

"Hey, Adam, that's really great," he paused in reflection. "You must be glad to be back," and he gave me a quick fist-bump. "Welcome home! Let's play darts. Cricket?" He never elicited another question about travel. His world ended with the immediate bar, the immediate dart board, and the rest of the world didn't hold much interest. He smiled with a huge advantage, "You're so rusty, I'm going to kick your ass!"

I reflected on this for a long time afterwards. When you go back to your home country, your experiences abroad simply disappear. They are no longer a part of you, and no one cares about them. While I was living in Korea, I could straddle both worlds. All my friends knew the previous existence and the new existence. We all carried both worlds with us, and we could switch back and forth constantly within our conversations with each other. Leaving Korea behind, I left all traces of Korea behind. No one would relate to those experiences.

Back to my immediate situation, I hadn't fully realized the implications of Richard's stolen bike. Or maybe I had, but I was suppressing it. Even though Sasha continued to talk about not wanting a boyfriend and wanting to enjoy the dating world, I didn't feel like things had really changed much. We rented films and shared dinners together. On the surface, it seemed like everything might be slowly going back to normal. "I don't like Richard like that," she told me once. "He's too young. But I still want to date other people."

So, on one particular night, we went out and bought some beer to make a night of it. It felt more special than an average night. We went back and forth to the fridge, accumulating empty cans in the living room. Then, about midnight, there was a hard pounding on the door. There he was, the one guy who could ruin a good discussion, a great evening. In the Bible, I thought sourly, they referred to him as Satan. Close friends might prefer to call him Richard, and I knew one person who called him the mystery man. I had other titles for him.

She answered the door, and he said, "Hi, Sasha. My friend Tom is in town, and we were thinking of going out tonight. Thought I'd stop by and see if you wanted to join us."

They stood in the doorway, and I sat hidden in the other room, deep in thought. I didn't want to acknowledge him. Soon they were out the door again, and it was just Sasha and I.

When she came back to the living room, she said, "They wanted to know if I wanted to go out with them tonight."

"Well, do you?"

"Actually, I sort of do," she said uncertain of my response.

"Do you like Richard?"

"I told you, he's just a friend. But I would like to go out tonight."

"And what about our evening?"

"We've had fun, haven't we?"

"Am I invited?"

"They didn't say."

"Are you going to go?"

"Yes." An empty feeling hit me.

She got her things together, and brushed her teeth for a full ten minutes. I asked again, "Am I invited?"

She said, "I'd prefer to have my own friends. Why don't you make new friends yourself?" With that, she went out the door.

I sat alone in her living room, staring blankly at Shaddow. I had so much beer in me that I couldn't relax. I paced around the apartment for a while. Figuring the bars were open until two o'clock, I made personal plans to be gone at that time. She could come home tonight and see me gone, experience the worry and anxiety for a change. I was sick of it! So I drank all her beer, put on my coat, gloves, and scarf, and walked out into the cold winter air at approximately 1:30 a.m.

I wandered half the city looking for a bar, but nothing was open. I wandered down the trolley line; I balanced my feet on the rails like I had as a kid. Eventually, at about 2:30 a.m., I figured she'd suffered enough. I'd go home now, and she'd be waiting for me, worried sick.

When I got back to the apartment, I unlocked the door, walked in, and looked around. No one was there. Now what? I scavenged the apartment for an overlooked beer, but found only empty bottles. I paced around for twenty minutes, peering out the windows. I wanted to go over to his apartment and look through the window, but I didn't know which one it was exactly, and it would be too embarrassing to be caught. The only thing I could do was go out again. I wanted to make it look like I'd had a good time without her. I put on my winter clothes again and left at three in the morning. At one point I thought I saw three people walking toward her apartment, so I laughed to myself—finally! Now I could make it look like I was having a good time, too! I hid my face from the three approaching figures, actually a slow run so I'd be far away and out of sight. I kept going, walking fast to fight off the cold. I looked at my watch. I would walk for thirty minutes, I decided, and then turn around. One full hour of anxiety for her.

Thirty minutes later, I was at a big parking lot. I loitered around for a while, rubbing my hands in the cold. The longer I was gone, the better. I embarked on the long walk back, trying to walk slowly, but it was too cold to walk slow. I thought about what I would tell her when I got home—"I won't worry you again, I promise!"

At the apartment, I once again unlocked the door. I once again wandered through the kitchen only to find myself welcomed by her purring cat—and a clock that said 4:30 a.m. I sat down on the empty bed, sad as hell. Shaddow jumped up on my lap, but I was unresponsive. I sat on the couch, in the dark, feeling sick to my stomach. I took Shaddow off my lap and paced the apartment floors again for another twenty minutes or so, looking out the kitchen window every time I passed by it. Damn! Damn! Damn!

At a little after five in the morning, I heard the door unlock. I wanted to shout, "Welcome home!" I wanted to give her the biggest hug I'd ever given her in her life. I wanted to tell her off. I didn't say a word or do anything, though. I just sat on her bed, fully clothed, at a little after five in the morning. She saw me and said, "I'm sorry." I didn't know how to answer her. "Are you angry with me?" I sat there in silence, took a deep sigh, and looked anywhere but at her. "I'm really sorry," she said. "We were talking in Richard's apartment afterward, and I didn't realize the time. I should have stopped by to tell you, and I didn't. I'm sorry." I sat there at the edge of the couch, shaking my head from side to side, until she said, "If you're not going to say anything, I'm going to bed. I'm sorry. What else can I say?"

I felt like Melvin. It was implied, Adam, it was implied. I was Melvin.

I sighed one more time. "You're excluding me. If he's your friend, and only your friend, it shouldn't be any problem to all go out together, right? Are you embarrassed of me?"

Of course I was twisting things, but I was only trying to make a point. She sat and contemplated, "You're right, I am ostracizing you, and I didn't realize it. I'll try to invite you to meet my friends if you'd like, but you're not meeting Richard. He's *my* friend."

With that, we pulled out the sofa bed. She slept with her back to me, as usual. I lied on the edge, my back to her. I couldn't sleep well. My vision felt clouded, my horizon limited.

***

44

***

A few days later, Sasha informed me that she wanted to invite Richard out to a movie. It would be nice for her—and again, her only interest was extending her network of friendships. I was still reading her files, and she didn't demonstrate any strong feelings for the guy. She was simply reveling in the fact that she had a choice between two men. Should she take Adam, the man she had dated for three years? Or should she go with the new guy and make some (much-needed) changes in her life? She just wanted to see where it would go.

Meanwhile, I felt emotionally attached. I knew it was time to move on, but walking away from those good years with her, seemed more difficult than walking away from that now fantastic half year in Korea.

"So what movie are you thinking of?" She told me the name, and I recognized it immediately. "That's the movie I recommended on Christmas Day, the one you said would be too boring! Not only that, but it's a love story!"

"I know, I know. But I was talking to Dora at work, and she recommended it."

"But you and I haven't been to the theater since I've been back."

"Things have changed, Adam." But I still felt like I was on that bumpy road, searing for a clearer sign to tell me to detour off this route permanently.

So a few days later, they made their plans. They developed a process for passing notes back and forth by taping them to the inside of her mailbox. She would wander off to get something from her car, and he'd have a note on his apartment door.

One of the first notes I saw was an electric bill taped to her door. I had thought it was odd, but figured it might have been from the landlord, so I brought it in and placed it on the kitchen table. A few days later, when I got back into her computer files, I understood what it was:

Richard is such an ingenious man. He taped an electric bill to my door with a note in it! I was worried that Adam might have seen it, but he apparently didn't even notice!

I felt sad the night that they went to the movie, but I was powerless to do anything about it. I wished her well and told her I loved her. I told her to have a good time. Then, when she left, I wrote a long letter to Joe. I explained what was happening. I told him that I planned to leave as soon as my boxes arrived, but that I wasn't sure where to go.

I'm thinking about going back to Korea, or I really liked Hong Kong. Or maybe I'll try something new, like Prague—a lot of American expatriates there, I heard.

The biggest thing on my mind was deciding if I should leave when my boxed arrived, or stay for a year or so, in another apartment. It made me sad to think of just leaving, because I knew that if I did, we'd lose any possibility of having the relationship we once had. But that possibility was probably already gone.

I told Sasha several times that I was thinking of going back to Asia or trying a European or another American city. Her first reaction was shock, but she gradually accepted it and she discussed my options with me. I hoped it would awaken her, make her realize I wouldn't be around if things continued as they were. She agreed with me, but she also talked about the possibility of me getting my own apartment. She told me she'd miss me so much that she'd call me every day. Little things like that kept me there. I felt I wanted that. The thought occurred to me, if I could only endure more pain, things would go back to the way they were. It's funny how the mind adapts.

The evening she went out with Richard, I was as calm as possible. I planned to watch all of Ken Burns's *The West* on PBS. Additionally I had two reading material books on standby, *The Great Plains* by Ian Frazier and *Black Elk Speaks* by James Niehardt. No pacing, no drinking, no tapping into her computer files—just the normal routine that I use to enjoy.

She came home late once again, but not as late as I was expecting. It's funny how you adapt to things. It was only one o'clock. But I hadn't totally adapted to things. She told me they had gone out for coffee after the film. "I don't like Richard that way!" she told me again. "It's not him in particular; it could be anyone!"

"But you're with *him*. I saw him, and he's not attractive. You could do so much better."

"I don't know, I just like the idea of a younger man. And I think he needs an older woman. Plus I can educate him. Maybe I can go from one young man to the next educating them. I'm just expressing my femininity, using my power. It's very flattering to be wooed by a younger man." She was only in her twenties, I thought.

I really didn't like any of this, but I was trying to be open to it. After all, I was living in her house, and I didn't have my boxes yet. Nor was I ready to wander out into Portland looking for somewhere else to live while I was debating what country I might be living in next month.

We had more soul-to-soul talks over the next few days. She told me she loved me, and I told her she was the most important thing in the world to me. Everything seemed to be coming back to me. I thought she might realize what a precious relationship we had.

Then, on a rainy night about halfway through the week, we were enjoying each other's company. We were drinking beer and lying on the couch when there was a loud pounding on the door. POUND POUND POUND. "Don't answer it," I said. "Not tonight," I demanded. She didn't answer it.

Forty minutes later, we heard it again: POUND POUND POUND. "It's like he's hounding me," she said. "I feel like he's creeping around out there, maybe even watching us."

"Yeah, me too. It's kind of creepy."

"Maybe I should answer the door. Maybe it's something serious."

"Don't worry about it. It's just you and me tonight." But she was genuinely concerned now.

"It'll just take a second," she said, and she was out of my reach and at her kitchen door. "Hi, Richard. You're all wet. What's wrong?"

"Can I talk to you for a second?" A pause. "Out here?"

I went around to the bathroom window so I could view them from the inside. They were just talking, and yes, Richard was completely wet. Then he leaned in to give her a big kiss, and I saw her arms go right up his back. She put both of her hands on the back of his head and pushed his lips harder into her own. I stood there, looking out the window in disbelief. My heart dropped, and I felt deceived, betrayed, and alone—without anyone or anything. I stood there staring out the bathroom window. They broke their embrace, he grabbed her hand, and they started walking down the driveway toward his apartment. My heart was smashed. I ran through the house and swung open the kitchen door. "Sasha—Sasha! Can I see you a moment?" She let go of his hand and began walking toward me, turning her head back to him with a look of understanding. Then she was back in the apartment. "I saw you kissing him!" I said.

"You were spying on me!"

"Sasha, you were right in front of the door! What do you mean, I was spying on you?"

"I don't care. I liked it. He's a good kisser."

The following Friday, I told her I wanted to go out and have a big evening out, just her and me. She was reluctant at first, but agreed that we would do that. When she came home that evening, I had bought a big bouquet of flowers. I inquired about every detail about her day and how it had gone. Of course, I had checked the mail before she came home, and I'd seen a letter addressed to her. It was obviously from Richard, as it wasn't postmarked. I opened it and it read, *See me tonight! Find a way!* I closed it neatly back up and pretended not to have noticed it at all. I left it at the bottom of the mail stack. Looking back, I should have thrown it away, but I felt incapable of containing what was occurring.

Once Sasha came home, I presented her with the mail. She wasn't herself after reading the note, but I ignored it, talking about how much fun we were going to have. I even got out a story I had started about our last day together before I had gone to Korea. It began, *Four long bulky bags and an acoustic guitar all sat in a row on the short green grass between the road and the sidewalk. I hovered nearby, peering towards Division Street searching for my cab. It was my last day living in Portland,*

Oregon—a city I had come to love—and it was my last night with the black-haired, green-eyed woman I'd been involved with for the last three years. For Sasha and me, it was no longer the beginning of the end: it was the end of the end. I was about to leave, I was about to go...

I read it to her slowly, crying at times. When I finished, she said to me, "What can I say to that? That was one of the hardest days of my life, the day that you left. What am I supposed to say to that?" I desperately tried to get her out on our date, but she told me, "Just wait a minute; there's something I have to do! Richard's hounding me with these notes! I just can't take it anymore! Between you and him, I just can't take it anymore! I'm going to go over there and tell him it has to stop! No more!" She went into the bathroom and closed the door—something unusual for us. Then she went storming out of the house, furious as hell. As soon as she left, I checked her toothbrush. It was sopping wet.

But I felt so relieved that it was Friday and she was with me. Things were coming back to my side. She was only gone for about thirty minutes. "Everything is settled," she told me when she returned. "I told him to knock off the notes. Let's go out and have a good time." And we did. We went to a quaint little bar, drank lots of beer, and talked. She told me again how much I meant to her. She also told me again that she wanted to date other men, but I thought that maybe Richard was out of the picture.

A few days later, I got on her computer once again and read the following:

> *Friday night. I received a letter from Richard telling me, "See Me Tonight. Find a Way!" I had made plans to be with Adam that night, and he was too excited to break them. So I made an excuse to go over to Richard's, and as soon as he opened the door, I gave him the biggest kiss of his life. We were making out all over the apartment, bumping into things. The kitchen table almost fell over. It was so powerful. We were at it for almost twenty minutes.*

After reading that, I knew it was just a matter of the boxed before I left Portland.

218

Then, that Sunday, Sasha did laundry. She stepped out regularly to check her clothes, and when she did, she was gone for an up to an hour each time. Whenever she came back home, she found more laundry to do. Of course I knew what was going on, but what could I say? What could I do? Everything had moved on. I was simply waiting for my stuff.

That week, I received my boxes in the mail. I was relieved. No more awkwardness. Now I could do anything I wanted. Now I had the freedom to leave. I felt like I had lost Sasha anyway. She was on her path, and I'd soon be back to finding mine—and this wasn't it.

My last days in the apartment weren't pretty. Sasha was tired of me being around, as she lacked the privacy to write on her computer. Up until that point, she would type while I read books, sitting on the floor, but she couldn't tolerate that anymore.

In one of the more enlightening evenings for me, she said, "Joe can have you!" It gave me insight into how she'd probably viewed our relationship for years. My constant desire for travel. An 'Okay Adam, follow your bliss, just don't end up on your parent's couch, okay?'

But she was following her own bliss, and who can blame her? She spent an hour or two each evening writing notes to Richard in the kitchen. She kept the door closed and became angry if I knocked. She stopped using discretion when she visited him. She would tell me, "I need to get some tapes out of my car," or, "I need to take out this trash." These were cues that told me that she'd be gone for the evening.

I reflected on the flower petal, the 'Should I' or 'Shouldn't I?' There was no indecision, just go forward. I felt empowered, and finally in choice of my own path. Why seek relationships, when you can just seek connections? Wasn't that enough? Wasn't that basically the problem back in Korea, just as it was in Oregon now?

Having my boxes, I quit my temporary job. I contacted a Drive-Away Car agency, as they needed drivers to take cars across the country for their owners. You had to pay your own gas and lodging, but you had a free car to use. They always had different routes, depending on which car owner put in an order from where to where.

I went to the agency with all of my documents, and hoped they had one to Detroit—it was the closest next couch that I could think of. There wasn't a car to Detroit, but they did have one to New Hampshire. Maybe I could visit my parents in Michigan along the way, get whatever I need, and settle down in Boston? I could start a new start.

When I signed the papers, I used Sasha's name as a local reference and as a local address. When I called her at work to tell her, she was shocked. She couldn't understand what I had done. Where would I go? She was worried.

That night she came home, she was sad as hell, but I was as matter-of-fact as could be. I told her, "I'll be okay. Everything will be okay. I just need to go." That was it. It all just ended. I had found my way.

What did I think of Sasha, in the end? Only the best. She had been an important part of my life, back when I was exploring up and down the West Coast, partly with her, and partly with Joe. Portland had ALWAYS been the end of the road for her, and only seemed a part of the road for me.

I had made the right choice the first time, when I first left. That was what I had always needed to do. Coming back wasn't as big of a mistake as it might have seemed. It gave me proper comparisons between Korea and Oregon that I couldn't see while in Korea. It gave me clarity and perspective.

It also gave final and complete closure with Sasha, and that was one thing I probably needed fully while in Korea. There was official closure now, and that wasn't a bad thing. It was a good thing.

***

45

***

The next morning, I couldn't look at her. I backed my car out of its space, my eyes stubbornly ahead. Then, slowly, I glanced out the driver's side window to where she stood—it was the last eye contact I would make with her. She was crying. My eyes drifted back to the road, and my own tears welled up and rolled down my cheeks. I thought back to our good-bye when I had left her to go to Korea, how we had both cried that day. I waved to her, and I drove on down the road.

I drove downtown one more time. When would I see Portland again? I drove around Powell's Bookstore a few times in my car, remembering the hours I'd spent exchanging books, browsing the stacks, and just plain people watching.

Soon I was on an Oregon highway, heading east. It was late January, and the roads were dangerously icey, so I couldn't drive half as fast as I wanted. I drove all day without stopping and spent the night in an Idaho hotel room. It was the loneliest feeling in the world. I wanted to call Sasha; I wanted to hear her tell me everything was okay. But I knew it was never going to be like that again.

The next day I got in the car again, and it was the same lousy feeling. I couldn't imagine feeling like this until I arrived in New Hampshire. And what would I do when I got there? How would I feel then? My friend Joe was in Korea, and my best friend—Sasha—was no longer in my life. There wasn't anyone in this country for me anymore, and I wondered if there ever had been.

On the third night, I decided to I would call Sasha. She wasn't home, which made me feel lonelier than ever. But having decided to allow myself to call her, helped me with the next day's drive through Nebraska and Iowa. When I called her that night, she was pleasantly surprised and asked about my trip. She told me how sad she had been when I'd left again; she just hadn't felt good about it either—in fact, she told me, she'd called in sick on Monday. I told her, 'That's too bad."

The drive across America was extremely beautiful at times, but it also created strong feelings of detachment and isolation. Everyone had something, everyone but me.

The following day, I drove into Michigan, where my parents lived. They welcomed me in the driveway. Their son had finally come home— long hair, goatee, old ragged clothes, back from seeing the world. It had been years since I'd been home for longer than a few days, and they were glad to give me a place to rest my weary head for a while. I slept on their couch for a couple of days, left all my boxes and bags in their house, and then took off across Canada towards New Hampshire.

In New England, I couldn't stop thinking of Sasha; as she had always loved the East Coast. She was a New England girl, so I bought some postcards and other souvenirs, which I sent to her in a big package. I hoped it would make her happy. While I drove around the region, I couldn't help but look for people who might look like her, but I didn't see any.

When I finally arrived at the destination, I gave the car back to its owner. He gave me a ride to the bus station in Laconia, New Hampshire, where I spent five or six hours wandering around until the bus left. There was snow everywhere; it was a quaint little place, typical New England. It was like a postcard that I might see in books. I found a bookstore in town, bought a Milan Kundera book, and settled into a little cafe until the bus departure. My hands were frozen, I tried to read, but my mind was preoccupied with what I was going to do in Boston that I couldn't concentrate. Later that evening, I boarded the bus and was on my way.

In Boston, I called local hostels until I found one called The Irish Embassy Hostel. They had many actual Irish people staying there. There were so many Irish bars in the area, it made me feel relaxed, with an exotic feel to it. I wandered downtown Boston for days, drinking by myself in the Irish bars at night. I didn't have enough money, and couldn't stay there forever, but I didn't have anywhere else to go. I had to do something, so I arranged to deliver another car. I found one that took me to Detroit.

Once I had the next car, I shot right up the Eastern Coast spending time in old Massachusetts cities like Salem. I wrote some letters to Korea, discussing my plight. I went all the way up to Portland, Maine, just to say I'd been there, and then turned around again. Next I drove straight down to Lowell, Massachusetts, where Jack Kerouac was born. I felt a sense of peacefulness in the restlessness. I wanted to linger around Lowell, but the car had to be delivered to Detroit. I had dallied too long off-route already, but something felt even more wonderfully Kerouacesque about that. I wanted to soak up as much Kerouacesque as I could get, before I Kerouacesqued off.

The next day, I went to Brattleboro, Vermont and looked at the School for International Training. I had been researching graduate school programs for years, and maybe now would be a good time to pursue one. I fell in love with the place; it reminded me of the summer that I'd worked at Yellowstone National Park. I was able to enjoy the beauty of the mountains every day. The connection between the two was immediate for me, and I stayed in Brattleboro, wandering around the entire day. I imagined what my daily life might be like here—where I would want to live, what restaurants and bars I would frequent the most. I even wandered around the School of International Training's library, imagining what kinds of books I might read.

From there I drove straight north to Montreal, where it was snowing hard. On the radio, I could hear the Simpsons being played in French. I found a hotel and spent the night in this French city, but wished I had more time for it too. I didn't. The moment I woke up, I couldn't afford another day on the road, so I took a marathon drive through Ontario all the way home. My parents' house was just on the other side of the Canadian border, in Port Huron, Michigan. I was asleep on their couch at approximately 3:30 a.m., just saving myself the expenses of another night in a hotel.

***

46

***

There I was, in Port Huron, Michigan, sleeping on my parents' couch. If I had known this was where I'd end up, I would never have left Asia. It would have been better to live up in the mountains of Nepal, shivering under a mound of blankets. But here I was.

Of course, my parents were glad to see me. "Let's buy a bed for the spare room," my mom told my dad.

"No, no," I told them. "It's only temporary. And I'm fine where I am."

It was pretty strange to see them again after all this time. The last time I had lived with them was almost four years ago, during an awkward two months after university when I had nowhere to go. I had packed up my car and went west across the United States, where I'd met both Joe and Sasha. Four years later, I was back, once again plotting my future course.

This house wasn't the house I'd grown up in. Honestly, I hadn't seen most of the houses I'd grown up in as an adult: there were just too many of them. I had recounted them up many times, and I came up with around eighteen by the time I left home. As an adult, my own propensity to move was exponentially worse, and I easily doubled that number in a much shorter time.

At least this house had character. It had a big balcony window overlooking the Blue Water Bridge that connected the city of Port Huron with Sarnia, Ontario. If you looked further down river, you'd see multitudes of factories pouring chemicals into the St. Clair River. But from the house, you just had a view of the Sarnia casinos underneath a busy international bridge.

I liked to lie on the couch facing the bay window and watch the car lights drift across the wall as big rigs and small cars went overhead at night. Near the couch was my parents' set of encyclopedias—from the year 1970. They had sat on the same set of bookshelves in various houses for the last twenty-six years. Little did my parents know that every map and geographical entry in those volumes was stained with my dirty fingerprints running up and down the side of the book—years of planning. I don't think anyone in my household had ever noticed.

There was plenty of other evidence of my desire for freedom throughout the house. For years, starting around the time I was about twelve, I carried a pocket calendar and marked off every day I had left until high school graduation. As with everything else, I destroyed the calendars as I used them; I didn't want any visible reminders of the past. It was all about the future for me. It wasn't that I had to get out of Michigan, it was that I wanted to explore the world beyond the borders of Michigan.

Sitting on this couch, I had time for some serious reflection. I thought back to myself as an eighteen-year-old, the day I'd graduated from high school. I'd spent most of my senior year spray-painting an old gas-guzzler truck with a top on the back. That was to be my escape from Michigan, my first time out of my home state. Two high school years of working at gas stations, supermarkets, fast-food restaurants, and summer factories, I finally had enough money to hit the road before my eighteenth birthday. I drove that truck south into Ohio, marveling at the sight of Ohio license plates and Ohio highway markers. I kept driving east until I hit Pennsylvania, where I was awed at my first sight of actual mountains. I had never seen them before, having never left the Midwest. I parked at a campgrounds outside Pittsburgh, up in the hills. I had a cot in the back of the truck, an old guitar, and a couple bags of clothing. I had thrown away everything else.

The next day, I drove to Philadelphia. Setting off, I knew I didn't have plans to go anywhere, but I had hoped to find jobs along the way, much like Peter Jenkins in *A Walk Across America*. But by the time I arrived in Philadelphia, I didn't see how I could financially make it work. I didn't know how I'd go about finding a job with money to sustain myself, and I didn't know how to find a place to stay. The old truck was guzzling too much gas, and my minimum-wage job savings weren't enough to sustain me. I had failed, but I learned. It was my first attempt at the hope of long-term travel. I would keep putting pieces together to figure it out.

It was now two in the morning as I sat on the couch, peering at the overnight traffic to and from Canada. It was strange to think that few in my family had thought of crossing that bridge. Here we were on an international border, but it had little meaning around here. People in these types of towns, viewed the world from their TV screens. Lying horizontal on a couch, taking in the world as it was presented by others' interpretations. Be it the evening news with horrific stories of the greater world, or mundane TV shows with much less of it. With the view of Port Huron's Blue Water Bridge, I always knew more was out there, but how to get it. A dreamer's couch. But dreamer's only know how to from A to B, in the dreamworld. Here I was again, stuck on this couch, contemplating, just like I always had.

I thought back to a drawing I had worked to perfection as a teenager, an image of an angel chained to the ground. I must have drawn that angel in different poses of escape a thousand times. It always had the same title: 'Left Tied When All Else Flies.'

But I had escaped, and South Korea represented an escape hatch to the other side. Through all the stress and frustrations, it made me feel free. I felt I could do anything from the experience. The bonding experiences with different types of people, the ways you cope and adjust and make the best of situations. There was an element to that, that I had always have craved, had always wanted. I wanted to extend that, repeat that, experience more of that.

47

Even though I initially left Sasha by my choice, feeling pressured to leave her by her choice, was taking its emotional toll. I called her occasionally, and she always seemed pleased to hear from me: "HELLO! HOW ARE YOU? I miss you." But in the same breath, she would make it clear that she stood by her decision that we had moved on. In many ways, this was the best thing for me.

It put focus back to my long-term dreams and goals. It rerouted me to the place that I had intended originally. On the other hand, to an observer, I appeared completely lost.

When asked about my plans, I made offhand comments like, "Prague is supposed to be really nice, especially in spring," or "I don't have money, I'll go back to Korea and save up," or, "Now that I have a car again, I'm going back out to Portland." The facts were that I didn't have money, and I didn't have many options. But, I had confidence. I felt like I could make anything work, that I wanted to work.

I spent time at a local Barnes and Noble Bookstore, planning my escape route. It was 1997, and there was a lot of talk of Eastern Europe being the next "it" spot. Both Prague and Budapest were featured regularly—many young Americans were starting new lives for themselves there. I imagined myself among those expats, forging another new existence. I craved that experience again, that community, regardless of how dysfunctional and temporary it felt. But, I was convinced I could find the perfect expat community for myself.

Logically, Budapest made sense. It would be a Korea-Lite existence, and that is what I wanted. I bought a postcard and addressed it to Kupo Hagwan in Pusan, South Korea.

February 11, 1997

Dear Paris, Louis, King, Huck, Kristian, Joe, Stefano,
Melvin, Monica, and Linda,

Here I am, back in Michigan, and the trip will continue onward. I am 100% certain it will be Budapest, Hungary! Any of you are welcome to visit me anytime in Budapest; you will always have a place!

I will have a couch there, which seems to be where I've been living since I left Korea. You are welcome to stay as long as you'd like. Maybe we can start a new community in Europe. We can't all stay in Korea forever, can we?

I hope this message finds you all well.
안녕히계십시오
Adam

Once I mailed it, I parked my car under the Blue Water Bridge, the international connection between Michigan and Ontario. I sat in the car, and I overlooked the benches too cold to sit on during winter. I watched the large ships pass through the narrow St. Clair River as they came in from the larger waters of Lake Huron. Wouldn't it be great to just jump on any one of those, simply to see where it went? All of these massive hunks of metal, moving products all over the world.

...And I wondered if I might even see one with a Korean flag...and I imagined it would have dropped off cargo in Chicago and was on a return trip back to Pusan...and wouldn't it be great...to just scale the Blue Water Bridge from the underside...poise myself to drop on a Pusan-bound freighter...and just...go...go...go...go.

48

My mom made dinner some of the nights. "I never got to do this when you were kids," she said. "I worked all those years, and we are still in debt. Maybe if I'd refused to work, your dad wouldn't have moved around so much."

"I really don't mind, Mom. It's not a big deal, really."

"I especially regret that last move, when you had to change schools in your senior year. I should have made a stand then."

"Mom, that was years ago. I forgot it already."

"Well, things haven't changed here much since you left. We went up to the Huskies game last night. Port Huron lost."

"Oh yeah?" I felt numb hearing about local sports. It was the religion of the region. It all made my eyes gloss over.

"We want you to stay here as long as you want," my mom said.

When my dad was around, he brought in the employment ads, "Look at all these jobs in the area. Why don't you try to get a job in the mall?"

"I don't even like malls. I don't want to live here. I'd rather teach English overseas. Or I could work in a national park again. Why would I want to work in the mall like a teenager?"

He argued, "Well, it's a good way to save money, and you could live at home."

My Mom added, "And we'd like to have you here."

My Dad and I sat up at night and had long talks. "You know your brother lives at home and puts all of his earnings in a 501k retirement plan. He's going to retire by the time he's forty-five. Maybe you should think about that."

"I don't have any money to put into a retirement plan."

"Well, you should look into a career like your brother. He has it all figured out."

"I can't live like that, Dad. Why would I want to?"

"Well, you can't just wander around. You need some stability. Even if you need to go back to school to find something you like."

"Why?" I would say. "What's the reason? So I can come home and watch television in the evenings? You guys work and work and work, and all you do is watch television in the evening."

"Well, when your brother retires, he'll have money to travel and do things. You'll still be working."

"But I'm traveling now. I'm doing all the things I want to do now. I'm investing in myself, and it'll all pay off down the road. I can't invest myself in a nine-to-five job; some people work their whole lives and everything falls out from under them in the end. They invest in their wives, and their wives leave them. They buy big houses, and they lose their house. I'm not going to live like that."

We went round and round like that, but in the end, my Dad would tell me, "Well, we're proud of you and the things you've managed to do," and left it at that.

I ended most evenings by reading books at the kitchen table well past the time that everyone else went to bed. The quiet of the night appealed to me, much like it had when I was growing up. I was still planning escape routes—Just like I always had as a kid.

My Dad was usually the last one to bed, and sometimes we'd talk about what he was interested in—sports, religion, politics, and gambling.

Of the four, I much preferred the last one. "I went over to Canada again," he told me, "and I was up about three hundred dollars."

"Oh," I said. "What were you playing?"

"Well, they have these poker games, and, well, here, I'll show you." He'd find the deck of cards and demonstrate every rule and strategy that exists in the game.

"If this guy places his chips like this, then you know he has something, you see."

"Oh yes, I see. Oh yeah."

"Okay, let's say you have four hands—no, five. This guy always bluffs, but this guy never does. Okay, here we go, let's see what cards they have."

"Okay, okay."

And it would go on like this. By the end of the night, he'd described all of the different characters he'd played with, how they played and how they bet, and his philosophy on the whole thing.

That was always one of the things I enjoyed about my dad. Sometimes he could be really funny and entertaining, and sometimes it was just a long-winded speech that you didn't care to hear, but overall he was like the great television itself—you just couldn't turn it off. And even if you could, there was always just enough coming out of it that you'd sit there and listen anyhow.

***
49
***

February 21, 1997

Dear Joe, Huck, Paris, Stefano, Melvin, Louis, King, Kristian, Monica, Linda, and all you other wonderful people,

Not so sure about Budapest now. I'll go to a travel agent and just find the best deal. The flight will go on a credit card anyway, but I definitely plan to get back to teaching English. Maybe Eastern Europe, South America, or different parts of Asia—Japan, Taiwan, etc. Who knows?

Maybe Chile? I could see myself there.

Here's to no more couches!

안녕히계십시오

Adam

Sometimes, when you write a postcard, you only want to convey the essentials. And the stripped down version is exactly where you are with things. When I analyzed this, everything made sense. The world was open to me. I wanted to recreate that South Korean experience. Once I had that clarity of vision, I was better equipped to enjoy what I would soon be losing again.

Having a car in Michigan, gave me chance to just drive and think. I went down to Detroit frequently, just to get to know my home state better than I did before. I would reflect on a different era, knowing I had a great-grandfather who was a Detective in this city back in the 1920s and 30s. I never knew that man, but I did know one of this 17 kids, one of which was my grandfather. Their Detroit was long gone, most of it torn down along with the American highway system being built up. Typical of many with Irish roots, I've heard many of those descendants had become politicians, policemen, judges, and boxers. One of the stories goes that one of our relatives was so good at boxing, they matched him up with later legend, Joe Louis, but that bout made him realize he was beatable. All of those men struck as people who didn't sit around on couches. They were active men, descendants from years of hardships in Ireland, who navigated streets and waterways that took them up river to Detroit. My grandfather himself, became a ball boy in the 20s era, having grown up within short walking distance to Tiger Stadium. I heard that they had lived all over the city of Detroit, and way up into the Thumb of Michigan as well. I was told that my Grandfather raised his kids in just one house, as direct consequence of growing up in Detroit in countless houses of moving around. My Dad seemed to raise his kids similar to my Great-Grandfather. I took well to moving, and thrived on it. Maybe I took on my Great-Grandfather's relocating proclivities. My grandfather himself was a train jumper, who had countless stories of how to catch moving ones. So I had a bit of his psyche integrated into my own, no doubt.

Port Huron was on Lake Huron, up in the Thumb. Go north from there and you followed expansive Lake Huron, as opposed to the narrow St. Clair River that went south towards Detroit. Going up, was an expansive of sorts. Lexington and Port Sanilac had breakwalls, which were places I might encounter my grandfather. I'd heard numerous legends of the man, as he dived and swam large distances off these breakwalls, in all types of weather and alcoholic conditions. He was one of the family who gravitated northwards Thumb-direction wise. Many people from Detroit had as well, and I enjoyed their stories, "Oh, so where in Detroit did you grow up?" When my grandfather answered, you could see the 'oh man, that was a rough area.'

But up north, I'd walk these Port Sanilac and Lexington breakwalls to clear my own mind. Lexington Heights had cottages, with benches overlooking the water on cliffs. With the cold weather, I could park the car, turn off the car engine, and simply listen to the sounds of the ocean. Shanties dotted the frozen lakes, another legendry tale I'd heard about my grandfather, always one to test the boundaries, he'd be the first to drive vehicles the farthest out on the ice, the earliest and latest in the season. I imagined I took on some his characteristics, in my own travel-focused way.

Closer to home, I had the Fort Gratiot Lighthouse in Port Huron itself, which was just on the periphery of a beach. This time in Michigan, the waters were frozen over, and I found it fascinating to see the paths that ships created or forced their way through the iced over lakes. That was how to do things, just push through, create your paths, and turn the ice into small workable pushable chunks. A lighthouse could guide all it wanted, but wasn't it better to just forge ahead, with or without guides.

I spent about a month in Michigan in total, and the time for me to go was approaching. I had too much time on my hands, and no peers my age to socialize with. Well, it's not like they didn't exist, they were just of a different mindset.

I still recalled the first time I made my escape westward. I told a good friend, "Hey man, I think I located a way to get out to Arizona!"

"That's great Adam, you still going to be back around on weekends?"

The more plans I made for this escape, the more I thought of the connections that I had made with like-minded individuals in South Korea. Why forge a new community somewhere, when I already had a community of connections? Perhaps lighthouses weren't used simply for guiding, but for grounding those who were on the move. I could push forward more easily, having already spotted that lighthouse.

Following through on the once seeming clarity of my letter to Korea, I found an airline deal to Santiago. So, I wrote a letter to the 'lighthouse of Deokcheon,' informing them that Chile was it. Immediately after posting the letter, I went back to that travel agency with my credit card, and found a better flight back to South Korea. I bought that ticket instead. Some might say I was floundering in my decisions, but I was just forging ahead, Great Lakes style.

The day before I left, Sasha randomly called me. I informed her that I was going back to Pusan. She was surprised, "Were you even going to call and tell me?" I hadn't planned that, but I told her that of course I was. But it gave a closure to everything. Having a connection, was still good. We all had to move on with our lives, and I felt I was back on track now. Couches, lighthouses, freighters, and that was it for Michigan. It was just the grounding I needed, to get moving.

So, after a little over a month at home, I had my plan. It was time, once again, to say good-bye. My mom told me, over and over, "You know if things don't work out, you can always stay here."

Then my dad would follow with, "Lots of jobs in the Port Huron area. You could live at home like your brother does."

"Good-bye couch!" I said to myself. "Good-bye, Mom and Dad."

There was a grounding support there, one a person might not suspect at first glance. Don't let that gravestone have your birthplace and death place in the same place.

***

50

***

The next morning, my mom drove me to the Detroit airport. She asked me, "When will I see you next?" I promptly responded that I had no idea. Then I boarded the plane, spent fifteen hours in a tense upright position, and arrived back in Korea.

It overwhelmed me when I first arrived. I couldn't believe I was back in this country again. I identified two other Americans on the plane, one of whom turned out to have been to Korea before, and immediately we went into Korea mode—much to the shock of the other American. We pushed and shoved, and we were sure to stand close to the person in front of us in line so that no one could jump ahead of us. Always, always, always, people were jumping in front of you—in the post office, waiting for a bus, in line at McDonald's, wherever. If you didn't have yourself firmly planted, nearly touching the person in front of you, you better believe some Korean was going to wedge his way between the two of you to cut in line.

So I was in line with the other American, jockeying for space going through customs, while the third American kept falling further and further behind, because he refused to nearly rub up against whoever jumped in front of him.

Before long, I was in the city streets of Pusan, calling a cab and weaving my way back to my old apartment. Sadly, Stefano was leaving Korea shortly; and he was one of the reasons I had booked my flight so suddenly. He was out that night—with a girl, I was told. That left friend Joe and myself to catch up on the changes that had taken place in the last four months since I'd been...been...what was I doing, exactly? Sometimes you do things so personal, you can hardly share or describe them. And even if you could, how would you convey them?

Before I could articulate anything, a new teacher entered the apartment. In Korea, particularly throughout the 1990s, they rotated the teachers almost monthly. Many language institutes were so shady and unregulated, so exploitative, that many teachers couldn't get through a year contract. Nonetheless, Clove from Montreal was living there now.

236

Clove had cropped black hair and fashionable attire. He moved, and spoke, quickly. He talked with us for a few minutes, pushed his long bangs behind his ear, where they met his shorter cut hair. He gave me a smile that looked like it might abruptly disappear and he excused himself in search of sleep. Little did I know, I'd become good friends with him, just like I did with all the others.

It occurred to me, this lifestyle, this constant coming and going of new co-workers. Clove was part of the new, Stefano would soon be part of the old. This was the quintessential Korea experience, in many ways, for many expats. This constant greeting and grieving of people you'd closely get to know. The emotional highs and lows of that attached as well.

After Clove excused himself, Joe updated me on everything I'd missed, which included the news that Melvin had left Korea. I laughed at the mere mention of Melvin's name, and Joe couldn't resist telling me about his last day. "Well," he began, "They let go of Melvin one month before his contract ended." I nodded my head. "Well," he began again, "Melvin had all this stuff, bags and boxes of comic books, posters, shit in general, tons of it," and I nodded my head again. "Not like us" he told me, "I don't know why he'd carry that much stuff around." I nodded my head in agreement, not like us—who essentially have nothing but books and clothes.

"So here's Melvin, with boxes and bags that he can't even carry, and he has them all lined up to go to Taiwan, where he'll be teaching next." I nodded my head again. "He finally got them outside the apartment, the elevator came, and he said to me, 'I've never done traveling like you guys, do you think I have too much stuff?' I just kept throwing his bags and boxes in the elevator and saying, 'Bye, Melvin, have a nice trip.' And all along he kept saying back to me, 'I don't travel like you guys. Am I okay? Is everything okay?' And I pushed him back in the elevator and said, 'Bye, Melvin. Bye!'" I was laughing. It was mean-spirited, but it was one of the funniest stories I had ever heard.

That's how we all learn though, just like a kid being thrown into the swimming pool, you learn to swim. You take too many boxes one time, and the next time you learn how irrelevant material shit is for your life. Especially when forced to carry it around from place to place, you become aware of how little of it you actually need. You get too caught up in it, and you become one of those people working their asses off to afford a bigger house, just to house the material shit you've accumulated. The quicker we learn to separate our stuff from our lives, the more flexibility we have to live interesting lives outside a passive couch-sitting, material-collecting stationary-grazing type of existence. Melvin would take something from the experience, no doubt.

We kept talking. "Can you believe what happened to me in Portland?" I asked.

"I never showed those letters to anyone," he immediately told me. I was surprised. When I wrote them, I assumed they were probably being read by everyone. I felt they conveyed all the romantic tragedy of my circumstances, which I liked.

Joe told me he now had a Korean girlfriend, but when I pressed for details, he was hesitant to give them. I could be the same way from time to time, particularly with the things that were most personal to me. I felt the more you shared your true intentions, the more others would question them—and perhaps make you question them yourself.

Joe blurted out, "Broccoli? But I don't even like broccoli! When did I buy broccoli?"

I smiled widely, "I don't even like broccoli! Why would I, Melvin, even buy broccoli?" I pushed up my pretend glasses, crinkled my nose, and squinted my eyes a few times.

"The real tragedy of Melvin was that they let him go after his eleventh month," Joe said. We both knew what this meant. Korean contracts were for a year, and if foreign teachers completed their twelfth month, they received a bonus thirteenth month pay and airfare home. It was common for a Korean hagwan to avoid paying up, by firing teachers in the eleventh month.

"Fuck the hagwans!" I blurted, half joking. "And fuck Stefano! He ain't even back yet on his last day, and my first day back! Time for bed."

"Yep, time for bed. Welcome back, Adam Wanderson."

"Good to be back. Good to see you too, Joe Moretti." With that, Joe shuffled off to bed.

Alone in the kitchen, I reflected on Melvin. His outsider status, the way he never quite fit in. The way he was almost symbolic of all of us foreigners, who never quite fit into Korean society. The way he came, never fully adjusted, never fully accepted even among us. The way he transitioned out, just as quickly as he transitioned in. His parting was no more dramatic than his arrival.

At the kitchen table, I browsed the things lying on the table and saw my postcard from Michigan. A couple of the lines that caught my attention:

> *I am 100% certain it will be Budapest, Hungary! Any*
> *of you are welcome to visit me anytime in Budapest; you*
> *will always have a place!*

Budapest, eh? I left it sitting among the half-read newspapers and random shopping advertisements. Now that I was back in the rotation for beds, I moved my stuff into the third most popular bedroom out of the four in the apartment. No one occupied the fourth at this time, it was just Joe and Clove, but that would change shortly. Things were constantly in flux in Korea, but I realized that I loved that aspect.

The third best bedroom had been mine before, and my Korean map still hung on the wall. South Korea was firmly in the middle, with the Americas to the right and Europe to the left. Many of the books I'd left behind remained on the shelf under the map, untouched. I sat on the warmth of the ondol floor, reached into my bag, and added more.

As I drifted off and closed my tired eyes, I swore I could hear Melvin's knocking, his voice calling out, "Heeee-woooooaaaa." He was gone, but his ghost remained. I had left, too, but my ghost had remained, and now my body too was inhabiting my old haunts. Here, where there were no couches. Here, where I was home.

***

51

***

After a long sleep well into the next day, I got a phone call from the girls' apartment. They were finished with their classes and wanted me to come on down. I collected some beer along the way and walked through their front door without knocking, as if I lived there. I gave a shout as I always had in the past, and received the warm welcome that always made me feel good—"Adam!"

Monica and Linda hadn't changed a bit. They were still gossip hounds. Maybe I was, too, as it all interested me. Once I distributed the beer, we got to talking just like old times.

"So Paris left," Monica told me. "It was about time, too! She was so stressed out. Every time someone would look at her, she would say, 'What the hell is your problem?' She really needed to go home."

"Yeah, Korea will do that to you," I responded to her.

I reflected back on Paris, her loud Texan voice, her blond exuberance, and her sparky attitude. "Aw, man. Paris."

I missed Paris. I had had a connection with her. We understood each other, and I understood why she left. I didn't need to have a physical relationship for a connection with a Korean woman or Sasha like I had assumed before. I just needed that mental supportive connection, and I had that with Paris, and most everyone who I had ever met in Korea as a fellow expat. I reflected back to Sasha, and realized she too supported my general nature, and even that situation had to happen to get back on track.

I thought of Paris' lows and what she must have dealt with. They followed my own trajectory. She came with the high hopes that we all had when arriving in Korea, and slowly watched things dissipate around her, Kristian leaving, the relationship with Stefano not working, the tight-knit group dissipating. She hadn't made it the full year contract, but she came close. She had all the experiences I had and even more.

"Monica's right," Linda continued. "You don't understand, Adam. She REALLY needed to go!"

Monica smirked in that way that she always did, with a slight grin from the side of her mouth, "Paris was getting downright abusive."

"That'll happen to the best of us," I responded.

"And your friend Joe," Monica launched into the next target. "I'm sorry, I know he's your friend, but my God, he's an asshole!" She shook her head, looking into my eyes for my response, "He's like a black cloud. When he's in the room, things go dark. It's incredible. I mean, he's witty when he wants to be, but he's usually a jerk!"

"Uh...okay." What could I say?

Monica launched into a monologue, taking a break from Joe-bashing to lay into Clove. Apparently, he wasn't socializing with them either.

"We used to be a unit, a family unit," she sighed.

I heard the front door open, and my old friend poked his bespectacled face through the door, his oversized shirt hanging from his shoulders. "Huck!" We sat around and reminisced about the old times—the Melvin Factor, the Minneapolis music scene, all those common interests rambling around in our heads.

We might have lost Melvin, Paris, and soon Stefano, but I still had Huck! "Oh, yessirree, Minneapolis. A lot of great bands in Minneapolis, oh yessirree."

Still suffering jetlag, and not wanting to miss seeing Stefano on his last night, I had to excuse myself. I wandered back up the hill, went into my old apartment, and knocked on Stefano's door. No response—he must already went out to celebrate his last night out in Korea. The house was empty. Joe was out with his girlfriend, and Clove asleep. I stumbled back into my old bedroom, avoiding my three somewhat unpacked bags on the floor, and went to sleep.

When I woke up from my much-needed night of recovery sleep, I figured it would be safe to wake Stefano. He answered the door nearly nude—apparently with a Korean girlfriend that he'd made while I was gone. He opened his door slightly, but blocking the view, to reserve the privacy of the girl inside.

"Good to see you, Adam!" His curly black locks hung in his eyes. "What time is it?"

"Um, not quite eleven."

"Eleven? I need to be on a bus by one!"

"If you need anything, I'll go with you," I responded.

"Yep! Just a second, be right back..."

Stefano disappeared behind his door, and I heard him trying to get in one more lay with the girl. A quick shower ensued. There was more discussion, and they apparently came to the agreement that she would wait in his room for him to get back.

His number one errand was to get to the bank and exchange his money. We hit the bus and tried to get to the busy Deokcheon rotary. It was strange how the ghosts spoke to you in these spots. I vividly recalled arriving and trying to learn the bus routes—Stefano's explanations only confused me more at the time. Now they were second nature. This time I shared with him how to navigate Bangkok. "Stefano, when you get to the Bangkok airport, make sure that you..." and on and on I went. Later I shifted the conversation to finances, as that was of my major stresses when I had left.

"Yep, I have all my savings from this year," Stefano told me. "I'm going to sit on a beach in Thailand and enjoy myself until the money runs out."

"Good plan. I'll be accumulating it for a while now, and I'll join you when I can!"

At the bank, Stefano withdrew a large chunk of Korean bills. The largest bank note that existed in Korea at that time were the ten-thousand-won notes, the equivalent of an American ten-dollar bill. In 1996, the standard teacher's salary was one point four million won a month, so to withdraw one paycheck, meant you had 140 bills to stuff into your pockets. Stefano had way more than just a single paycheck saved up.

We continued to catch up on the last four months, Stefano too time-stressed, occasionally exclaiming, "I gotta get back to the apartment and back!" I had no idea how he managed to get back there for that one last lay and then pack, but he did—Stefano was an advanced expert on procrastination and getting it all done. But it worked for him.

When Stefano emerged from his bedroom once again, he had money bulging in his pockets, and probably throughout his bags, and he had his girlfriend on his arm. She would be taking him to the airport. Clove, Joe, and I stood at the door to say farewell. I was already sad to see him go. "Bye, Stefano! Good luck!"

I would miss that guy as well. From Day 1, we had connected. I recalled Haeundae Beach, even from my first weekend, I felt like I had already known Stefano for years. We'd been through a lot as hagwan colleagues and roommates. We had a significant amount of similarities, and anyone willing to make a move way out of their comfort zone, to South Korea, that kind of person, was always the kind of person, that I would relate to. But saying goodbye to him, was much like saying goodbye to Joe. I knew it didn't matter, as I knew I'd see him again.

After Stefano left, I felt an urge to make my way to the Happy Town convenience store next to our apartment.

I entered through a plastic cover that doubled as the front door. The couple was always there, and they didn't miss a beat to greet me with a hearty Korean hello. I don't know if they had realized I had been gone, but it didn't matter. They knew I was one of their local foreigners.

We did the typical Korean gestures symbolizing respect, this involved the left hand touching the right arm, as you handed something to someone else with your right hand. "I love you," the old ajusshi said, as he handed me my change.

"And I love Korea," I said back to him. "I really missed you all."

Stefano loved the connections just as much as I had. He always got a kick out of the Happy Town 'I love you.' It occurred to me that I used to ignore their 'I love you', and Stefano would respond to it. But I just responded it Stefano-style myself.

While others of us had simply been burned out, and left through the contract for various reasons, Stefano had completed his entirely. He had weathered the storm of his relationship with Paris, as well as the Middle School stuff and all the rest. I was on his path. But he was off towards Thailand, maybe he was on my path? We were all interconnected.

52

After my arrival and Stefano's departure, we all settled in to wait for the new teacher. Our world resembled MTV's *The Real World*: we could end up with a roommate from one of Dante's seven layers of hell, or we could get a real cool person. But it didn't matter who arrived, as it was all about the experience. I'd learn something from anyone, regardless of who it was, and I looked forward to that now.

The new teacher arrived, and I'll always remember how we met. I was sitting on the toilet with the door unlocked, enjoying the relative privacy of my own mind behind closed doors, when these big long arms applied a tremendous force to the outside my not-very-well-fortified castle door. I immediately applied pressure back of my own. There was a power struggle, the door gave, and I looked up at a blue-eyed, blond-haired Adonis of a man with a very surprised look on his face. His otherwise tan face turned red, and he wordlessly turned around and went back into his bedroom, where he began unpacking in a whirlwind of nervous activity. I locked the bathroom door, checked it several times over, and hurriedly resumed another few minutes of my toilet usage.

I came out, still not having formally met the new teacher, and busied myself with a breakfast-related activity—it involved setting a container of juice next to the *Korean Herald*. I settled in my chair and began flipping the pages of the newspaper. The new guy—who would shortly introduce himself as Kendall—and I, seemed to be at an impasse; neither of us ready to break the ice.

Eventually, my old friend Joe shuffled out of his bedroom, Kendall wandered in and joined us, and the awkwardness dissipated as we sat around and gave him the rundown on teaching and living in South Korea. Anyway, that's how I first met Kendall.

Since I was now just a visitor to the apartment, I left my bedroom largely empty, much like Joe's minimalist room. I didn't sign up for another Kupo contract, because they were too exploitative the first time around. Melvin getting shafted out of his bonus was yet another confirmation.

My only real plan was to be back with my community of like-minded friends and ideally take on private teaching gigs, which required no contract and frequent visa runs. King helped me land a key part-time teaching job out at Haeundae Beach, where I taught kids three days a week. Ironically, it paid more than the 7-days a week Kupo Hagwan job.

I had no idea that little Haeundae hagwan would later install classroom cameras that would project live video streams from my classroom to throughout the hagwan. This seems harmless, but disciplining young learners in English, was a consistent struggle, that I didn't want broadcasted. But it didn't matter, as overall it paid more and I worked less.

Despite the long commute to Haeundae, it was fantastic to still have the bedroom at Taekyung Happy Town Apartments. With their busy schedules, I seldom saw them. It gave me a quiet place to read, write, and study. But not so isolated, that I wasn't plugged into our social group.

53

I spent more time in our apartment than my roommates did. It didn't matter, as I had great relationships with everyone there, and always felt welcome. Usually Joe was the first to come home. A snippet of one night might go something like this, and Joe would tell me, "I haven't spoken to Li in a week. Haven't seen her in class. The last time I saw her, she was thinking about whether she wanted to pursue a relationship with me or not. I told her I would be here."

"Don't force it, just wait it out." I was done with my Catcher in the Rice Field shtick. I wanted it to work out for him. I was going to immerse myself into Korea now and I could learn all the subtleties of that by observing his connection with Li. I was going to be an active participant in Korea from now on.

He usually brushed the personal stuff aside, as his preferred discussion was about politics or popular culture. He brought up the situation in North Korea, "What're they thinking up there?" he asked me. "Don't they know the United States would support South Korea? They'd literally destroy them if they tried to attack!"

"Yes, but I don't think that matters, Joe. They're desperate; their economy is falling apart. It's a matter of saving face. There's no way they're going to just hand over rule to South Korea. It has to escalate to the point of no return, because the rulers have a nice lifestyle up there." I would spurt this out while I drank from a large carton of Korean peach juice at the kitchen table.

Joe played music from his room, usually the Rolling Stones or Jimi Hendrix. He busied himself in the kitchen, making his healthy dinners that featured broccoli. "But North Korea doesn't have a chance," he would tell me. "WHY? Why don't they know communism doesn't work? Why don't they just give up?"

Things had been escalating again between North and South Korea, and there were constant rumors of war in the news. No one knew when the attack might come, but it seemed inevitable. Sometimes we felt like we were all just waiting around until it occurred. It was a constant concern for newly arrived teachers who brought it up as a discussion topic in and out of the classroom. But the students didn't find it very interesting; most pretending the conflict didn't exist.

When I switched topics to my favorite conversation of travel, he'd say, "The one country I really want to see is North Korea. Very few outsiders have ever been there, but I'd like to see what really goes on there." Each night, we rehashed these topics, and I never tired of them.

Clove would come home next and make dinner for himself. Joe would be in bed by that time. I'd still be sitting at the kitchen table, maybe having finished another seven or eight pages of whatever book I had. The carton of peach juice would have dropped by three or four inches, and Clove would come through the door. Clove was usually tired at night, so he would talk for fifteen minutes or so before going to bed. Most afternoons between classes, he went swimming, or he taught some private lessons, or he slept. We had some serious conversations, but usually not at that time of night.

Then, once Clove went to bed, Kendall would arrive. We talked about traveling, or ex-girlfriends—we both had that experience in common. Or we'd talk about writing.

"That's what I'd like to do," he told me, "travel and write." He paused and reflected, "I wrote one this week entitled, 'The Crazy Ivan.' Because, you see, during World War II, there were these submarines. When they thought someone was following them, they'd turn and go after the pursuer. Here in Korea, with everyone staring at us, and sometimes following us, I like to suddenly stop and start walking in the opposite direction, just to see what happens." He smiled, and I couldn't help but laugh.

Most nights went like this, but some evenings, Monica would call and ask, "So what are you guys doing up there? You and Kendall want to come on down?" Sometimes we would, and sometimes we wouldn't.

Clove and Joe didn't want to do anything after work, so usually it was Kendall and I who would go down. We played cards and drank beer. Kendall was a great storyteller, and I always listened, but if you let Monica go, she would talk and talk and talk. I would have liked to hear Linda speak more, as I'm sure she must have had actual opinions on things. But that simply wasn't to be. But she was one of us, regardless.

Kendall and Clove represented the constant change, the constant greetings, and the constant farewells. More people left, and more people came, and absolutely nothing stayed the same. I felt like by the time you analyzed and made sense of your current situation, everything would once again be different, with all different people.

I thought about how everything was just being recycled. New people reincarnated to play old roles. Sasha's new boyfriend, Stefano's trip to Thailand, Kupo's constant stream of new teachers—everything changed only to retain frail images of what had once just been there.

My head spun with the rapidity with which strong friendships were created and their bonds broken in this country. Everyone I was familiar with upon arrival in this country had moved on. Skate, Caden, Melvin, Paris, Stefano, Louie, and Kristian— all moved on—just as we all would. Their replacements were now here, but for how long? It was all one big rotation.

***

54

***

In the spring of 1997, no one would have guessed that Korea's current run of prosperity would lead into a financial catastrophe ending with an IMF bailout. The economy was exploding in Pusan, with more demands for English and a sudden influx of foreign faces.

Places like the Monk Bar were so packed with foreigners that the clientele expanded to occupy other nearby bars around the Pusan National University area—Tombstone Bar, Crossroads, Hard-N-Heavy, Road House, Rock & Roll, and others with appealing western names. It seemed there was always another around a corner vying for some of the expat foreigner crowd coming in. The previous year, foreigners anywhere in this city of millions were a major reason for any Korean local to stop and stare for a while. Now unfamiliar foreign faces were becoming more of the norm. A newsletter entitled *The Expatriate* emerged, and the foreign community began writing stories, and soliciting business ads to target the expats in the city, predominately in the PNU area.

The *Lonely Planet* travel guide for Korea, the previous year, described Pusan as a concrete jungle to be quickly navigated on the way to Japan. It insinuated there was nothing noteworthy to see in this city. The latest edition exploded with information, derived almost entirely from the expat community that was being created that summer. Every one of our new hangouts would be recorded for future visitors in the next Lonely Planet guide.

The Monk Bar was still the nucleus to the community. It had an actual bar with bar stools, which was a rarity in Pusan in 1997. Most Koreans socialized at large tables that could accommodate all of their drinks and many snacks. They focused solely on the group of people that they went out with. Monk Bar appealed more to foreigners—it was a place where people could go by themselves, have some drinks, and interact with people at the bar. Even better than Monk, in my opinion, was Tombstone, another foreign-friendly establishment without the required Korean anju purchasing system, and an entire wrap-around bar with barstools.

The Monk was still the center of it all, as you'd meet the most eclectic types of people. There was one face I would regularly see at Monk, even if it didn't have much significance at the time. His name was Gary. A few years later, at a different time in my life, I would turn on the TV back in the States and see Gary on one of those dating shows coming out of Los Angeles. The premise of that show was that a couple agreed to go on a date with different people. They recorded the date for the TV audience, and discussed live whether their relationship was worth pursuing for them, based on a first date comparison with a different person.

Gary failed miserably on the show. His girlfriend accused him of being a lost soul who didn't know what he wanted in life. "My boyfriend was living in Korea, and he always talks about going back. He doesn't know if he wants to get married or get a real job. He's rootless, and he doesn't have focus. He complains about Korea—but he always talks about going back."

In 1997, he didn't know he would late be on national American TV projecting a common theme among Korea expats—the love/hate relationship they had developed with their second country. A certain strain of us regularly returned to Korea over the coming years. When I saw him on TV, he represented a pull that many of us old expats in Korea had with the country, when we weren't actually in it.

In the spring of 1997, the Pusan expat scene was a happening place, and few would have guessed that the owner of Monk Bar would commit suicide when IMF hit.

Joe wouldn't know that later this year, he would lose all his savings—nor did he know that he would marry the Korean girl that he was dating. He didn't know his Korean won savings in dollar terms would be cut in half because of the 1997 Asian financial crisis, and that he would wait out the financial crisis for his Korean won to recover. A time when many Koreans would donate their own gold to help pay off government debt.

No one knew any of these things in the spring of 1997.

***

55

***

In 1997, as I was running to Haeundae to teach consistently, and I had more free time, so I became a regular of the PNU expat scene. I now had time to explore, get to know more people, and understand Korea better. It also meant that I didn't always get to see my old friends as much.

But, one night at PNU's Monk Bar, I ran into Louie. He spat at me, "Adam! Dude! I never see you. It's a whole other world on this side of the mountain!" Pusan was a large city sandwiched between mountains and the ocean. It was nice to be frequently be out of Deokcheon, which had little access to anywhere.

"It's hard to get ahold of each other once we leave the house, isn't it?" We could call each other at home, but we were otherwise out of communication. The big challenge of the city was the getting places in a large construction-filled city. It was impossible to coordinate plans in an efficient manner. Now that my social circle kept expanding with old friends spreading around the city, it became a major coordinating challenge.

"Just use the payphone when you get near my place, dude!"

"Yeah, but just getting near your place!" Louie was living near Seomyeon, not an area that I frequented as much as PNU.

"Aw, c'mon, dude!" Louie spat. "I have a base pass! I can get you on base. You can see western movies, eat western food. It's like a little mini America." Camp Hialeah was the U.S. Military base near Seomyeon, the location of the late night haunts of Dallas Club and Legion where Skate indirectly caused Stefano's broken arm incident. For me though, I wasn't interested in that area, I mostly just wanted to go to PNU.

But, being that Louis lived there, and I hadn't seen him much. "All right, it's a deal. I'll make my way over there next weekend."

As for that weekend, we were near the mandatory 2pm bar closing time. It was set by government law, and enforced throughout the country. This would be hard to imagine a few years later, when everything went 24 hours, and nowhere ever closed.

But in 1997, we dealt with it. The system dictated that you had to be in a place before it closed; and as long as you stayed there, you could drink all night. But you couldn't barhop, and you couldn't go anywhere new. Additionally, bars had to be kept quiet, as if they were actually closed. If they were loud and disrupted anyone outside, the bar could be raided by the police, and everyone kicked out. The key, at this time of night, was to find a place where you wanted to stay—one with a crowd you wanted to be part of, and one that wouldn't be raided.

Louie spurted out at me, "Where should we settle in before the bars close?" He towered above me with his large body frame.

"How about Crossroads?"

"Nah, dude, I got kicked out of there."

"What? How'd you get kicked out of Crossroads?"

"Dude, some dude was being an asshole, and he poured a pitcher of beer over my head."

"And you got banned?" I knew Louie well enough to know he was probably being evasive on some front.

"Yeah, dude, I know..."

Louie was the first guy I had ever met in Korea, and I still thought back to the first offering of beer, during his lunch time. He was also the first to meet at the hagwan. The first guy I knew to move to this more interesting side of Pusan. Flash forward twenty years, he was also one of the guys who made Korea a home for himself for the long haul. He enriched my life, by knowing him.

Nonetheless, before official national bar closing time, we escaped Monk Bar for Tombstone. It was a good choice. Tombstone was larger, and it had a long wrap-around bar, a rarity for Korea. It was also tucked away from the main strip, slightly under the radar for being raided.

I saw familiar faces in the bar, as much as the expat scene was expanding, it was still somewhat limited. My new roommate Clove was coincidentally sitting next to my old Kupo Hagwan co-worker friend, Kristian. I immediately joined both of them, and I asked her, "Where are you now, my old Christian noraebang singing friend?"

"HEY," she exclaimed, follow by, "Just a second guys, I need to check my *bee-pee* (삐삐)." Excusing herself, "Can you hold my seat?" She made her way to the payphone in the back of the bar.

As Louie was also with me, I asked him, "Bee-pee? Is that some kind of code word for something?"

Clove pushed the hair out of his eyes. "Nah, it's a pager. We need to get those things, Adam. Enough with not being able to contact anyone until you get home at the end of the weekend."

"Pager? How does it work?"

"It vibrates when someone leaves you a message."

"Crazy!"

When Kristian got back, I extended my hand for it. "This thing stores your messages?" I examined it closely, "So, if I want to contact you with this, what do I do?"

"You just call my number, it vibrates. Then I call my own number on the payphone, and I can hear what you said."

"That's crazy! I can get messages while I'm out of the apartment? Crazy!"

"Yes, you can buy them everywhere now. Only 10,000 won for a month."

"Can I try this right now? Can I call you right now?"

"Go ahead, here's my bee-pee number."

I navigated my way towards the bar's payphone, next to the bathrooms. There was a long line to wait, which wasn't normal. A line for the payphone, at this time, inside the bar? This pee-bee thing must be exploding.

In time, the peebee culture continued to advance. It was based on a system that you could leave a message, or punch in numbers for people to call you back. In time, those numbers took on various codes. For example, '1004,' meant 'angel,' '8282' meant 'hurry,' and '18' meant 'screw you.' These were mostly phonetic-based, for example, '8282' sounded like the Korean word, bali bali (빨리 빨리), which means hurry, hurry. It didn't take long for every foreigner to have one of these.

It was interesting how quickly these beepees became obsolete with the emergence of cellphones. Korea grasped onto those quickly, and when I was to leave Korea and come back a few years later, they were deeply ingrained into the culture.

Quite a contrast from the United States, where post-Pusan, I ended up living in New York City for a couple years. The U.S. didn't embrace it with nearly as much gusto. In fact, I recalled going back and forth between the U.S. and South Korea, and seeing the Korean cellphones continually getting tinier and more pocket-size all the time, whereas the U.S. had a nearly non-existent cellphone culture, where people pulled out large shoebox-looking phones, usually purchased for emergency usage only. Of course the U.S. did get into them later, but it was at a much slower pace.

Korea was endearing in this regard. Just how quickly it embraced technology and change. Even the subways and bullet trains throughout the country. Things were always happening in South Korea. Whereas the United States, they didn't embrace things like public transportation or any public or social good, in fact, those things were largely met with strong resistance. It made South Korea a very dynamic place in which to live.

56

The following weekend, I went to visit Louie near his Seomyeon apartment.

"Have you heard from King?"

"Nah, But I have his beepee number," Louie spat that out nonchalantly.

"Yeah, what is it?" He gave it to me. I was getting connected.

Off to a pay phone to give him a message, and later I got my own 'Buzzzzz Buzzzzz'.

I ran back to the same pay phone, and listened to his message. He was telling me to get to PNU, as he had something he wanted me to see. He wanted me to look for Dream Internet Cafe, on one of the streets just outside PNU Station.

When I found his location, I saw a coffee shop with computers along the walls. Computers? In a coffee shop? They called this coffee shop an 'Internet Cafe.'

I saw my tall, soft-spoken, goatee-faced, old friend in front of one of the computers.

"Hey, King. What's up with this place?"

"Adam, this is just my second time here myself."

"What are you doing on the computer?"

"If you sign up through Internet Dream Cafe, they will give you a free e-mail address. You can go back as much as you want, only 50,000 won for a month.

"What's an e-mail?"

"It's like a written letter, but it goes through the computer."

So I signed up for my first e-mail address through Dream Internet Cafe in Pusan. I could write any name I wanted, then follow it with @dream-net.co.kr, or whatever it was at the time.

My understanding was that each computer had its own address. I assumed I had to find the same computer to check my e-mail each time I went. King and I exchanged a few e-mails, so I could see how it worked.

On the third time that I went back to Dream Internet Cafe, there was someone else at my computer. I asked if he would be done soon, as I wanted to check my email.

He gave me that look. You know *that* look. "Hey man, you can check your email on any of the other empty computers."

"How do you figure?"

"You have a Dream-net.co.kr email address, right?

"Yeah."

"Check it over there, it'll work anywhere in here."

I tried it, and he was right. I opened up my email, excited to see that I had mail. I had something from King again, I had something from Joe, and I had something from a good friend who later introduced me to Hotmail. Getting an email was much like getting a letter in the mail. It offered excitement, even if it said nothing more than a simple, "Let me know if you get this email."

"Yes, I did," I responded to all three of the emails individually, followed with, "How are you today?" This was at a time well before spam mail and junk mail and Facebook. If you received an email, it was always personalized, and instantaneous. This was in direct contrast to regular postal mail such as the postcard I sent from Michigan, which arrived in Korea well after I did.

Buzzzz Buzzzzz. The bee-pee again. I ran to a telephone to see who left me a message. Amazing. I called King back, and told him, "I was just emailing you. Check it out later. I'm at the Dream Internet Cafe today."

Another weekend, I made my way back to Dream Internet Cafe, when I ran into a friend named Brad, in the streets. Brad represented that new type of friend, as I expanded my horizons in Pusan, getting to know more people every weekend. Louie and Brad, they were both two people who still lived in South Korea twenty years later, in 2016, just as they had in Pusan in 1996.

"Hey, are you off to check your email?"

"Yep, there's a second internet shop now, called Soloriens. Only 25,000 won/month."

"Do I have to get another email address for that too?"

"No, just use Hotmail."

"Hotmail? What's that?"

"It's a free email address. You can check Hotmail at any computer, at any computer cafe."

"Weird! How does it store your messages?"

"I don't know. It just does."

I got it, and he was right. I emailed my three friends, letting them know my new email address.

From that time on, it became my habit. I would buy a large Cass bottle of beer from outside, bring it in, wait for a computer, and then email people all the time. Every day you wondered who might 'find you' of past friends, and I equally spent time looking to connect with my own friends. Prior to this, when you relocated, you lost complete contact with most everyone you knew from the previous place.

Soloriens served food and drinks, and sat you in comfortable sofa chairs. They had them pushed up to a long rows of computers that stretched across both walls. It was completely different than the later partitioned, compartmentalized, pc-bang style just a few years later. They would take over all of Korea, filling every niche and cranny of the country, making South Korea one of the most wired countries in the world.

57

All of these new and old people at Kupo Hagwan, living over in Deokcheon, began to fade away from my daily existence. They were stuck there, working seven days a week, from six in the morning until ten at night. I simply wasn't able to see them as often as those who had made it into their second contracts, away from that hagwan. I always had 'my room' with them, but my schedule pushed me out of the apartment more, and throughout city. They were stationary and fixed, and tired.

With that, my wanderlust was kicking in. Seeing more of Pusan, made me want to see more of everything. I saw myself originally arriving in Deokcheon as a baby, not knowing anything. Not knowing what a horrible contract I was in, not knowing that dog markets weren't typical, and not knowing that Deokcheon people were more a type of person, representing a completely different time of Korea. I saw all of my expat connections there as family, we weathered something together.

I saw myself as a young boy, on a mountainside. To the left, remained that narrow little existence, that familiar mother figure nearby representing all that I had known. To the right, represented a long uphill narrow road, one that appeared to go in multiple directions, taking me various places, leading ever upward. However narrow and limited the view might have been starting that path, it would ultimately lead upward, until the view and scope was so much larger than I could have ever imagined before.

I saw that I wanted to keep taking that unknown path. I saw Korea as the starting point for that greater perspective, and I wanted to experience more, with Korea as the springboard. Initially it was hard for me to get over all of the staring and attention, but I adapted, and Korea adapted. It was a minor stumbling block that initially seemed like a major one. But, it's always that way when you step outside of your element. You should be expected to get stared at, to get the attention. You're blazing the trail, you're the freighter moving through the ice, that kids want to view and talk about.

Understanding the realities of Korean relationships would be another issue. But I knew that knowledge didn't just apply to Korea, it applied to everywhere in the world. Korea would be but the beginning to understand all the bigger pictures, of everything.

With that, I began plotting further escapes, thinking back to Michigan, as I dreamed of cities like Budapest expat scenes and Santiago expat scenes, and anywhere in the world's expat scenes. I thought of 1920's Paris, filled with American writers. I had no doubt that the entire world had this, and there must be stories all over the world, and I wanted to interweave with those stories.

I slowly weened myself away from Pusan altogether in the late summer of 1997, luckily just prior to when IMF would shortly arrive.

I made that plan a reality, and I went to Budapest, and I sent those postcards back to Pusan, telling them they all had a permanent bedroom available for them, free of charge, at any time they wanted to escape their Korea reality for a different one. But I found myself comparing it to Korea. Hungary simply wasn't exotic enough as Korea had been. I spent nearly two months there, and decided that I needed to find a different home that was more like Korea, but not Korea.

I flew to Istanbul, determined that it would be my new home. It had so many Asian elements to it that reminded me of Korea, but it too, wasn't Korea. It was equally exotic, but it felt like a different type of Korea. I accepted a teaching job there, but a few weeks of traveling around the country waiting for it to start, and I felt like it had the same plusses and minuses of Korea. I dwelled on the language, and felt that Turkish or Korean, would equally have the same hurdles, and maybe I didn't want that at all. A Spanish speaking country was more my thing, one that I could learn the language. I felt free to go anywhere, so I did.

I flew to Santiago, Chile, and I sent postcards to Pusan, about how I had a new home. I would stay here, and any of them were always welcome to come there at any time, stay with me, and I'd help them adjust to yet a new culture and country. This country had all the elements that I ever wanted. But weeks later, I found myself seeing Asian people in Chile, and felt an immense longing to be around them. I wanted to interact with them, I wanted to be closer to Asia, but my money was nearly gone, and I had few options. I was almost stuck.

I craved that ability to learn a language, and I craved to have some Asiatic people of some sort around, and I craved a culture that I could find a connection with. Sao Paulo, Brazil became that place. Staying at a hostel in Santiago, rotating roommates and travelers on a daily basis, a common thread began to reveal itself. A Chilean hostel clerk, daily, told me how much better Brazil was on every account. Chile was okay, but BRAZIL...now that's where you want to be.

Then Rob checked into the hostel. What was he doing in Chile? He was an American who had just left Brazil, looking to instead teach in Chile. He had left his roommates and his job, and if I acted fast, I might be able to assume his teaching position, and potentially move into his old apartment, that is if either was still available.

I left the next morning, direct to Sao Paulo, with just a few days of money left in my pocket. Because of a confusion of who I was to Rob, everyone assumed I was some long lost best friend. I was hired the exact day, and began teaching the next morning. I told them I had nowhere to stay, they called his old roommates, and I moved into Rob's old flat, living with three Brazilian girls and a guy. I didn't have the language skills to refute being his best friend from back home, and I didn't have any money to risk it either.

Having future income, and a place to sleep, certainly helped a lot. With the remaining coins I had, I lived on faucet water, and day old bread from a nearby store. My stomach ached every day, and I felt odd being this American who couldn't contribute to any of the meals, but being offered to eat at times with them, and trying not to devour it down.

In fact, from the day I arrived in Brazil, until day I left, Brazil was such an experience, I just wanted to write about it. But I couldn't start writing about it, without first writing about that crazy Korea experience before I would forget it. With that, I began to reflect on Pusan, and what an unusual place it had been. I wanted to write down the dialogue and show the characters and their stories. I didn't want to forget any of it, or anything from there, so I filled up notebooks with my writing. It became something I would do passionately, as unlike Korea, I didn't have access to English books. I didn't have the money for them, and I didn't have the community to come across them. I had to write my own book, so that is what I did, all day long, whenever I wasn't teaching.

Via Hotmail, not only could I keep in contact with my Pusan friends, but I could go deeper into my past reconnecting with others too. For example, Jin, a Korean-American, who I used to work with at in an American National Park out west. It was a small world when you stepped out of your hometown. I emailed him that he should visit me in Sao Paulo. He said he would, and he did.

Up until his arrival, there was a Korean-Brazilian girl that I would sometimes see in the Jardins expat bars. I always told her, "Annyonghaseyo," in Korean. I couldn't say much more than hello and a dozen or so other words, unfortunately. I tried my best to convey to her that I actually had lived in South Korea. She didn't believe me.

She always gave me *that* look, that *whatever* look. I must have looked peculiar to outsiders, that I would be speaking to her mixing up a little Korean, a little Portuguese and a lot of English. I would have thought I could have made some connection with her in some way. I could not.

Then Jin visited me, the Korean-American. The two of them gelled right away, talking days on end. I couldn't connect with the Korean-Brazilian girl, but Jin certainly could. It made me feel great. It made me wished I'd connected more with Korea. It made me wish that I could better convey that I had a connection with Korea, and that it, in turn, had made an impact on me.

Meanwhile, I kept writing as much as I could about Pusan. I reflected back on South Korea as being so insular, so unvisited, and so incredibly unfamiliar with anyone non-Korean. The place seemed to be one of those forgotten anomalies on the planet. Meanwhile, even in faraway Santiago and Eastern European Budapest, they had plenty of hostels, backpackers, foreigners, travelers, and all the rest. If for some reason you had found your way to Seoul, at that time, then it was said that Pusan was just a concrete jungle to navigate on your way quickly to Japan. It certainly felt that way when I was there.

That manuscript would follow me around for the next twenty years, as I was unsure what to do with it. But, I was sure of one thing, I wanted to share that connection that I had made there. I wanted to share my story of that time, with anyone who might be interested in reading about it. I didn't want to give up on it, even though I didn't know what to do with it.

***
58
***

I was sitting at work, in New York City. It was 1999. I had a job where I created presentations for investment bankers on Wall Street. In between jobs, I checked my e-mail, occasionally receiving messages from people like Stefano and Joe and Huck.

I also browsed the net to keep informed on Pusan and Korea. As I did, a Caucasian guy next to me asked why I was viewing a website titled "PusanWeb."

"Ah...I used to live in Korea, and this keeps me in contact with people there."

He responded back at me in fluent Korean.

"Whoa!"

"Well, I used to live in Korea too."

Instant friends. Carl was a science-fiction writer. He told me about Rolf Potts, a fellow ex-resident of Korea who had written for Pusan's zines and websites during the same 1996–1997 timeframe that we were both there. Just two years later, in 2002, Rolf Potts would have his book *Vagabonding* published. Later, I would spend time clicking on PusanWeb interviews of Rolf Potts and exchanging e-mails with him. His style of writing stood out, making me feel like Korea certainly could attract an element of expat writers just like Paris once did.

Each day I saw Carl at work, we talked about Pusan—about Monk Bar, Tombstone, Pusan National University, the first Internet cafes of Pusan, Haeundae Beach, Pusan's First International Film Festival, and many other things from that wonderful little city on the other side of the world.

I missed that city. I missed it madly.

From work, I would go back to my apartment, which was up in Washington Heights. I took the subway to 168th Street, and walked to Fort Washington Avenue, passing by the same homeless junkie I always did. I sometimes gave him a dollar, and sometimes I didn't.

I lived in a four-bedroom apartment, and one of my roommates was from Seoul. His last name was Rhyu, and he told me he received a letter from his parents.

"Adam, I cannot marry my girlfriend here in New York. My father gave me his answer, and his answer is no."

"No? But she's Korean. And he's never met her."

"Yes, but her last name is Rhyu."

"What does that mean?"

"Traditionally, we are not allowed to marry someone with our same last name. Particularly someone like me with an unusual Korean last name like Rhyu."

Rhyu and I sometimes went to Korea Town on West 32nd Street. While there, I asked him what a PC-bang was, and he told me it was a Korean internet cafe. They had begun sprouting throughout Korea to such a quick degree, that spinoffs of them were arriving in Korea Towns across the United States. When I used their computers, I had to reset their displays from Korean to English. Even more interesting was that New York, the heart of business-minded United States, had so few internet cafes, and the few they had, were overpriced and expensive compared to the Korean ones. In New York, I was getting a taste of just how much Korea was continuing to change.

The funniest thing about Ryhu, is he did something unacceptable in the U.S. that many Koreans found normal in Korea. When we hung out, he would lean over and put his hand on my leg or knee, as he talked to me. He did that regularly to me while in New York bars, and I found myself squeamishly moving away from him. It made me reflect of a later Seoul experience where I would be in Itaewon, where American military would often interact with Koreans in the same bars. Some young Korean guy would put his hand on the thigh of a G.I., and the soldier would negatively react to it. He grabbed and threw the Korean so far up the wall, that the man slid down, and passed out limply on the bar floor. People immediately went up to the G.I. and asked him what happened, "The guy tried to make a move on me. He put his hand on my thigh!"

So Carl and Rhyu were the people I would regularly see at work and home. Additionally, before I moved to New York City, I also knew two other people, who made up my social life. One of them was Jin, the same Korean-American guy who had visited me in Sao Paulo. Jin was an artist, and he invited me to art events. He moved in two circles of friends, one were Korean American artists, and the other were young Caucasian hipsters, all interested in the New York art scene. Both of his social scenes were a bit exclusive and elusive, but Jin had enough interest in Korea that he occasionally asked me questions about it from time to time. I think I sometimes disappointed him, as I didn't know that I loved Korea yet. I didn't give the types of answers I would later—in 2001 or 2008 or 2016, might give. In 1999, I was only starting to realize the truth: I had absolutely loved Korea.

That being said, he represented that American side of Korea. That immigrant's son, who exceeded in education, and he represented the artist. The Asian-American artist, with that unique view on the culture, the life, and the world. He also represented a world that I couldn't tap into well, either the artistic community, or the Korean-American one, but he helped me connect to it. He was yet another person, who made me realize that knowing Korea more, was something I was interested in doing. Korea had connected with me after all, even though I wasn't aware of it yet.

My other friend in New York wasn't a Korean connection. His name was Mason, and I knew him from working in the national park system prior to Korea, just like I had known Joe, Sasha, and Jin. Mason was a white guy from Maine.

Mason and I didn't have conversations about Korea. He had no interest in searching out Korean restaurants with me. He and I did white guy things. We sat in bars, a lot. We never talked about Korea, but he must have known that I loved it a lot. Years after I left New York City, he decided that he wanted to teach English in Korea, too. About a decade later, he would find himself teaching and living in Korea, and he would stay there for a very long time.

Even when I wasn't aware of my Korea connecting, I must have been emitting that off somehow, someway.

All the while, I took my 250+ page story about Pusan 1996, and I typed it into a word document, and I printed it out. This would stick with me, but I still didn't know what to do it. In the end, it was a part of me. It remained a part of my Korea experience. I wrapped it up in a large manila envelope, put layers and layers of tape around it, and left a copy of it in my parent's Port Huron house. It seemed the appropriate place. Someday I would know what to do with it.

Lastly, while living in New York, I had discovered the Korean communities of Flushing, Queens. I met Koreans who had never known white Americans. They continued to want to study English, just like many Koreans had in Korea itself. Many lived in something called a hasook (하숙), which was a Korean-style boarding house, with an ajumma who cooked Korean food for their tenants. They studied in hagwans that looked much like the one I had taught at in Pusan. They even talked about trying to do language exchanges with native English speakers, much like they had talked about in Korea itself. I liked the fact that Korea existed in large bubbles in places like Flushing, Queens, New York.

Once I discovered that large community, I would talk to Carl at work as if I was just in Korea over the weekend. I might as well have been.

And that was my New York. My New York was a Korean-filled New York.

***

59

***

By 2000, I had returned to South Korea. All my Korea connections in New York City, compelled me to want to re-experience Korea from a Seoul point of view. My colleague Carl talked about his visits to Seoul from Pusan, and the depth that Seoul conveyed, and I shared that same feeling. I wanted to know that city. By a recommendation of soon-to-be life-long Korea expat friend, I opted for Shinchon (신촌·新村). It was a neighborhood where four universities converged in Seoul. I couldn't have been more content.

Shinchon Seoul was nothing like Deokcheon Pusan. It was mostly young adults, college students, and all of the amenities that would appeal to those demographics – i.e. bars and restaurants. One major difference on top of that, was that there were now Internet cafes everywhere, seemingly on every corner. I didn't see bee-pee pagers anymore. Now everyone had tiny cellphones. These new cellphones you clicked a numerical button sometimes several times to get to your letter, than push enter. They were addictive. You could write out entire messages with words, something different from the beepee capabilities. I never considered getting one in New York, but they seemed essential in Seoul in 2000.

The Internet was commonplace and Koreans commonly went on 'lightning' Internet dates. They even had a Korean word for it, they called it Bun-Gae-Ting (번개팅). You got online, contacted a Korean girl, and she would agree to come out and see you. Few people had pictures to share, but people were eager to meet someone this way. It was so epidemic, that Friday nights, I would go to the Burger King, outside of Shinchon station, only to see other Caucasian guys waiting for their lightning meeting dates as well. It was a struggle to know who you were meeting, as there were few photos online, and so many others meeting at the same places. A few years later, internet dating evolved significantly, and you simply wouldn't see or experience it in quite the same way. But in 2000, you would. It was the emergence of a new kind of dating, and it was very raw and unorganized.

Living in Seoul, I had a different set of friends. Pusan was a memory, along with what seemed to be a different era. In Seoul, in 2000, people never stared or looked at me, and kids no longer shouted hello at me. All of that disappeared. Subways were more orderly, or at least changing rapidly. Government campaigns instructed passengers on how to wait for people to get off trains and buses, and they more or less followed the instructions—at least those of the younger generations did. You still had old ajusshis yelling loudly into those new things called cellphones. You still had old men coughing hard on the back of your neck, while on buses. But they were aging a little more year by year, or at least beginning to do that.

As I was living in Shinchon. I frequently patronized the Woodstock Bar—it was an institution. It had graffiti everywhere, and you ordered large pitchers of beer. They played loud music requests, and people sat at large picnic tables spread out across the bar room floor. Think of an Oktoberfest setup, in that your group could sit next to any other group, and start a conversation. Your social network could expand significantly with this type of bar arrangement. The atmosphere of loud music, graffiti, and close proximity made something special. The design was then copied by other bars—such as Nori's (놀이하는사람들), which became my favorite. Nori's was a downstairs bar with a stairwell to an upstairs alley which served as the men's official bathroom. Both of these venues, and others around Shinchon copied the Woodstock model. They had record albums lining up and down their walls behind, in vinyl. They had DJ's and Bartenders, and they took vinyl music requests.

Nori's started as a Woodstock-like equivalent, when Woodstock was standing room only due to popularity. Step out of Woodstock, go to the left, hit the first corner, and then turn right. When you saw the words 'The Bar' in big letters, then you went downstairs into Nori's. Since Nori's was written in Korean, and 'The Bar' was written in a larger prevalent English sign, most people simply called Nori's, 'The Bar' or they translated Nori's into English, as 'People's Bar'. 'The Bar of the People.' Initially a spin-off from Woodstock, it suddenly became an institution as well. Within a year, it too found its way into the Lonely Planet guide. Then suddenly, an influx of new teachers, from all around Korea, would find their way into Seoul's Shinchon, and look for that bar, just as they had for Woodstock's all the years prior. It was a weird feeling to realize you were the beginning crowd of what would later become an institution.

If Seoul expats wanted dance clubs, they went to neighboring Hongdae (홍대·弘大). Dancing in Hongdae meant Hodge Podge (하지파지). Just say the words, "I'm going to Hongdae," and people would respond, "Okay, I'll see you at Hodge Podge later." Five years later, Hongdae would have multitudes of dance clubs, hip-hop clubs, techno clubs and everything else. Entire streets would be filled with new restaurants and bars. In 2000, though, there were four main choices: Hodge Podge and Joker Red were around the corner in an alley, and Route 66 and Saab were on the main road. They were all clustered together around this corner, and a few others would spring up along this alleyway. They were not far from the Hongik University's front gate, going towards the Sangsu metro station. If you visited Hongdae in 2000, you would poke your head into all of these few places, just like everyone else who might go there. Then you would decide if you were better off going to Shinchon or Itaewon instead. Hongdae simply didn't offer more than that little corner of four to six places maximum. By 2005, HongDae's bars and clubs would explode, easily eclipsing what Shinchon was offering for expats, and even for Koreans alike. Later, I would visit small towns in Korea, and meet locals who made Hongdae pilgrimages once a month, it changed that quickly. By 2010, I would see hostels and guesthouses popping up, bringing in international backpacker travelers from around the world. By 2015, it was a full-on international hipster mecca. It oozed internationalism in all respects, mixed with the artistic tinge that Hongdae provided being the premier Art University of South Korea.

Way on the other side of Hongik front gate, and much closer to the Hongdae Metro station, rested Macando Latin Music Bar, the first salsa joint in Korea. An American expat, Kelly, initiated it five years earlier in 1995, the first of its kind. The Spanish-speaking community, as well as Latin music lovers both had this as their nucleus. It would remain the only one of its kind far longer than you'd expect. As always, Seoul was years ahead from anywhere else in Korea, including Pusan where that would have been inconceivable.

Itaewon was a neighborhood around the Yongsan (용산·龍山) US Army Base, including the infamous "Hooker Hill." It featured dive bars with either billiard tables or dart boards, and US military guys were everywhere. I seldom made my over to that area. Fifteen years later, it would become a trendy area of Seoul among Koreans. Any foreigner from 2000 would hardly recognize it as the same place.

In 2000, it catered to mostly military guys and some long-term English teachers, seeking a foreigner-friendly refuge. Just a few years later around 2003 or so, it would explode with people from the Middle East, who would gravitate towards a nearby mosque. Nigerians and Africans would descend as well, and the street below 'Hooker Hill' began to see African haircut shops, and some African restaurants. Little restaurants with Iraqi food, or Mexican food would pop up. You would occasionally see Russians or Turks or Nigerians fight it out on the streets, with the Korean police having no idea how to handle a situation like that.

Ten years later, it would transform again, and become significantly upscale, with money from around Seoul coming to the area, and some of those ethnic groups would disperse to the suburbs of Seoul. Meanwhile, the U.S. military was continually being discussed to move further south of the Han River, and out of the area completely.

But, in 2000, Itaewon was still that little U.S. military personnel meets English Teacher area, all looking for the few places that served some western food like hamburgers, or one of the few Mexican taco restaurants in the city. One little institution was a street vendor in Itaewon who sold eggburgers. It was a nightlife feature of Itaewon, and its very existence for many expats, meant a mandatory visit. It wasn't often we could treat ourselves to a fresh burger patty with a fried egg on top. It was just below 'Hooker Hill', and to the right. Fifteen years later, all of Itaewon was filled with Mexican and Indian restaurants, and just behind the Egg Burger street venue, a rarity in Korea, slices of pizza were being offered. By 2016, The Egg Burger stand suddenly seemed like a strange relic from another time, or a really strange idea, if someone thought it was new. But, in 2000, that eggburger meant a lot to expat teachers visiting Itaewon and looking for a change from the regular staple Korean food all of the time.

Meanwhile in 2000 Seoul, I was once again teaching at a hagwan, but a very well-organized one in Shinchon. They had teacher resources, and books that were written by an established company according to student level. This alone amazed me, as my days in Pusan, I wouldn't have imagined that teaching materials could have been available or organized at the Korean management level.

In one of the lessons they had a reading discussion centered on, 'The Korean Wave.' It was a hard concept for me to follow. It meant there were people interested in Korea, who weren't Koreans. A few years later, I would hear of, 'The Korean Dream,' which was a play on words from the 'American Dream.' It implied there were many other Asians who dreamed to live and work in South Korea.

These interests were difficult for me to understand in 2000. I had never heard of anyone having interest in South Korea. But a few years later, I would travel extensively throughout Asia, and see it often. In countries like the Philippines, I would meet Filipinos who watched Korean TV all day, listened to K-Pop music all the time, and were enthralled by all things Korean. In Vietnam, I would hear K-Pop music on their radio, intermixed with American music, with the same level of popularity. It would be another decade that I would meet young American college students who equally had this interest in K-Pop, Korean culture, and Korean TV. These were hard concepts to understand in 2000, particularly based on my 1996 experiences, where Korea seemed to be some remote, hidden, isolated, backwards, corner of the planet.

On the other side of the coin, there was a different hagwan in Shinchon that I was considering teaching at. I arranged a job interview at noon. When I went there, I met the hagwan owner. He had me sit down in a dingy back room, which looked like it doubled as the teacher's room.

He was one of those typical hagwan-owner sketchy guys, and he immediately said, "Can you start teaching on Monday? Someone pulled a runner." He then proceeded to pour me a shot of soju.

"Nah, too early for soju, for me," I told him. "Can you tell me a bit about your hagwan? Classroom sizes, hours a week...." Then I paused, as I saw a dirty long-haired blond foreigner pass through our space, entered what looked like a small college-like room or a closet, or something. He walked in there, did something momentarily, and then walked back out. I asked him, "Hey, are you teaching here?"

"Yep, five years now."

"Really? Where do you live?"

He pointed right back to the little hole he came out of, "Right there."

"Ahh...."

I didn't take that job, but I could see that some things hadn't changed. As much as I was getting a different perspective of Korea, there were certainly many elements of the old Korea I had known back in Pusan. That type of hagwan owner and employee situation certainly was one of them.

***

60

***

By 2005, I had come and gone a few times, in and out of South Korea, just like many other foreigners I had known. I went and received an MA degree in TESOL, so that I could teach English more effectively. I had went back to the United States a second time, San Francisco, and met my future spouse. I tried living in Europe for a year. But, all of that, and Korea kept pulling me back, like it had with many of my good friends.

One of those evenings, I went to the Seoul Pub, to meet my old Pusan friend, Louie. Seoul Pub was one of those older establishments with pool tables, dart boards, barstools, and large windows that overlooked the street scene below. It was a mainstay in the Itaewon area, one that continued to last the test of time. It was the type of place that would have U.S. army types drinking all day long, and by night, you'd just have military contractors and English teachers. When I did go to Itaewon, this would be one of the places I might pop my head into, for a while. Five years ago, I wouldn't have had much interest in Itaewon, and it would have taken a lot to get me out of Shinchon. Now, I frequently went to Hongdae or Itaewon for a night out, but seldom to Shinchon.

Louie had always been tall, but now he was expanding outward as well. He had still retained his boyish looks, however, and was just as active going out as he ever was.

"Remember how we met?"

"Of course, Louie. You were the first person I met in Korea!"

Louie stopped his beer mug just before his lips, "Yeah? What do you remember?"

"You tried to give me a beer at lunch time! Between classes!" A brief laugh, and a moment's reflection between old friends.

"Hey, whatever happened to our friend Stefano?"

"Oh, I stayed with him in San Francisco a few years ago."

"Yeah? What was he doing there?"

"Dot-com industry," I paused. "That fell apart while I was there." I put my own mug of beer to my lips. "But you do know that he is back in Korea, don't you?"

Our mugs hit the bar at the same time. "You can check out, but you can never leave."

"And here we are, sitting at Seoul Pub, ten years later."

"Cheers to that!"

I received a few text messages, as I often did. I left Louie in Seoul Pub with his beer, his bartenders, and his regular barstool.

Next I went over to Hongdae, where I met up with Stefano, my old roommate from Deokcheon, Pusan. He was more of a late night clubber type.

"Adam, there's this new club—I'm heading that way now, if you want to come with."

"Let's do it."

Many of my old friends from different Korean experiences were still around. When I met new people, however, I avoided telling them just how long I'd been around Korea. For one, they seldom believed me. Also, they were too busy having their own Korean experiences. And my Korean-speaking abilities were nothing to boast about.

Traditionally, all you ever saw in Korea among the foreign community was English teachers and American military. But around this time, we started hearing more about the "Korean Wave," and it seemed to be becoming more of a reality, quite shocking to us long-termers who simply hadn't known Korea's impact outside of Korea. Suddenly, people were coming to Korea from all around the world, but it seemed odd to us. I had never met a foreign tourist visiting Korea prior to this time.

As Stefano and I were walking, a wide-eyed man stopped us and asked, "Where can I find the dance clubs in Hongdae?"

"We're going there now. We'll show you."

"Yeah!"

"New to Korea?"

"Just visiting."

"Visiting?"

"Yeah, for two months."

"For two months? Visiting?"

"Did you say you were visiting for two months?"

"You mean you aren't teaching English?"

"No, I just want to visit Korea."

"Visit Korea? Where are you from?"

"Israel."

"Israel?"

"What's an Israeli doing here?"

"I just want to see Korea."

"What made you want to visit Korea?"

"Kimchi. I worked in a Korean restaurant in New York.

"Yeah? New York?"

"I wanted to go to the source of their food."

"Korean food?"

"Yeah, Korean food."2

"I've never met anyone who traveled to Korea for two months for Korean food."

"Did you say two months?"

"Where are you going to go here for two months?"

"I think you can see the entire country in two weeks?"

"Two months? In Korea?"

And so it continued. Throughout the rest of the night, we had a variation of that conversation with every long-term expat that we introduced him to. I felt like us long-timers in Korea, had become like 1996 Koreans in Pusan. Just amazed that any foreign visitor was here, and wondering if they even liked it, and what they would even do while in Korea.

It was a far cry from ten years ago, when most expat bars were filled with people complaining about contractual disagreements, cultural shock differences, and overworked and underpaid teaching days. Now there were backpacker tourists in Korea? It was a small sign of things to come.

Later that night, I went back by myself to Itaewon. Many long-term expats hung out in Itaewon, so it was a great place to run into people you hadn't seen in a long time. I ended up in a place called Debut Bar, the place that funneled all of the late-night drinkers into one spot until the sun came up the next morning. The Debut of 2005, as opposed to the 2016 location when gentrification forced them to move, was located in the narrow upward alley of 'Hooker Hill' in Itaewon. There was also another hill, parallel to it, called "Homo Hill," a new scene which would have been inconceivable a few years ago. But Hooker Hill had what its name implied, and it had many late-night bars and clubs that socializers, drinkers, and long-term expats would converge at. Outside Debut, the usual three in the morning drunks spilled out of the small venue and into the narrow alley. While there, I overheard one obnoxious foreigner boasting about how long he had been in Korea. "I came here *five* years ago!"

Unable to recognize him, I told him, "Plenty of people did."

He confidently crossed his arms. "You don't understand. I have never left Korea!"

"Yep," I paused. "I know plenty of people who have never left."

"You don't know what you're talking about."

"I got here in 1996," I told him.

"You did not. No one was here in 1996. I got here right at the beginning, in 2001."

There was a small part of me that felt that my arrival, in 1996, was when things really took off. But even for me, there was always someone who had been there longer, still lingering around. Now I was that guy—if this 'new' guy had believed me.

The night wore on, and the sun would come up soon. I never liked being in Itaewon in the morning, so I took a taxi to my old neighborhood of Shinchon, which was an easy walk to my apartment. It was five in the morning, and sometimes graffiti-filled Nori's was still open at this hour.

As I stood outside in the alleys of Shinchon, not far from Nori's, I heard, "Makkoli (막걸리·農酒). Makkoli. Rice Wine!"

The infamous Makkoli Man, was pushing his familiar cart of Korean rice wine up and down the narrow alleys. Smiling widely, he took one look at me, "Very good!" He gave me the thumbs up sign.

"Not tonight," I sadly told him. He was a long-term fixture of times past walking the streets—the old kind of Seoul.

Not too far away, a white-haired, long-legged foreigner sat at a plastic table outside a convenience store, legs spread out, empty beer cans around, blabbering about everything and nothing all at the same time.

"Tom!"

I joined Tom, a guy who I had met many times, who had been in Korea the longest of any foreigner that I had known. He had fought in the Vietnam War, gone home to write screenplays for Hollywood movies, and decided that he simply couldn't handle "America." He packed up for Korea for good in the 1980s, and had spent the last thirty years losing jobs from hagwans, dealing with age discrimination, and just being unable to function well in society.

I was home in Korea. These were the kinds of people I wanted to drink with. These were the kind of people I wanted to hang out with. These were the kinds of stories I wanted to hear. These were the kinds of people who made me love life, love Korea, love being an expat, love beer, love people, and simply celebrate this short little existence we call being alive. There was no better place than this little corner of the world to celebrate just that, and I was celebrating. We clinked our store-bought beer cans and stayed right there drinking until one that afternoon—or was it three?

Clink.

***

61

***

Twenty years later, in 2016, I looked again to my four bulky bags of *No Couches in Korea*, sitting at my feet. One copy in my hands. The main copy in my heart. I had finally decided what to do with that old manuscript, I had it published, and made it available to distribute. I would empty out these bags, and fill these same bags up with Korean memorabilia to bring back with me. Having last lived in Seoul in 2008, I was reflecting on how much Korea had changed from 1996 to 2016. I was seeing food choices that I couldn't have imagined when I first arrived in South Korea twenty years ago. For example, Philly Cheesesteak sandwiches, Korean tacos, Mexican tacos, and not only they did they exist, but they existed in large numbers throughout Seoul. But, more than anything, I was wondering how much Pusan had actually changed. When I had returned to live in South Korea in 2000, it was with the goal to know Korea better, and I achieved that in Seoul. Little ol' Pusan, I managed to visit as a tourist occasionally, but usually only Haeundae Beach. All of my old haunts throughout Pusan remained dormant to me for twenty years.

So, I purchased a ticket on the KTX, a speed train that would take me from Seoul to Pusan in 2 ½ hours. Twenty years ago, that would have been a regular train in 6 ½ hours. I dragged bags of books with me, all intent on promotionally distributing them throughout the expat scene in Pusan.

The moment I stepped on the KTX, I intended to give a free signed book to anyone on the train to Pusan. I walked throughout every car, and I didn't spot a single other foreigner. I resigned myself to just find my seat, and start signing a dozen books. I would find my foreigners soon enough. It was Korea 2016 after all, not Korea 1996.

As I signed them, a foreigner, approximately my own age, came in for a seat in the same car. KTX trains have half of the seats facing one direction, and the other half facing the opposite direction, so that in the middle, we are all looking at each other. Where I was sitting, I had a clear view of this other foreigner facing my direction, but several rows back.

I observed the potential recipient of my first signed promotional Pusan-bound book. He was tall and skinny, middle-aged, with a beard, and had curly hair. The man stood up continuously, and pushed his glasses up over the bridge of his nose several times a minute. Each time he pushed up his glasses, he crinkled up his nose. My heart raced, could that be Melvin? Wouldn't it be ironic if Melvin was on this same train as I was, after not having seen him for twenty years? I needed to see Melvin. I wanted to spend part of my return trip to Pusan, with him. My heart raced. We could get back to Deokcheon and Happy Town Apartments, explore around. He must be completely different now, but his mannerisms hadn't changed a bit. The beard looked great on him, he looked more mature, more knowledgeable, more informed. My heart raced, I didn't even know if I wanted to approach him, how might he receive this book, how might he perceive my perception of him?

I approached him and my heart raced, because if that was him, it was meant to be. "Hey, by chance, is your name Melvin?"

"Who?"

"Melvin. You remind me of a guy that I know."

He pushed his glasses back up with his fore finger. "Nah, my name is James."

"Oh, alright, you just reminded of this guy I used to know."

He crinkled up his nose, as he looked down through his glasses once again.

"You want a free book? I wrote it myself, and you are welcome to have it. You might enjoy it for your train ride.

"Sure. Yeah, thanks."

And with that, I turned back around. I was in disbelief that it wasn't Melvin. But then again, what possible chance could it have been Melvin? Why would he be on this train twenty years later, of all the random times in life, and be in the same car train as I had been. It was crazy that I had entertained the idea.

I imagined this strange scenario that could have taken place. Melvin and I exploring Pusan. We would go up to our old apartment, way up in the hills. We would go above and beyond our apartment, up to the mountain top that overlooked my apartment building and that part of the city.

Somehow we would run into King, who would now be the 'King of the Mountain,' in some run-down shack. He would be some wise old western guy, with a cane, and a long grey goatee, and a whole lot of Peace Corps and Korea living experiences to continually share with any new or old hagwan teacher that wandered up that hill. We'd sit up there overlooking our old city, with a fire pit. We'd reminisce about the old times. I'd apologize to Melvin for not having embraced him twenty years ago, for having left him as the eternal outsider. I would have understood him for the first time, and he would have understood me for what I was before. King would overlook it all, with a slight grin, with a monotone voice, and a knowing smile.

But, in the end, I was simply alone with my books on the train, contemplating how cool all that might have been. Instead, I strolled up and down the train, looking for other foreigners to share No Couches in Korea as a gift for them on their train ride. I didn't see any other new arrivals on the train, nor did I see any at Pusan Station when I arrived. Quite a contrast to the enormous amount of foreigners strolling around throughout Seoul.

But, it didn't matter. I was back in Pusan, twenty years later, and I was going to see all of my old haunts.

***

62

***

After having spent so much time in Seoul, I was used to a more cosmopolitan type of Korean. When I arrived in Pusan, I saw those same old types I remembered from twenty years ago. The ones with their old man haircut—short, unstyled, conservative, conventional, and probably consistently trimmed with the same barber shop throughout most of their lives. The same guys with the buttoned-up shirt with a collar, but the shirt that looked like they'd worn it every third day for the last thirty years. The mandatory slack pants or hiking zipper pants. That kind of typical-looking aging Korean type of man. Not the flashy newer Seoul clothes, but these old market clothes, that a poor man would buy and wear every day, day in and day out, as a way to attempt to not look so poor.

The guys at the taxi stand were standing around looking at everything around them. When I approached them and gave them a simple 'annyonghasaeyo' in Korean, they beamed with Korean pride that a foreigner could say hello to them in their language. A few acknowledgeable grunts of satisfaction and congratulations for being able to pronounce the five simple syllables. That was a common Pusan experience twenty years ago, but not one that I ever encountered in Seoul.

Minutes later, I was being whisked away to my hotel in Haeundae Beach. The taxi driver played the 1970's hit song, 'Just the Two of Us' on his old stereo system. I half expected to hear the click of a cassette player, even though none was in sight. I reflected to how often I had heard old 70's American songs back in 1990's Korea. Just how different that was from Seoul, where I mostly heard current pop or dance songs or K-Pop.

In the Korean language, he asked me if I was an American, and I said I was one. He gave me the 'I love USA' thumbs up, with a big smile. That reminded me so much of the 1990s taxi drivers, way back when, so different than the ones I'd get in Seoul. I felt like I was being transported back into time with this taxi driver. More 1970's American music was played, and I gave more thumbs up, as he whisked me away, transporting me back to 1996, in the 2016 present.

Over in Haeundae, I saw foreign tourists from Russia, Europe, Australia, and the United States. Many of the Korean people were from Seoul. I put most of my books in my hotel, and immediately hit the subway trains, determined to get this book out there to people in this city. I wanted to find Pusan expats, not just visiting tourists.

Mostly I just wanted to see my old city, and observe everyone and everything in it. I rode the trains, and noticed the age demographics of Pusan was titled with a much older population than Seoul. Seeing old ajumma ladies, complete with the big wide visors and permed hair, were the norm in Pusan, not the exception like in Seoul. Old women with plenty of loosely fit clothing, and floral patterns which clashed in color. The people hadn't changed much in twenty years.

I saw men with what I'd refer to as fishermen jackets. They were a type of fishnet vest, that you could imagine people hanging their fishing lures on. They had plenty of pockets with zippers, which seemed to me like another fisherman accessory type of thing. They'd wear this fishnet vest over their buttoned-up shirts. It was very practical attire, and Pusan being so close to the ocean, maybe they never needed to stop selling that possible top seller item in the region? But, more than anything, I was getting a taste of the same attention that I used to get on the train twenty years ago.

As I made one subway transfer, I had an overweight, middle-aged Korean woman with a Mickey Mouse sweatshirt stare hard at me, reminding me of the feel I used to get years ago. As I stood on the platform, I gave her that look that said, 'You know, I can see you staring daggers into me, don't you know?'

She saw my look as an invitation, and quickly asked me, "Where are you going?" I answered her in Korean, and she responded in English, "Where are you from?" I responded again in Korean, and she quickly asked me in English, "What do you think of Korea?"

I couldn't answer that in Korean, and I didn't know how to answer it in English either. "I like Korea. I used to live here. It's nice." I wanted to move away from her, far down the platform. But the subway train pulled up, and I had no choice but to enter at that moment. You might wonder why I would care if someone wanted to make small talk for the next twenty minutes? Mostly it was because the questions were predictable and repetitive, and they wouldn't be able to understand my answers. Worse, is the questions were filled with assumptions – i.e. that I didn't live in Asia, that I hadn't tried Asian food, etc.

As the doors opened, I let her go in front of me, with the intention of moving the opposite direction for a seat. As fate worked out, she took a seat, and the only other open seat on the train, was directly across from her. I sat there. Then I took out my notebooks to write, and she just uncomfortably stared at me. I tried not to make eye contact, but I could feel the stares, and every time I looked up, sure enough, she was still staring. "Excuse me," she said, "Do you like kimchi?"

"Yes."

This flooded my memories of Korea, all the attention, all of the constant questions, almost all of them the same exact questions. Pusan hadn't changed at all. It was still Pusan, and the people in Pusan might have aged twenty years, but the questions were passed down, or preserved, or left completely undeveloped. It was intriguing, weird, frustrating, and interesting.

As she sat across from me, and I had my notebook, I wanted to record exactly the type of person who would ask me this, as it was definitely a type of person. Even twenty years ago, it was someone of about her age, in her forties, but usually a man. This overweight lady had grey tights as pants, her green Mickey Mouse shirt, a pink backpack, and a pink, wide, visor over her permed hair.

But, I thought it wasn't fair that I pinpointed her as typical. I had my pen, and I began recording the other generations. The younger ones never stared or gave a foreigner undue attention. Most of them had now grown up with foreigner teachers throughout their school years. I noticed the young females on the train, the ones who were in their early twenties. Most of them wore blue jeans or denim shorts. High heels was mandatory, and their tops were usually black. Every one of them on this train had a large black purse sprawled out across their lap, half of the time, half open. They were busy staring at their cellphones to notice me. Younger Koreans were oblivious to anyone around them. It struck me as I reflected throughout the years, that younger women were so focused on mirrors, cellphones, that they seldom even saw the people around them. I wondered if this was generational.

The doors opened again, and a very old, bull-legged woman entered the train. The same kind that you'd assume spent their life working in the rice fields. The type that had stunted growth, a horribly disproportionate back, and bones that ached tremendously. But equally the same that would be carrying, pushing, or pulling something heavy down the street. Someone ready to squat anywhere on the sidewalk, and lie out a dozen vegetables with the hopes of a few customers. The type that would never ask any of those mundane questions in English, because they never knew any English at all. The kind of woman you envision could be sharing that same mountain top with King, but with a different perch to overlook everything. The kind that was born into a different Korea, one that must have been foreign in every capacity compared to the one that existed currently in Korea. The one that you have no connection to whatsoever as a foreigner, but the kind that you notice everywhere in Korea.

I took trains to the old familiar haunts of Pusan. The first destination was Seomyeon, one of the two largest most active areas of the city. When I arrived in Seomyeon, it was still that neon-lit restaurant and nightlife area, but a much cleaner organized version of what I remembered before. It was as busy and crowded, and as difficult to navigate due to its expansiveness. I looked desperately for a foreigner, partially to share *No Couches in Korea*, and partially to have them tell me where to find the center of Seomyeon, and where to locate the foreigner haunts within it. I reflected on how international Seoul was these days and it shocked me that Pusan hadn't become that too.

When I did see an ambiguous English-speaker, as I couldn't identify his nationality at all, I asked, "Do you speak English?"

"Yep."

"Where's the central part of Seomyeon? And I can't find any foreigners here, you are the first."

"Oh, you won't find foreigners here. But if you want to find them, you have to go to the beaches. They are crawling with foreigners over there. Try Haeundae Beach, Gwangalli Beach, and Kyungsung University area."

Throughout the week in Pusan, that would be a theme I would hear from the very few occasional foreigners that I would encounter outside of those three mentioned foreigner areas. Still though, seeing all the places that I knew back in 1996, was still a higher priority.

"Hey do you want a promotional copy of a book about Pusan? I used to live here twenty years ago."

His eyes lit up, and being that he expressed much interest, I gave him several copies to distribute a couple to Pusan expats as well. I was carrying forty books with the assumption that I would see forty foreigners easily, but it occurred to me that I might not even see forty foreigners throughout the day. I didn't want to spend any time at the beach areas, until I saw Nampodong, Deokcheon, and PNU again. If Seomyeon was foreigner empty, surely Nampodong and especially Deokcheon would be just as empty.

Nampodong was just down the same subway line, and I saw the occasional Russian just like I used to see. That area was close to the international docks that brought in sailors and ship passengers. I approached a few to share about this Pusan book, but they didn't speak enough English to understand what I was saying. I scoured the entire area, and found one foreigner, an English teacher from Seoul, visiting for a few days. I gave him a couple copies, and that was it for that area. Nampodong was even more crowded with narrower streets, so after spending a couple hours there, I wandered off towards Pusan Station.

Again, another few hours went by, and I saw very few foreigners going in or out of the station. Prior to this, people had been thankful to receive a free book. At the station, people were more hesitant to be approached by anyone. They assumed the worse, and I wasn't seeing foreigners anyways, so I moved on as it was still mid-afternoon. The day was still full.

Outside of Pusan Station, there existed a little Russian town. I didn't expect to see English-speaking foreigners there, but I certainly saw Russian-speaking ones. A few snarled at me, as I withdrew my camera to take a picture of some of the Russian signage. Other Russian sailors staggered down the street, mid-afternoon, with vodka bottles dangling just at the tips of their fingers. I expected they would accidently drop their bottle any second, as they stumbled over jagged sidewalk.

I could come back to these neighborhoods again, to soak up the vibes. It was time to move on, for the day.

I then went back to my old neighborhood of Deokcheon. I was looking for foreigners, but I didn't find any there either, nor did I expect to. I went back again during the week, and I only saw one the entire time. A Brazilian guy married to a Korean girl. Finally. A foreigner. Finally. But he was it. I gave him a book.

But the ghosts that I saw, from twenty years ago, ran rampant in those streets. I could see Skate giving Caden the big F-you, as he ran to work. I could see the schoolgirls giving us flowers, in this busy alley, on my first weekend here. I could see Eun-Hee and Kamm, as she hid behind him, unsure what to say to the foreigner who was trying to invite her to his after-work party. I could see Paris losing it, yelling at someone for staring for the umpteenth time before she walked in and gave her resignation to the hagwan. I could see Huck lost wandering around for hours, realizing those landmarks he thought were unique, to be commonplace. I could see Joe courting his future wife, trying to hide his tattoos, possibly from her, and definitely from everyone that she probably knew. I could see Melvin popping in and out bars, just looking around for who knows what. I could see the odang stands where I would live on my fish hot dogs for a few weeks until I could read Korean menus. This very familiar little alleyway, and here I was holding *No Couches* looking for more foreigners that I could find. But, I didn't see any others.

Then I wandered up to Taekyung Happy Town Apartments on the same 169-1 bus. The bus number hadn't changed, and neither did the bus itself. It was still the same setup of seats, handles, paying the fees and so forth. The road up was even steeper and windier than I remembered. The route was a bit different, as the construction was gone. The main roads were wider, and when the bus took me closer to the mountain side, it meandered more than I ever remembered. As soon as I was near my stop, I recognized the steep hill I always had to climb. I saw the little Happy Mart that I had always frequented. I noticed my old apartment building towering above me, even more self-imposing than I remembered. I hadn't noticed how close I was to the mountain peaks though. It seldom occurred me to go to the nearby peak when I lived there, but I desperately wanted to get up to the top now, and overlook everything. Maybe I'd see King up there after all? Maybe that was Melvin on the train, but he hadn't heard his name quite right, but he'd be up there waiting for me, possibly even doing the same thing I was doing, wanting to see it all from a new perspective.

As I ascended, I was surrounded by schoolgirls, shouting hello. I hadn't experienced that in twenty years since 1996. It was on a small scale, but it was the same thing, just like before. When I climbed to the peak, I overlooked Deokcheon and beyond in Pusan. A Korean man spotted me, and asked, "Where are you from?" I smiled, it was nice, and this was so Pusan, I thought. He followed up with, "What do you think of Korea?" I wanted to shout, this is fantastic! Instead, I just thought it out loud, gave him a big smile, and meandered around a bit more, wanting to be more alone with my own thoughts. Other people saw me, stared at me, and said their hello, and all the while I was thinking, Pusan hasn't changed one iota in twenty years. The only difference now, is that are no foreigners here, when years ago, we had a little group of us wandering around amongst them on a daily basis.

I went back down to my old apartment, passing the school girls again, and they again shouted whatever English they knew. I meandered my way to my old apartment, found the apartment guards, and gave them several copies of my book. I conveyed to them, that anytime they see a foreigner around there, could they approach them, and give them a copy of my book? They examined the book title, and horribly mispronounced every word they read, but they conveyed back that they understood what to do with the books. How cool would that be for some native English speaker to receive this book, right in the location of where most of the story occurred?

Then I walked down the hill toward Deokcheon Rotary. I passed that old familiar dog market, and contemplated how none of that had changed either. The streets down the hill had certainly changed though. The construction was gone, and the streets looked nicer, cleaner, and wider. But, the overall neighborhood was still just as old style Korean as you could get, authentically so. Several days was enough exploring it though, I felt like I had relived it enough, and I was anxious to interact with the new expat scene of Pusan.

Pusan National University, how I missed you. The view from the station exit, was just as expansive as ever. I could still look down the busy streets with college students who meandered about. The mountains still loomed in the far off background. Mostly, I could see my old familiar paths that I would take to get to my Monk Bar, Soloriens Internet Cafe, Dream Internet Cafe, and Tombstone. I saw some foreigners in PNU, but it became strongly evident that the bulk of the expat community had moved on. I couldn't locate the exact buildings of the internet cafes or Tombstone. They were long-gone without any trace. I did find Monk, but it appeared to be a shadow of its former self. A nearby bar owner told me that Monk was only open for special jazz events, but otherwise closed. It looked so bland, so non-descript, so dated from the outside. If the place hadn't had such significance to the expat community in 1996, I would have passed it by in 2016, without any notice of it whatsoever.

Crossroads was the only old haunt that I could recognize that lasted the test of time. They proudly had a sign that said, 'Since 1997.' They had fantastic vinyl albums and a request music DJ, with a fantastic view.

But whenever I saw a foreigner in PNU, they all referred me to the Basement Bar. It appeared to be the heart of the expat scene in PNU, and when I went downstairs into it, I knew that I was 'home' again. There were long-term expats, and a bartender who had lived through the 1996 time period and IMF. A person who bought a bar in PNU, because back in the day, that was the heart of the expat community. That was my old world, and he was a standing element of that world.

The Basement Bar was a fantastic venue, complete with barstools, live music, a pool table, dart boards and everything we would have loved to have had in 1996. It was the perfect dive bar, and if anywhere was to remain as the heart of PNU in 2016, I was very pleased that Basement Bar was that spot. It embodied everything we had ever wanted.

Having visited PNU again, I could see that it was no longer the heart and soul of the expat community. I needed to get to Gwangalli Beach. I was referred to Beached Bar and HQ Bar, among others. A couple nights later, I focused on that area, and that is where I saw that things in Pusan had really changed. That is when I became comfortable to use the name Busan for this city, as it really had no connection whatsoever to the Pusan that I had once known.

Gwangalli did indeed have the foreign community. Not only did they have a beautiful well-lit bridge, and a gorgeous beach, but they also had Seoul influences. Some of the popular expat clubs and bars from Itaewon, had also opened a business on the beach in Pusan. Places like Wolfhound Irish Pub and Thursday Party were in both cities.

The bars and beaches were filled with foreigners, and an active population of just interesting people. HQ was one of the recommended ones, and the views of the beach, the bridge, and the entire scene was fantastic. This was a new Busan entirely, and I loved it compared to my old Pusan. It wasn't the only foreigner friendly bar though, the entire beach scene was filled with them. It felt to be an extension of Hongdae and Itaewon, but in the best possible location you could put them in.

Beached Bar was the heart of the reading community of the new Busan expat community. Used books filled up an entire wall. They did book readings, and had book groups. But, more than anything, it was just an amazingly fantastic dive bar. The kind of place that you could interact with a large number of old-time and newly arrived expats. All that with a view and an ocean breeze, or just pull up to a barstool and enjoy the banter. The books were what pulled me in, particularly in contrast to 1996, when finding any book in the English language was a challenge. I liked this new Busan, I like this new Busan a lot!

Once I stepped outside of Beached, the greatness of the area just continued. I could find Mexican restaurants, Indian restaurants, and pretty much everything else, along with beach goers and beach events. I saw very little of anything international anywhere else in Busan, but it was all in Gwangalli, and Haeundae. The main difference between the two, was that the former served the larger expat community, and the latter served the tourists. I preferred Gwangalli, and being among my brethren, the expats of Korea.

That being said, I also felt I needed to do a few touristic things in Busan, as I was straddling two worlds now – perpetual expat, and temporary tourist.

Gamcheon Cultural Village, touted as the Macchu Picchu of Korea, or the Santorini of Korea, was a must. It was a different element of Korea altogether, way up in the mountains, filled with newly painted houses. It was once a run-down neighborhood that became revitalized due to a lot of paint, some already incredible views, and a whole lot of innovation. Gamcheon didn't exist as a tourist site when I lived in Pusan, it was a Busan invention well after I had left. But, it made me reflect on my old Pusan neighborhood up on its own respective mountainside. But this one looked mesmerizing with the kaleidoscope of painted houses. This new Busan, was a very appealing one. While the people hadn't changed much, the city had continued to dynamically change on into the future, as it always had, but wonderfully so, in different ways than I had ever expected. I didn't pine for the old Pusan at all, I felt that I was beginning to pine for the new Busan, the one that now existed.

Equally, I made it to Bosu-Dong Book Alley, another aspect of Busan that I simply had never heard of before. But unlike Gamcheon, this Book Alley had existed for a long time, but I just wasn't tapped into it. Buso-Dong was the largest used book market in all of Korea, and there it was, eternally under my nose in my same old city. I felt compelled to explore it, despite knowing it was almost entirely Korean books. But an interesting thing happened when I went there, I found western hipsters. They were being photographed, as they casually browsed the old Korean books. The man had the face and body of a model, but his beard was as hipster as you could get. It was so long and full, and trimmed. The woman had a hipster dress, a perfect body, and long straight blond hair that gave off an essence of Russia, and an essence of San Francisco combined.

It was my first time to see that type of interest, in this part of Korea, by a foreigner. I saw it strongly in Seoul's Hongdae, but I had never expected to see it in Pusan, particularly after a week of exploring all of the immensely crowded non-beach areas of Busan, and seeing so few foreigners anywhere. Was it a sign of things to come?

With that I felt my time in Pusan was complete, and I felt that I could finally begin to call it Busan for the first time. It had a lot of the Pusan elements that I remembered, but the future of the city, was all Busan. It had new and different things to see and do, and anyone arriving in the city now, would find themselves in a different scene and situation than the one I experienced twenty years ago.

Even more than that, of the many long-term expats that I met in Gwangalli, few ventured as far north as PNU. Somewhere like Deokcheon, where I had lived, few had even heard of the name, despite it being where two subway lines converged. A few expats at Beached Bar, exchanged stories on how strange it was in those 'northern' regions of Busan, far from the beaches. Just how different the people behaved up there, and the attention they'd get. I just thought, 'Yep, that is the typical Pusan that I remembered, the one I attributed to the entire country. The one that still existed, but would eventually die out generationally. That was my 1996 Korea, and even more so peculiar twenty years ago.'

With that, I felt content with what I'd seen.

Pusan and Busan.

***

63

***

Koreans don't generally use couches or traditional furniture; they often throw a small table in the middle of their living room and sit cross-legged around it. This was a land where I always felt foreign, but I always felt welcome. As much as I might want to sleep on someone's couch, there was always a permanent extra bedroom available to me. I would do the same, anytime any of my old friends would revisit Korea as well. In the end, I had connected deeply with Korea, but in a way completely different than I expected.

I had sought out connections with Koreans themselves originally. But my deepest and strongest were with the Korea expats themselves. Particularly outside of Korea, if I met another individual who had also lived in Korea, we had an instant connection, every single time. We shared a similar life decision, a similar experience, and understood multiple realities.

I thought back to years ago, my flower petals with the 'Should I' or 'Shouldn't I'. Years ago, I completely lost that flower, having realized that anything that didn't hurt another human being, should always 100% be 'I should.' That *Catcher in the Rye* book, the one I used to see as myself connecting with possible Korean relationships, the same one I later tried to dissuade a few others from trying those relationships. I long got rid of that as well. I didn't believe in phoneys anymore. All people were good people. All people had immense value. All of them were worth the connections that I could make with them.

Genuine Koreans with their curiosity and kindness, I would welcome them. People I used to know like Caden, Melvin, Skate, Monica, Linda and others were always true to themselves, and I respected that more than ever. I became aware of the fact that I learned deeply from them, through their flaws and strengths. My old dear friends that I loved to death like Joe, Huck, Paris, Stefano, King and all the others, always remained in my heart, as they always would.

And Joe? Sasha's eternal words, "...and Joe can have you?" Well, Joe went back to Portland years ago. Maybe I'd been the one with the strongest pull all along. Maybe I met my destiny just as I had intended, a young boy escaping a living room couch with his eyes on the international. A provincial Michigan boy shuttling ahead into his own beloved unknown, just the way he had always hoped.

And in Seoul, I reflected at how international it had become as well. I met Portland people studying fermentation in Korea, and ways to improve kimchi and makkoli rice wine. I met foreigners around the park in Hongdae, who were artists, and selling their wares. "I'm from San Francisco, but I used to live in Austin," was one such disclaimer. In 2016, Hongdae of Seoul was descended upon by backpackers, travelers, tourists, exchange students, and international hipsters.

The sheer amount of hostels and guesthouses that permeated all the niches and crannies of Hongdae put me in awe. I stumbled upon one with a Michigan theme, filled with young Koreans who had all studied abroad at Michigan colleges. All of these changes, and all of these people from all around the world, descending on Korea, to experience Korea. People talking about how cool Korean food was, and how much K-Pop or Korean film or movies had impacted their childhoods positively.

I was now in this other Korea, excelling full-speed into the future, Seoul at the helm, dragging the entire country behind it, all of them happily going along, with little resistance, and all pride. This Korea that used to desire so deeply to 'beat' Japan, in regards to international influence, and it dawned on me, that it might have done just that.

This Seoul, that continued to mesmerize me, but in different ways than I would have expected twenty years ago. Even a 'best-case scenario,' I never would have dreamed up how cool this new Korea had become. Every international food item I could imagine, was now available. All the things that I loved about Korea, seemed to be suddenly discovered by young people from around the world.

Back twenty years ago, Joe had to search all of Pusan for broccoli. Huck would have ordered most of his American food through his parents back home. The rest of us turned Korean in our eating habits. Old friends from various Korea experiences, still haunted the streets throughout everywhere I had ever known in Korea, as they always had. All of my previous ghosts haunted the streets I had frequented.

If I looked around hard enough, I could still see myself talking to Ms. Key, to Eun-Hee, to Melvin, to Louie, to Paris, to Kristian, to Stefano, to King, to Skate, to Caden, to Joe...and to the multitudes that I had come to know in my subsequent post-Pusan years living in Seoul. Many of them still around, and others long gone. I reflected on them and I swore I could see them, just out the window, out on the street, walking around the corner, whistling ever so slightly, giving me a slight wink, giving me a thumbs up— "Hey you, here we are, where we've always been." This constant welcoming me back, and this consistent connecting in the way I always wanted to connect.

All the Korean beers, the Korean memories, the Korean ajummas and Korean ajusshis, the Korean soju and the Korean makkoli, the Korean beaches and the Korean trees. The Korean ways they build the houses, that never seen to have been built quite right. The expat friends you meet and bond with, always without judgement, who share your crazy existence of living in this Korean corner of the globe filled with Korean things. The way the air smells and the way the alleys meander. The way time goes on with lingering memories of fantastic times that could never quite exist anywhere else in quite the same Korea-like way. The way Korea is just Korea.

Three weeks went by. *No Couches in Korea* was released into the alleys, into the streets, and into the bars.

Four long bulky bags and an acoustic guitar all sat in a row under the green and pink neon signs as I hovered nearby, peering down the wide Seoul Boulevard, looking for my cab. It was my last day in Korea, a country I had come to love. It was my latest session of soaking in all the memories from the last twenty years. For me, it was no longer the end of the end; it was the continuation of a long-term love affair. I was about to leave, but I'd be back. As I always had, time and time again.